FIRST KISSES

A NOVELLA COLLECTION

LINDA GOODNIGHT

JANET TRONSTAD

DEBRA CLOPTON

MARGARET DALEY

CAMY TANG

LACY WILLIAMS

The Rambler's Bride Copyright © 2014 Linda Goodnight

Lovebirds at the Heartbreak Café Copyright © 2014 Janet Tronstad

Her Mule Hollow Cowboy Copyright © 2014 Debra Clopton Parks

Deadly Hunt Copyright © 2014 Margaret Daley

Necessary Proof Copyright © 2014 Camy Tang

Kissed by a Cowboy Copyright © 2014 Lacy Williams

All rights reserved.

ISBN: 0-9915284-0-9
ISBN-13: 978-0-9915284-0-0

CONTENTS

Dedication	i
The Rambler's Bride by Linda Goodnight	1
Lovebirds at the Heartbreak Café by Janet Tronstad	63
Her Mule Hollow Cowboy by Debra Clopton	133
Deadly Hunt by Margaret Daley	221
Necessary Proof by Camy Tang	311
Kissed by a Cowboy by Lacy Williams	387

DEDICATION

We'd like to dedicate this anthology to our many readers. You live around the world from Australia to Canada to the hometowns in our own country. If you're not already part of our Facebook group, please join us at www.facebook.com/inspykisses .

THE RAMBLER'S BRIDE

LINDA GOODNIGHT

CHAPTER ONE

So that's where she lived-the harlot who had killed his brother.

Jericho North shifted in the well-worn saddle and stared down upon the small ranch spread in the valley below, his lip curled in loathing for the woman he'd never met. He'd warned Silas against her, hadn't he? He'd done his best to stop his brother's foolish decision. And now Silas was as dead as Jericho's insides.

Beneath him the paint horse stomped, blowing nostril smoke into the chill March afternoon as if to question his master's pause. A swirl of wood smoke rose from the cabin into the slate gray heavens, the promised warmth a lure. Like the woman had been to his brother.

For a hundred miles or more he'd considered exactly what he'd do when he arrived at Silas's homestead on the Kansas prairie. He still didn't know if he'd stay. One thing for certain, the harlot had to go.

While he squinted, thinking, a red roan horse came into sight and stopped in front of the log cabin. A woman came out onto the porch, hugging a blue shawl to her chest. Esther. The harlot.

Anger unfurled inside him, a snake ready to strike. He'd been angry so long he didn't know how to feel anything else.

A man in a suit and black bowler dismounted and approached the porch. He grasped the woman's arm and she shrank back, resistant.

Jericho frowned, more interested than he wanted to be.

FIRST KISSES

Leaning forward in the saddle, he squinted hard, saw the woman struggle against the man's superior grip. Struggle and fail. Jericho should be happy to see her in trouble but he wanted to be the cause. Not some dandy in a black bowler.

Whatever the dandy wanted couldn't be as troubling as the news Jericho carried inside the pocket of his duster.

A grim smile flickered.

A man against a woman. He didn't like the odds. Might as well make it two.

He clicked his tongue softly and tapped his heels to the strong brown flanks that had carried him hundreds of miles for this moment.

Time for a reckoning.

Esther North was as mad as a wet hen. She should have grabbed the shotgun the moment she saw Theodore Perkins perched on his horse like a vulture on a dead tree limb. She yanked, but Theo's hand gripped her upper arm tight as a smithy's vise.

"Leave me be, Theo."

"All I want is to help you. Can't you see that, Esther? Kin cares for kin."

"I'm not your kin." She sneered, not quite as stupid as he thought. She knew what he wanted. She also knew he'd have to kill her first.

She shivered at the thought. A woman alone, especially here on the lawless prairie, could fall prey to many evils, not the least of which was a man like Theodore Perkins.

"Go back to your saloon, Theo. I want no part of you."

His gripped tightened, his beady eyes gleaming hard as Minnesota ice, the smell of his hair oil pungent enough to turn her stomach. "Don't make me angry, Esther. I'm trying to help you."

Neither of them heard the horse approach but suddenly a man's voice intruded. "Howdy there, folks."

Esther jerked her head toward the stranger seated high on a handsome paint. A different kind of shiver ran through her. A dark pirate of a man who'd not seen a barber in some time casually leaned on his saddle horn, his gaze shaded by a battered hat.

"Who are you?" Theo's scowl deepened. He didn't take kindly to interference.

"The lady requests you unhand her." The man's voice was soft and calm but held a steel-edge, like a sharpened blade. A slight smile, not a bit friendly, edged up his cheeks.

Theo glared. "Mind your own business."

The cowboy shifted forward in the saddle. His nostrils flared. "*Now.*"

Theo growled in the back of his throat, dropped her arm and charged toward the paint horse. Esther's heart thudded as the stranger slid from the saddle to face Theodore, a man most people in Twin Springs knew not to cross.

There was about to be more trouble than she could afford. More trouble than the helpful stranger knew.

Before she could think of any other way to avoid an impending disaster she cried, "You're here!" And threw herself into the arms of a man she'd never seen in her life.

She'd expected the leap to knock him backwards, at least to make him stumble, but he stood sturdy as an oak. As if in reflex, a pair of steel-corded arms snagged her in mid-jump and reeled her in. To convince Theo the man was a long-lost love come to save her, Esther did the natural thing. She pulled down his shaggy head and kissed him.

The stranger stiffened, resistant for just long enough to make her realize what a foolish thing she'd done. But in the next instant he changed, shifted, softened.

Every bit of reason shot out of Esther's head. She'd only meant to give him a peck, a quick, dry-lipped touch to throw Theo off the scent. Instead, her knees gave way as the stranger scooped her closer, murmured something deep in his throat that set her blood to humming, and returned the kiss. By the time he stopped, Esther couldn't remember her name, much less why she was standing in the chilly wind in the front yard.

Never had she been so thoroughly, completely, wonderfully

kissed. Her blood hummed, her pulse pounded like stampeding buffalo, and she wanted to kiss him again.

Oh dear. How foolish could a lonely woman be?

When the man started to step away, Esther wobbled like a one-legged turkey. As if he'd known her forever, the stranger pulled her close again and held her up with one of those tree-trunk arms.

"You probably should head on back home, Mister," he said to Theo. "As you can see, me and Esther have some catching up to do." One diabolical eyebrow twitched upward and that small, dangerous smile returned to his lips. Oh, those magnificent lips!

Not one to give quarter, Theodore bristled, mouth thin and tight. "Who is this man, Esther? You never said anything about having a new man."

Esther regained enough composure to toss her head. It still swam and she was ever so grateful for the kissing stranger holding her upright. Let Theo think she had a new man. Give him something to worry about. "I owe you no explanations. Please go."

"You heard the lady." Pirate man pushed open his sheepskin coat. The handle of a six gun gleamed bronze in the weak sunlight. In a voice cold enough to cause frostbite, he said, "Leave."

Theodore's gaze flicked from Esther to the gun butt and back again. "This conversation is not finished, Esther. For your own good, I plead with you to—"

"Goodbye, Theo."

Theo sputtered and postured but mounted his horse and in a fit of temper, slapped a whip across the animal's flanks and galloped away.

Good riddance. She'd grown weary with listening to his pretend concern.

As Theo disappeared on the horizon, Esther became acutely aware of the heat and strength of the man beside her, a man she didn't know, a man she'd kissed like a brazen hussy.

Oh my. What had she done? Slowly, cautiously, she tried to

ease away from her rescuer. He held tight.

"I—thank you—" she stuttered, searching for words. "You—you've been kind."

And her toes still tingled from that kiss.

"You can turn loose now." She dared to lift her head and look at his face. What she saw there made her heart rattle against her rib cage. Fury. Loathing. And fire.

Esther stepped away quickly, yanking the shawl tighter. She'd lost her mind. What had she been thinking to throw herself at a stranger? And why on earth had he returned the kiss like-like-that?

But he'd come to her rescue. He must be a kind man, a gentleman.

She'd no more than had the thought when he said, "I figure you owe me."

Esther bristled. "What!"

Spurs jingling, he stepped up on the plank porch. "I'll take my payment now."

A hot panic tingled to the ends of Esther's hair. She'd left her Winchester inside, certain she could handle Theo. But this man? After what she'd seen, she wasn't sure anyone could handle him.

"I am not a loose woman." Though some in Twin Springs would disagree.

"No?" The wicked black eyebrow winged upward. He pushed the door open as if he owned the place.

"Absolutely not." She yanked at her skirt with both hands and hurried to the doorway, blocking the entrance with her body. She could not allow him to come inside. "That kiss was...desperation."

Looming over her, the stranger braced a hand on either side of the doorposts. The movement stirred his scent, the sage and leather smell of an outdoorsman.

Voice soft and dangerously probing, he asked, "Are you often desperate, Esther?"

Something in the question, in the voice, in the tilt of his shaggy head, set her head to spinning. Something familiar.

FIRST KISSES

A new worry tickled the back of her neck. She licked lips gone dry as jerky. "Who are you?"

He dropped his gaze to her mouth, reminding her of the kiss. She went hot, then cold as he found her eyes, pinning her with the intensity of his black, black gaze.

"Why, Esther, I thought from your rather exuberant greeting that you recognized me."

"Recognized?"

His jaw clenched. "The name's Jericho."

The blood drained from Esther's brain.

"Jericho?" she whispered.

"That's right, Esther. I'm your brother-in-law. Don't you want to kiss me again?"

CHAPTER TWO

The stunned woman-Esther-wobbled. It was all Jericho could do to keep from reaching out to offer assistance. He didn't. He couldn't touch her again. Ever. The unexplainable kiss had his mind shooting images a man ought not to think about his brother's widow. Especially a woman like her.

She'd kissed him. And he'd kissed her back. At the time, the idea had seemed like a good one, a kind of humiliation he could heap upon her head. Revenge.

But somewhere in the process something had snapped. Sparks had shot out of his eyeballs. She'd scorched him.

Had this been what she'd done to his brother? How she'd lured him to marry her and settle down out here so far from everything he'd ever cared about? A place-and a woman-that had cost Silas his life?

The thought so incensed Jericho that he pushed past her into the cabin and stalked to the fire. Out of habit, he held out his hands to feel the heat. And as he did, a bleak realization swamped him. Silas had built this fireplace with his own two hands, gathered every rock, toted every pail of mud chinking.

Throat thick with emotion, Jericho stroked his fingertips over the wood mantle, a chunk of oak polished by time and undoubtedly by his brother. He hadn't expected this, to feel Silas in this place. To miss the brother he hadn't seen in years with an ache that pushed at his chest and eyes.

Behind him the door clicked shut. *Her.*

He snatched his hand away from the mantle but didn't turn around. With thoughts of Silas and the unexpected kiss strong in his head, he wasn't ready to do battle with the harlot.

He heard her move into the cabin, the soft shuffle of feet against the plank floors. The sound stopped and the hairs on the back of Jericho's neck quivered. Features carefully steeled, he drew in a deep breath of broth-scented air and slowly turned.

Esther stood quietly before him, hands clasped at her narrow waist, watching him from gray eyes. Esther. A harlot shouldn't have a Bible name. Unless it was Delilah.

He didn't want to call her Esther, the queen whose grace and beauty had won a king and saved her people. This Esther was no great beauty. Too thin and plain with ordinary brown hair bunched around her shoulders in thick waves. A decent woman put her hair up.

"Silas built this," he said.

Something flickered in her November gray eyes.

"You're Silas's brother."

"In the flesh."

"Have you journeyed far?"

"Far enough."

His terse replies didn't seem to affect her, though he could see the questions she wanted to ask.

Instead, she said, "Would you like some coffee? I have a stew boiling."

"Coffee sounds good." So civil, the pair of them, as they circled around each other. She must wonder why he was here after all this time but he wasn't ready to let her in on the secret just yet. Not until he knew more. "What was that about? The man in the yard?"

She went to the cook stove at the other end of the cabin. Her back to him, she plunked a coffee pot onto the black step-top stove. "Nothing for you to be concerned about. And for the record, the kiss was a mistake, though you didn't seem to mind at the time."

Jericho brushed aside a truth he didn't want to deal with. "What did he want?" A thought struck him. "Are you behind on a mortgage?"

"No."

A cord of tension left his shoulders. He liked what little he'd seen of the homestead with the barn and corrals and the pleasant woods running along the back. The thought of the dandy in the bowler putting his snaky hands on Silas's farm wasn't a welcome one. The place had cost his brother everything.

The cabin, though rough hewn and homespun, was tidy and clean and well-put together, a bit of a surprise. His brother had never had a love for farm work or carpentry, had never planned to settle. Somehow this woman had convinced him to give up his life of adventure to buy a homestead, to build this cabin with the money he'd earned in the Colorado silver mines.

Where, Jericho wondered, was the rest of Silas's nest egg? There was nothing fancy here. Braided rag rugs on the floor, though warm and homey, cost nothing but handiwork. He shot a hard stare at the woman. Had she made them? He hadn't pictured her as the domestic type who spun cloth and braided rugs.

The rest of the cabin was every bit as ordinary. A plain, square table of dark wood surrounded by cane bottomed chairs, the cupboard and stove and a pair of slat-back rockers. He couldn't imagine his adventurous brother in a rocking chair.

To one side, beyond the table, a quilt covered the entrance into another room. The cabin was spacious, likely at the woman's insistence. She'd have wanted more, he was convinced, but like most women in her situation, she'd settled for what she could get.

The woman motioned toward the table. "You can sit if you'd like."

Watching her, he moved to the chair. Her eyes met his, then skittered away.

Was that shame? Remorse? Fear?

Jericho shrugged out of his duster, doffed his hat, and placed them on one of the hooks beside a door. Silas's hook, no doubt, a connection that struck him at every turn. He hadn't expected this.

The woman put a steaming mug on the table and went back to the cast iron stove to lift a pot lid and scoop a thick stew into a tin bowl. This, too, she sat in front of him.

"I can make cornbread."

Had she said those things to his brother? What kind of wife had she been?

The uncomfortable questions poked at him, burrs in his saddle.

"The stew is fine." More than fine. He'd not expected hospitality. Brooding a little, he stirred the boiling mix of vegetables and meat, the brothy scent pleasant. His mouth pooled. He was hungrier than he'd known. "Aren't you eating?"

"Later."

"Sit. We need to talk."

Her hands twisted at her waist, fiddling with the apron she'd tied there. "Why have you come, Jericho? Silas has been—been-" She bit her bottom lip, an enthralling puff of dark pink skin. "-gone more than two years."

"I received your letter in early November."

"That's only four months ago. I wrote you shortly after his death." Esther pulled a chair from the table and sat down. "I suppose you have questions."

She didn't know the half of it. He had a million questions, not the least of which was what was his brother doing here? With her?

"First tell me about that man." Jericho was here, maybe to stay, and he wanted to know as much as possible before he sent her packing. "I made an enemy. I need to know who he is so I know how to watch my back."

She folded her hands primly on the tabletop and studied her thumb. Her hands were cracked and dry, her nails to the quick.

"Theodore Perkins owns the Golden Cage Saloon in Twin Springs."

Twin Springs, a town less than an hour's ride north. Jericho had ridden through yesterday. He'd seen the saloon as well, a typical establishment for small towns west of the Mississippi.

"Was that where you worked?"

She blanched. "Silas told you?"

"I had a letter." Two to be exact.

"It isn't the way it sounds."

Jericho lifted his spoon to wave away her excuses. "Tell me about Perkins."

"Theo owns a lot of land in and around Twin Springs and holds interest in several of the businesses. He's also the town mayor."

"He's your kin?"

She bared her teeth. "He's married to my cousin, Hannah. God help her."

"Is he dangerous?"

"If you mean, will he shoot you in the back, no. At least, I don't think so. But he is a dangerous man to cross. He has...ways. Power."

"How?"

She glanced to the side and he watched the play of worry move across her features. He also noted, to his annoyance, the smooth white curve of her neck and the pretty arch of cheekbone. For a plain woman, she stirred him too much, and he didn't understand why. He knew what she was, what she'd done.

"Theo's involved with the railroad."

Jericho frowned into his stew bowl. Railroad officials were known to run roughshod over towns and settlers, bribing and bullying their way across the country. "How?"

"I don't know exactly. But he wants the railroad to come through Twin Springs very badly."

Which meant Perkins stood to make a fortune. "Bad enough to threaten you?"

She pushed up suddenly from the table and moved to the window. "I shouldn't have imposed my worries on a guest. This doesn't concern you."

Jericho slowly put down his spoon and pushed the empty bowl aside, stomach warmed and satisfied. She made a good stew.

"Oh, but it does concern me."

His tone must have warned her. She whirled toward him.

The document inside his duster waited. In one minute, he could exact the retribution he'd ridden hundreds of miles to get. He'd dreamed of this moment, imagined the look on her face, and the reaction when he turned her out in the cold.

With the fire crackling behind him and his belly filled, the time had come. He pushed back from the table to reach for his duster when he heard a sound that stopped his breathing.

"Mama."

Esther hurried to push aside the quilt-covered doorway. "Mama's here, precious."

Jericho's heart banged like a Colt 45. Not this. Anything but this. A child would change everything.

The woman went to a crouch, her brown skirt pooling around her. As she stood, she turned holding a long-gowned, blue-eyed boy in her arms.

Her face had gone soft as rain water and stunningly beautiful. While Jericho reeled with the unwanted news, she came at him, her rosy mouth softly bowed. A Madonna smile. The child yawned and rubbed sleep-clouded eyes.

"This is Samuel," she said, proudly. "Samuel, baby, this is your uncle Jericho."

The man looked as though she'd run at him with a hot poker.

He rocked back in the chair, eyes wide, large fingers strangling the table edge.

Esther clutched Samuel to her side, suddenly nervous again.

She still didn't know why her brother-in-law had come to Kansas. Silas was long dead and buried and there was nothing his brother could do here. One thing for certain, Jericho was not the cheerful, loving man Silas remembered. Hard, cold, and suspicious, he both frightened and intrigued her. There was something he wasn't saying. He carried secrets. The west was full of men with secrets. Outlaws and rogues, adventurers and those running from the pain of a war they couldn't forget. A woman who'd worked in a saloon had met her share. She wondered which he was.

He knew about the saloon and had judged her for working there. She wondered if he'd believe her if she told him the truth. His brother had.

But she wouldn't bother to share her situation with a stranger. A handsome, kissing stranger who seemed to bear her no sympathy. In a day or two, he'd move on, having satisfied whatever itch had brought him to Twin Springs.

"Your letter never mentioned a child." Jericho spat the angry accusation.

She hadn't? She barely remembered writing the letter. Grief had surprised her, consumed her, and left her frightened for her future and that of her unborn child. Silas, for all his faults, had cared for her. And somewhere along the line, she'd come to care for him.

"I don't—don't remember. It was a terrible time. I was with child and Silas died—those days are a blur."

The chair slammed backwards. Samuel startled. Esther tightened her arms and stepped away. Was her brother-in-law violent? Would he harm his own nephew?

"I didn't know. You should have told me. This changes everything." Jericho stalked to the fireplace, back turned as he stared into the licking flames.

"I don't understand."

His wide shoulders heaved once. "I don't expect you to. I have to think."

He strode to the coat rack and donned his duster and hat. Without a backward glance, he opened the door and went out into late afternoon.

Jericho took his horse around the house and into the barn, unsaddled him, brushed him down and turned the paint into the barn lot with a bucket of hay. The woman had done an adequate job keeping the farm going. The animals were healthy, the barn stocked with hay, though how she'd done the work alone, he couldn't imagine. Especially with a little one.

He didn't want to think about the nephew, the son his brother had never known. He leaned against a wooden stall gate and squeezed his eyes shut, imagining his brother's reaction to the news that the woman was expecting. How had Silas felt? Tied down? Or would he have whooped with joy and whirled the woman in a circle, kissing that soft, sweet mouth of hers? Would he have held her and loved her the way a man should when his wife tells him such glorious news?

He shook his head against the imagined scene. Silas was not a sentimental man.

The perverse part of him wanted to believe the child did not belong to his brother, but one look at Samuel had wiped away all doubt. The boy was handsome, his eyes as blue, his hair as pale as his father's with that particularly identifying chin dimple. Samuel belonged to Silas.

With a sigh, Jericho stroked a hand over a muscled red mule that had ambled into the barn, probably hoping for an early supper. He fed the animal a handful of hay and resumed his exploration of the property. His property.

But the will was made before Samuel's birth. What would Silas expect him to do now? How could he take the boy's birthright? But how could he not? Didn't Silas's early death demand retribution from the woman who'd brought him to such an early end? The property rightfully belonged to Jericho, not the harlot.

He found the busy creek running through the stand of woods, and in a quiet glen he spotted a single grave marked with a wooden cross. His heart clutched inside his chest as he approached and saw his brother's name inscribed in wood.

She'd buried Silas here on the property. Jericho didn't want to be grateful to her, but he was glad for that.

Though the March wind flapped at the hem of his duster and cold ran down his spine like ice water, Jericho removed his hat. His hair blew into his eyes, a good excuse for the moisture gathered there. He didn't pray much, but he believed, knowing the Almighty watched over all, so he murmured the Lord's Prayer. Then he donned his hat and after a few more contemplative moments, moved on.

He walked the woods and fields until the sky shot fire and faded into dusk. A pale yellow moon rose, and his stew and coffee wore off as he thought about the woman, the kiss he couldn't get out of his mind, and the baby he hadn't known about.

A baby didn't change what she had been or the trouble she'd brought to his brother.

When he stepped back inside the cabin, cold and every bit as muddled, she sat in one of the rockers reading a book. The boy played on a rag rug at her feet with a bowl and spoon. The fire still crackled with a pleasing warmth that Jericho's bones sorely craved. A peaceful, domestic, welcoming scene completely at odds with his expectations.

If his unannounced entrance startled Esther, she didn't let on. She tilted her face toward him, expression serene, never questioning his right to invade her home. Her calm angered him. He was confused and tormented because of her. Disgruntled, too. She had no right to be serene.

He stalked to the fire, facing her with his hands behind his back, soaking up the heat. The child, Samuel, babbled something that Jericho couldn't understand but appeared to make perfect sense to the woman. She gathered the boy into her lap and began to read quietly from the Bible.

The incongruity was too much for Jericho. Hungry and irritated, he strode to the stove. The stew had cooled but the coffee was hot and fresh. He helped himself to some of each. Beneath a dish towel, he found a partial pan of cornbread.

He looked over his shoulder at the pair in the rocker. The woman was watching him.

"You're hungry," she said. "I'll heat the stew."

"Don't bother." He should thank her for the food, for baking the cornbread. She'd not so much as flinched at feeding him, a stranger for all intents and purposes, and his grandmother would have his hide on the wall for rudeness. But the words stuck in his craw.

She went back to reading the Bible in her gentle voice, her

son listening raptly as if she read to him often. Did she claim to be a Christian?

He didn't want to think she'd changed since he'd received the letter from Silas telling him about the saloon girl he would wed. Or the letter she'd written admitting Silas had died because of her.

"Are you a religious man, Jericho?"

The question clogged the dry cornbread in his throat. He'd just prayed over his dead brother's grave. Had she been spying on him?

With a gulp of coffee, he washed down the thought along with the cornbread. "I believe in God."

"So does the devil."

The reply surprised him so much, he laughed. A short, startled bark, but a laugh nonetheless. She smiled.

Something inside him chipped loose, like a chunk of ice in the Colorado snow melts. She had a pretty smile, the way her soft mouth tilted upward at the corners and pushed a light into her cool, gray eyes.

"A person needs God out here, Jericho. I would have crumbled without Him to keep me going."

"Since Silas died?"

"Since coming west four years ago."

Jericho frowned. Was she saying she'd come to Kansas a Christian woman? Yet, she'd worked in a saloon? She didn't make sense, at least not according to his understanding of decent, Godly women. Women like his grandmother who'd raised him and Silas.

"What brought you west?" he asked, suddenly curious to better understand the woman his brother had wed. Where had she come from? And why? "Did you come out here alone?"

In the glow of lamplight, Esther's pale eyes saddened. "My family in Pennsylvania died in a diphtheria epidemic. Only I amongst six did not contract the horrible disease." Her voice faded. "I've still to ponder why God spared me and no one else."

Sympathy tugged at him and loosened his lips. "I'm sorry."

"Thank you." Loss shadowed her face, a despair he understood. He'd lost parents he didn't remember, a woman he might have loved, and comrades on the battlefield. Losing Silas, his only remaining kin had ripped him deeper than a mini-ball.

"Half the town died," she said, "and there was simply nothing left for me. My cousin, Hannah, wrote urging me to come to her in Kansas."

Like him, Esther was alone in the world, her closest kin beneath the hard soil.

The fragile moth's wing of sympathy fluttered stronger in Jericho's chest. He kept that unwelcome response out of his reply. "So you came west looking for a husband?"

Her head snapped up. "There is no shame in desiring a home and family. I'd seen the advertisements in the papers. Hannah fostered the idea, assuring me there were decent farmers and settlers in need of a good wife. There was need on both sides of the coin, to my way of thinking, and both parties benefit."

He knew about mail order brides but knew Esther hadn't been one.

Jericho's lip curled. "But you worked in a saloon instead."

Head high, she held his gaze. "After less than a week as a guest in his home, before I had opportunity to make many acquaintances, my dear cousin's husband, Theo, the scoundrel, decided I should earn my keep or get out."

Scoundrel, indeed, if what she spoke was true. "Not very hospitable of him."

"Theo is not a kind man, though I had no way of knowing this until I'd spent every penny to come here. With no money and nowhere to go—"

"—And no man rushing to be your husband?" he interrupted.

Esther's chin went up another notch. "I cleaned rooms and cooked for the upstairs girls." She pinned him with her cool gaze. "There are those who choose not to believe a woman can work in a saloon and remain a Christian. Are you one of those,

Jericho?"

Was he? Or was this a story she'd concocted to hook Silas? To regain a smidgen of respectability?

"Couldn't your cousin have intervened?"

"Hannah was beside herself, but no one in Twin Springs stands up against Theodore. Certainly not a woman."

"So you latched onto my brother as a way out."

"Latched onto?"

"My brother was an adventurer, a rambler. He was not the settling kind."

"Perhaps you didn't know your brother as well as you think."

He jerked up from the table. "What do you mean?"

"When was the last time you saw Silas?"

"Six years ago, though time and distance matters little. I know my brother." . Their joint history had now ended. Never again would he and Silas concoct some money-making scheme or ride off on a grand adventure. The reminder that his brother was gone seared a path through him.

Esther sat across the small space, her rocking chair turned toward him, the child dozing in her arms. Her gaze was mild and quiet and there was knowledge hidden there that he must come to understand before he'd know what to do. But not tonight. He was too weary, too befuddled, too stirred by the unexpected events of the day.

He must think. And yes, pray, if the Almighty would listen to such as him.

Long shadows stretched from the lantern across the cabin floor. The day had disappeared and he still hadn't told her about the will. Tomorrow was soon enough.

Itchy with uncertainty, he pushed away from the table and stood. "It's getting late. The boy needs his bed. I'll sleep in the barn."

"You're staying on tonight?"

"Tonight and indefinitely. I'm here, Esther. I'm not leaving any time soon."

She blinked, her calm countenance disturbed at last. Jericho felt a smidgeon of satisfaction in ruffling her feathers.

"May I ask your purpose?"

"Maybe I want to know my nephew better." He warmed to the idea, as good an excuse as any for now. "He's all the kin I have left."

Her posture softened as she rocked the baby in her arms. Samuel was her tender spot. He could see that and didn't know what he would do now that he knew Silas had a son.

Esther seemed to consider the validity of his statement but could find no reason to refuse him.

"Very well, then. But not the barn. The night's are too cold."

"I've slept under the stars for weeks."

"You're Silas's brother. His home is yours. He'd want that. You will sleep here in front of the fire. Samuel and I sleep there." She motioned to the quilt-covered room.

His jaw flexed. "Aren't you worried about your reputation?"

"Should I be?"

After the kiss they'd shared? Perhaps. But he'd vowed not to think about that unexpected, foolhardy moment in the yard again. Esther North was the last woman on earth he'd let touch him. Again.

CHAPTER THREE

Jericho awakened slowly to the sound of a cock's crow. A misty gray light penetrated the single east-facing window. Dawn.

He blinked the sleep from his eyes, needing a second to remember where he was. Silas's cabin. But Silas wasn't here.

Heaviness bore down on him. He'd always expected to see his brother again. They'd promised to meet somewhere on the trail or in a silver camp or back home in Indiana. Together they'd survived war and mining camps, blizzards and scorching heat. It wasn't supposed to happen like this.

He sat up, noticed the fire had been stoked at some time in the night. That bothered him. Esther had stood a few feet away and he'd not awakened. What was the matter with him? A man who slept on the trail learned to awaken at the snap of a twig. But last night, he'd slept like the dead.

No sound came from the room behind the patchwork quilt. He shoved away the bedroll and went in sock feet to the water bucket. It was empty. So, too, was the hook where the woman's cloak had hung next to his duster.

He spun to stare at the colorful patchwork quilt hanging between him and the mysterious space where she and the child slept. Where was she? Where was Silas's son?

Slipping into his boots and coat, Jericho swung the bucket up and headed out to the well. The March morning hung crisp and clean with the sun peeking above the horizon like a fresh egg yolk.

In the quiet dawn, he heard sounds coming from the barn

and followed them. Inside a stall, the woman milked a soft fawn-colored Jersey—and she was singing. She didn't hear Jericho's approach, so he stood out of sight in the dim barn watching her. A man could learn more about his enemies from observation than all the conversation in the world.

But she didn't seem so much an enemy this morning. For hours, he'd stared into the fireplace and considered all he'd learned and had fallen asleep with a prayer for wisdom on his lips.

Now, here he was, secretly watching her milk a cow with the smell of hay and warm bovine in his nostrils and his emotions, as well as his belly, running on empty.

To keep her son safely out of the way, Esther had tied his gown tail to a post. The little blue-eyed boy with the shock of blond hair looked as content and happy as the cud-chewing cow. He was a charming cherub, a toddler that reminded Jericho so much of Silas. His heart strained toward this remaining piece of his brother. His only kin.

"Onward Christian soldiers," the woman sang in a high, pleasant voice, to which Samuel marched in place like a tiny soldier, giggling now and then. Esther's hands worked in rhythm to the tune, squirting rich milk into the bucket at her feet.

Amused and oddly content, Jericho settled against the side of the opposite stall and chewed a piece of straw, watching the baby, observing the woman. As he did, he took in the barn, the tasks left undone, though the major ones were secure. Still, there was work to be done, repairs to be made. A man was needed here.

While he considered his brother's farm, Esther sang and talked and told stories to occupy the little boy. Whatever else she might be, she cared for her child.

When she rose to set the filled bucket aside and let the cow out, Jericho spoke up. "Let me take that."

She gasped and whipped around inside the small space, her skirt twirling dangerously close to the milk pail.

"Whoa, now. Easy." Jericho opened the gate and stepped

inside to rescue the milk.

"You're awake." Her cheeks flushed pink and she sounded breathless. This morning her hair was tied back in a braid, making her face look small and delicate. She was prettier than he'd first believed. Pretty enough to remind him again of the kiss.

What would she do if he kissed her again?

The thought disgruntled him. He grabbed the bucket handle and moved to open the stall while she untied Samuel's skirt and scooped him into her arms.

"Ingenious method of keeping him out of the way."

"I didn't know what else to do. Brownie is a patient cow, but Samuel is getting more active every day." She rubbed her nose against the baby's neck. "Aren't you, precious?"

The woman, the child, the motherly affection made Jericho uncomfortable. He pushed out of the stall and headed toward the house.

Esther didn't know what to make of Jericho North. One minute he was harsh and condemning, the next he carried the milk pail and paid her a compliment.

With Samuel on her hip, she fed the mule, then collected two eggs from the henhouse and went into the cabin. Jericho was coming out again as she entered.

"The woodpile's low."

"I'll get to it."

He made a huffing noise and stalked away as if she'd made him angry.

He was a bewilderment, this big, dark man who shared little in common with his late brother. He seemed angry with her for some reason. Perhaps he was disappointed that Silas, not she, had died an untimely death. Interestingly, she'd have felt the same had it not been for Samuel. Life for a woman alone was not easy, especially on the rugged, unforgiving frontier. Marrying Silas had saved her in many ways because she'd not known how long she could hold out against Theo's pressures. Even now she wondered what would become of her and this farm. Theo was determined to have it, to push the railroad through, no matter who was displaced and bankrupt in the process. As long as it wasn't him.

But neither she nor Theo had counted on Silas's brother coming into the picture.

What did he want? Why was he here? And why did he dislike his brother's widow?

With a sigh and a head full of unanswered questions, Esther set water to heat for the weekly wash and went to the shed for the wash tub.

With Samuel riding her hipbone and her arms already tired though the day was early and the work load considerable, she heard the rhythmic crack of an ax the moment she stepped outside.

Curious and more grateful than she could say, she stepped to the corner of the cabin and saw, near the barn, Jericho splitting logs on a tree stump. He'd tossed his tan coat aside and worked with his sleeves rolled back. Mesmerized, Esther saw the thick muscles of his back bunch and flex with each blow of the gleaming ax blade. His black hair shone in the bright spring sunshine, flopping onto his forehead to be repeatedly shaken away by a quick toss of his head.

Jericho North was a splendid looking man.

The thought jerked her back from the corner of the house. Whatever was she thinking to gaze moon-eyed on a man, especially one as surly and suspicious as Jericho North?

She touched her lips, remembering that moment of fire and tenderness, the way his initial assault had gentled and he'd made a sound deep in his throat as though he, too, was surprised by the feelings the kiss had engendered.

She was simply lonely. That was all. Lonely and tired. Tired of fighting with Theo about the land rights, tired of the unending work load. Tired of being alone. Jericho North had nothing to do with her errant thoughts.

Samuel needed kin. He needed to know his uncle. That was reason enough to welcome Jericho into her home.

And if thoughts of a dark stranger and warm kisses haunted

her dreams, she would simply ignore them. She, of all women, did not believe in love at first kiss.

"Sweet pea," she said to Samuel, "We have work to do. We can't stand here and ogle a handsome man all day." No matter how much pleasure the few minutes had given her.

A flock of hens pecked the ground and squawked as she carried the baby and tin wash tub back into the cabin.

Sometime later, she was elbow deep in hot suds scrubbing Samuel's soiled diapers and dresses. Her back ached from toting bucket after bucket of water into the house. Her fingers cramped and her knuckles were raw from the scrub board.

As if that wasn't enough, she still couldn't get Jericho off her mind, and Samuel was fussy. At sixteen months, the child was into everything and, worrying the hot water would burn him, she'd hooked his dress tail under the table leg. Unused to being confined inside the cabin, he took exception and cried.

She sang his favorite song. He cried louder, his tiny hands reaching for her. "Up, Mama."

"Hush, baby. Let Mama finish the wash."

His face grew red and distorted. "Mama!" He wailed at the top of his little lungs.

Resigned to the interruption and a delay in getting the wash hung out, Esther dropped diapers into the hot water to soak and reached for a drying rag.

The cabin door slammed back against the wall. Esther jerked, hit the washboard with her knee and splashed suds onto the floor. Samuel turned wide, shocked eyes toward the doorway. Mercifully, he stopped crying. His nose ran and tears streaked his cheeks.

Jericho's face was a thunderhead. "Is he hurt?"

Esther grabbed her knee. She'd have a bruise, though only one of many.

"Angry."

The man's relief was palpable. "Thank God. I thought, from the sound of him, he'd cut his leg off."

The reference made her shiver. Anything but that.

Hands fisted on his hips, his hair disheveled and sweat

gleaming on his forehead in a most attractive manner, Jericho surveyed the scene and seemed to come to a decision. He lifted the table easily with one hand and Samuel with the other.

"Come on, lad. Your mother is busy. No more crying. You scared your uncle out of five year's growth."

"I'm sorry he disturbed you."

Jericho simply said, "The woodpile's replenished."

"Thank you."

As if her gratitude irritated him, he grumbled, "The fire will warm my back as well as yours."

She bristled. "Fine."

What was wrong with the man? Had he not a trace of civility in him?

Jericho, gazing at her as if she was a spider, jostled Samuel in his arms. Her son, usually anxious with strangers, patted his uncle's cheeks and gurgled.

The sweet gesture caused a reaction in the big man. He smiled and tweaked Samuel's chin. "You're a fine boy."

Esther's heart swelled with pride and love. Samuel a fine boy but hearing the words from so disagreeable a throat made them even more true. She stuck her reddened hands back into the tub, the heat and smell of soap thick in her nostrils. She wasn't sure what to think of Jericho North.

"I have room in the tub if you've clothes to wash," she offered.

He seemed taken aback by the offer. "You'd wash my duds?"

She couldn't help but tease. "I'm fond of clean smelling clothes."

Amusement flared in his dark eyes. "Are you implying that I've ripened on the trail?"

A smile bloomed inside Esther. "A lady never mentions such things."

"No, but she carries a handkerchief to protect her sensibilities. Have you a handkerchief, Esther?"

She laughed. "Several."

They stood for a long, pleasant moment grinning at each

other. Esther could hardly believe this was the same man who'd all but called her a whore yesterday.

"Get your clothes, Jericho," she said mildly. "Do us both a favor."

"All right, then." He chuckled. "Shall I occupy Samuel while you finish the wash?"

"You'd be willing?"

"A fair trade I'd say." He chucked Samuel under the chin and caused a giggle. "He and I have some catching up to do."

"I would be deeply obliged."

He looked at her a moment longer, those intense black eyes burning with something she couldn't comprehend. "As I'm obliged for the washing."

He tucked the boy inside his duster and went out the door, leaving Esther scrubbing clothes with a puzzled smile on her face.

Sunday morning, Esther rose earlier than usual, eager for the day spent at Twin Springs Church. Jericho's place in front of the fire was already empty, his bedroll neatly placed in a corner. He was, she'd noticed in the three days since his arrival, an early riser who wasn't afraid of hard work. He spent most of each day making repairs, chopping wood, mucking the stalls. So she wasn't surprised when he came inside with the pail already filled with rich milk.

"You don't have to do that. Milking is my job." She clattered an iron skillet against the metal stove top and began to lay out strips of salt pork.

"Want me to pour it out?" The tone was gruff but his eyes twinkled.

She smiled. "Silly."

"Work's work. You're going to church." He spoke as if her announcement, made last night at supper, still surprised him. When he learned she made the trip every Sunday, he'd become quiet and moody. Jericho North was a complicated man.

"You are welcome to join us."

He didn't answer but disappeared to the barn after

breakfast while she'd dressed Samuel and filled the picnic basket with fried chicken and canned peaches.

When she stepped outside, Esther discovered the mule hitched to the wagon and waiting by the porch. Jericho sat in the driver's seat, freshly shaved, combed and wearing a clean shirt.

Delight glowed through her. She didn't understand him one bit. "You--?"

He hopped down, helped her in and handed Samuel up. Then he regained the reins and the wagon rattled out of the yard.

A bright, cold sun lit the way and Esther snuggled Samuel beneath the quilt. On the narrow wagon seat, she jostled against Jericho's warm, sturdy side. He kept his eyes on the road and the mule.

Esther chattered about the people in Twin Springs, acquainting him before they arrived, though mostly she talked to cover a sudden case of nerves. Sitting close to Jericho had her thinking things she shouldn't. About how nice it was to have a man around and how his manly presence filled the cabin in a way a woman and child alone couldn't do. About how handsome he looked with his face smooth as Samuel's and his hair neatly combed.

Her son had taken a liking to him as well, and now reached for him, babbling in his baby talk that only she understood. Last night, Jericho had stretched on the floor before the fire and Samuel had bounced on his chest. Both man and baby had laughed and played.

Her heart pinched to remember the sweetness, the swell of tenderness, the longing that had come over her.

"You're good with him," she said when he took Samuel's reaching hand and jiggled it up and down.

"I like little ones."

"Did Silas?"

Her question turned his head. "You never got to find out, did you?"

"No. And he never said." There were many things left

unsaid between her husband and her.

For a moment, his silence was broken only by the bounce and rattle of the wagon.

No doubt, the stark reality of Silas's sudden death and the fact that he'd never known his child weighed on Jericho's heart. It weighed on hers.

"When I was maybe ten," he said at last, "a mother with two babies came to live with us. I don't know who they were, if they were kin, but it fell my chore to tend the young 'uns while Grandma and Rose preserved the vegetables."

"Silas told me about your grandmother."

"She was a good woman. We were an ornery pair of boys." He tapped Samuel's cheek. "You'll promise not to give your mother fits. You hear me, son?"

Something quivered inside Esther. Son. For the briefest moment, a fairy tale danced through her head. What if Jericho had been Samuel's father? Just as quickly, she blinked away the errant thought, disturbed at the attraction to Silas's perplexing brother.

"Look." She pointed, saw her finger tremble and yanked it down again, her heart thudding strangely against her ribs. "You can see the church steeple from here. We're almost there."

Jericho jangled the reins and set the mule trotting the rest of the way.

CHAPTER FOUR

Jericho still questioned his decision to attend church. But the last three days had been different than he'd expected and perhaps a trip to town, in the company of the people who knew her best, would shed some light on his brother's widow.

He didn't want to admire her but she tended her son with loving care and worked harder than any man he'd ever known. Yesterday, when he'd returned from riding the hundred and sixty acre spread, she'd been in the field, plowing. The sight had weakened his knees and made him mad. Plowing was man's work. No wonder she was thin as a bed slat.

He'd taken charge, a bit gruffly, and finished the job, sending her and Samuel to the house. He couldn't understand why she'd take umbrage at his offer of help.

Now, he stood in the church yard surrounded by the gathering worshippers who'd come early to visit with neighbors, to share recipes and catch up on the news. They'd no more than arrived when a plump woman in a fancy dress and a jaunty blue hat above bouncy yellow ringlets had hurried toward them.

"And who is this?" The woman had said prettily, stretching a small hand toward him. Jericho couldn't help comparing the smooth, pampered skin to Esther's work-reddened hands.

"My brother-in-law. Jericho, my cousin Hannah Perkins."

Hannah's bow mouth tipped up in a smile. "So, you're the man who put such a bee in Theo's bonnet."

"I did my best."

His reply brought a laugh from pretty Hannah and a

worried frown from Esther. She jostled a wiggling Samuel. Jericho took the boy from her.

He wanted no trouble, though he knew he'd made an enemy of Theodore Perkins. He glanced around the yard but didn't see the disagreeable dandy.

"Jericho's been wonderful help on the farm."

"I see that." Hannah's eyebrows twitched at the baby happily tugging at Jericho's hair. "It's about time you had a real man to help you."

"Hannah." Esther shook her head slightly, but Jericho caught the signal. What was she keeping from him?

"You knew my brother?" he said to Hannah.

"Everyone in Twin Springs knew Silas. He spent considerable time in the saloon."

"Hannah!"

He saw Esther's consternation and didn't understand. He knew they'd met in a saloon. "At the time he met Esther, you mean."

Hannah batted guileless blue eyes. "Well, of course, then, but before and after, too."

Jericho's mood darkened. "What are you implying?"

Esther gripped her cousin's arm, eyes widened in desperation, but Hannah gave her a sharp look and kept talking. "Esther should have told you, but she protected him too much. I liked Silas. He didn't have a mean bone in his body, but after the accident, he gave up. He quit working on the farm. He didn't even finish the cabin. If not for Esther..." Hannah's voice gentled as she looked at Esther. "She took pity on him. She saved him."

Jericho's whole body went on alert. A sense of foreboding, dark as a crow, hung in the Sunday air. "What accident? Silas never mentioned an accident."

Both women turned horrified eyes in his direction. Esther's chapped fingers touched her lips.

"Oh, dear." Hannah reached out to him. "Jericho, forgive me. I am deeply sorry to have spoken out of turn. I thought you knew."

"Knew what? What happened?"

Esther slipped her hand into his elbow and squeezed, an offer of comfort about something he wasn't going to like. What had happened to his brother?

"Just tell me."

"Silas had a wagon accident a few years ago." Esther bit her lip and swallowed, gray eyes as wide and pale as the overcast sky. "His right leg...had to be amputated."

All through church service, Jericho prayed and fretted. The last four months of his life were unraveling all around him. Silas had lost a leg in a wagon accident. He'd taken to drink and self-pity. Why hadn't Silas written to him? And why hadn't Esther told him before now?

But he knew why. He'd forced his way into her life, certain she'd caused his brother's demise, and he'd given her no reason to trust him with anything.

He slid a glance at the woman sitting next to him on the hard wooden pew. With serene and rapt attention, Esther held her baby and listened to the sermon.

Stunned and heartsick, Jericho tried to focus on the preacher, too, a red-faced man with a shiny bald head. He was reading a scripture.

"And Ananias went his way, and entered into the house; and putting his hands on him said, Brother Saul, the Lord, even Jesus, that appeared unto thee in the way as thou camest, hath sent me, that thou mightest receive thy sight, and be filled with the Holy Ghost.

And immediately there fell from his eyes as it had been scales: and he received sight forthwith, and arose, and was baptized."

"Have you scales on your eyes, brethren?" The preacher leaned over the pulpit and gazed into the group of listeners with a penetrating stare. The words spoke straight to Jericho's soul. "Is there something God wants you to see but you've turned a blind eye?"

The rest of the service faded away as Jericho wrestled with a truth he didn't want to believe and a faith he'd stuffed in his saddlebags and forgotten for too long.

He'd been wearing blinders like some out-of-control mule, refusing to see because he needed someone to blame. That someone had been Esther.

The two of them were headed for a long conversation. And this time, he'd keep his mouth shut and listen.

When the service ended and they'd filed outside with the other congregants, Jericho took Esther's elbow. "Do you mind if we don't stay for dinner?"

"Aren't you hungry?"

"We could eat in the wagon or wait until home." He had to know the truth. All of it. Food wouldn't settle until he did. "We need to talk. But not here."

Esther's pale eyes searched his face before coming to a decision. "Of course. Let me say goodbye to Hannah."

Jericho took Samuel from her, holding the boy while she, in her simple brown dress, wove amongst the gathering in the journey to her brightly feathered cousin. Church-goers spoke to her, smiled. Would they do that if she'd been a conniving harlot as he'd believed?

He watched her, realizing he admired her. The memory of that troublesome, dangerous kiss danced around the edges of his mind, as sweet as her lips. If such a thing was possible.

Baby Samuel patted his cheeks. Wryly, he said, "Keep slapping me, son. I deserve it."

Just then, Theo Perkins broke away from a group of men and headed toward the two women who were deep in animated conversation.

Jericho straightened, alert and watchful. He didn't trust Theo Perkins as far as he could throw a buffalo.

A warning, like cold fingers, raised the flesh on the back of his neck. He'd known such men in the silver fields of Colorado. Men who, under the cover of respectability, took advantage of anyone for gain.

He had news for Mayor Perkins. Esther had nothing to give him.

"Time to mosey on over, Sammy." He tucked the child close and strode quickly toward the women.

As he approached, he saw Theo's oily smile aimed at a bristled Esther. Jericho smiled a little. He recognized that bristle, like a porcupine when riled.

"I have already refused your offer, Theo. Your railroad can build across the back of the acreage where I showed you, but I won't sell."

"I'm offering you a fair deal, Esther."

"Fair for whom?"

"Theo, please," Hannah begged, her hand on her husband's arm. "We're at church. You're the mayor, an important public figure. You don't want to be overhead haggling in the shadow of the steeple."

Jericho stepped up beside Esther. "It was a pleasure to meet you, Hannah. We're leaving now."

Without so much as a glance at Theo Perkins, he tucked Esther's hand into his elbow and led her to the wagon.

"I could have handled Theo," Esther said as the wagon pulled out of the church yard and rumbled toward home. Though the truth was, she didn't know how. "But thank you for intervening. I've grown weary of his bullying."

"Why didn't you tell me about Silas?"

The abrupt change of subject didn't surprise Esther. She'd known he'd want more details, but how did she tell him without breaking his heart, without sullying his fond memories of a beloved brother? "Would you have listened?"

"No." Reins in both hands, he turned his head to look at her. Samuel, weary from the long sermon, lolled across her lap, eyelids drooping, thumb in his mouth. "But I'm listening now."

"Why now?"

"Let's just say the scales have fallen from my eyes."

Holding his gaze, she considered his words, her heart softening toward him. She'd felt his tension during the church service, seen him bow his head with hands clasped tight against his forehead. "What do you want to know?"

"Everything. How did you come to know my brother? Is it true what Hannah said? Was Silas a drunk?"

"Silas was—" She stopped and sighed, grappling for the right words. "Theo introduced us. Though I hadn't heard of the railroad coming through at that point, I think Theo pushed the two of us together believing I'd convince Silas to sell out. Silas's heart wasn't in homesteading-he'd built a shed and not much else. Even I wondered why he didn't sell."

"That sounds more like him. Sell out and move on. Why didn't he?"

"He was secretive about his reasons, but Silas wanted to mine the property for silver."

"Here? In Kansas?"

She'd been every bit as incredulous.

"There is no silver, Jericho. It was just a dream." Her arms grew heavy from holding Samuel. Tenderly, she shifted his weight and eased his thumb from between his bow mouth. "After the wagon accident and the amputation, Silas lost his ambition. He came to the saloon more and more. He was quickly falling apart."

"So you did Theo's bidding? You convinced Silas to marry you? Is that what happened?"

"No, it isn't. Please believe me." Suddenly, she urgently wanted his trust. "Silas needed help. So did I. Theo threatened to...force me...upstairs." A hot blush rushed through her body and heated her cheeks, the humiliation still fresh and painful. "One day, after Silas overheard Theo pressuring me, he offered a solution that would help us both. We married that evening at the preacher's house."

Silas had been drunk, but she didn't tell Jericho that.

She'd been scared out of her head to marry a man she barely knew, a man she'd seen inebriated more often than sober, but she'd believed they could help each other. And she'd been certain she had to get out of the saloon and away from Theo's grasp. Silas had been her best hope. And she'd been his.

Jericho's fingers tightened on the reins. "Did you ever care for him?"

"Of course I did. I wouldn't have married him otherwise. From the beginning he was a friend. I knew he had a heartache he didn't know how to handle, but he was a kind man who treated me well." She warmed to the fond memory. "And he gave me a home, Jericho. Even though he cared little for the farm, he was glad I did. He wanted me there. I tried my best to make his life better, easier, happier. I didn't mind the work. It was far preferable to the saloon, and I had a home and a gentle, if broken, man. I was not unhappy with your brother."

"Was Silas content?"

The cold air seeped into her toes and fingers and bit at her nose. She snuggled the quilt closer around her son, buying time while she pondered the best way to describe the man Silas had become.

"I believe he was as happy as he knew how to be. He had moments, days even. But losing his leg stole something from him beside a limb, and when the pain became unbearable, he'd go to the saloon."

His jaw flexed. "While you worked the farm."

She refused to put Silas in a bad light. Jericho didn't deserve that, and neither did Silas. "My husband's memory is valuable to me, Jericho. Silas is Samuel's father, and I won't have him dishonored in death. Silas and I worked out an arrangement that benefited us both. And when he learned I was with child, he was the happiest I'd ever seen him."

"Did he stop drinking?"

She bit down on her bottom lip. "He tried."

She fell silent, waiting for his questions, wishing she could give him a rosier picture of his brother's last years.

The wagon rumbled along, past tall stands of prairie grass and another homestead with smoke curling from the chimney in a silver ribbon. Samuel slept in her lap, the chicken and peaches in the lunch basket ignored.

Her throat thickened with pity for Jericho and with the need for him to understand why she'd done the things she'd done.

Marriage for other than love was a way of survival in the west. Surely, he understood that. Love was a commodity she'd longed for but had never been able to afford.

The homestead came into sight. Chickens scattered, squawking, as they pulled the wagon alongside the porch and unloaded.

"I'll put the horse and wagon away," Jericho said, not looking at her. His tone was short, almost harsh, and her empty stomach sunk low.

Just when she'd thought they were finding their way...

Was the truth too hard for him to bear? Did he despise her more for telling him about his brother?

She prayed he didn't. She cared very much about Jericho's opinion. Too much, she realized with a deep dawning, like a flower bud opening in the cold spring, afraid of the exposure but yearning to bloom.

He was more than her husband's brother, this man of moods who, in a few short days, had shouldered the farm work as if it was his right and responsibility. He was more than a farm hand, more than a playmate who delighted Samuel.

From the moment he'd ridden into the yard, she'd thought of little except him. Now, throat tight with realization, she understood why.

Jericho was the man she'd dreamed of meeting when she'd come west full of girlish hopes. The man she'd prayed God would send. The kind of man she wanted to love her.

While Esther stood on the porch, shocked and reeling from her heart's unexpected revelation, Jericho shook the reins and drove away.

CHAPTER FIVE

Long after the mule was fed and the wagon stored, Jericho lingered in the barn. He prayed. He thought. He wondered.

There was one thing she hadn't told him. Yes, he believed her now, though the newfound acceptance cost him dearly.

"Silas," he muttered into the bits of dust and hay stirring up from the barn floor. "My brother. Why didn't you tell me? I would have come. I would have helped."

But he knew the answer before he asked. They'd been brothers, but they'd parted ways for a legitimate reason. All their lives, they'd competed, besting one another each time the opportunity rose. They'd been the same in the silver fields and on the cattle trails. A broken, crippled Silas would have been too proud to ask his able-bodied brother for help.

Heartsick, Jericho went to the tack room and retrieved the letters from his saddlebag. Two from Silas and one from Esther.

As he reread, infuriating moisture pushed behind his eyelids. Now that he knew the truth, he could read the false cheer in his brother's words. Why, though, having married, had Silas willed his property to Jericho instead of his bride? He could see nothing in the letters that resolved his questions, but there had to be a reason.

And Jericho had to tell Esther that he, not she, owned the homestead.

But how? When he'd believed her to be a conniving harlot who'd used his brother mercilessly the way had been clear.

Now, he thought of Esther, of her back-breaking work and

her rough, damaged hands. He considered the way she loved her son and cherished Silas's memory even though times must have been hard. He remembered the way she'd welcomed him into her cozy cabin with food and kindness.

He could keep the contents of the will to himself, saddle his horse and ride away, though his chest pinched at the thought of never seeing her and Sammy again. But what if Theo pressured her into selling? What if times became too hard for a woman alone and she gave up his brother's land? land.

"Lord Almighty," he breathed, stuffing the letters into his pocket. "Nothing is clear anymore."

"I have one more question." Jericho hung his coat and hat on the hook inside the door and extracted Esther's letter from his pocket.

Samuel was nowhere in sight and Jericho suspected he was asleep behind the quilt. He missed the little critter even in those short times of napping.

The fireplace had been stoked and he was proud of the pile of wood he'd put by for her. For them, he supposed, because he couldn't leave. Self-preservation said he should. Ride away and forget the will, but he couldn't. Not now. Not after he'd come to know her better.

His need for retribution had become tangled with the truth and with admiration. Revenge was easier.

She'd put the chicken and peaches on the table along with thick slices of yeast bread made fresh yesterday. The woman could cook.

Two plates thudded softly as she set them out on a muslin table cloth he hadn't seen before. Sunday best, he supposed.

But right now, food could wait. Before he could decide what to do, he needed one more answer.

"What is it?" she asked, straightening.

"Something you wrote in your letter." There was no question of which letter. She'd only written one to inform him of his brother's death.

She arranged a fork next to each plate, her expression

serious. "And?"

He held up the rumpled pages he'd read many times. So often he'd memorized the words as well as her small, precise handwriting, the script tidy and pretty and clearly feminine. "You said Silas died to protect you. What did you mean? I thought I understood but--"

He hadn't. He knew that now.

A pained look flashed in her eyes. She swallowed, hands white-knuckled against the table edge.

"Did you think he died fighting with one of my former—customers?" She spat the word as though it was nasty. For indeed, it had become so.

Jericho shifted, his boots scraping the wood floor like a guilty school boy. "I was wrong."

Two pink circles dotted her cheekbones. "Yes, you were."

He'd hurt her, embarrassed her. For that he was truly sorry. He fought the unexpected urge to pull her close and say her part in Silas's death didn't matter. But it did. Nothing would be right again until all the scales fell from his eyes. Even those concerning his brother.

"What happened?" He turned the letter over in his hands. "You gave no details."

That fact loomed large now, though he'd not seen it before. He'd been too busy blaming Silas's widow and her disreputable past. A past that had existed only in his angry imagination.

Esther's skirt swished as she came around the table, fingers nervously working the folds of worsted wool. "Silas saved my life. Mine and our baby's."

"How?"

"We had a barn-raising. The weather was as hot as any June day could be, but the church men came to help. I was proud of Silas that day. He was out there working right along with the men while the ladies and I prepared a meal."

"He didn't normally?"

She glanced to the side, hedging. "Sometimes. When he felt up to it."

Jericho heard what she didn't say. She'd been the laborer,

not Jericho, and it broke him in half to know how far his brother had fallen.

"He was in a happy mood that day. I'd told him about the baby a few days before, and he'd been making plans."

"Silas liked to make plans."

She smiled as they exchanged a shared memory. "Yes, he was always making plans. One of them was to build the barn, a big change from the wild plans to return to Colorado or head to Alaska."

"He talked of leaving you?"

She shook her head. "Only on the bad days. He'd say he was no good for me or that we'd never have anything here on this desolate prairie. After he learned of the baby, he seemed happy. I thought he was moving in the right direction. We'd build a wonderful life here on the homestead and he'd be strong again. He would have been a good father, I'm sure of it."

"You loved him."

"In the end, I did. I miss him still."

"How did it happen?"

The story wasn't easy for her. He could see that by the way she gazed off into space, her mouth pulled down at the corners.

"The men were raising a wall. I'd come out with a pitcher of cool tea. Without warning, one of the men tripped. I heard a shout and looked up to see the wall falling toward me." She gave a small, sad laugh that broke his heart. "Before I understood fully what was happening, Silas slammed into me. We both hit the ground. His body was across mine. I felt the impact of the wall and heard him grunt as something struck his head--" Her voice broke. Tears like drops of silver glistened on her eyelashes. "He saved me, Jericho. And he saved our baby."

Jericho squeezed his eyes shut, but the vision of her description was hiding in the darkness, vivid and bloody. In a raspy voice he barely recognized as his own, he asked, "Did he suffer?"

"I don't think so." She put a hand to her chest as though

her heart ached. He understood because his did too.

Jericho moved closer and put his hands on her upper arms. She was trembling. Again, he battled the urge to hold her. "Was he...drunk?"

She raised her head to look at him, eyes soft with compassion. "Your brother was a hero, Jericho. That's how I want to remember him. That's how I want Samuel to know him. Nothing can lessen his final, courageous act."

Her loyalty touched him as Jericho understood what she refused to admit.

"I won't make you say it, but he was. Drunk to the end."

"No, no. We prayed. He was conscious for a while and completely sober by the end. He accepted the Lord before he—before—"

His throat filled. He squeezed her arms in gratitude. "Thank you."

But gratitude wasn't the only emotion coursing through his blood.

Time stopped. Jericho's heart raced inside his chest as fast as the thoroughbreds he'd watched in Missouri. All thought and feeling became centered on the woman.

Jericho gazed down into soft gray eyes that looked at him with heartache and something he couldn't quite understand, but something the man in him responded to. He moved closer, inexplicably, enticingly drawn to plain and simple Esther as he'd never been drawn to any other woman.

He'd been wrong about her. She was nothing, like he'd imagined. Silas had been the luckiest man alive to find her.

The scales had truly fallen from his eyes.

"Jericho," she said softly, and he was as lost as a child in the desert, thirsting for what only Esther could give him.

He cupped her cheek, awed by the contrast of his dark hand against her milk-pale skin. So delicate and lovely.

He'd kissed her before but this time was different. Before had been selfish and angry. But this. .

As he slowly drew her to him, relieved and bolstered that she came to him without hesitation, he lowered his head and touched his mouth to hers.

A rush of sensation washed through him, a river out of its banks. Esther, as beautiful to him now as her namesake, melted into him, sweet and soft and giving, pliant within his embrace. He tasted the peaches she'd snitched while setting out the food and felt the gentle fire her love would be.

Love? Could this be love?

The earth moved beneath his boots, rocking him. And for the first time in his life, Jericho felt centered as if he'd come home. He, a rambler and adventurer like his brother, felt at home in the arms of a woman.

His brother. Silas. And the woman was his brother's wife.

A mix of guilt and longing warred within him. She was Silas's wife. She didn't know about the will.

She was everything he wanted.

This couldn't be happening. But it was.

Esther shivered with pleasure and wonder. Jericho's fresh-air scent and masculine warmth filled her head. She didn't know how it had happened, but her arms were around his middle and the muscles of his back were strong and hard beneath the palms of her hands.

And though she admired his strength and physical beauty, it was his tenderness that brought tears to her eyes.

Long after the kiss ended, Jericho held her, cradling her head against the smooth cotton of his shirt. She'd rested there as content and safe as she'd been since losing her family. They said nothing for a long time. The fire crackled and the house settled around them, and he held her as if she was a delicate flower he didn't want to crush.

Did he understand how easily he could crush her heart, this man who'd arrived with anger only to give her wild hope?

She raised her head to tell him, but he kissed her again and she let go of the worry.

A familiar sound invaded her consciousness. She stiffened and pulled back, putting hands to her scalding cheeks. "Samuel's awake."

The words came out breathless and husky.

His gaze searched hers but he offered no clue to his thoughts. Should she regret the kiss? Did he think less of her for allowing liberties?

He simply said, "I'll get him."

She nodded and stepped away, feeling the loss of his comforting strength all the way to her toes. "Dinner's ready...when you are."

His boots thudded quietly across the floor of her cabin and disappeared behind the quilt. While she stared, stunned and yearning, she heard the rumble of his voice and the responding gurgle of happiness from her son. When she managed to force herself to turn away, she heard the quiet cadence of "patty-cake" between man and baby.

Everything inside her turned to warm pudding.

She clasped her hands to her waist and listened to the precious sound of man and baby playing.

If she hadn't been falling in love with Jericho before, she was now. Was such a thing possible?

Her heart responded with a leap of joy. Yes. Yes, it was.

Dear Jesus, what was she going to do? She was in love with a man she barely knew. A man who had come to Kansas only for answers about his brother.

Now that he had them, he was bound to leave again.

And he would take her heart with him.

CHAPTER SIX

Theodore Perkins rode into the yard just after noon the following day.

From his knees in the garden's soft, freshly turned dirt, Jericho watched the dandy ride in astride the tall roan horse. "Got company."

Esther, on her knees beside him, set back on her feet and ran the back of a wrist over her forehead. He'd never imagined a woman could be appealing with her hair flying loose around the edges of her calico bonnet and dirt on her hands and cheeks, but Esther was.

He'd had a time this morning watching her make biscuits and gravy while he brought in wood and then repaired a broken bridle at the kitchen table. He'd wanted to kiss her again but kept a distance. He didn't know what he was going to do about her, about the land and the will. Kissing her without promises wasn't fair to either of them.

But oh, he wanted to.

Now here was Theodore Perkins again, and Jericho didn't expect a friendly visit.

"Want me to send him down the road?" he asked, seeing the fretful crease in Esther's brow.

She pushed to a stand and dusted the dirt clods from her brown skirt. "This isn't your fight."

The statement stabbed a bit. She was wrong, for more reasons than she knew, and he couldn't tell her. Soon, but not yet. Not until he knew how to break the news without breaking her.

She mattered. As much as he hadn't intended her to, Esther had woven a soft yarn around his heart and mind.

"How do you know there will be a fight?"

"With Theo there always is."

Jericho tossed a potato back in the tow-sack. "I'm going with you."

With Samuel on her hip, Esther went to greet her visitor. Jericho, determined to help whether she liked it or not, joined her stride for stride.

Theo waited on the porch, the glossy roan tied to the railing. His face hardened when he saw Jericho. He turned his attention on Esther.

"My dear cousin, how nice to see you again." He chucked Samuel under the chin. "Your handsome baby is growing faster than poke weed."

With a serenity belying her worry, Esther ignored the man's false niceties and said, "What can I do for you, Theo?"

"Could you spare a cup of coffee for a friend?"

Jericho didn't want the man in the house, but the ever-hospitable Esther hesitated only a moment before giving a nod and leading the way inside.

Perkins, he noticed, made himself at home in one of the rockers beside the fire. Jericho left the other for Esther and took a spot behind it. Esther lowered Samuel to the floor and heated the coffee. Jericho took the mug from her and carried it to Perkins. He didn't want her waiting on the man like a servant.

"Here's your coffee, Perkins. Now, state your business. We have potatoes to plant."

"We?" Theo ignored the rudeness in Jericho's demand and lifted an eyebrow. "Esther, have you taken in a paramour?"

Esther's shoulders stiffened. "What brings you out here, Theo?"

He crossed his legs and sipped at the coffee, as relaxed and confident as a sunning rattler. "Concern for you, of course, as always. Though you doubt my intentions because of some unfortunate misunderstandings at the saloon, I have your best interest in mind. You are, after all, my dear wife's cousin, a widow alone in the world, and as such, I bear a certain responsibility."

Jericho fought not to roll his eyes. Of all the smarmy men, Theo won the prize.

"I'm not selling this land. Silas entrusted our home to me and I won't give it up. This is Samuel's legacy." At his name, the baby toddled to his mother and smiled.

Perkins sighed a beleaguered sigh. "You will certainly find my price more agreeable than the railroad's. Have you heard of the law of eminent domain?"

Jericho's gut knotted. He had.

"I have not."

Theo picked a bit of invisible lint from his trousers. "The railroad has a right to purchase your property regardless of your wishes."

Esther thrust forward in the rocker, shocked. "They do not!"

Jericho put his hand on her shoulder and squeezed. "They do."

"How can that be?" She twisted to stare up at him in anguish. The sight tore at him. "That's wrong!"

"I agree. But it is the law."

Perkins, clearly enjoying her discomfort and his advantage, sipped at the coffee, a half smile on his lips. Jericho's fists itched to knock it off.

"The railroad will offer you very little, Esther." Theo uncrossed his legs and leaned forward. In for the kill, Jericho thought. "I, on the other hand, because you are a relative and a widow, will offer top dollar." He reached inside his coat. "I brought the papers today. All you need to do is sign and the bank will issue a check."

Esther shrank away from the offered documents. "I don't believe this. I want to speak to the railroad superintendent myself."

"That's quite impossible. He's out of state." Theo's obsequious smile hardened. "I'm doing you a favor, Esther.

Don't let this opportunity slip by. The railroad is moving forward. I had a wire yesterday concerning this property. They take possession. The paperwork is on its way. You must act now. Once the railroad steps in, my hands are tied. I'll no longer be able to help you and your son."

Beneath Jericho's hand, Esther trembled. He'd kept quiet as long as he could. "You're upsetting your *dear cousin*, Mr. Perkins. I suggest you take your offer and your papers and leave."

Esther reached back and placed a hand over his. "I need time to think about this. There has to be another solution."

Theo plunked the cup on the floor. A bit of coffee splashed out. He ignored it. "There is none."

Jericho released Esther's shoulder and moved from behind to beside her. "She's not signing those papers."

She couldn't. The land wasn't hers to sell. Mind racing, he sought for answers and came up empty. Even though he owned the property, if the railroad exercised their power, there was nothing he or Esther could do to stop the sale.

"This is none of your business, North." Theo dropped the paperwork in Esther's lap. "I'm showing you a kindness, my dear. Don't listen to this stranger."

Esther clutched at the legal-looking documents and gnawed her bottom lip. Jericho ached for her. She loved this farm. She'd put her sweat and tears and toil into making a life here. Why had Silas willed the property to him? Why had his brother put both of them in this predicament?

"I can't do it." She handed the document up to Theo who loomed over her like a vulture.

Perkins snatched the forms from her. "You have two days before I rescind my generous offer and let the railroad steal your farm. You know where to find me."

"I don't understand any of this." Esther crossed her arms, stared into the dying fire and rocked. "How could this happen?"

Aching for her, Jericho kneeled in front of the chair and

made a promise he didn't know if he could keep. "I won't let you lose your home."

"You heard Theo. There's nothing anyone can do." She stopped rocking and stared at him, bereft. "Perhaps I should go ahead and sell now while I can get a good price. He's offered enough to buy a little place in town."

"And do what for a living? Work in the saloon again?"

Her eyes widened with horror. "What if I must for Samuel's benefit?"

"I won't let that happen, Esther." No matter what he had to do. "Perkins seems in a big hurry to me. I don't trust him. I think there's more he's not saying."

Hope flared in her eyes. "I thought the same, but what?"

"I don't know, but I aim to find out."

"Why? Why would you get involved? This isn't your property or your problem?"

But he couldn't. She had too much on her mind already. Later, when things were settled. When he could make her understand.

"I think you know why, Esther." He gripped her fingers with one hand. The baby wiggled in between them and babbled something. Jericho patted his little back.

Her eyes searched his. "For Samuel? Silas?"

"Yes, for my brother and my nephew. But most of all, for you."

"Oh, Jericho."

"I...care for you, Esther. No matter what happens, I'll see that you and Samuel are taken care of."

She touched his face. A shiver of pleasure ran through him. "Silas was right about you. You're a good man."

Not good enough. But he could change. He had changed. Esther and the Lord had taken the scales from his eyes, and now he could not only see her for who she was, but he saw Theo Perkins as a slimy snake oil salesman out to swindle a widow.

But the dandy mayor hadn't counted on her brother-in-law coming along to object.

"Perkins is pushing too hard too fast. I think you're right. We need to talk to that railroad boss before any decisions are made."

"I don't know how to contact him."

"Someone does." And Jericho planned to find out today.

Two days later, Esther dressed in her Sunday best and nervous as a cornered mouse, straightened her shoulders, tucked her hand into Jericho's elbow and walked into the Twin Springs Hotel. From the dining room came the savory smell of roast beef. Her belly rumbled in appreciation but too much was at stake to concern herself with food.

Jericho paused at the lobby desk and said to the clerk, "Has Alfred Howard arrived?"

The clerk rubbed ink-stained fingers across his thin mustache. "Yes, sir. Mr. Howard came in on the morning stage. He's in room six."

Jericho turned to Esther. "Are you ready?"

She nodded, too nervous to reply. The next few minutes held her future.

"Hey now," he chided softly. "Hold to hope."

"What if he doesn't listen?"

"Then, we'll think of something else. Now, stop fretting. We're in this together." He touched her cheek with a tenderness that generated an ache of longing.

Together. Did he know how much she wanted that to be true? Did he have any idea she was in love with him or how sad she'd be when this was over and he moved on?

Drawing on his strength, she took a deep breath. "Let's talk to Mr. Howard before Theo discovers why we're in town."

He winked, the smile edging up his face. "That's my girl."

Then he strode away, boots pounding with confidence on the wooden stairs. She'd never known anyone like Jericho North. In such a short time, she'd gone from fear to love and trust. He made her believe everything would work out for the best even when the odds were so clearly stacked against her.

With Samuel toddling at her side, she led the way to the

settee along one wall overlooking the main street. She lifted her son onto the sofa so the outside could entertain him. Rain had fallen yesterday but already the relentless prairie wind had turned the ruts hard and dry. Wagons and carriages bumped past. The blacksmith's wife went into the dry goods store, three children in tow. Normal, everyday activities played out around Esther while her future-and Samuel's-teetered uncertainly in this hotel.

Esther squeezed her hands together in her lap and thanked God for Jericho. She feared she would have folded under Theo's pressure to sell except for his unexpected support and determination. A simple telegraph had revealed that the railroad superintendent would be in Twin Springs today.

Theo must have known, yet he'd chosen to keep that information to himself.

Just then, Jericho reappeared on the stairs behind a portly man in a brocade vest. Esther's body froze, so nervous was she.

Smiling and appearing relaxed though she felt his tension, Jericho made the introductions and they were all seated.

"So you are Mrs. North, the lady who owns the property south of town." The portly man seemed friendly enough.

"Yes, sir. That's what I wanted to speak to you about. I'm a widow, sir, with a son, as you can see. We've built a good life on my farm. I sell eggs and butter and raise my own hogs and crops. The prairie is vast. Can't the railroad build somewhere else besides my land?"

"Begging your pardon, ma'am, but if we accommodated every settler who didn't want the railroad on his land, there would be few trains. Months of preparation go into the decisions. We need that strip between the springs."

Esther's hopes disappeared like wood smoke in a gale. She dropped her head, fighting tears. It wouldn't do to cry in front of a businessman. "I see."

"What if she deeded you that strip, free of charge?"

At Jericho's voice, Esther's head jerked toward him. What was he doing? They'd agreed not to sell. And now he was offering the land for free?

Jericho's hand covered hers. "If one strip of land is all the railroad requires, then why take the entire farm?"

Mr. Howard straightened in his chair, a bewildered look on his round face. "Pardon my confusion, but as I told Mrs. North's representative months ago—"

Esther leaned forward, pulse thudding. "I have no representative."

"Theodore Perkins is your cousin, is he not, and therefore able to represent you in matters of business?"

"He is neither."

"Mayor Perkins gave me to understand that you would not sell any part of your land for any reason. This is why I had no recourse but to invoke the power of eminent domain."

"Theo said nothing to me about selling part of the land. He's trying to force me to sell my whole farm to him."

"Really?" The man leaned back against the gilt-edged chair, contemplative. "This does cast a different light on the situation. Perhaps we should begin again, Mrs. North. I see you are not the hysterical, difficult female Perkins led me to believe. The railroad is interested in securing a strip of land between the springs that runs across the back edge of your property."

"Only that strip?" Her pulse banged in her ears with such hope, Esther felt light-headed.

"Only that."

"The answer is yes, Mr. Howard. As long as my home and my husband's grave are left undisturbed, I will gladly sell you enough land for your railroad to come through."

A wide smile broke across the man's face. He rose and extended his hand. "Ma'am, it is indeed a pleasure doing business with you. I do believe we have a deal."

Thirty minutes later, Jericho and Esther walked out of the bank in high spirits. It was all he could do not to hug her close and twirl her around on the street.

"We did it."

"You did it," she said. "Without you—"

"--You would have found a way. You're a strong, smart woman, Esther."

"I still can't believe Theo lied. All this time, he knew the railroad only wanted that one section, but I was too ignorant to question."

"He stood to make a great deal of money if he could convince you to sell. He would own the water rights, rights the railroad will now lease from you instead."

"I know." She pressed both hands to her cheeks. "This is unbelievable, Jericho. Samuel and I will have a regular income."

Yes, they would. For as long as the railroad ran, because Jericho had made up his mind. Esther need never know the farm and the water rights belonged to him.

"Appears so." He gazed across the street toward the saloon. "Want to pay Theo a call?"

She grinned. "I think Mr. Howard will give him the news soon enough. I'd rather celebrate."

"Let's have dinner at the hotel."

"Splendid idea, Mr. North." She laughed, the first full blown laugh she'd experienced since Theo's dire warning two days ago. "I smelled roast beef the entire time we were talking to Mr. Howard."

Jericho laughed with her. He'd been the same.

They looped elbows and started off down the boardwalk, smiling like children on Christmas morning. Samuel bounced on Jericho's hip and clung to his neck.

They ordered beef and potatoes with thick brown gravy and freshly baked bread. Jericho scooped bites of potato into Samuel's bird mouth and laughed along with Esther at the faces-and the mess-the boy made.

He listened to Esther talk about plans for the spring planting and her desire to buy yard goods for sewing while they were in town. He shared boyhood stories and if those included bittersweet tales of Silas, they both enjoyed them, nonetheless.

Over thick slices of apple pie, the mood shifted. The joyous relief of today's successful enterprise left them trading smiles and touches until Jericho could think of nothing but Esther.

He didn't care about pie or the railroad or the farm. But he cared about .

If this was love, he liked it.

"What will you do now, Jericho? Will you stay in Twin Springs?"

He pushed his pie aside and leaned toward her. Even though she was only a table away, she was too far. He wanted to touch her and hold her and tell her about this crazy feeling rising in his chest like a tide. "Do you want me to?"

She ducked her head, her long eyelashes sweeping suddenly pink cheeks. "I wouldn't be opposed."

His heart hammered hard enough to break a rib bone. "Samuel--."

She glanced up. "—of course. You'll want to be here for Samuel. He'll need his uncle to teach him man things."

"He needs more than an uncle. He needs a father." Leaning in, he clasped her hands. They were cold. "Will you marry me, Esther?"

Esther thought her heart would burst. Jericho wanted to marry her so Samuel could have a father. She wanted that too, but she wanted so much more from Jericho North. She wanted love.

She hurt to think of another convenient marriage, a marriage without kisses or declarations of love. But she would do it. Jericho loved her son and Samuel adored him. Her baby would have a good man to raise him. And like Silas, maybe someday Jericho could love her too.

Mind made up, she tipped her chin and said, "Yes, I'll marry you.

If he looked disappointed, she didn't understand why.

"The day is early," he said. "We could stop at the preacher's house now."

"All right. Fine." She pushed back from the table, her happy mood dampened slightly.

Jericho rose, too, and came around the table. Standing close, he murmured, "Esther. This feels all wrong."

He'd already changed his mind. "You don't have to marry me. Samuel and I will be fine."

But tears prickled her eyes and she couldn't stop them from splashing onto her cheeks.

With a frustrated huff, he gripped her arms. "Why are you crying? What did I do wrong?"

"Nothing."

"I know better." Gently, he pulled her closer. "You can tell me anything."

She sniffed. "I love you."

Suddenly, she was engulfed in a powerful embrace. Her feet lifted from the floor.

"Are you sure? Are you sure?"

She nodded against the smooth linen of his shirt. "Very."

"Thank God. I thought I might be rushing things, that I'd spoken too soon."

"Do you mean--?" She was afraid to ask.

"I love you, Esther. I want to be the man you need and the man you love. Marry me for me."

Suddenly, the joy she'd yearned for and the long-held romantic dreams exploded into reality. He loved her. "That's all I wanted to hear, Jericho. I thought you cared for me, but love—" Tears filled her eyes again, only this time they were happy tears. "Love is all I ever wanted."

With a final hug, he asked, "Ready to see the preacher?"

Smiling through tears, she answered, "Absolutely."

Jericho held her coat, his calloused fingers lingering on her neck as he gazed at her with such tenderness, she wanted to melt like candle wax.

She leaned into him. "Can this day get any better?"

He pumped his eyebrows. "I hope so."

"Mr. North!" She gave him a little slap, teasing because she, too, looked forward to what the rest of the day, and the night, would bring.

Jericho reached for his own coat and something made of paper fell from inside and landed at her feet. With a joyous laugh, she scooped it up.

He stiffened and a strange expression darkened his face. "I'll take that."

Something in his voice gave him away. Fear began to creep up her spine. He didn't want her to see the stray piece of paper.

Jericho felt the world crumble beneath his feet. To have won her and lost her in a single day seemed too painful to bear.

But bear he must. This was his fault. His mistake. He should have told her from the beginning.

He could lie. But she deserved better than that. She deserved his honesty.

When the scales had fallen away, they'd exposed more than the truth about Esther. They'd exposed the truth about himself.

"Can we sit down again?" he asked, gently removing the will from her hand. "I have to tell you something and if it changes your mind about the wedding, I'll understand."

"You're scaring me, Jericho." But she returned to her chair and picked Samuel up to hold like a shield between them.

Seated again, Jericho slowly unfolded the will and stared down at the words and his brother's signature. "Silas left a will."

Esther's head tilted to one side. "A will? Why would he-"

He couldn't say the words, so he scooted the paper across the table to her. "I'm sorry. When I came here, my intentions weren't good. Then I met you and God changed me. I can't start a marriage on less than the truth."

"I don't understand." She sat Samuel on her lap and reached for the will.

"Read it."

With his future in his throat, he watched her scan the document and knew when she understood by the small gasp of distress and the way she clutched her son tighter. Still, she didn't look at him, and Jericho despaired.

She folded the will and sat with her eyes down. She was so still, Jericho feared she might faint. "I'm sorry. I don't know why Silas did this, but the farm is yours to keep. No matter what you decide."

At last, she looked up, gray eyes shining with unshed tears and something else. "Did you think this would matter to me, Jericho?"

"Doesn't it?"

She shook her head. "No."

"I should have told you. I didn't want to hurt you. I--" He looked at her helplessly.

"Which is exactly why I'm not upset. Your brother..." She stopped and a nostalgic smile lifted her lips. "Silas talked about you all the time. He adored you. I think I know why he willed the land to you."

"You do?"

She nodded. "He knew you'd come."

Of course, Silas had known, or at least had believed his brother would come to claim his prize and find the greatest earthly prize waiting instead.

"Silas knew I'd fall in love with you." What sensible man wouldn't? He and Silas had always loved the same things, the same people. More than once, they'd courted the same girl.

"Or maybe he simply we would find our way together and a will afforded us that opportunity. Silas wanted to take care of us both, Jericho, and after losing his leg this was the only way he could think of." She laid the will on the table. "Always tell me the truth even if it hurts. Lies and secrets hurt more."

"Always and forever." The words were more than an answer, they were a promise. Of his honesty and his heart.

He reached for her hand, relieved when she turned her palm up and laced her fingers with his. "I love you, Esther. I'm not much but I'll love you and Samuel, and I'll work hard to be the man you deserve."

"You already are."

Humbled and joyous, he bent his head and kissed her, quick and light, but a reminder of that first, powerful kiss that had started it all. In a husky growl, he murmured, "Let's go find that preacher."

With a smile that melted him, Esther, his queen, looped her arm in his and said, "Yes, let's do. And then let's go home." Home. His home and hers. Together. "I'd like nothing better."

Then with forever on his arm, Jericho led the way out of the hotel, down the street, and into a most unexpected future with exactly the right woman.

ABOUT LINDA GOODNIGHT

NY Times and *USA Today* bestselling author Linda Goodnight is best known for her emotional, heartwarming stories and realistic characters. Her books have won numerous awards, most notably the RITA, the Booksellers' Best, the ACFW Carol and the Reviewers' Choice Award from *RT Book Reviews*. She has authored over 45 books that have been translated into more than a dozen languages. An avid reader from early childhood, Linda has always loved the power and beauty of words and feels blessed to write stories of hope and light in a sometimes dark world.

Linda's great love is her family, and she especially enjoys holidays when all eight children of her blended family come home-and bring the grandchildren. In her spare time, she loves to read, bake and travel and is involved in orphan ministry. A former nurse and teacher of the year Linda lives in rural Oklahoma with her husband and two Ukrainian daughters. Readers may connect with Linda and sign up for her newsletter through her website at www.lindagoodnight.com or on Facebook and Twitter.

LOVEBIRDS AT THE HEARTBREAK CAFÉ

JANET TRONSTAD

CHAPTER ONE

July 1958
A fly buzzed outside the screened window of the Heartbreak Cafe while, inside, a truck driver named Buddy Hamilton sat in a worn booth and nursed his tall glass of lemonade. He'd seen the *Waitress Wanted* sign in the café window for the past month, but he hadn't paid it much attention. Jobs were scarce, but working at the Heartbreak couldn't be anyone's dream come true.

Besides, the place with its white and black cracked linoleum and slow-moving ceiling fan was practically deserted. Right now, it was only him and another trucker – a man he called Shades in honor of the movie star sunglasses he wore. Buddy and Shades never spoke, but they nodded hello and good-bye the way truckers did with each other.

Buddy was starting to stand up and make his farewell nod to the other man when the door opened.

Whoa, he thought, as he stood there, trying to keep his mouth from hanging open. A gorgeous blonde woman stepped into the cafe. Well, not so much stepped as bounced. Then she stopped and pointed at the waitress ad with a red-tipped finger. Buddy had always been a sucker for polished nails on a beautiful woman.

"Well, hello there," he said in his friendliest voice.

She smiled back at him and his heart raced.

He was trying to think of something clever to say when Fred Norris, the middle-aged owner of the cafe, came out of the kitchen and saw her. Bubby couldn't help but notice Fred's appreciative look turn a little sour when he saw where she was pointing. The man always said he didn't hire young women because they didn't stay on the job and this one looked like she couldn't be much past twenty-one. Still, Fred set down the coffee pot he had been carrying and motioned for the woman to take a seat.

Buddy sat back down, figuring he should stay around to console the woman when Fred refused to hire her. She was a looker, all right. Now that he saw her up close, he could see she was more wholesome than he'd first thought with her shining golden hair pulled into a sleek ponytail and the ends of her white long-sleeved shirt knotted tight around the waist of her denim jeans.

Her cheeks were rosy and Buddy didn't think she was wearing any makeup. But then he could never tell those things. He did notice she had a bit of what looked like grape jelly on one cuff of that blouse of hers. She probably didn't even know it was there.

Buddy enjoyed looking at the woman, but Fred was right -- she didn't belong here. He figured she'd taken a break from a cheerleading squad on some college campus. When she got the full picture of Webster Crossing though, no amount of rah-rah optimism would make her stay. The place was so nondescript that he wouldn't be stopping himself if it wasn't the only place to eat along this stretch of desolate highway.

He had almost missed it on his first trip through. He had been driving along comparing the tight barbed wire fences of the Dutton Ranch on one side of the road and the scruffy winter wheat crop trying to grow on the other when he noticed a cluster of buildings a few miles up the road in a slight hollow. It had been hardly worth slowing down for – not much more than a dozen old clapboard houses, a two-story general store in need of paint, a gas station with one pump, a wide swath of tumbleweeds, and the Heartbreak Café & Hotel.

The café sign is what stopped him that first day. Buddy pulled off the road and read the sign twice. The structure itself was painted dark lavender with white trim and there were red geraniums trying to grow in a neglected window box.

But he didn't see a hotel -- unless one counted the rusty trailer peeking out from behind the squat building.

Very funny, he'd thought with a dry chuckle when he finally saw the trailer door had a crooked Vacancy sign on it and striped towels hanging from the porch rail like they'd been stolen from some swanky resort.

Elvis had sung his song for just such a place.

Not that the blonde was what Elvis had in mind for an occupant of his hotel. She was holding a piece of white paper in her hand and she announced to everyone in general that it was a resume. She drew the word out and made it sound French. Her name, she said, was Penny Rose and she was asking about the waitress job.

Then she grinned until her teeth twinkled.

Even if there wasn't much chance of it, Buddy suddenly hoped she'd get the job. He stopped at the cafe three times a week now that he driving his old flatbed truck along the ribbon of highway that ran along the eastern edge of Montana. He was delivering railroad ties to the crews working on the Hi-Line up by the Canadian border.

With a steady route, he had saved enough money to make an offer on a small farm he'd found down by Miles City. His offer hadn't been approved by the bank yet, but he could spare a few dollars to take the blonde out to dinner.

Buddy saw that Fred was frowning as he studied the piece of paper. Maybe Penny really was a college girl. That wouldn't set well with the other man as he was not too impressed with higher education, maybe because he'd only finished the eighth grade. Buddy felt a moment of sympathy for the girl; he didn't see how she was going to get the job.

A balding man, Fred covered his paunch with a series of identical white T-shirts, grease spatters on the front and sleeves rolled up to hold a packet of Camel cigarettes in the fold of cloth at the high beefy part of his arm. He was reaching for one of those smokes now.

Then he stopped and read more of the paper instead.

All of a sudden, Buddy watched the blonde sneak a peek out the side window. That was twice now that she'd done that; both times like she didn't want anyone to see her. It made Buddy curious enough to move over on the seat so he could glance out that window himself. His jaw dropped and he sat up straighter in the booth. Children seemed to be crawling out of every opening of an old beat-up Buick sedan and there wasn't a grownup in sight.

Buddy stood so he could see the full width of the window. If you took away his flatbed truck, Shade's dump truck, and the jeep Fred drove that only left one vehicle there.

He looked back at Penny. The gray sedan, with the dent high in the front fender, had to be hers. She was barely tall enough to see over the steering wheel in that tank. He was twenty-nine years old and he guessed she had to be over thirty if she was mother to those kids. He sat back in the booth and casually counted them through the window. Six children. He searched some more, but that was it unless some were hunched down and hiding on the floor of the car like kids did from time to time. The oldest, a girl, didn't look any more than nine or ten years of age. The two littlest boys, barely toddlers, looked like twins.

What inclination Buddy had to romance the blonde died right then and there. She must be married. Even if she was divorced, she wouldn't take dating lightly with all those children and he had no intention of marrying. Just then he heard Penny say she was a widow. He wondered if the man had tripped over a toy or just laid down in weariness and died to get away from it all.

"Do you have any experience waiting tables?" Fred asked as he looked up from the sheet of paper he'd almost worn through with his twisting and turning.

"No," Penny said. "But I learn fast."

Buddy had to admit he didn't know much about family life. He'd seen the inside of more foster homes than he cared to count until he was finally old enough to seek refuge in the army.

Lately, now that he had finally saved enough to buy a farm, he felt like his life was turning a corner. Granted, the farm was the cheapest one he'd ever seen. There was barely enough acreage to support a man and the house was nothing but a shack with roof problems. Not that the place was meant to be a home.

He didn't need one of those, especially not one with six ready-made children in it. That wouldn't be so much a home as it would be an institution, and not the good kind. He could almost feel the lock of the cell door behind him just thinking about it.

Fred shook his head and handed the white paper back to the woman.

"I'm sorry," the café owner said. "Business is down and I just can't afford to hire—."

A scream from outside interrupted him.

Fred looked over at the window as if he was a bird dog on point.

The woman turned to look too and, for the first time, Buddy saw the full force of worry on her face.

"I've tried every other place," Penny said, clearly at war with herself on whether to go to the window or to keep sitting in that chair. "Billings. Havre. That's why I came back here. There's no jobs anywhere."

Buddy craned his neck so he could see the car out of the nearest pane of glass. The children didn't seem to be in any distress. Besides, the scream sounded more like a battle cry than a frightened call for help.

"They look fine," he said, loud enough for her to hear. He'd counted six – or was it seven – heads moving around so, unless there was a dead one in the trunk, he was pretty sure there was no medical emergency. For the first time, he noticed a shiny red bicycle leaning against the tree and that puzzled him for a moment until he decided he must have overlooked it earlier.

"What's out there?" Fred asked as he stood up. "Is it that black crow? He keeps coming around expecting scraps. We ain't running no soup kitchen for birds though."

Fred had Navy tattoos on the top half of both arms: pink roses entwined with faded anchors. That poor old crow needed to find a new home before he riled Fred too much.

"It's just some kids," Buddy said and then saw the panic on the blonde's face. He was sorry he'd spoken up. She looked as guilty as if she'd kidnapped those children. Although only a lunatic would do something that foolish and Penny looked quite sane.

"Kids?" Fred repeated as though he'd never heard of such things. He looked at the blonde again. "You never said anything about having kids."

Buddy could see right away this was a bigger problem than the crow for Fred.

"They won't be any trouble," Penny assured the man although Buddy didn't see the point since she'd already been refused the job.

Fred pressed his lips together, as if he was trying to think of a polite way to say what he was thinking. The whole place was silent.

Then Shades cleared his throat. He sat at a table with a half-eaten tuna melt sandwich in front of him. Buddy thought tuna melts were a sissy kind of a meal for a man. But that was Shades. He hadn't taken his sunglasses off and Buddy could see the man had a movie star tan as if he sat around a swimming pool all day instead of moving gravel for the county in that dumpster of his.

"I wouldn't mind some kids around here." Shades spoke for the first time and Buddy frowned a little as the woman sent the other trucker a dazzling smile.

"They're good kids," Penny said, with enough eagerness to her voice that Buddy wished he had thought to say what Shades had. He could see right away how much the woman liked it.

"How many kids?" Fred demanded to know.

Penny hesitated, but finally whispered, "Six."

Fred's face went pale. "And you say your husband died?"

She nodded. "Two months ago."

She paused then added. "He'd been sick for a long time. Cancer in the lungs. He farmed a few miles south of here. A bit of dry land wheat crop."

She sounded discouraged when she described it.

"Not that piece off the Dutton place?" Fred asked with enough heat in his voice to make Buddy curious. "Every year some fool tries to grow a crop there. Old man Dutton makes more renting that piece of worthless land than anyone ever has on crops."

The blonde nodded.

Buddy figured that meant she had the pathetic-looking wheat crop he'd been seeing every time he drove by.

"Well, that ground there isn't much," Fred conceded. "But with the kids, you should have stayed there for now. The lean-to isn't a real house, but you don't need heat this time of year anyway. I know it is hard work for a woman, but —"

Penny shook her head and her face pinked up. "The owner had certain conditions I couldn't meet."

"Like what?" the café owner bellowed.

"Intimate things," she whispered and then looked down at her hands.

Buddy got her meaning and had half-risen out of the booth before Fred swallowed.

"Someone should get the law on Harold Dutton," the café owner said and took the cigarette out of his mouth. His indignation was gone, but the edge to his voice had hardened. "Tomcatting around the country with a wife and kids of his own at home. He's got no call to be making that kind of trouble for young widows."

Everyone was silent for a minute.

"I could pay him a visit," Buddy offered. He'd boxed some in the army and could hold his own. He wouldn't mind hitting this Dutton fellow once or twice just to let Penny know someone was on her side. "I could give him a heart to heart, so to speak."

Then he punched one hand into the other.

Penny looked at him, surprise in her violet eyes. Buddy felt the jolt of their loveliness all the way down to his feet and he put his hands back on the Formica table. He was suddenly self-conscious about how chapped his fingers were.

"Oh, I wouldn't want you to hurt him," Penny protested. "I don't believe in violence."

"I'll pray for Mr. Dutton," Shades said then, looking innocent.

Buddy opened his mouth to protest. He'd heard the trucker curse up a storm at a café south of here because the waitress hadn't put any ketchup on the table. Buddy told himself he couldn't judge any man. He hadn't been in church for some time since he'd taken on an extra trucking route, but the unfairness burst out of him anyway. He at least had enough respect for God not to pretend to pray.

Before Buddy could say anything, Penny gave the other man a little smile.

"Thank you," she said solemnly. Her voice was respectful like Shades was a preacher of some kind.

Buddy grit his teeth.

"It was almost a mercy that we had to leave," Penny said then, folding her own hands together like she was thinking of praying herself. "The wheat is burning up out there in the heat. We couldn't have stayed. We didn't have enough food put by to see us through the summer."

"We could pass the hat," Buddy offered. He'd missed out on the prayer comment, but he did want to show his support "Get you a few dollars at least."

"I don't take charity," Penny protested, her tone aghast and her eyes looking at him as if he'd suggested something indecent. Her back was straight and she turned her head away from him.

"No, ma'am," Buddy mumbled. "Of course not. I'm sorry."

Shades flashed him a triumphant grin and Buddy had all he could do to curb his tongue.

Fred was silent for a moment before he spoke. "That crop that you planted is yours. No charity there. I know the lease laws and the Duttons always run their leases fall to fall. They collect up front, too, so your husband likely paid them."

"We were planning to borrow Dutton's machinery for the harvest," she said and her shoulders slumped. "He's already said he's refusing to lend to me now unless I ... I ...."

Her voice drifted off.

Fred grunted in disgust.

Buddy didn't open his mouth for fear of what would come out. Even Shades had abandoned his pious look and appeared ready to tear into the man if he had a chance.

Then Buddy saw the strangest thing. The café owner held out his hand and asked to see that sheet of paper again.

Penny gave it to him.

Just then the door to the café opened and a small boy poked his head inside. He had a look of quiet distress on his face and Buddy wondered at first if he needed to use the bathroom.

"There's blood," the boy finally whispered looking at Penny. "Ellie said not to tell you, but it's getting all over."

Penny gasped and stood up. "What happened?"

Then she was moving toward the door. She found it hard to make the handle on the door work and, since Buddy was right behind her, he reached around and pushed the thing open. She mumbled some words of thanks to him, but she didn't turn around.

Buddy followed her right out of the café without even asking himself if that was the smart thing to do.

CHAPTER TWO

Dust was blowing around, but it was easy enough for Buddy to see most of the kids standing next to the car, forming what looked like a huddle for defense.

"She hit me," a boy stepped forward. He hadn't been in the circle with the other children and Buddy could see right off that he didn't belong. For one thing, the boy wore a crisp white cotton shirt and the rest of the children wore ragged T-shirts of various colors over patched jeans.

Of course, the white of the shirt was spoiled some by the blood from his nose bleed, likely caused by Ellie hitting him.

"My father will have the sheriff out to arrest that girl of yours," the boy said pointing at the only other child not in the huddle -- a scrawny looking girl with a scowl on her face and a cloud of dust at her feet. Her hair was wild and short. A man's shirt, much too large for her, was tied around her waist and some chopped off men's jeans hung on her hips.

"Yah?" the girl took a menacing step toward the boy. She was a good three inches shorter than him and had a new bruise on her cheek. "You started it. Picking on the babies like a coward. And then when I hit you –"she stopped to spit. "I barely tapped your nose and you go around sniveling about it like a – a—sissy little girl."

Buddy lifted an eyebrow at her words, but she and her mother seemed to accept the insult without surprise.

"Ellie," Penny reprimanded the girl sharply.

Then the woman turned to the boy. "I'm sorry." Her words were stiff, but Buddy had no doubt she meant them. "I've told

Ellie to come get me when there is a problem."

"There wasn't time," Ellie defended herself. "He would have had the babies crying if I didn't step in. He was calling them naked savages. Then he threw dirt on them trying to cover them up – like he was going to bury them alive. He wouldn't stop until I hit him. And he hit me first. I just didn't blubber about it."

The huddle of children nodded in support of that statement. They looked at their sister with something akin to hero worship in their eyes. As the ragged bunch moved around, Buddy saw the two toddlers sitting in the middle of their circle, a faint sprinkling of dirt on their heads, but otherwise looking healthy and unharmed even if all they were wearing was a diaper each.

"Then he called me a heathen," Ellie declared, the glint of tears in her eyes unmistakable. "On account of me not having a dress. He said the school won't let me come this fall."

Buddy was surprised she was that upset about a dress, but then he saw it was the ridicule that hurt more than the lack of wardrobe.

"What's your name?" Buddy stepped forward to ask the boy, more to stop him from saying anything more than because he had any real desire to know.

"Matt Dutton," the boy said like he was proud of the fact.

"Ah," Buddy said. That was a twist he hadn't figured on.

He couldn't help but look at Penny to see how she took that information. She took it right well which made him realize she had known who the boy was all along. Which only made sense when he thought about it.

"My father owns this place," Matt continued with a swagger to his voice that got on Buddy's nerves. "All the land around here. He rents to the café and the store people." He sent Penny's children a contemptuous look. "He's also the head of the school board."

The boy sneered at Ellie as he added. "He'll say the school has standards. No ragged girls allowed – not ones that can't even afford a dress. And no babies with nothing on but diapers."

Buddy watched the flush rise on Penny's face. She was embarrassed, but Ellie was ready to fight.

"You tell your father she'll have a dress to wear to school," Penny promised even though Buddy could tell the woman was bluffing. "She's just grown lately. That's all. Her old dress doesn't fit."

Buddy looked over at the Buick again. "Where do you keep your stuff?"

"In the car," the woman said.

Buddy knew the trunk might be big, but it didn't add up to much when it came to holding a family's possessions.

Something about the way the woman held her head, as if she would beat the world, made Buddy want to help her. He didn't know what he could do though.

"Who wants a hamburger?" he made the offer impulsively.

He saw the kids' eyes all grow big, but they didn't say anything. They looked at Penny.

Except for Matt Dutton who said, "I'll have one."

"Maybe if you apologize to the ladies," Buddy said.

A sneer grew on the boy's face. Buddy lifted an eyebrow.

"Well, she doesn't have a dress," Matt finally said, his voice defiant. "And the school rules say girls have to wear one unless it's Friday or snowing."

"No one's in school today," Buddy said. "And Fred here makes a good hamburger."

Buddy looked over to where the fry cook was standing in the doorway of the café, watching the whole thing play out.

"I'll throw in some fries," Fred said as he turned to go back inside.

With that promise, even Matt's eyes went big.

"I'm sorry I said you were a girl and needed a dress," the boy mumbled in the general direction of Ellie as he tucked his head down and went toward the café door.

Buddy didn't figure it was a full apology, but he decided to let it go. His more pressing concern was the huddle of children around Penny, looking at him with their faces full of misery and longing. Penny was deciding about the hamburgers and it didn't look promising.

"We have our food packed in the car," Penny finally turned to him and said serenely.

"But —" One of the tangle of boys protested until Penny gave him a look.

"It is most kind of you, of course," Penny added. "But we can't take charity."

Buddy could tell she was going to usher her children into that car and take off with some notion that stale crackers or whatever she had would be enough to quiet their stomachs — if she even had anything.

"The kids could wash my truck," Buddy offered in desperation. He'd finished his run; the back was empty. He didn't think they could hurt anything. "It'd be a fair even trade that way. I need to keep it clean for inspections."

That last part gave it an official feel, but Buddy never had anyone check over his flatbed. All he carried was wood ties for the railroad.

"I can scrub real good, mister," a scrawny towhead boy said as he stepped closer to Buddy. He was the one who had protested when Penny said they had something to eat.

Hope caught in the eyes of the other children and burned bright. Buddy knew Penny could see it, too.

"I guess if we work for it, it will be fine," she finally agreed to the arrangement. "But we won't finish the truck until it's spotless."

A half dozen heads bobbed and Penny led them into the café like a mother duck leading her charges. Ellie and the towhead boy each carried a toddler on their hips.

Buddy waited for all of the children to go inside before he followed them. Fred was already directing the children to two booths in the corner. He'd set them up with three bottles of ketchup per booth and glasses of water all around.

When they were settled — with a wide space between Matt Dutton and the others — Fred handed one of his white work aprons to Penny.

"Might as well get started if you're going to work here," he said to her.

She looked at him in surprise. "I got the job?"

Fred grunted and gave Buddy a sly look. "Business seems to have picked up. So, yeah, you got the job. At least for now. You get the use of the trailer in back and five dollars a week plus tips."

Buddy figured that wasn't enough, but Penny was already grinning and nodding.

"You won't regret it," she promised.

Fred gave a skeptical glance at all the children in the booths and shook his head as he went back to the kitchen.

Buddy stood and watched the kids pour ketchup into their water glasses.

Shades came and stood beside him.

"I thought you left," Buddy said as he looked over at the other man.

"I was in my truck," Shades admitted. "Then I came back. You really going to let them wash your flatbed?"

Buddy shrugged. "What can it hurt? The sun's so hot nothing will rust."

"I guess," Shades agreed hesitantly.

Ellie was the first to drink her ketchup water and she pronounced it delicious so the others followed. The towhead boy burped after his.

"You're all going to die," Matt Dutton pronounced ominously as the younger children drank their brew. "You know what's in ketchup, don't you?"

"What?" the towhead boy looked at Matt in fascinated terror. "Rat blood?"

Matt seemed stopped by that possibility. Whatever he was going to say, it obviously had not been as awful as that.

"Stuff," Matt finally answered. "Yucky stuff."

Penny chose that moment to bring the hamburger platters out. She held one high in each hand and placed them on the tables like they were steaks in a high class restaurant.

Buddy looked close at the green on the side of the plates.

"What's that?"

"Parsley for color," she answered with flair.

"I thought that's what a pickle was for," he said. "Why isn't there a pickle?"

"You got the hamburgers," she said. "Fred gave the fries. There's no money for pickles."

"Hamburgers always have at least a slice of pickle," Buddy protested. "That's the vegetable part."

Fred stuck his head out of the kitchen door. "Order up."

Penny hurried back to get the other platters.

When everyone had their hamburgers, Fred made a plate for Penny and brought it out to her.

"You'll need your strength," the café owner said as he sat the food in front of her.

Fred then came to stand by Buddy and Shades.

"You got any buckets?" Buddy asked the café owner. Now that he'd had the idea, he'd begun to wonder how the children would be able to wash his flatbed.

"I've been meaning to get a new one," Fred said. "The mop bucket has a crack in it. I can't put more than a quart of water in it or it drips all over the place."

"They'd have a bucket at the store across the street," Shades said. "I stop in there once in a while. The old lady who runs the place has everything – even a granddaughter that visits."

Shades raised his eyebrow at this as though Buddy was supposed to take some meaning from it.

Buddy was clueless.

"Tell her what it's for and she'll give you a good deal," Fred added. "I'll throw in some grease soap if you want for the kids to use."

"I don't have any tar or anything back there," Buddy said.

"That soap makes suds though," Fred added. "The kids will like that."

Buddy grunted and gave a general nod. He figured he'd better get a bucket or two before the kids finished eating. Knowing them, they'd start without him if they had to. He gave one last look at Penny, but she wasn't facing his way so she didn't see it.

He reminded himself that he wasn't planning to date her anyway. She was strictly off limits. She was sure pretty though. And, if a man was given to impossible dreams, he could almost imagine her standing in the kitchen on that farm he was hoping to buy. After a second or two, he frowned. The kitchen was small even for him. There'd be no room for kids and no place for a table. He'd have to eat standing up at the sink. Which was fine for him, but he couldn't imagine Penny and those kids doing it.

She turned finally and gave him a shy smile.

He didn't waste any time in getting out of the café. It didn't do any good to yearn for things he had no hope of getting. Besides, those six kids deserved a man who knew how to be a father. They sure didn't need a man like him who'd never been anything but the thorn in the side of a dozen foster families.

CHAPTER THREE

Buddy stopped outside the café and looked across the highway to the store. The white sun was hot and a wind blew a cluster of tumbleweeds past him. He'd driven this road long enough not to be surprised that no traffic was coming in either direction. The two-story building looked like it had been there for years; the shingles on the side of it a weathered white and the window trim a more recently painted blue. A sagging porch ran along the front of the place and the three steps each creaked as he made his way up them. A rocker sat in one corner of the porch and a big display window stood on the other side of the door.

He was just wondering if this place had any Elvis overtones when the screen door opened and an old hound dog ambled out, followed by a thin young woman with hair like faded copper. The wind picked her hair up and blew it around until it was tangled. Apart from that, she looked pale as if she might be ailing. Her eyes also had dark circles under them.

"Oh." The woman stopped when she saw Buddy standing there. She had an old beige sweater wrapped around her shoulders even in this weather. "I thought you were the trucker who comes by."

Buddy turned to look behind him.

"His truck's over there," she said with a nod toward the café.

"You mean Shades?" Buddy asked.

"I don't know his name," the woman answered with a blush. Her face was so pale that it flamed in her embarrassment. "He buys stuff from my grandmother sometimes. And I thought I'd let him know the crows are still here."

"Shades cares about some crows?"

The woman shrugged. "Probably not. But one of them has a wing that doesn't work. The other one brings her food. The trucker was wondering why they didn't fly away."

Buddy nodded. "He's right to be curious. Crows don't take care of each other."

"This one does."

Buddy didn't have time to argue. "Shades isn't his real name. I just call him that for the sunglasses."

The woman grinned and her face looked more alive. "It fits him. I always thought he should be in the movies. He's so handsome."

Buddy was glad she'd stopped talking about the crows, but he didn't want to hear someone sing the other trucker's praises.

"I came to see the woman who owns the store."

"That would be Granny. She's over at the gas station getting a permanent in her hair."

"What?" Buddy wondered if he was hearing wrong.

"Lizzy Monroe, who runs the station, cuts hair and gives perms when she doesn't have enough mechanic work to do," the woman explained. "She also does sewing when business is slow. She likes fixing truck engines best though. Granny will be back soon."

Buddy processed all of that and nodded. "I was hoping to buy a bucket."

"A bucket of what?" she asked.

"Just a bucket."

"Oh, well, I can help you with that," she said as she turned and opened the door so they both could enter the store. "I'm Irene, by the way. Irene Potter."

The inside of the store was dim. Shelves ran in every direction, stacked high with canned goods and an assortment of other things. Hair ribbons, bolts of fabric, rubber boots. A narrow staircase ran to the second floor and a wide counter sat along the other side of the store, small shelves behind it and a brass cashier register on top of it. Everything smelled of spices. Cinnamon mostly.

"The buckets are in back," Irene said as she opened a door and went through it into a room.

Buddy heard a car pull up in front of the store and wondered if that was the grandmother returning. Before he could make it over to the window though, a middle-aged woman, wearing a yellow cotton dress and a growing frown, stepped inside the store and demanded to know. "Has anyone seen my son?"

She obviously hadn't looked around enough to see that Buddy was the only one there, but she fixed him with an impatient stare anyway.

"I saw his bike over by the café," she added in a voice that was vaguely accusing.

"Matt's having a hamburger," Buddy told her. "He should be out soon. He's eating with the Rose children in the cafe."

"That hussy!" the woman arched back and literally hissed. "I don't want him having anything to do with those children. That woman's a disgrace. And eating with them! Who knows what kind of germs they have."

Just then Irene came back with several shiny metal buckets.

"This one is seventy-four cents," she said as she held up one.

Buddy didn't consider his decision before saying, "I'll take all three of them."

That seemed to set Matt's mother back a little.

"What trucker needs three buckets?" she asked, suspicion strong in her voice. "You planning to steal gas or something? The county sheriff comes by here regular and the woman who runs the station keeps a gun behind the counter. I don't know if she keeps it loaded or not."

Buddy wondered if that last bit was anything to tell a potential thief, but he didn't want to argue with the woman.

"I'm getting my truck washed," he said, deliberately making his voice sound positive. Then he finished walking over to the window and glanced out. "Looks like your car could use a wash, too. The Rose children would be grateful for the job. It'd make up some for the teasing Matt gave the little ones."

"I'm not going to let those heathens touch my car," the woman said and pursed her lips in disapproval.

Before Buddy could think of a reply, a thundering roar sounded and the door burst open. All of the Rose children spilled into the store with Matt coming behind them at a more reluctant pace.

"Get in the car," Matt's mother commanded him before he even got all the way through the door. "We're going home."

"But --" The boy protested. "We're washing the man's truck."

"You're doing no such thing," his mother pronounced and walked over to grab his ear. "You're coming home with me right now, young man. And what in the world happened to your shirt?"

She turned to scowl at everyone, but no one said anything and she obviously didn't want to spend any more time talking to them. She pulled her son completely out of the store and Buddy couldn't help but notice the hint of sympathy on the faces of the older Rose children. It didn't last long though, not around the excitement of the store.

The towheaded boy nudged Ellie and she edged her way over to the counter where Irene stood.

"Do you have any perfume?" she whispered. "The kind that gets you a prince to marry you?"

"You mean Royal Enchantment?" Irene asked, bending over to match the girl's quiet voice. "They have that ad."

The girl nodded.

Buddy was surprised at the request but didn't have time to hear what Ellie wanted with perfume because he suddenly saw that Penny was standing on the porch outside with an older woman. They were both watching the Dutton's car throw gravel as the woman behind the wheel slammed the car into gear and backed out onto the highway.

"Don't pay any attention to her, dear," the older woman

was saying to Penny as they opened the door and entered. "She suspects every woman around here of trying to seduce her husband."

"It's him she needs to worry about," Penny muttered.

The older woman shrugged. "Who's going to tell her that?"

"She should watch her mouth anyway," Penny said, her cheeks red from either anger or embarrassment. "There are children present. And her son doesn't need to hear it."

The two women had no sooner stepped into the store than Shades came loping across the highway, taking the steps up to the porch in one leap and opening the door. Buddy couldn't help but notice the admiring glances the women sent the man's way. Even in the dim light inside, the trucker kept those shades of his on.

Buddy couldn't be bothered with him though. He edged over to Irene who was still standing behind the counter looking bemused. Even though her eyes were focused on Shades, Buddy reached in his pocket and pulled out three silver dollars.

"I'll take the buckets now," he said as he put his money on the glass topped counter. "And I'd like six brand new dimes, too."

That got Irene's attention.

Ellie was still standing in front of the cash register, her gaze fixed on the bottle of golden perfume standing on the shelf behind Irene. For a girl that didn't own a dress, she was showing a remarkable longing for that bottle of scent.

"Like the color, do you?" Buddy asked her. It was the only thing he could imagine. The bottle even had a tiny gold crown on top of it. With the liquid inside, it made a pretty picture all right. He noticed the store had the perfume in several sizes.

Ellie sighed and whispered. "It's my aunt's birthday coming up and I thought —"

The girl stopped and stepped closer.

"She already has dozens of ashtrays all of us made," the girl confided with some disgust in her voice. "She doesn't even smoke."

Buddy knew it wasn't any of his business, but he couldn't help himself. "Why doesn't this aunt help you?"

He kept his voice low so that Penny wouldn't hear. She was proud, but surely she would accept help from a relative. He wouldn't bet on Penny's purse having more than a few dollars in it.

"She does," Ellie said simply as she turned away from the counter.

By then the older woman who owned the store was in some long explanation about how the community meets on Sundays on the top floor of her establishment and they have church services when they are able to convince a preacher to come.

"The pastor in Dry Creek is always happy to make the trip over," she was saying. "But he has laryngitis and can't make it this Sunday and it's too late to get anyone else."

"Does it have to be a regular preacher?" Penny was asking. "My new boss already told me I can have time off on Sunday to take the children to church. I'd sure like to do that. We haven't been in a while."

The older woman shrugged. "We can't be fussy about preachers. We take pretty well any man who has a good relationship with the Lord."

Penny beamed. "Floyd here prays."

Buddy looked on in astonishment as Penny nodded her head toward Shades. He wasn't sure what was more shocking – that she knew the man's given name or that she was offering him up to preach this coming Sunday.

Shades obviously thought the latter was more alarming.

"I'm not sure about–" Shades got out before he froze all together and looked around for a bolt hole. "I mean, I –"

"You're a praying man?" Irene asked, awe in her voice as she looked up at the trucker.

Buddy was beginning to enjoy watching the other man decide whether he wanted to bask in all of the attention or run for the door.

"Well, I'm not really a preacher," Shades managed to say.

"I suppose I could read some from the Bible though."

"That would be just fine," the older woman said decisively. "With a few words of explanation as to the meaning of what you read. And maybe a couple of hymns. Irene can help with those."

The older woman smiled at her granddaughter. "She's home from college this summer helping me in the store. I don't know what I'd do without her."

"Oh, Granny," Irene said as she blushed again.

Buddy nodded rather absent-mindedly. He was looking for an opportunity to ask Penny about the children's aunt. He wanted to be sure Penny had told the woman how things stood with her and the children.

By this time, the children were leaving the store though and Buddy figured they'd need the buckets he'd just bought if they were going to make a stab at washing his flatbed.

He turned to the store owner before he stepped outside and asked, "Need a car wash?"

"We don't have a car," she called back. "Me and Irene make do with using a cab when we need to go somewhere."

That stopped Buddy in his tracks. "A cab comes out here?"

"Lizzy," Irene muttered near his shoulder. "She has a cab service for locals."

Buddy nodded. "Of course she does."

"It's just an old pickup that she uses," Irene confessed. "But she takes us."

With that, Buddy looked both ways at the highway and crossed to the café side of the road. He was going to step inside and ask Fred if he could fill the buckets with water when the café owner came outside and told him there was a water hookup with a hose beside the old trailer.

Then Fred went back into the café. Buddy followed him so he could pay his bill for all the hamburgers.

The money must have put the café owner in a generous mood because he told Penny when she came in that she could take a half hour to direct the children in washing the truck.

"Then you might as well get yourself settled in the trailer," Fred added. "You can hear if any customers drive up. Most likely though we won't have anyone come until closer to supper."

Fred smiled like he was a benign boss, but Buddy was beginning to frown.

"So Penny works breakfast?" he asked.

Fred nodded. "We start serving at six o'clock sharp. That's when the first truckers stop."

"And she works through supper?" Buddy asked. "When does that end?"

"Usually around eight in the evening," Fred replied. "In the winter, it's earlier since there are fewer trucks on the road after dark."

"That makes how many hours?" Buddy was going to protest further when he saw the look Penny gave him.

"That's just fine," Penny said.

Buddy saw her adding it up in her head though and her face went a little pale when she realized she was going to be working fourteen hours a day.

"Maybe we can close Sunday mornings." Fred frowned like he was doing the math, too. "No one comes in until after church anyway."

Fred didn't seem too sure about what he was promising.

"I think I'll come up for church," Buddy declared. It was fifty miles from where he rented a room in Miles City, but he didn't have his truck route this Sunday so he could do it. It was good for a man to sit in church.

The shock of his announcement silenced everyone in the café. It even seemed to stun Shades who had just opened the door.

"You're coming to church?" Shades asked like he thought he might have heard wrong.

Buddy grinned and nodded at the other trucker as he stepped through to the outside. Shades looked decidedly uncomfortable after the nod. Yes, Buddy decided he might enjoy hearing Shades pretend to be a preacher.

With that thought, a whoop came from across the highway and Buddy knew the children were on their way.

"Watch the road," he yelled and they all stopped to look each way.

It gave him a warm feeling to know they had obeyed him, especially because Penny had stepped out of the café behind him and saw it.

"Impressive," she muttered as he motioned for the children to come and they obeyed again.

It was like being the conductor of an orchestra. Maybe being a parent wasn't such a difficult job, after all, he thought to himself a little smugly. He'd learned a thing or two about command in the army.

"I can get the water," Ellie said as she walked up to Buddy and Penny. Then she held her hand out for a bucket. "You both just sit back and watch us."

The towheaded boy brought two folding chairs out of the café for Buddy and Penny to sit on. Buddy tried to relax, but Penny was wound up tight, ready to jump up the moment the children needed her.

Those kids all worked together like a well-oiled machine with Ellie and the towheaded boy bringing the water and the younger children on their knees using the scrub brushes Fred had brought out earlier.

It wasn't long before Buddy discovered it was Ellie who was the sergeant. The children obeyed her. It's just that, during the truck washing, he was the paying boss and she had decided he warranted sharing her power. It was a humbling realization.

By the time the flatbed was sparkling clean, Buddy had tried three times to ask Penny out on a date. Each time something interrupted them and he lost his nerve. Well, maybe it wasn't so much losing his nerve as it was regaining his senses. Even if they could work together, six children were a lot for a man to take on when all he wanted was a bit of quiet. He'd never thought about setting up a family of his own before and he shouldn't start now.

And then he heard Penny sigh and realized she'd had a

family with a man he didn't even know.

"I never did say how sorry I am about you losing your husband," Buddy said, realizing it was not quite how he felt so he added what was true. "I hate to think of you going through that kind of grief."

"Howard was a good man." Penny smiled at Buddy like he was the first person who had given her an ounce of sympathy after the man's passing. And then he wondered if it was true. The Duttons certainly hadn't sent any bouquets to the funeral. She hadn't mentioned any other friends or neighbors.

"It was hard to lose him," she said then. "Especially with the children."

Buddy felt like a heel for even thinking of asking her out on a date.

"If there's anything I can do--" His voice was thick from the swirl of emotions around them both. "--just let me know."

"Thank you."

And, just like that, she leaned a little closer to him and he figured they were friends. Within minutes, he was telling her about his dream of owning a farm and the property he was in the process of buying down by Miles City.

"Does it have a house?" she asked.

Buddy nodded. "More of a line cabin really. One bedroom is all."

And that was just separated off with a thick curtain.

Her eyes dimmed as though she could tell what kind of a man he was to buy such a place.

"It's got a root cellar though," he added.

Penny nodded, her enthusiasm back. "That's always nice if you have a large garden. I love a garden."

Her eyes went dewy-eyed. "I always thought -- if I could only have a garden – how perfect everything would be."

Penny sighed at the longing. "You're so fortunate."

"I didn't see a garden when I looked at the place," he said. The ground had been hard and no one had planted anything but field crops for decades.

Now that he thought about it, he didn't remember seeing anything in that root cellar. Maybe the old bachelor who owned the house had used the space to store grain for the mule he was said to have. The image of the old man and his mule, living on that farm day after day, suddenly didn't seem as appealing as it had last week.

Just then a black crow swooped down and landed close to where they were sitting. Buddy remembered what he'd heard about the birds.

"There's another crow across the highway," Buddy muttered. "Irene thinks this one goes out searching for something for the wounded one to eat."

Penny looked at him.

"It can't be," he added. "He might have done it once or twice, but there's no meaning to it. He wouldn't understand what he was doing."

Penny nodded and reached into the pocket of that big apron Fred had given her. She pulled out a French fry.

"It fell on the floor," Penny said as she tossed the fry to the crow. "I planned to throw it away. Let's see what he does."

The crow gave a squawk before picking up the food and flying off, only to land on the other side of the road and offer up the fry to a bird that must be his mate.

"Well, I'll be," Buddy said.

They were both quiet after that.

"It isn't natural," Buddy finally added. "Not for crows."

"Maybe sometimes birds are better than they're supposed to be," Penny said.

Buddy didn't know what to say. He'd always thought things were set somehow. That a crow acted a certain way just as a foster kid acted a certain way. He didn't want to say that to Penny though so he just sat there.

CHAPTER FOUR

Buddy had been in such a hurry to shave, trying to get to church on time, that he nicked his chin Sunday morning. A drop of blood landed on his only tie so he threw the thing back on his bed in disgust. He didn't have much use for a white shirt, but he did have one and he pulled it out of his closet. It had some fraying around the cuffs, but that couldn't be helped. He hoped his gray dress slacks would make him look pious enough. He had shined his shoes last night and brushed up his black hat. It would have to be enough he thought as he looked around.

The room he rented was cramped, but it came with a hot plate and a wooden table sturdy enough for him to sit and whittle as he listened to the radio in the evenings. The single bed was lumpy, but he'd be moving soon anyway. The bank had promised him an answer to his loan request by the end of this week.

He was trying not to worry about the bank's decision, but he hoped God would take note that he was showing up in church today just in case the banker needed any nudge from the Lord to say yes to his loan.

At the last minute, Buddy dug through the box of belongings at the end of his bed and found his old Bible. He'd gotten it in one of his few visits to Sunday school decades ago, but as far as he knew, it still worked. He'd kept it with him during the army and his years since even though he didn't open it often. He figured sin and redemption made up the main themes; he didn't need to review to know that.

Several vehicles were parked around the general store when he arrived in Webster's Crossing. He was surprised to see the Dutton car parked up front, but he didn't recognize any of the other vehicles. He'd driven his Chevy instead of the old flatbed.

A note taped to the front of the store invited people to 'Come in – church is upstairs.' He went inside. Buddy could hear people singing a hymn as he climbed the narrow steps along the left wall. Listening to the tune, he thought the hymn might be *The Old Rugged Cross* and, when the folks sang the chorus, he was sure of it.

When he reached the top of the stairs, Buddy found himself at the back of a large single room. The area, painted beige, was wide and each side had rows of folding chairs set out. The ceiling rose to the rafters. About thirty people were standing and that didn't count the Rose family who took up the front row of the left side.

A large round window filled the wall behind the wooden pulpit at the front. Standing where he was, Buddy saw nothing but blue sky and clouds when he looked out. The window, more than anything, made the room feel like a church. Two other windows, small square ones, flanked the round one and the morning light was streaming in from the east. Those two were open.

Shades didn't look comfortable standing in front of the congregation. Buddy could see that right off. The trucker was smiling stiffly and twisting his neck as if his collar was choking him even though his pale blue shirt wasn't buttoned high enough to warrant it and he didn't have on a tie either.

"Why don't we try another song?" Shades asked as the sounds died down.

Buddy shook his head. If the man didn't know these were hymns and not songs, he was in trouble.

It was silent for a moment and then Irene raised her hand. Shades nodded to her in relief.

"I always like *When the Roll is Called up Yonder*," she said.

"Good." Shades lifted his arms in a signal to begin.

Several soft voices started the tune and the hymn continued in a halting fashion, no thanks to Shades who clearly didn't even know the words. The whole hymn would have floundered if Buddy hadn't added his baritone to the mix. It was a song they used to sing in one of his foster homes.

Shades sent him a look of pure gratitude.

It was then that Ellie craned her neck and stared toward the back. Her face lit up when she saw Buddy and she motioned for him to come to where they were. That's when he noticed one of the chairs among the Rose family was empty.

Buddy felt warm inside as he walked up to the folding chair. They'd saved him a spot.

"Thanks," he whispered.

The girl had squeezed him between her and the towheaded boy who he'd learned yesterday was called Jason. They both looked so pleased to see him that he suspected they were angling for free hamburgers after the service.

He smiled back. Maybe he could work some kind of a discount with Fred. He figured his food bill would rise until the family got settled. And that was fine. It did his heart good to see them looking so pleased to be here. He already knew Penny set a lot of store by them coming to church. All of their faces were washed and everyone's hair was slicked back. He couldn't see a speck of dirt on any of them, not even the littlest ones who now wore white T-shirts with their diapers.

When the hymn died down, Shades just stood for a minute, looking frantic.

Everyone was silent.

Apparently that was invitation enough for Mr. Dutton to rise in his beige pinstripe suit and clear his throat. He ran his hands around the brim of his Panama straw hat.

Buddy shook his head. Only a rich man owned a suit he couldn't wear to fix a tire and a hat that wouldn't take any rain.

"We need to remember we are in the house of the Lord," Mr. Dutton said, his voice pitched low and serious enough to carry a funeral. "I think we should urge everyone to dress appropriately."

With that pronouncement, his eyes came to rest on the front row where the Rose family sat. At first, Buddy thought the man was upset about his lack of a tie, but them he saw that Mr. Dutton was staring at Ellie.

The girl was looking forward, with her back stiff like she could feel the man's eyes targeted on her.

"The Bible says it's an abomination for a girl to dress like a man," Mr. Dutton continued.

"Why —" Buddy stood up and faced the man. There was no call to be mean.

Buddy could see, out of the corner of his eyes, the embarrassment that covered the Rose family and suddenly he didn't know what to do. He could hardly punch the man out in church.

"God isn't like that," Buddy protested, his voice deep enough to stir the waters. He didn't rightly know; he'd only heard about God here and there. But he didn't believe the Almighty would pick on a little girl when she was doing her best.

The silence grew deeper.

Then Irene spoke up. "We should say the Lord's Prayer together. The Dry Creek pastor always had us do that after our hymns."

"Good idea," Shades said, relief giving body to his voice until he almost sounded like a preacher. Shades looked at Mr. Dutton, but the other man didn't sit down. So the trucker lifted his hands and solved the problem by saying, "Let's all stand."

Everyone stood and looked ahead at Shades.

Buddy could tell the exact moment when Shades realized he didn't know what to do next.

Buddy grabbed his Bible and flipped through the pages until he found the Gospel of Matthew. He stepped over and handed the other man the book.

"Chapter 6, verses 9 to 13," Buddy whispered and he pointed to the place on the page where Shades needed to start.

The other man nodded and then removed his sunglasses. Buddy figured that was a move of pure reverence on the part of Mr. Hollywood. Then Shades bowed his head and began to read the words to everyone.

Buddy noticed that the pink on the cheeks of the Rose family gradually subsided as Shades ploughed through his reading.

After they finished the Lord's Prayer, someone who Buddy didn't know mentioned that they needed to take an offering. With that word, another man stood and two baskets were passed.

Buddy put in a silver dollar and noticed that each of the Rose children put in a shiny copper penny. He figured they could scarce afford it, but Penny watched them with a look of immense satisfaction on her face. Then he realized they were giving a tithe on the dime he'd given each child for washing his truck.

When the baskets had made their way to the end of the rows, the man who had started the collection brought the baskets to the front of the church, set them on the floor right close to where Buddy sat and bowed his head. The man then started to pray.

Buddy had his eyes closed, as befit a man praying to the Almighty, but he saw the shadow of an arm anyway and opened his eyes just in time to see Ellie reaching over and fishing out all six of those bright new pennies from the basket. She was so quick, he almost wondered if it happened. But then he looked close and saw her fist clenching around something.

He waited for someone else to cry out that the girl had stolen from the offering, but no one did so he concluded no one else had seen her. He wasn't keen to say anything himself, but he didn't feel right just letting it go. She had only taken back what she and her siblings had put in though. He wasn't sure that could be counted as theft as much as a person having second thoughts about giving something away.

Everyone else was standing up and shaking hands, but Buddy stayed sitting where he was even when the towheaded boy, Jason, stood up on the other side of him and walked away. Ellie sat there, too, and he suspected she knew he had seen her.

Buddy wished Ellie's father was still here to talk to her and he suspected she must long for the same. But he wasn't. Buddy figured he was the last person in the word to guide a child, but God had seen fit to let him see what the girl had done. And, one thing he did know -- Penny would be heartbroken to have one of her children turn to theft.

"What do you need the money for?" Buddy asked, thinking that was the place to start. He wondered if she was saving up for a dress. He couldn't even blame her for that after the ridicule she'd received from the Duttons.

"The perfume is ninety-nine cents for the smallest bottle," Ellie whispered. "And my aunt's birthday is next week. We don't have enough money. Just the ten cents you gave each of us."

She raised her eyes to him and he could see the misery in her. For a moment, he felt a flash of irritation for this aunt who meant so much to the girl and yet was so glaringly absent.

"I can't ask you for more," she said as though she knew what he wanted to do. "Not even to wash your truck again. I'll get in trouble."

"Well, then you're going to have to ask your mother for the money," he said.

Ellie blinked back a tear. "I can't. My mother's dead."

"But--" Buddy was speechless.

Ellie waited a minute and then it all poured out of her.

"When Aunt Penny came," she whispered, her voice obviously straining to stay low so no one would hear. "Mama said she was giving up her prince so she could take care of us kids. I just want her to have her prince back."

After that, Ellie stood up and walked as quickly as she could to the stairwell. Buddy was so dumbfounded he let her go.

He looked around and everyone but a knot of men had gone downstairs. He noticed Shades stood with them so Buddy went over. He heard the word Dutton mentioned several times before he got there.

"It isn't right," one of the men was saying when Buddy got close enough to hear. The man looked familiar and Buddy realized he was a trucker. Buddy looked closer at the group and counted half of them as truckers.

"You the flatbed?" One of them asked as they made room for Buddy in their circle.

Buddy nodded. "The railroad ties."

"I'm the 18-wheeler." The man introduced himself as he held out his hand. "George over there is another 18-wheeler. We haul grain mostly."

"He's got the county dumpster," the same man added with a nod to Shades. "Gravel."

"We know each other." Buddy smiled and then added. "Friends."

Shades inclined his head in agreement.

"We're all steamed about the way Dutton is ruining this little town," the man said then. "Fred at the café told us about the raw deal he's giving that new waitress of his – the one whose husband died. We truck through here. We've all seen that field of wheat. It isn't right."

Everyone was silent for a minute.

"I wish it would rain," one of the truckers said then.

The quiet stayed.

"We might not get any moisture here until winter," another man said. "It's supposed to be a scorcher all summer."

With that, the truckers turned and started to walk toward the stairway. Buddy expected most of them would stay to eat before heading out.

"Don't forget to tip your waitress," he called after them, his voice echoing down the stairway.

Fortunately, he was pretty sure Penny and the children had already gone across to the café.

CHAPTER FIVE

Buddy felt the push of the heat as he opened the door and stepped out on the store porch. He looked across the highway and was surprised to see that Penny was leading the children into the trailer instead of the café. When she had them almost all of the way in, she turned and looked right at him before motioning for him to join them.

He hoped that didn't mean Ellie had confessed her misdeed. He knew Penny would frown on what the girl had done. He also knew Ellie would accept any punishment rather than spoil the surprise so they might be at a standoff.

A half dozen trucks were parked around the café, some of them loaded and others not.

Buddy passed by the café door on his way to the trailer and decided to stop a bit.

"Anyone riding empty – now's a good time to get a truck wash," Buddy announced to the café at large. "There's a special going for this afternoon only. Trucks washed for a dime each."

None of the men looked too enthused until Buddy added, "The Rose children will do the scrub down. You pay them."

A ripple of interest swept the café and, within minutes, Buddy had orders for five trucks to be washed.

He hoped the added business would take the sting away if Ellie had to give the pennies back to the church. Something about the sharp eye she gave him when he stood on the steps of the trailer a few minutes later though made him suspect she hadn't said anything to her aunt.

He nodded cordially, hoping the girl would take that as a

sign he wasn't going to say anything either. She nodded like she understood.

Then Penny was at the door inviting him in.

They had set up a card table and an assortment of chairs in the front part of the trailer. He noticed Fred had provided a few crockery plates from the café. A stack of what looked like ham sandwiches stood on the table.

"We wanted to invite you to share with you, after all those hamburgers yesterday," Penny said as she gestured toward a chair.

Buddy sat down, feeling a little out of place. He hadn't had many experiences with family dinners and he suspected Penny would make as much of a production out of sandwiches as she would a roast beef meal. He nodded when Penny bowed her head and the six smaller heads followed.

"Thank you for our blessings this day," Penny prayed. Her voice had a lilt to it that he admired. "We thank you for our new home and our new friend, Buddy."

He was so startled that he blinked and looked up at that those words. No one had ever thanked God for him before. It was as out of place as the foolishness about that old crow caring for his mate.

Penny continued to pray like what she had said was nothing unusual. Finally she added, "Amen."

"Thank you," Buddy mumbled.

By that time, Penny was passing around the plate of sandwiches and no one was talking.

"Good," Buddy said after he took a bite of his sandwich. There was mayonnaise and a touch of mustard with the ham.

Penny nodded her thanks.

It wasn't until everyone was almost finished eating that Buddy told the children they had some customers for truck washes, if they wanted them.

Ellie brightened at the mention.

"I told them it was a dime each," Buddy said. "Five trucks are ready."

They were all beaming at that.

Buddy was satisfied. That would give the children enough for the perfume and they'd still have enough pennies left over to give their ten percent to the church. The slight nod Ellie gave told him she'd take care of putting the pennies back in the right hands.

When the children finished their sandwiches, Penny told them they could go outside and get ready for the washes.

"Wait for Mr. Hamilton and me to come out before you start though," she cautioned them. "No climbing on the trucks until Mr. Hamilton is there."

"I need to get over to the café," Penny said to Buddy when the children had scattered. "Mr. Norris will be busy with the truckers."

She kept sitting there though.

"Do you have a minute to talk first?" Buddy finally asked.

He wasn't given to fancy words, but he had to know.

"I'm wondering about the children," he said when she nodded. "When did they lose their mother?"

Penny was silent for a bit. "My sister died a week or so after giving birth to the twins. Some kind of fever."

"And you married their father?"

"It wasn't a real marriage," she said, looking over to meet his eyes. "Howard knew he was dying even before my sister passed. They were both worried about what would happen with them gone. No one would adopt the six children together. We all knew that. I was single and I didn't think the state would give me all of the children either. That's when we came up with the scheme to make me their legal guardian by marrying Howard. I couldn't stand for the children to go into foster homes."

Buddy nodded. "Had you been planning to marry someone else?"

A shadow came over her eyes. "My high school boyfriend. He was captain of the football team when I was only a freshman. He swept me off my feet. His family had money. He's in college now at Princeton."

"A prince of a fellow," Buddy echoed softly.

"How did you know that?" Penny looked at him with a little frown on her forehead. "That's what my sister always used to say about him."

Buddy watched the worry settle back on her face.

She stood up then. "It was not true, of course. He wasn't a prince. And I need to get back to work."

"I'll help," Buddy offered as he stood.

Eating sandwiches hadn't taken more than five minutes so Fred was still frying up the orders for the truckers who were eating there.

The café owner gave instructions to Penny about who had which platter and Buddy helped her carry plates to the various truckers. He made it a point to whisper to every one of them that any tips all went to the Rose family.

Buddy watched Penny as she moved around the tables, always with a cheerful word for anyone she saw. He didn't know how she managed to do it. He might not have had much experience with families, but he knew what kind of a life she'd given up to take care of her nieces and nephews.

Buddy waited until everyone had their food before stepping into the kitchen of the café. Fred was scraping down the grill.

"Could you ask Penny to come back here?" Buddy asked quietly. "I have something I want to discuss with the men out front."

Fred shrugged. "Remember those are my customers. Don't upset them."

"I won't."

When Penny was safely out of hearing distance, Buddy asked the other truckers to gather around him. He explained that Penny wouldn't take what she saw as charity and, the only way for the family to get on their feet again, was to make a good profit on that pitiful wheat field they had on the Dutton ranch.

He didn't tell the others, but he figured if the Rose family made enough money, Penny might be able to go to a community college someplace. It wouldn't be Princeton, but it might give her a chance to marry a doctor or a lawyer.

Buddy wasn't sure whether it was the sight of the children in church or the dislike most of the men had taken to Mr. Dutton, but they all agreed to help carry out his plan to get that wheat field growing again.

After they finished talking, the men slid back into their booths and waited. Fried chicken was the special on Sundays and it came with a slice of apple pie.

Fred poked his head out of the kitchen before he had Penny bring out the dessert.

Buddy nodded. About that time, he told the truckers who wanted a wash that the children were outside, ready to scrub.

An hour later, Buddy and four very wet children were sitting on the steps of the trailer. Even the toddlers had gotten their share of water as the others flung it around. But it was Ellie, perched at the bottom of the stairs, who looked the most satisfied as she counted the five new dimes.

Penny invited Buddy to sit with them for a while. Everyone was tired, adults and children alike, but there was a sense of companionship that Buddy had known little of in life.

It didn't quite seem fair, he thought as he looked around at the Rose family. He hadn't wanted a family until he met this one. And now that he had met them, he hoped for something better for them. He knew why Ellie was so intent on finding a prince for her aunt. If ever a woman deserved the best in life, it was Penny Rose.

And then, as if he wasn't sad enough, Penny invited him to her birthday party.

"It'll just be us," she said shyly. "Unless, of course, anyone else wants to come. But I only know Mr. Norris and your trucker friend to ask."

"Shades?" Buddy asked with a frown. He could see why she might want to invite Fred since the man was her boss, but how did Shades fit into this?

"Of course, the kids know how to celebrate," Penny was continuing without answering his question. "And I plan to make a big cake for the boys to decorate. Ellie will be in charge of blowing up the balloons. I'm going to try and buy some cake candles from the store across the street. It'll be next Sunday after the café finishes up with the noon meal."

"I'd be delighted," Buddy managed to say. He'd never been to a birthday party before unless he counted the monthly announcements in the army. They were more in the way of bulletins though even if sometimes there were pieces of stale cake to pass around.

"Now don't be getting me a present," Penny admonished him. "Unless it's something you make. Those are the only kind of presents I allow for my birthday."

She gave a stern look at the children. "Homemade presents only, remember. They are the best kind."

They nodded obediently although Buddy saw Ellie roll her eyes.

Buddy agreed with the girl. If he ever did get a birthday present, he hoped it wasn't an ash tray. He wondered what kind of a gift Shades might bring Penny. The other trucker wasn't likely to settle for anything homemade.

Suddenly, Buddy felt unsure of himself. Ellie had the perfume already. He could get Penny chocolates, but he knew the kids would eat them. He'd like to get her a month's supply of groceries, but that didn't seem like a very sentimental gift. He knew she'd refuse any article of clothing as being improper. Although maybe a pretty scarf would be acceptable. Or some fancy stationary.

That pesky black crow came back to the trailer then, clearly eyeing Penny in hopes of another piece of food. The woman threw the bird a piece of bread that looked like it had come from one of the sandwiches.

It was like Penny to adopt the crows, Buddy thought – as though she didn't already have enough mouths to feed.

He was still fretting about what to get her for a gift when he started his car some hours later and drove away from Webster's Crossing. He'd hoped to take some time and drive by the farm he was planning to buy, but it was getting late and he was scheduled to take his truck route tomorrow.

Right then, he decided to call the railroad office and see if he could adjust his schedule. They had a backlog of ties up there as it was so it wouldn't make any difference.

He'd be busy at the wheat field tomorrow, putting his plan in place. He'd forgotten to swear the other truckers to secrecy, but he'd ask Fred to help him with that. The café owner had already told him he'd like to do his part to help the Rose family.

Penny and her children had gotten everyone's attention around here. Buddy was determined to make their crop grow. They deserved a good life.

CHAPTER SIX

Buddy stopped at Penny's field on Monday morning. The heat was just starting for the day, but the wheat was already beginning to shrivel and fall down. It wouldn't last much longer without water. The gray ruts were visible where the plow had gone between the rows in the planting. Everything was dry as dust. Even the birds weren't coming by to peck at the weathered stalks.

Shades and another trucker were already there, sitting inside their cabs. Buddy had fixed the buckets before he went to bed last night, taking a hammer and nail to the bottom of each. He could tell Shades had already visited the Olson ranchers, two elderly brothers from the church, who had promised to let Shades fill his dump truck with all the water he wanted.

"Let's go then," Buddy said after he stepped out of his truck. He reached back and grabbed the three buckets. He'd tied a barrel on his flatbed earlier and it was there, ready to work.

Shades had two other buckets when he climbed out of the cab of his dump truck.

"The Olson brothers lent me these, too," Shades added as he held the buckets high. "Said they'd come by in an hour or so and help us. They don't think much of the way Dutton operates either."

Buddy knew a few other truckers were scheduled to pull in soon. And three other ranchers from church had agreed to come when they could.

It took him and Shades a few minutes to get the angle right, but finally they were able to start a trickle of water going from the back of the dump truck to the barrel sitting on Buddy's flatbed. The barrel had a spigot on the bottom that hung over the edge of the truck so they could fill the buckets easily. Once a bucket was full a man would take it out to the field and fling it wide. The water came down like rain.

It was slow dusty work, but as they did it, the gray dirt turned brown until the whole field was covered. When one shift of truckers left, another shift came. Each man only had an hour or so in their schedule, but together it had been enough.

During the day, Buddy had been drenched several times. But, when the last of the truckers left, he walked out to the middle of the field and saw that the wheat stalks had revived. They were standing straight and soaking in the sunshine like it was welcome.

Joy spread through him at the thought of saving this wheat field. If things continued like this, Penny and the children would have a harvest.

Buddy was so close he couldn't resist driving up to the café even though he didn't want to give the secret away. A harvest was never a sure thing until the wheat was in the storehouse. He didn't want to promise something that might not happen.

But he was happy. He left the window on his truck open so the breeze would dry his shirt as he drove down the road, singing. Even Webster's Crossing looked better today. Maybe it was the row of little socks pinned to the clothes line beside the trailer.

It was the middle of the afternoon so he wasn't surprised that there were no other trucks in front of the Heartbreak Café. He pulled off the road anyway and walked over to the business. He opened the door and no one else was in the dining area.

"Hello," Penny said as she poked her head out of the kitchen, a bright smile on her face. The smile faded when she saw who it was. "Oh."

That took the happiness right out of Buddy's step.

"What's wrong?" he asked, a little defensively as he sat down in the booth nearest to the door.

Penny sat right down with him.

"The truckers don't like me," she confided, her whole manner defeated. "I was so glad to get this job – and now Mr. Norris left me in charge and–"

Her voice trailed off. "I know you're my friend, but I was hoping it was one of the other truckers. Someone who wasn't stopping because they felt they had to."

"They like you," Buddy interrupted, confused about how to reassure her. If she only knew what they had been doing for her and the children this morning, she would have no doubt that everyone liked her.

Penny shook her head. "None of them stop to eat. They all want a sandwich to go and that's it."

"Oh. Well." Buddy stammered. He couldn't argue with that. The truckers couldn't take their normal meal break since they were spending the time on her wheat field. "I'm sure it's just because –"

Buddy had no clue how to finish that sentence, but Penny was looking at him with an expression of hope on her face and he didn't want it to dim.

"Because you're so pretty," Buddy finished in relief. He figured all women liked to hear that.

Penny snorted. "I can't be that pretty if I put them off their dinner."

With that, she stood up and stomped back to the kitchen, only turning when she got to the door to ask what he wanted to order.

"A cheeseburger," he said.

"To go?" she asked

He shook his head carefully. "No, I'll eat it here."

She nodded, her satisfaction showing, before going into the other room.

Buddy looked out the window. He thought Fred would be back by now. The café owner had gone down to the wheat field this morning, but everyone had left there an hour ago.

Not that the café had that much business now. It's just that Fred was always in the café, playing records of Elvis songs if the day got slow.

Suddenly, Buddy noticed a black bird flying by his window. It landed on the edge of the window box and stared inside.

"Hi, there," Buddy said even though the crow's beady eyes didn't invite any warm feelings. It took some effort for Buddy to maintain his smile. He'd been haunted by that old crow lately, with its scruffy visage and ruffled feathers. It was trying to do right by its partner even if there was no reason he should. That bird had no natural instinct to guide him and yet he did it. Buddy had more empathy for the bird than he figured he should.

Right then, Buddy saw Ellie come out of the trailer onto the porch and throw what looked like an apple core toward the bird. The old thing hopped over and picked it up in its beak. Then it flew across the road to where its mate waited.

Persistence, Buddy told himself, that was what the bird had. It refused to leave without something in its beak. Even an ignorant bird could do that.

In a few minutes, Penny came out of the kitchen with a cheeseburger on a platter. She didn't look any happier than she had been earlier, but she set the plate down on the table and sat down on the other side of the booth.

"The pickle is to say I'm sorry." She pointed at the green spear beside his burger. "It's not your fault the other truckers are treating me like I have the plague."

Once again, Buddy was speechless. But he felt inspired by the crow to try and give Penny what she needed even if he didn't know how.

"Thank you," he said. "It will all work out."

That much he knew for sure. The truckers weren't going to keep flinging water around that field forever. When they knew it was going to work, they could announce what they were doing even if the field wasn't ready to harvest.

"You're a good friend to me," Penny said.

Buddy felt like a heel. He should have thought of

something more inspiring to say. Shades would have. So would Penny's high school sweetheart. "Yeah, well —"

Just then Fred came back into the café through the front door.

Penny stood up like she'd been caught violating some policy.

Fred waved her back down.

"No one else is even here," the café owner said. "I hope you fixed something for yourself, too."

"I was going to wait and eat with the children when you got back," Penny said.

Fred nodded as he walked toward the kitchen. "Well, I'm here."

Penny sank onto the booth again.

"Sandwiches with the kids?" Buddy asked.

She nodded. "I'm going to make fried egg ones this time and I got them all some apples to eat. And a big jug of milk from the store."

Buddy figured that sounded pretty healthy. He wouldn't ask if she had enough money for groceries since she obviously did.

"Before you —" Buddy had to stop and swallow. "Before you got married, what were you going to study in college?"

Penny looked at him in surprise. "I hadn't decided."

"I bet you could be anything," Buddy answered, trying not to sound like an army recruiter. He didn't know anything about college, but he supposed a lot of people had to take a few classes before they knew the direction they wanted to go.

Ellie came into the café then and Penny turned to look at the clock on the wall behind her.

"I guess I better get those sandwiches," Penny said as she stood up.

He let her go without protest, but was surprised when Ellie slid into the booth after her aunt walked out the door.

"I got the perfume," she whispered, after checking to see they were the only ones in the café.

"Good," Buddy said, cutting his cheeseburger in half and

offering the girl a piece of it.

Ellie spread out a paper napkin on the booth table and carefully set the cheeseburger half on it.

They ate in companionable silence for a few minutes.

"I'm going to get a dress," Ellie finally confided as well.

"Oh?"

She nodded. "Irene over at the store said there was some pink cotton that no one was buying so they were going to put it on sale, but then they wondered if I'd like it. My aunt said if I agreed to sweep their porch every day for the rest of the summer, I could accept the fabric." Ellie paused. "My aunt said it worked out to a nickel an hour for my sweeping."

Buddy grinned. He could imagine Penny making that deal.

"They have an old hound dog at the store," Ellie continued. "He's nice. I think they named the store for him."

Buddy nodded. He hadn't realized the store had a name, but then he recalled a sign on the side of the building that was so faded no one could read it.

"And then there's a lady at the gas station who said she'd sew my dress for me if I sweep her porch, too," Ellie added and then frowned. "Only she doesn't have a porch."

Buddy smiled. "I guess you'll have to sweep the inside of the station for her then."

"I could do that," Ellie agreed, her frown clearing up. "She said she'd sew me a fine dress. Something for church and for school, too."

"That would be real nice," Buddy agreed.

"I'll show Matt Dutton that I have a dress," she said fiercely then. "Better than his, anyway. If he had one, I mean."

Buddy knew what she meant. "I'm sure it will be everything a dress should be."

Ellie seemed content, having given him all of her news.

When they finished the cheeseburger, they both walked over to the trailer. The boys were still outside and they tackled Buddy when they saw him coming. He swung the youngest up high and then the others wanted to fly as well.

"Don't bother Mr. Hamilton," Penny called a halt to the

swinging a few minutes later. "Come in and eat your sandwiches."

Buddy followed them in just so he could share the blessing Penny gave for the food. He'd missed some meals in his life, but he didn't think he'd ever been as grateful for food as Penny was when she prayed.

He liked listening to her talk to God, thanking Him for the day and the provisions He'd given them. After she prayed, Buddy said his good-byes, being sure to tell Penny he was working tomorrow.

"I'll honk when I go by," he said. "But I won't have time to stop."

"But you'll be hungry," Penny protested.

"I'll bring some sandwiches with me from home."

Everyone nodded at that, but Buddy was the only one who realized he didn't have a home, not like the kind Penny had already made for the children in the trailer. He looked around, unable to decide what it was that made the difference. There was no fine furniture in the trailer. No fancy curtains or overflowing cupboards. It was the laughter, he thought as he listened to Penny chuckle over something one of the boys said. A man living alone didn't have much reason to laugh, Buddy told himself as he left.

When he got back to his room, he felt the urge to whittle. Suddenly, he realized there was something he could make for Penny's birthday. He'd been saving a block of soft pine for something special and this would be it. His room felt more like a home that night than it ever had before as he sat and whittled, thinking about Penny.

CHAPTER SEVEN

The next morning, Buddy took his whittling knife and wood with him as he drove his flatbed up to the Hi-Line. He'd stopped to help water the wheat field again, but then had to leave to make his delivery. After he helped unload the railroad ties in Havre, he'd spent a few minutes working on Penny's birthday present before he headed back to Miles City. He worked the water buckets then, too. It was after dark when he walked into the house where he rented his room.

He was tired and he'd forgotten all about his bank loan. So, he was surprised when he found a note taped to his door saying someone had called and left a message that he should stop by the bank in the morning.

He smiled when he read it. The loan papers must be ready to sign sooner than anyone had expected. The old bachelor who was selling had seemed anxious to leave so maybe he'd rushed things along.

The next morning, Buddy took his time getting ready for the meeting. He didn't have a delivery scheduled for the day. He shaved carefully, aware that this was the biggest day of his life and that he should look good. He had scrubbed the blood off his tie earlier so he wore that with his freshly ironed white shirt. His dress shoes still shone from Sunday and his dark hair lay back from his forehead like he wanted it to. He looked in the mirror as he set his hat at a rakish angle. No one could say Buddy Hamilton didn't look like a property owner.

Before he opened the door, he glanced toward the table at his whittling. He wished Penny could be there when he signed

the papers. In a few minutes, his dream would come true.
If Penny knew it, she would be getting up a celebration about now, he thought. Then he remembered the telephone poles that lined the highway going up to Webster's Crossing. He'd never seen a phone in Fred's café, but there must be one close by.

Buddy decided to surprise Penny with his good news. He went out into the hall of his rooming house and picked up the phone sitting there. Then he dialed the operator and asked for the Heartbreak Café. She said there was no phone number for the place. Furthermore, she said the only phone in Webster's Crossing was at the gas station.

"Connect me there then," Buddy said.

"Lizzy?" he asked when a woman answered.

It didn't take him long to ask Lizzy to take a message to Fred, requesting that the café owner set out a special spread for him and the Rose family at noon.

"His fried chicken dinner would be good," Buddy said. "I'll pay extra – within reason, of course."

"You're also invited, Lizzy," he added. He hadn't met her yet, but it was the least he could do.

"Tell Irene and her granny to come too," he finished.

Buddy hung up before he spent all of his money. Then he started to grin just thinking about it. He'd have to watch his pennies when he started making his mortgage payments, but a man should do something to mark the day the biggest dream in his life came true.

Buddy drove his Chevy to the brick building that housed the Miles City Bank. He parked on the main street. A barber shop stood on one side of the bank and a dry goods store on the other. Twenty businesses were lined up and down that street. He wondered if Webster's Crossing would ever grow that large.

There was enough brass inside the bank lobby that it made him feel prosperous just walking in. He gave a clerk his name and he was ushered back to the row of offices.

The meeting only took two minutes. His heart had sunk

when he saw the loan officer's face. The farm he was hoping to buy had been pulled off the market. Apparently the old bachelor's nephew had decided he wanted it. The loan officer tried to console Buddy with the news that he still qualified for the loan and would be welcome to present a different farm at the same price.

No one mentioned that there were no other properties for sale that cheaply, not in the entire state. Nor had there been any for the past year. They both knew it.

Buddy had waited a long time to find this farm and now it would be much longer until he found another. It might never happen. He walked out of the building, telling himself he should have known better. Things never worked right for a guy like him.

He looked up at the sun in the sky and decided there was nothing to do but to carry on. By now Lizzy would have spread the word. The children would be looking forward to their fried chicken and he wouldn't add their disappointment to his.

He headed up to Webster's Crossing and pulled off the road early when he came to the wheat field. The ground was moist so he knew the truckers had watered it earlier. The stalks were looking better. It would take a few more weeks, but the crop was thriving.

A pickup drove up to him and stopped. Mr. Dutton rolled down the window. The man hadn't shaved for a couple of days and his eyes were rimmed with red, likely from the dust.

"What are you up to out here?" the other man asked with a scowl on his face. "And don't say nothing because something's going on. Last week this field was drying up and now it's looking better than my crop. It isn't natural."

"I'm just doing a good deed." Buddy said and then chuckled when he saw the other man was so astonished that he didn't know how to respond.

With that, Buddy put his car into gear and headed down the highway.

Maybe his dream wasn't going to come true, but there were

better days ahead for the Rose family.

When Buddy parked at the café, he saw Shades dump truck over by the store. The kids had evidently posted a lookout on the steps of the trailer because Buddy had scarcely pulled his keys out of the ignition when all six of them raced out of the trailer.

Buddy stood facing them as they squealed and rushed to him. Ellie and the oldest boy, Jason, were bringing up the rear since they had the toddlers on their hips again. That's why he didn't fully see Ellie at first. Then she set down the twin that she'd been carrying.

"You got your dress!" Buddy grinned as he motioned for her to twirl. The skirt swirled out in a blur of cotton candy pink softness. A strip of white eyelet edged the bright white collar around the girl's neck. "It's the prettiest dress I've ever seen."

Ellie had a white barrette in her hair and white socks peeking out over her black shoes.

"Aunt Penny said I could dress up for the party," the girl said beaming.

"Well, I'm honored." Buddy gave the girl an exaggerated bow and tipped his hat to her.

The door to the café opened and Penny stepped out.

Buddy looked over and, just seeing her in the sunlight, made him feel better.

"What's the party for?" Penny asked as she hurried over to him. "I can't wait to hear. Did you sign the papers for your farm?"

Buddy grinned at her for no good reason.

"I guess the party is to celebrate Ellie's new dress," Buddy said. He didn't want the children to know of his difficulty. When Penny got closer, he leaned over and whispered, "I'll tell you about it later."

She nodded like she understood.

Buddy had never laughed as much as he did at that party. Ellie pranced around in her dress until Fred gave her one of his old aprons to put over it, saying he'd had a little daughter once and she liked to keep her dresses clean.

Fred refused to answer any questions about his mysterious daughter. Instead, he ducked back into the kitchen and brought out a whole apple pie, cutting everyone a slice while grinning at the antics of the boys.

It was dusk by the time the party wound down. Ellie marched the children over to the trailer to start getting ready for bed. But Penny lingered a bit. The two of them were alone in the café.

"Tell me about the loan," she said, sitting across from him in a booth.

"The owner took it off the market and is giving it to his nephew," Buddy said.

"Lucky nephew," Penny said.

Buddy nodded.

"Well, one thing I do know," Penny continued. "If God doesn't give us something, it's because He has something better in mind."

She said it with such confidence. Buddy had never seen faith like that.

"Did you feel that way about the Princeton guy?"

She was quiet for a minute. "Not at first."

Her hand was on the table and he covered it with his own.

"But it's true," she whispered. "God does have someone better for me. My old boyfriend didn't really love me. He didn't stick when times got hard."

Buddy figured even a doctor or a lawyer wasn't good enough for her. Maybe she should marry the President of the United States. Not the current one, of course. But there was time for the next election.

CHAPTER EIGHT

The wheat field grew thick and golden during the week of water. Buddy stopped every day and, when he didn't have a delivery to the railroad, he chased away the birds that were now attracted to the growing stalks. Regardless of what he was doing, however, he stopped by the café and talked to Penny. His days spun around her. He knew it couldn't be forever, but he basked in their budding friendship.

Sunday morning dawned bright. Buddy had stayed up late the night before, finishing his gift for Penny. It was the best work he'd ever done and he hoped she liked it.

He'd purchased a new white shirt on Friday and, before he headed out to Webster's Crossing, he adjusted the knot of his tie until it was comfortable. He figured he'd be wearing this white shirt and tie every week in the future, at least on those Sundays they had services at Webster's Crossing. He was getting to know God through Penny's eyes. He'd had some faith as a child, but nothing like he needed. Church was a place to start.

The vehicles were parked on both sides of the highway when he came up to the small town. A good number of trucks were parked next to the café and pickups and cars stood beside the store. Buddy didn't see either of the Dutton vehicles, but he saw Shades' dump truck.

Buddy climbed the stairs inside the store, after glancing at his watch to be sure he was early. He heard the chatter stop when the people heard his footsteps.

"It's only me," he said when he got to the top of the stairs.

By then his head was visible in the church area.

He looked around. Irene and Shades were holding a giant card with a big sunflower on it.

"We can't decide if we should say Happy Birthday or Welcome to Your New Home," Shades said.

"Maybe both," Buddy walked closer.

"We're not going to give it to her until we're at the wheat field, are we?" Irene asked. "I brought a bandana so we can blindfold her until we get there. That'll make it a surprise."

"We need to be sure and tell her that the men are committed through the harvesting," Fred said. "The Olson brothers said we could use their combine to do the wheat. It's an old machine, but they've kept it working and it does a good job."

"That's a lot to get on a card." Irene frowned.

"Buddy should give a speech." Shades had enough of a twist to his smile to let Buddy know the other man would enjoy seeing him up in front of everyone.

Suddenly, the door shut downstairs and everyone went still.

Muted voices came up the stairway and then Buddy heard Penny laugh.

"It's her," he whispered.

Everyone scattered to their seats.

When Penny and the children arrived, Shades was already up front with a Bible opened. Buddy glanced at the other man. He didn't think the trucker had a Bible and this one had an embroidered bookmark hanging down. He guessed the Bible belonged to Irene.

It didn't take long for the Rose family to get settled in their chairs. The children saved a place for Buddy and he slipped into their midst like he belonged.

Shades cleared his throat and the service began.

"We had a special request today for the hymn, *Bringing in the Sheaves*," Shades said with a grin.

More people came upstairs as the song was underway and, before long, the singing was strong.

Shades lifted his arms and the voices soared as they all sang,

"We shall come rejoicing, bringing in the sheaves!"

Everyone was silent as the hymn died away.

"And now Buddy Hamilton has an announcement," Shades said as he stepped to the side.

There was a sprinkling of applause as Buddy walked to the front. He hadn't glanced at Penny before he walked up, but when he stood there his eyes wouldn't look anywhere else.

"We are pleased to have you, Penny Rose, and your family here in Webster's Crossing," Buddy began. By then, the woman was looking curious. "We know you've had your rough patches in life lately and we want to say we're on your side."

His words were inadequate, Buddy knew, but he couldn't tell her all that was in his heart. Not in front of everyone like this.

But he didn't need to say anything more because Irene was bringing the big card out.

"You can't have this until you see your surprise," Irene said, waving the card, but keeping it far enough away that nothing could be read. Then she brought out the red bandana. "Come downstairs and we're going to put this over your eyes as we drive you someplace."

Buddy liked the delight on Penny's face.

"I love surprises," she said as she gathered up the children. "And I haven't had one like this for a long time."

Buddy had brought his Chevy and, after he settled Penny in the passenger seat, he wedged the children all into the back seat. The twins needed to sit on the laps of the older children, but he suspected they were used to doing that.

Driving down the highway, Buddy felt like the Rose family was his family. He liked it more than he should, with Penny chattering away about her week and the children in the back asking how long it would be before they got where they were going.

"Just be patient," he called back to the children after he answered the question about what color of curtains he thought Fred should put in the trailer. He was glad the café owner planned to fix up that old trailer some, but he hoped the Rose family would have a better home soon. Maybe with the wheat money, they would.

When they arrived at the field, Buddy put his finger to his lips to silence anything the children might say. He could see the questions in their eyes though. They all sat in the car together for a few minutes while the rest of the people from the church arrived and took up positions along the edge of the highway.

Then, suddenly, everyone was there and Shades gave a nod. It was time.

"I'm coming around to help you out," Buddy said to Penny. "But don't take off your blindfold just yet."

"I just can't imagine--" Penny said, the excitement making her voice rise.

Buddy nodded for the children to leave the car and then he walked behind the car to open Penny's door.

"Don't stand up too quick," he said as he put his hand on her head to make sure she didn't hit the door frame as she got up.

He helped her walk a few feet until she was in a perfect spot to see.

Everyone was silent while he untied the bandana from her eyes.

"Oh, my," she whispered when she saw her wheat field. Then she turned to Buddy. "What happened?"

"Your friends have been watering it," he explained and then he saw tears form.

"It's not charity," he whispered urgently.

She smiled at him then, her face beaming. "I know it's not. It's friendship at work."

Buddy felt warm inside as he grinned back at her like a fool.

"We're going to keep with the field through the harvest," Buddy said as he looked up and gestured to include all of the people there. "All of us."

"I don't know what to say," Penny said as she looked out at the faces. "It means so much to me."

"It will give you a new life," Buddy said quietly.

He hadn't thought she had heard him because of all the chatter around them, but she turned to look at him. "I have a new life. Here."

"A better life, I mean," he said. "Maybe college —"

Just then a pickup screeched to a stop along the highway and a horn blasted so loud that everyone stopped talking to look.

"What's the meaning of this?" Mr. Dutton demanded as he opened his pickup door and swung himself down all in one angry motion. "I knew something was going on here."

"We're holding a church service," Shades said as he stepped forward.

Buddy put his arm around Penny to protect her.

"Out in the middle of the highway beside my wheat field?" Mr. Dutton asked, his tone scathing.

"It's not your wheat field," Buddy said. "It belongs to the Rose family."

"Only until the first day of September," Mr. Dutton said, eyeing his neighbors like he was taking their names down. "Remember, I own the land."

"God owns the land," Buddy protested. "All of us are just renting from Him."

Buddy felt the tension leave Penny's shoulders and she looked up at him with admiration in her eyes.

Mr. Dutton sputtered, but he couldn't seem to think of anything to say past that. Maybe he did realize it was a church service, Buddy thought.

"It's not fair," the man finally muttered. "That field never grows anything. And now it's looking better than mine."

Just then a flock of birds flew down and landed in Penny's wheat. They started to peck at the grain.

"None of us are going to have any wheat if we don't get rid of those birds," Mr. Dutton said then, his voice strong again.

"I guess I better get out my birthday present," Buddy said as he removed his arm from Penny's shoulders. "I'll be right back."

Buddy went to the trunk of his car and came back.

"Oh," Penny said when she saw what he held. Tears filled her eyes and then she laughed. "Why it's a perfect picture of those crows!"

Buddy was pleased at the delight on Penny's face. "It was a bit of a challenge to get their beaks just right."

His carving had one crow flying down and giving a piece of apple to the other crow.

"They look like lovebirds." Fred had walked closer and studied the life-size crows that Buddy had mounted on a short piece of wood. He'd nailed the piece of wood to a pole tall enough to be stuck in the ground.

"Why they're kissing!" Fred announced in further astonishment. "But crows don't kiss. Not even the two up by the café do that."

Buddy saw the pink flood Penny's face. Everyone else must have seen it too.

"I have a shirt," Buddy blurted out. He didn't want Penny to feel uncomfortable. He had brought his old white shirt back from the trunk and now he put it on the wood shoulders.

"A scarecrow!" Penny said then, her face smiling once again.

"It'll scare all those birds away," Buddy said. "The flapping in the wind will make them leave."

Shades cleared his voice as he stepped closer to the scarecrow and looked at Buddy.

"We'll leave you and Penny to plant that thing out in the middle of the field," Shades said. "You don't need all of us tramping around out there. The rest of us are going back to get the party ready."

"There's more?" Penny asked, her eyes widening.

"Give us fifteen minutes," Irene said. "And the children can ride with us."

With that, everyone walked to their vehicles.

Buddy and Penny waited for the last car to leave before they started to carefully make their way to the center of the wheat. Buddy carried the scarecrow over his shoulder and they walked until Penny pointed to a spot.

Buddy had sharpened the end of the pole and it didn't take much for him to push it down far enough to hold in the ground.

"That's the best present I've ever received," Penny said solemnly as they stood there.

"Well, it's hard to compete with an ash tray," Buddy said.

She smiled. "The children told you."

He nodded.

They stood there silently, each staring at the crows Buddy had carved.

"They really do look like they are kissing," Penny said softly.

"That's because —" Buddy started and then stopped.

"What?" Penny nudged him.

"Because I was thinking of you when I made them," Buddy finally admitted. His voice was little more than a whisper.

He watched her face change as she realized what he'd said.

"I know crows don't kiss," he hastened to add. "Not like people do."

Penny smiled. "I think it's wonderful that they're kissing."

Buddy stared at her a moment. "You do?"

Her smile faded, but her eyes remained steady. "Very wonderful. I wish --"

He had to strain to hear her voice, but her eyes were looking at him in a way that made him hope.

"What's your wish?" he murmured.

"You."

That was all he needed to know. Buddy dipped his head and kissed her. Sweetness exploded between them and he had all he could do to finally pull back. Penny had choices now and he didn't want to push her to take him when the whole world awaited her.

Love might be enough for those crows, but Penny had the children to consider. And Ellie wanted her aunt to marry a prince.

"Our first kiss," Buddy said softly. He'd remember it forever even if it was the only one.

They held hands as they returned to his car.

CHAPTER NINE

Buddy pulled his car off the road and parked next to the café. They had given the others enough time to prepare and he knew he was supposed to lead Penny into the café.

"Aren't they having church still?" Penny asked as they walked toward the café.

"I think they're just changing the location for today," Buddy said as he opened the door.

A shout went up from the dozens of people inside. Balloons of every color were strung from the booths. Twisted garlands of gold dipped down from the light fixtures and rose back up to the corners of the dining area.

"Happy Birthday," Buddy whispered as others called out congratulations in louder voices.

Shades cleared his throat and silence reigned again.

"We're finishing our church service here this morning so we can praise God for all the good things He's given to us," Shades said and then people found places to sit at the tables and booths.

Buddy looked at the trucker. The other man was taking to this church business better than Buddy would have thought.

He looked down at Penny then. She was sitting next to him in the booth and the children were crowded into the other side. She glanced up at him with a smile so wide it broke his heart.

He supposed the reality of that wheat field hadn't quite sunk in for her yet. He didn't know how to tell her she could aim higher now so he sat back and listened to the hymns and the reading of some Psalms.

Finally, Fred slipped back into the kitchen and the smell of his fried chicken filled the café. By the time Shades called for a final prayer, everyone was hungry.

Buddy had never seen people eat their fill of fried chicken like they did that day. He had opened his wallet to pass some money to Fred but the café owner assured him that a collection had already been taken to cover the expense.

"We all wanted to welcome the Rose family," Fred said before he hurried back to the kitchen. "Best thing that ever happened to my business."

After the food was gone, Ellie brought out the chocolate cake that Penny had made. The boys had decorated it with white frosting and ribbons of licorice that spelled their aunt's name.

Most of the truckers had to leave then, since some of them had deliveries still. Almost all of the ranchers left, too. So there was only a handful to see the opening of the birthday gifts.

The toddlers each proudly gave Penny an ash tray with an impression of their tiny hands in the middle of it. She thanked them sincerely. The boys had made a bridle out of leather strips in case they could ever afford a pony. Penny admired it as well.

And then Ellie stood up. "This is from all of us."

She had wrapped the present in a scrap of the pink material from her dress. The girl carefully handed it over to her aunt.

Penny removed the fabric and drew in her breath. "Why it's beautiful! How'd you ever?"

"We bought it with what we earned on the trucks," Penny said proudly.

Penny held the perfume bottle up to the light. "Absolutely gorgeous."

Ellie and the other children beamed.

Buddy was proud of them. And then his whole world teetered on the edge of despair.

"It's to find your prince," Ellie informed her aunt. "It says right on the bottle."

"Really?" Penny sounded impressed as she opened the bottle. "Shall we see if it works?"

Penny daubed perfume behind her ears.

"It smells like chicken in here," Ellie said with a frown. "How's a prince supposed to find you?"

"Maybe it will take a while," Penny said as she put the lid back on the bottle.

Ellie turned to Buddy and screwed up her face in concentration. "You need to help me fan."

Ellie gave him a paper napkin. She already had one in motion.

Buddy fanned for all he was worth. Penny was smiling and playing along with her niece, but Buddy could hardly look at the woman. Everyone knew there was no prince worthy of Penny around here.

"Can you smell the perfume yet?" Ellie leaned over to ask him.

"I think I do," Buddy answered.

Ellie looked at him expectantly then, her eyes shining with excitement. He wasn't sure what she wanted.

"I'm sure I do," Buddy clarified.

That only turned up the wattage on the girl's smile.

Penny leaned close and whispered in his ear. "She wants you to kiss me now."

"Me?" Buddy was dumbfounded. But he looked at Ellie's face and he thought that must be what she wanted. He still couldn't do anything.

"She thinks I'm a prince?" Buddy asked.

Penny nodded. "We all do."

Buddy looked around then. A small circle of friends – Shades, Fred, Irene, and the Olson ranchers – were all staring at him.

"They think I'm a prince," he repeated for his audience, waiting for someone to tell him he was mistaken. No one did.

Finally, Shades cleared his throat. "The prince generally kisses the birthday girl."

Buddy grinned. "No one needs to ask twice."

With that, he leaned over and kissed Penny soundly. He still wasn't sure though so he said, "I was thinking, with the money from the wheat, you might still be able to go to college and meet –"

Penny interrupted him. "I don't need a college boy."

"You're sure?"

She nodded.

That was good enough for Buddy and he kissed her again.

"Lovebirds," Fred said in resignation a few minutes later as he turned to go back to the kitchen. "They're all over."

"I've got to be going to," Shades said and Irene walked with him to the café door.

"We've been hoping to have a word with you," one of the Olson ranchers said to Buddy then with a nod to the corner of the café.

Buddy obligingly got up from the booth and followed them over.

"If it's about the water," he began.

The men shook their heads.

"We have plenty of water," the older of them said. Buddy thought the man's name was Seth. "You're welcome to all you need for that field."

"It's the ranch," the other one of them said. Buddy didn't remember that one's name.

The two men looked at each other and Seth continued, "We are getting too old to handle the ranch and we've been looking for the right young man to take over for us."

Buddy caught his breath. "You need a ranch hand?"

He might not make as much as he was now with his trucking, but his heart wanted to work the land.

"More than that," Seth said. "We know you've been looking at ranches to buy and we want you to consider ours."

"I can't afford –" Buddy began.

Seth waved his concerns away. "Money is not that important to us. We don't have any heirs to leave the place to and our mother always said the ranch should have a large family. She only had the two of us and she'd wanted a houseful."

"But it's just me," Buddy protested.

"It's a good-sized spread that we have," Seth continued like he hadn't heard. "And the house is built to last. Two stories with four bedrooms upstairs and large rooms downstairs."

"I don't qualify for that much of a loan," Buddy said.

"We figure we'll share crop with you for the first couple of years," Seth said. "See that you get on your feet. We plan to rent an apartment in Miles City so we'll be close for questions. And we'll take the price down for each of those years. We'll make the money work if you want the place."

"Want it?" Buddy asked. "Of course, I want it."

And then hope hit him.

"I don't suppose it has a garden?" Buddy asked.

Seth nodded. "A big one. When my parents were alive, my mother used to can all of our vegetables. The place has a root cellar, too."

Buddy was almost speechless so he reached out and shook hands with the men.

"You have no idea," he started to say.

Seth cut him off with a look and whispered. "I think we do."

Then they all three turned to watch Penny and the children as they gathered the balloons that had come loose from their ties. The children were laughing as Ellie chased a runaway red balloon and then the toddlers got tangled up in the ribbons.

"Some things are worth more than money," Seth said.

Buddy nodded. He marveled at how he had found this family.

About that time, Penny came over to stand by him and he put his arm around her. She snuggled next to him and he bent down to kiss her. It was enough to make a man feel like a prince, Buddy thought as he kissed her again.

EPILOGUE

September of That Same Year
Buddy purchased a black suit. Penny joked that it was his lovebird suit and he didn't correct her. What else should he wear to his wedding? He wanted a reminder of the crow who had shown him that the most unlikely males can change into good mates if they have God's help.

Besides, no one was looking at him once Penny started walking down the aisle. Actually, they had stopped looking at him when Ellie waltzed down as the maid of honor in a frothy dress of yellow chiffon. She held a basket and sprinkled yellow rose petals along the aisle between the folding chairs. The windows up front cooperated and sun shone through and landed on Penny like she was receiving a blessing from on high as she made her way forward.

The pastor from Dry Creek had come over for the ceremony and the whole upstairs of the store was packed. Truckers from up and down the state were there. Even the Dutton family had squeezed into a corner of the church. He noticed Ellie made sure Matt saw the fullness of her dress as she waltzed by him.

Buddy had moved into the Olson house last month and he'd gotten the place ready for his new family. It was helpful that the two bachelors claimed they had no need for the furniture and left most of it in the house -- from beds to tables to hundreds of canning jars. Fred confessed he was relieved at the way things were working out because the trailer behind the café didn't have any heat and he wasn't sure where the Rose family would have gone for the winter.

Finally, Penny reached his side and Buddy was so proud he felt like he had grown an inch taller in the short time it had taken her to come down the aisle.

The two of them recited their vows without stumbling and, almost before Buddy knew it, the pastor said, "You may now kiss the bride."

Buddy didn't hesitate.

He wasn't sure if it was his heart that thundered in his ears or if people were really clapping that loud. It didn't matter though. Not with Penny in his arms. No matter how many years they had together, he was determined they would always be lovebirds.

ABOUT JANET TRONSTAD

USA Today and *Publisher's Weekly* bestselling author, Janet Tronstad, has 35 titles published by Harlequin's Love Inspired line. *Romantic* Times says her long-standing Dry Creek series is a "quirky small town...with witty characters." Don't miss out on her new Webster Crossing stories (just down the road from Dry Creek). Tronstad has over 3 million books sold around the world.

HER MULE HOLLOW COWBOY

DEBRA CLOPTON

CHAPTER ONE

"Get in there, you ornery hunk of steaks," Maddie Rose gritted out through clamped teeth while thrusting all of her weight into pushing the cattle trailer's rear gate closed. A hard task since her hundred twenty pounds didn't hold up against Buford's two thousand pound bulk. Needless to say, despite all of her shoving and pushing. Despite all of her exertion. Buford's big, hairy rump hadn't budged even an inch! Nope, there it was—hanging out over the back end of the trailer.

Firmly in the way of the latch.

"C'mon, only a few more inches," she coaxed, pushing, giving it everything she had. But the bull wasn't buying it. He didn't budge.

"*Arrg,*" she growled, frustration nearly getting the better of her.

This should have been a piece of cake—an easy load-up. Ha!

Bull-headed Buford messed that up deciding he wanted off rather than on.

Just Maddie's luck.

And what was new about that? "*Nothing,*" she grumbled.

She wasn't a whiner, but there was no getting around the hard truth that most things in Maddie's life hadn't come easy. She'd been fighting for survival since the moment of her existence—a sickly baby only a few weeks old at best estimation, found alone, sitting in a carseat. Yup—just sitting on the steps of the post office like she belonged there.

Obviously, she didn't belong anywhere.

Maybe before that, but unlike most people Maddie had no recollection, no records, nothing...as far as her life record went she hadn't existed until that day in the post office when she was found.

If she'd been a whiner she wouldn't have made it.

No, Maddie was a survivor so she'd grown used to days like today. But it sure was getting old.

Buford's attitude was a sharp reminder she'd better not get comfortable with the good fortune that had recently come her way.

Owner.

The thought dazzled her. Like a beautiful sparkly gift under the Christmas tree that she knew had to belong to someone else...and yet it was hers.

She really was part owner of this magnificent New Horizon ranch. An amazing cattle ranch sitting on the outskirts of Mule Hollow, the most embracing little town she'd ever known. For a gal with her past, raised in an orphanage and then the foster care system this homey community was as close to family as she'd ever gotten.

But she felt like an impostor.

"What had C.C. been thinking when he'd made me an heir?" The question plagued her since the reading of the will two months ago. The day it was revealed that her boss, God rest his sweet soul, had left his ranch to five employees: four cowboys and her.

She could understand why he'd leave her four amazing partners a share. After all, he had no children of his own and these men had been here on the ranch for years, despite not being much older than her. They were cowboys who'd had a bond and a dedication to C.C. and they loved the ranch. She'd noticed it from the first day she'd walked onto the premises two years ago. They deserved the gift.

But why her? Had he felt sorry for her?

It wasn't as if she went around telling everyone her past. She told no one. But intuitive C.C. had guessed some facts during a conversation once.

Sympathy was the only valid reason she could come up with that she was here.

The very thought soured her stomach as life-long insecurities ran rampant inside her head. Despite those insecurities she was still an owner and she was determined that she'd earn this gift if it was the last thing she did.

Teeth grinding down hard she met the ill-tempered glare of the bull. Her palms went slick on the sun warmed metal of the trailer gate. Her insides tensed—but she'd had enough.

Digging her boots into the dirt, Maddie refused to give up or to run away. Letting the bull get the better of her was not the way to prove herself.

Working harder, accomplishing more, being competent and reliable...that was how she became deserving.

For the first time in her life she'd been given a shot at something big—it didn't matter that she didn't deserve it—she was going to do her fair share to see that her former boss never looked down from heaven and regretted the faith he'd shown in giving her this opportunity. She'd already decided that any dream she'd had prior to the reading of that will was going on hold...there would be plenty of time for them later.

Buford snorted sending Maddie instantly on alert. He never did anything he didn't want to do and Maddie knew the ornery bull could make mincemeat out of her if he chose.

He chose—one powerful kick sent the gate slamming into Maddie. A scream ripped from her as the bone crunching impact knocked her off her feet. Flying backwards like a rag doll she slammed into the pipe fence. The hit was immediately followed by the heavy, steel gate. Pain exploded everywhere, glazing everything as it seared through her, dazing her.

Got to stay on your feet.

The gate swung away from her and instinct had Maddie clawing, grasping for its rungs.

Stay off the ground or be trampled.

Buford kicked the gate again, this time, all Maddie's breath whooshed from her, her lungs locked up—the impact so excruciating she hit the ground instantly.

Right in Buford's pathway.

She landed face first in the dirt and her mouth filled with foul tasting grit. Fighting for breath she couldn't help herself, she was helpless. A flashback to her childhood crowded her mind.

Wheezing, she willed herself to move. To breathe.

But, as she'd been unable to help herself all those years ago when she was a sickly abandoned baby, she was helpless now.

Suddenly, boots attached to denim-clad legs thudded to the ground between her and Buford.

"Yah," yelled the cowboy, planting himself directly in the line of danger as the bull bolted from the trailer like a runaway tank.

Where the cowboy had come from, Maddie didn't know, but from her position he looked like a gift dropped straight from heaven.

"Go on, now," he yelled then stomped and waved his arms—held his ground—Buford cut sharply to the right, away from Maddie.

Though her lungs still burned with the need for air, relief surged through her watching the cowboy herd the bull away from her and into the holding pen. Within moments he returned and dropped to his knees beside her.

"Here you go," he drawled, easing her to her side. "Try to relax. The breathing will get easier. Come on, now go easy."

She struggled to relax. He was right, after a few more inhales the breaths did come easier, though there was a sharp edge to each breath if she inhaled too deeply. "Thank. You," she managed, giving him a weak smile.

He didn't smile back, concern etched his rugged, handsome face. "Glad I was here. How are you feeling now?"

Maddie's pulse fluttered, she was mesmerized by his penetrating indigo eyes. Flustered, she yanked her gaze off her gorgeous rescuer and rubbed her ribs, wincing. "Like I've been kicked by a two-thousand-pound bull."

His soft chuckle sank over her like warm honey.

"You may have broken some ribs," he said, kindly then

demanded. "What were you doing out here by yourself in the first place?"

"Loading a bull," she retorted, humiliated by the entire pitiful ordeal and the fact he'd witnessed it. This cowboy probably thought she was some greenhorn who didn't know beans about bulls or cattle.

Needing more control she struggled to sit up without groaning. Honestly, she was feeling better—but who wouldn't? Her cowboy rescuer would make any woman forget she'd been almost stomped to a pulp by a bull—even her.

And that those eyes of his were lethal weapons.

The guy was gorgeous—even oxygen deprived and in pain as she'd been she'd realized that immediately. Touchable dark hair curled from beneath his straw hat and enhanced his firm, chiseled jaw. His high cheekbones underlined those penetrating, strength filled, blue eyes.

He flashed an enticing crooked grin. "You're one tough lady, Maddie Rose."

Maddie got hung-up on that smile—suddenly thinking about long, slow kisses... There was an understandable delay in her fogged brain relaying the message that he knew her name.

And she'd never met him. She knew because she would have remembered him if she'd met him *anytime* in her entire life. And yet, she realized there was something slightly familiar about him.

"Have we met?" she asked, as dawning hit her dazed brain and she saw the resemblance. "Wait, you're Cliff Masterson, Rafe's twin brother. The bull rider." Rafe was one of her ranch partners and a good friend.

"Some nights. Some nights I eat more dirt than you just did." His expression was a mixture of humor and ire—one that made him look more like his brother than he had so far. Rafe had said they weren't identical by a long shot. He'd been right.

They were both dark haired, good looking and with similar face shapes and body builds, but other than the occasional similarity of expressions a person would never mistake them for twins.

She relaxed, some. "Rafe said you were coming but I thought it wasn't until next week."

His left cheek twitched. "My plans changed."

She'd caught the way his expression tightened and pain briefly dulled his eyes. "Oh—"

"How about we get you up to the house?" he asked and before she could answer or even nod he'd moved behind her and in an instant his strong arms slipped around her, gently lifting her up.

Momentarily all pain disappeared. His purely masculine scent wrapped around her, drawing her like a hummingbird to sugar water. She fought the overwhelming urge to lean into him.

"Lean on me," he said, as if he could read her mind.

Ha! Like she needed any encouragement. Even the sharp pains shooting from her ribs overrode the initial shock of his touch, Maddie's awareness of the man stunned her.

She didn't let men get too close. Held them at bay and even though she got lonely and hoped one day she'd have the guts to change that...this kind of reaction had never been a problem.

Never happened.

She chalked it up to the fault of the ordeal she'd just gone through.

It didn't matter anyway. Not right now. Finding the guts to knock down her emotional barriers. To risk her heart for her dream of falling in love and having the family she longed for—that dream was on hold for now.

She had other priorities. Like not flubbing up any more. To prove to herself that she was deserving of this gift.

Needing a hero to ride to her rescue was not the way to do it.

CHAPTER TWO

Cliff Masterson's stomach clenched thinking about how close Maddie had come to being trampled by the huge bull. If he'd arrived at the ranch a moment later he wouldn't have seen Maddie fly through the air and hit the pipe fence like a sack of concrete. He wouldn't have heard her scream when the trailer gate slammed her. And worse, he wouldn't have seen her crumple to the ground in the path of Buford's hooves.

He hadn't thought he was going to make it to her in time.

When he'd scaled the fence and landed between her and the crazy bull his pulse was exploding. Even now, his heart hammered and his mouth went dry thinking about her being crushed beneath the bull. What if he hadn't shown up?

"You're doing great," he encouraged, squeezing her shoulder gently as they eased their way toward the ranch house. "Hopefully those ribs are only bruised and not broken. But I speak from experience--there isn't too much difference, bruised ribs are as painful as broken ribs. At least in the beginning. Broken take a lot longer to heal though."

She huffed out a shaky laugh. "I guess you would know about that—being a bull rider."

"More than I care to think about. Think about something else to put the pain out of your mind." He glanced down at her and her pale caramel hair tickled his nose. She felt slight in his arms and he found himself willing her to look back up at him with those huge green eyes. Eyes that had zapped him like a hotwire the moment she'd rolled her over and she'd planted them on him.

He never felt anything like the electric surge that had arched instantly through him—or the protective instincts still driving him where she was concerned.

He forced himself not to think too closely about his reaction to her. He knew full well that he had issues fogging his head right now. Until a week ago he'd thought he had his life figured out. Had grown good at ignoring his past.

He'd thought he'd left it behind the day he and Rafe had struck out on their own when they were barely seventeen.

But now his dad was dead.

And for reasons he wasn't sure about, Cliff was now questioning everything he'd ever thought about himself.

"That was really stupid of me," Maddie said, her disgust filled words yanking Cliff out of the past. "I should never have gotten in there until he was far enough into the trailer."

"True," he said, not wanting to make her feel worse but the danger she'd put herself in was still too fresh on his mind. "I certainly didn't expect a rooky mistake like that from you—not after the description Rafe gave me."

The minute the words were out of his mouth he knew he'd said something wrong. If he'd been hoping for her to look at him, mission accomplished. Her head jerked back against his shoulder, her expression guarded she stared up at him, her gaze narrowed suspiciously.

"Why were y'all talking about me?"

Their faces were mere inches away, so close he could see the deeper flecks of green dotting the huge pools of emerald. His mind went blank looking into their luscious depths—the sudden desire to lower his head and kiss her nearly overwhelmed him.

He swallowed hard. *What's wrong with me?* Instead of getting a grip his gaze wandered from her tempting lips, over her jawline to the reckless beating pulse at the base of her throat.

Whoa there, hotshot, he warned himself. He hadn't come here to get infatuated with his brother's partner. He'd come to figure out what he wanted out of life. For a man who'd always thought he'd known the answer to that, it had come to quite a blow when he'd realized that he might have been running from his past instead of reaching for a dream.

"Don't get all riled up," he said glad they'd made it to the house. He used the time it took to cross the patio and get inside to try and get his thoughts on track. Once they were in he headed across the large kitchen to the table where he pulled out a chair for her.

She eased onto the seat and looked up at him. "Well?" she prompted, her pretty mouth twisted into a small frown.

Obviously she was prickly about being talked about. "Rafe talks about all of his ranch partners. He says y'all are all good at your jobs. Says you in particular are one of the best cowboys he's ever seen despite you being female and all," he teased.

"Oh." Her brows dipped and her cheeks flushed a pretty pink. "Well, I do my work."

"And then some, from what Rafe said," he offered, then planted his hands on his hips and voiced what had been eating at him from the moment he saw her flying through the air. "My question is, *why* in the blue blazes were you out there loading that bull by yourself? Where is my brother and all of those partners who are supposed to be so good at their jobs?"

Sure he'd already picked up on the fact that she felt like she could do it on her own. That didn't mean it was right.

It also didn't make it any of his business, but he'd never been the best at minding his own business when it came to females getting a raw deal. It probably was a psychological effect left over from watching his mother get a raw deal from his good for nothing dad. She'd taken it for years before her premature death when he was seventeen.

It didn't matter what it was born from. Fact was if Cliff saw a woman who needed help he stepped in. Even if it was one like Maddie who he'd figured was too stubborn to want help. Or too independent to ask for it.

He told himself he should back off, not let himself get any more involved than needed, but that was Cliff's trouble—he tended to acted on instinct in situations like this.

And since learning his dad was dead he'd come to realize

his instincts were off-kilter.

Looking into Maddie Rose's luminous green eyes every protective instinct he had went on high alert.

But from the jut of her chin and the tension filling the room he figured she was about to tell him and his instincts to back off. However, that wasn't happening, because the way he saw it, his brother or one of the other cowboys should have been here helping her out. And he aimed to know why she'd been in that pen attempting to load that bull alone.

He'd been the one to witness her nearly get trampled by a bull—that invested him in this as far as he was concerned. After all, he'd have been the one rushing her to the hospital if he'd arrived any later than he had.

Yeah, he wanted to know why...and he felt like he had a right.

"Because Buford is due at the auction today by five and I'm the one taking him, that's why," Maddie said, irritated at her reactions to the man. Still stunned that the instant he'd wrapped his arm around her all coherent thought had abandoned her.

The clock on the solid brick wall beside the kitchen table ticked a few beats into the silence as Cliff held her gaze. She was glad there was a little distance between them at last. Hopefully she'd start thinking clearer again.

She rubbed her neck and wondered what his story was. Wondered what had caused that shadow in his eyes moments ago.

All things she didn't need to be concerned with.

If there was one thing her life had taught her it was to keep her guard up. The few times she'd relented in the past she'd regretted it. Maybe one day she'd find the courage to risk being hurt one more time, if it meant she could have the family she always dreamed of. But that was on hold for now while she gave everything she had to this ranch.

Besides, she told herself, she'd reacted so strongly toward Cliff out of a sense of gratefulness. She hated to think what would have happened if he hadn't shown up when he had.

"It's not safe," he said, at last. Frowning. "For anyone—especially a woman."

She bristled. "I can take care of myself."

"Hey, I'm concerned for you. And glad I happened by or you'd be out there right now, hurt and alone with a one ton bull tap dancing all over you. And I for one don't like the thought of that." His voice dropped an octave on the last part, softened enough to cause her heart to knot dangerously. Suddenly he knelt beside her and before she knew what he was doing his warm hand splayed open palmed over her left rib cage.

She jumped, gasped, at the intimacy of his touch.

"Easy there. I'm just testing your ribs."

Her heart knotted tighter. "Okay," Maddie quipped, trying for nonchalance, trying hard not to be affected by his touch and nearness. But she was though.

Her breath warbled when he pressed gently while his gaze searched hers. Held. She bit her lip as she held his azure gaze, feeling as if she were freefalling.

"Breathe in and tell me if it hurts. Any sharp pains?"

Only at his urging did she realize she'd been holding her breath since he'd spread his long fingers over her ribs. Trying not to focus on his touch she inhaled slowly. "It's okay. No sharp pains." He moved his hand to the other side.

"And this side?"

"Fine," she said, tightly.

From his kneeling position she had a close up view of the easy smile that spread across his face, crinkling the edges of his eyes.

"That's great news. You still may want to see a doc." He stood and moved to the kitchen counter where he started prowling through her cabinets. "Do you have some pain killers for the soreness that's certain to set in?"

"In that cabinet." She pointed him in the right direction and watched him locate it. She was more than a little aware that the warmth of his touch still lingered and her heart was still behaving oddly.

After being directed to the glasses he brought two pills to her with a glass of water.

"These will help."

"Thanks." She was grateful to have them. Though she was beginning to feel more like herself, she knew even if her ribs weren't broken a tough few days were ahead for her. She didn't want to think about the pain, she would have to find a way to make it through. She was good at that. She'd make it.

"I'm sure Rafe is going to be happy to see you." She knew they weren't real close, at least that was what she'd gathered when she'd overheard Rafe talking to two of her other partners, Dalton and Chase. From what he'd said, Cliff basically lived on the road, zigzagging across the country from one bull riding event or rodeo to the other. And honing his skills in between. He hadn't held on to his spot as a Pro Bull Riding favorite because he was bad or undedicated.

She didn't want any part of that kind of lifestyle and didn't understand it, but she had to admire his dedication.

"They should be back before evening," she said. "They're branding cattle on the far side of the ranch. It's a big job."

"I'm in no hurry—you're a whole lot prettier than my brother."

Maddie knew she looked a mess. Her honey colored hair was stringing loose from her ponytail, one long pale strand hung at the edge of her eyes, tickling her cheek.

She found herself smiling at him anyway. "No doubt about it. You are definitely Rafe's brother. You're as full of nonsense as he is."

That crooked white grin flashed across his face again and tickled her insides. He'd relaxed against the counter, one booted foot crossed over the other, his arms loosely crossed.

"Darlin', I'm only stating the facts. You do own a mirror, don't you?"

His drawl and the way he called her darlin' was pure Texas. And that grin and those twinkling eyes—well, it was no wonder her pulse kicked in again, even despite knowing it didn't mean anything. It probably came natural, especially to a cowboy used to laying on the charm for the cameras and crowds he encountered at the Pro events he participated in.

Faking an unaffected air, she shot him a look of mild disbelief. "Does that line work for you most of the time?"

"What line? You have a little dirt on your face doesn't change the facts."

She laughed, surprising herself. He was good. Maddie had been living among cowboys for several years now and she'd heard her fair share of the slow drawled pickup lines.

"Right." She curbed the laugh. "Well, this dirty-faced cowgirl's got to try and load up a bull." Her ribs rebelled as she eased to a standing position. She ignored them.

"Whoa. You aren't serious?" Stepping in front of her he blocked her path to the door.

"Yes. Now that I've caught my breath and can tell nothings broken it's time to get back to work. I've got a job to finish."

"But your ribs?"

"They'll be fine. Thanks to you and that pain killer you gave me I'll be able to get Buford to the sale. I can still make it."

"But." His eyes flashed fire as Maddie sidestepped him and made it to the door. "This isn't right. Rafe needs to get back here and take care of this."

Maddie swung back around—instantly regretting it as sharp knives of pain stabbed her good. "Hold on, cowboy. This is *my* job and I always finish my jobs."

"Your ribs could be cracked."

"We've been over this already. You know perfectly well that other than wrapping my ribs there is nothing the doc can do for me. If it was you, you would already be out there loading that bull. Don't even try to deny it. I'm no different. I have to do this." He had no idea how much she meant that statement. Her concience wouldn't let her slack up.

His expression tightened as if he wanted to deny it and couldn't because it was true. "Right." It was a frustrated growl.

Ignoring the nagging pain, she went out onto the back porch and tromped from the patio a little more forceful than necessary, punishing herself unduly.

Cliff caught up to her. "If you have to do this then I'll load the blasted bull. You sit down."

She didn't like his tone, but she could actually understand his frustration. He had witnessed her in a terrible situation that could have been a total disaster.

"Look, I'm very grateful you showed up when you did. I truly am. I can't thank you enough. But, if you keep bossing me around, we're going to lock horns."

His brown brows dipped in consternation or aggravation she didn't really care, at least he was listening.

"You're as stubborn as Rafe said you were."

"You better believe it. So either help or leave. But back off for certain."

And there it was, one of two reasons why Maddie Rose was still a single woman. Men, dad-blame their hides, might *think* she was beautiful. Might *think* they could control her. But they always had a rude awakenin', because Maddie was the driver now. She'd been at the wheel of her life ever since she'd walked out of the last foster home when she was ten days away from being eighteen.

And that was the way it was staying.

Since the day she was born other folks had dictated every aspect of her life. And she wouldn't ever let that happen again.

Ignoring the pang of regret, she undid the chain on the holding pen gate and let herself in. Cliff could follow if he wanted. She didn't care one way or the other.

He followed.

Maddie's heart jumped in her chest when he winked at her, tipped his hat then headed toward Buford with the confidence of a man who knew what he was doing.

Watching him saunter across the pen Maddie's mouth went dry and a shudder swept through her. Every instinct she had told her there was something about this cowboy that might be more dangerous to her than Buford the pig-headed bull...

CHAPTER THREE

Despite the pain she had to be in, Maddie helped get Buford back into the loading chute by waving one arm and holding her ribs with the other when he ran her way. Cliff had to battle the urge to hoist the spitfire into his arms and carry her out of the pen kicking and screaming if need be. He decided the best course of action was to help her.

The woman acted driven. Like if she didn't get her job done she'd miss out on making the National Rodeo Finals or something. It didn't make sense to him. He and Rafe might not have spent a lot of time together over the last few years, because he was on the road all the time, but he knew Rafe wouldn't make Maddie feel like her loading this bull was a do or die deal.

So what was up with her? It was just a bull.

"There you go, mission accomplished," he said closing the trailer's gate shut with Buford safely inside and Maddie safely on the outside.

Maddie stood with her hands on her slim, jean clad hips and watched him, green flames flickering in her eyes. It was like she knew she needed help but she didn't want it.

"You like taking control don't you?" It wasn't a question but a statement.

He hiked a brow at her. "Funny, I was about to say the same thing about you. I'd say we have something in common."

Her eyes softened, the fire faded as some of the fight went out of her. "Look, this isn't easy for me. I'm not normally so careless. Thanks for loading Buford."

Either she didn't like accepting help at all. Or she didn't like it from him. Either way, saying thank you was obviously hard for her.

"You're welcome." He went to the truck's passenger door and opened it for her. "Hop in, I'm driving."

"No, that's okay. I'll take it from here."

"I'll drive you and the bull to the auction Maddie. All you have to do is show me the way."

She didn't move. "Can you not hear?"

He chuckled. "I have selective hearing. Do we really have to go through this again? You're injured whether you want to admit it or not, and I'm not about to let you do this alone. You warned me earlier to back off or we were going to lock horns. Consider our horns locked. Either you hop in and I drive, or I'll take the keys and your bull won't make it to the sale today."

"Of all the nerve," she huffed, moving past him to ease into the passenger's seat.

The Dodge had running boards that came in handy, making it easier for her to climb into the cab than if it had been his truck. She kept one arm wrapped across her ribs and he caught the strain in her expression. She was still in a heap of pain and trying to hide it—or ignore it. He laid his hand on her waist to assist if he could.

Fiery eyes met his and had him fighting the sudden, strong urge to kiss her. Not a good idea on any fronts, but especially now—he'd just met her for one, and he didn't figure her ribs could handle the pain when she took a swing at him.

"So, when are you leaving?" she snapped, sliding into the leather seat.

He grinned. "Trying to get rid of me so quick?"

"I'll buy you a tank of gas if you need me to spell it out any clearer."

"Rafe didn't mention it?"

"You are not a topic of conversation your brother and I discuss."

He chuckled. "Well, for your information I'm here for a little while. I'm thinking of buying a place in Mule Hollow.

Time to put down some roots."

Her face went slack as he closed the door. He jogged around and slid behind the wheel and glanced at her. Yup, she still wore that oh-no-tell-me-it-ain't-true expression of shock and dismay.

"Makes you nervous, doesn't it."

She went all prune faced—not her best look but somehow she managed to pull it off. "I don't care what you do. It's a free country." Reaching for her seatbelt she gasped when she couldn't twist her torso to grab it from its dock beside her shoulder.

"Here let me." Leaning over he reached across her to grab it. Neither of them said anything as he made sure it wasn't too tight before securing it.

He hated she was hurting and didn't like having to push her around like he'd been doing, but he couldn't figure any other way to make her let him help her.

He headed the truck and trailer out of the loading area and the endless, high dollar pipe fencing. They circled around past the massive tan and red trimmed metal barn and then on past the ranch house that was a showcase of sandstone rock and redwood logs. New Horizon ranch was a showplace. From what Rafe had told him, C.C. Calvert had been worth a bundle and this ranch had been one of his hobbies, but he'd loved it.

Hobby or not, the man hadn't made the money he'd made without knowing how to put people in place who could maintain his hobbies and businesses in his absence. For the ranch that had been Rafe and his partners.

"This is a beautiful place," he said as they drove down the fence-lined lane leading from the house to the black top road. "A little bigger than what I'm looking for though." He shot her a grin, hoping to ease the tension that filled the cab.

She didn't say anything, instead looked like she was mulling over when would be a good time to push him out of the truck. He had to smile at that thought.

"Which way am I going?" he asked when they reached the road. She nodded left and he eased the truck out on the road and pressed the gas.

He slid a peek at Maddie, curious about what her story was. "It's pretty country around here." They'd gone about five miles down the road heading away from the direction of Mule Hollow. This was prime cattle country, right on the edge of Texas hill country it was a good combination of flat land mixed with the rolling hills and deep ravines that made it both interesting and beautiful. He'd seen a lot of country over the last ten years. While not as breath taking as the Colorado vistas or some of the other places he'd been there was something about this area that spoke to him. From the moment Rafe had settled here almost five years ago he'd said it was a good place to make a life. Cliff figured it was time he at least gave it a try.

He was a thirty year old man who'd spent the last ten years moving fast and light. Everything he owned fit into a gear box that held his bull riding gear and a large duffle bag. He didn't live so sparse because he couldn't afford anything more, he lived that way because he had goals and dreams and riding bulls filled the empty holes in his life.

At least that was what he'd always thought. Told himself. Believed.

Since he'd learned last week that his dad was dead, something had snapped inside of him and he'd suddenly began to question everything he'd ever believed about himself. He wanted to chalk it up to the fact that it was getting easier and easier for him to get injured. The thirty year old body of a professional bull rider wasn't as resilient as that of a twenty-two year old. He wanted to chalk it up to the fact that after ten years of hard work and dedication he was road weary.

But he knew that wasn't true.

Sure he'd always had a plan for when it came time for him to hang up his spurs. But he'd kept putting it off over the years. Now, suddenly it almost seemed like he couldn't make it happen soon enough.

And that sudden change of heart had slammed him like Buford had slammed Maddie the moment he'd learned his dad was finally dead.

Funny thing was, he'd already planned on making the trip to Mule Hollow and checking out land. He'd already put the wheels in motion before the call.

But the call, it had changed everything.

Suddenly starting his business of breeding bulls, warriors for the circuit couldn't happen fast enough. He was still sorting through why this change had come over him.

"Do you know of any small, good places around here for sale?" he asked, needing space between him and his thoughts.

"Me?"

"I was thinking since you live here, you might know of a place or two."

He glanced back at the road but out of the corner of his eye he caught her bite her lower lip.

"What um," she cleared her throat, "sort of facilities do you need? What plans do you have for it? It'd help to know."

He shot her a grateful look and she gave him a small, not-quite-certain smile.

"Bulls. I'm going to raise bucking bulls for the industry. I have some young stock housed at different breeders across the country and I figure it's time to gather them all together and get down to business. And now that Rafe is going to settle here for good, since being named partner in the ranch, I'd like to be near him." It was true.

"That's nice," she said, but didn't look exactly thrilled at the prospect of him hanging around.

He realized that he on the other hand, found the prospect of being around her intriguing. He laughed. "Don't look all gloomy. I promise not to come over every day and fire you up."

Her cheeks flamed. "I wasn't worried about that."

But they both knew that had been exactly what she'd been thinking about.

He had things about his past that he needed to come to terms with, to try and make sense of...but for reasons he was suddenly interested in figuring out, getting to know Maddie Rose put a whole other spin on things.

CHAPTER FOUR

Maddie spent an hour soaking in a sea salt bath. The rose scent lingered on her skin as she eased into soft, sweat pants and an oversized, poppy colored top. When she and Cliff finally made it home from dropping off Buford, she'd been worn out and nearly doubled over from the pain radiating through her back and ribs. She hurt everywhere.

Despite the tension that still stretched between them like a thick rubber band, tensing and giving, but threatening to snap at any given moment, he'd helped her from the truck and she leaned on him as they entered the house.

She'd barely pointed him in the direction of the upstairs guest room before shuffling through the lower level to her room down the hall from the kitchen.

The soak and more pain killers had eased some of her discomfort. Her stomach growled, reminding her that she hadn't eaten since grabbing a couple of pieces of bacon that morning. But though she felt better, she did not feel like cooking. She didn't even feel like making a peanut butter sandwich.

But most of all, like a big chicken, she didn't want to run into Cliff again. Chicken was the right word, too, because she really wanted more than anything to go back in there and see if she was as attracted to him as she thought.

And if so, what was she going to do about it? She had to have a little talk with herself during her soak about the way she'd treated him all afternoon. And she'd had to ask the Lord to forgive her and to also help her understand why she was so affected by him. No answers had come, but it hadn't even been an hour—she should probably give the Lord a little more time than that.

Cliff was bossy and infuriating. *And gentle and caring.*

True. How could a man rub her the wrong way one minute and make her all gooey inside the next?

She'd known him all of one afternoon so this conversation seemed premature anyway. Wasn't it?

She needed to focus back on finding a way to feel deserving of owning this ranch. It was proving to be a hard thing to accept—especially after days like today. It had taken her a long time to accept God's love too, but she'd finally understood that John 3:16; For God so loved the world that he gave his only begotten son. That whosoever believeth in him should have everlasting life...

For a sick kid abandoned by her parents—rejected, unwanted for adoption and then raised in the foster care system like she'd been, it had been hard to believe that God actually cared for her. Much less loved her and gave His son for her.

She'd learned to trust God. But she was still having trouble trusting that anyone other than God would leave her something like the partnership in this ranch.

She was also having a hard time believing she could ever trust someone with her heart. Abandonment issues were tough. They were real. And they scared her to death.

Because unless she ever got past them, she would never be able to let a man get close enough to her to fall in love...and if she couldn't do that then she'd never have the family and the white picket-fence-happily-ever-after buried deep in her heart.

She'd never found a man who tempted her to throw caution and fear to the wind.

But Cliff Masterson was different.

As emotionally unavailable as she'd always been, her emotions had been electrified today. She stared out the window to the back yard as thoughts of how she felt when Cliff looked at her. Her skin tingled thinking about it, as if she'd been out in the cold for too long and his warm gaze was bringing her back to life.

Someone knocked on her door.

"Maddie, I've made some dinner."

Dinner? Cliff had cooked!

Her stomach rumbled again at the thought.

"Are you awake?"

It crossed her mind to pretend she was asleep, but...he'd cooked for her. She'd *never* had a man cook something just for her. Sure the guys took turns like she did with kitchen duty, but that was for everyone.

Unable to stop herself, she padded slowly in her bare feet across the cool tile floor and opened the door. Her heart dropped to her toes, Cliff was smiling like he was thrilled to see her.

It was too irresistible to deny. Her defenses were down already. Her pulse raced unevenly as his gaze slid over her, dropping to her bare feet. Awareness danced across her skin.

She loved the way it felt.

"You look good and relaxed. Exactly what the doctor ordered. Now he's ordering food, if you're up to it?"

"I'm starving. I skipped lunch today and barely ate breakfast. And it smells fabulous out here."

He chuckled. "Cowboy Mash. It's got a real romantic ring doesn't it?" He stepped aside so she could move past him in the hallway, her pulse jumped at his nearness.

"I don't know about romantic, but I'm attracted to that spicy scent." She could have said the same for him and his fresh showered scent. Instead she clamped her lips tightly shut on that and ignored the temptation to linger beside him.

As it turned out, he'd set the table out on the stone patio. C.C. often had eaten his meals out there. When she'd come to the house to report to him they'd sit here and go over the details of the day. C.C. hadn't done a lot of business in his ranch office. Said, he spent enough time in offices when he was away from the ranch.

"This is one of my favorite spots," she said, seeing the two plates of food and tall glasses of iced tea. "I can't believe you cooked."

"We have to eat. And I figured you'd probably curl up and go hungry if I didn't do something."

She laughed. "Bingo."

He pulled a chair out for her and she eased into it. Her heart hammered in her chest.

"This is one of the nicest things anyone has ever done for me." She hadn't meant to blurt that out.

A look of horror flashed across his face. "I hope not."

She laughed again. "I meant, you could have simply fixed a sandwich. Or at least left it on the stove and said dig in. There really is a nice guy behind that controlling attitude."

He sat across from her. "I'm going to ignore that remark." He lifted the lid on the pan and the aroma instantly filled the space between them.

"Please do if it means we can eat. I'm dying over here."

"Patience, and stop trying to control me." He hiked a teasing brow then scooped out a large portion of the pasta and meat dish onto her plate.

"Funny." She matched his raised brow with her own. Warning bells of caution rang inside her head, but at the moment she was too hungry to heed them.

"I learned this from an old friend on the road. It's easy to make and delicious. But then, anything with green chilies, cheese and tomatoes is going to be good in my book."

"I totally agree." And she was right, one bite proved it. Cliff could cook.

"So, how did you get mixed up with this rough group?"

"They're a great group. Like brothers to me. I--" she caught herself before she blurted out that she was a foster kid. She didn't tell anyone about her past. C.C. had figured out some of it and she suspected knowing had spurred his decision to include her.

He finished off a bite of Cowboy Mash. "So they have you fooled. But really, what brought you out here to do hard labor on the ranch? Labor you're excellent at from what Rafe says.

C.C. must have thought the same."

"I didn't feel excellent this afternoon. I felt like a beginner."

"Nah, things happen. So, what brought you here?"

He sounded genuinely interested. "I was on my way to a ranch in Corpus Christi for an interview and the tire of my truck blew out right in front of this ranch. Your brother and Chase happened by when I was changing it. They stopped and, a little like you, they tried to take over. In the end we compromised and then they invited me up to the ranch. Turned out C.C. was hiring. So here I am. I fell in love with the ranch and Mule Hollow. It's a wonderful community." She didn't mention how for the first time in her life she'd felt like she belonged. Belonging was a very strong need.

Almost as strong as needing to be loved.

Two hours later, with the red glow of the sun settling on the horizon, Cliff stood out by the arena watching the horses when Rafe and Ty Calder drove into the yard. Chase Hartley and Dalton Bourne followed in a second truck pulling a trailer. The sun was disappearing and the heat of the day fading to a low simmer rather than high boil of a Texas afternoon in July.

He'd met Rafe's partners a couple of years ago when he'd banged his shoulder up and spent a couple of weeks at the ranch with Rafe. That had been the last time he'd been to see his brother and the longest time they'd spent together since walking out of the battleground they'd called home.

Maddie hadn't been here then. He'd missed her by a month or so if he remembered correctly.

Rafe bailed out of the truck first, a wide grin on his face. "Hey, brother!" he called, crossing in long strides to meet Cliff, giving him a hard handshake and then yanking him into a quick hug. They hadn't been around each other but they were twin brothers and their bond remained strong.

They'd also been through a lot together. What doesn't kill you makes you stronger. And closer.

"It's been too long," Cliff said, knowing it was true as he stepped back from their hug and grinned. "Man, it's good to see you, Rafe."

"Tell me about it, world traveler." Rafe's expression teased.

Chase and the others came up and greetings were exchanged. They were dust covered, sweat soaked and smelling of cattle.

"Y'all look like y'all've had a day of it." He shook their hands as they held them out. "I still haven't figured out what in the world y'all's boss was thinking though, leavin' yall in charge." He chuckled.

"Believe us, we wonder the same things," Chase said. Unlike Clint, he wasn't joking. "But C.C. was a good man and he always knew what he wanted and he did it."

"True," Ty added, scrubbing the stubble on his lean jaw. "I have to say I've had my doubts about a couple of these fellas. Especially your brother. I don't think C.C. ever saw him rope. He hasn't gotten any better with one since you were here two years ago."

That got chuckles from the rest of the group.

"Whoa, now." Rafe warned, a grin in his voice. "I'm good with a rope and y'all know it. It's the hopping from the horse at a dead run that had me stumbling."

Cliff knew that seven years ago when Rafe had blown his knee out had been hard on him. It had forced him to give up calf roping as a sport and take up cowboy'n full time. Shutting the door on a dream wasn't ever easy but Rafe had come to terms it. Cliff had been lucky to have remained relatively uninjured in bull riding. He'd been blessed to see his dream in the rodeo fulfilled for the most part.

"So, what happened?" Rafe asked. "We thought you were going to drive out to the branding and meet us there."

Cliff hiked a shoulder. "I got sidetracked. Speaking of which I have a bone to pick with you knuckleheads. What were y'all thinking abandoning Maddie? Leaving her to load that bull by herself was a blamed bad move. If I hadn't gotten here when I did she could have been killed."

All of them went on alert.

"What happened?" Dalton Bourne demanded first. "Is she

okay?"

He quickly filled them in on the situation and when he finished they understood full well how he felt about the situation they'd placed Maddie in.

They all looked uncomfortable and relieved that she wasn't harmed more than she was.

Chase's serious gunmetal gray eyes locked on him. "I'm glad you were here, and sorry she got hurt? But Maddie's adamant that we treat her like we treat each other. Truth is, she can load cattle with her eyes closed and her arms tied behind her back."

"True," Dalton grunted. "Still, I've never liked it. But she'd look at it as an insult if we tried to hang around and watch over her while she loads a bull. You've seen how tough she is."

Cliff saw their point. "She's tough, but still, I'd do what I thought was best. Even if it made her mad." His temperature spiked all over again thinking about seeing her going down in that pen.

"Oh, you'd have made her mad all right," Rafe chuckled along with the others as they headed toward the house. "Since you're out here and she's nowhere to be seen. I'm thinking you probably already did."

They'd reached the house and as he said that he entered the empty kitchen, looking around for Maddie.

"She's already turned in for the night, said she'd see y'all in the morning. And all I can say is she's something when she's mad. Those gorgeous green eyes are more beautiful than a roman candle exploding."

Four sets of eyes pinned him to the wall.

He held up his hands. "Hey, just because you idiots and all the other cowboys in Mule Hollow are blind doesn't mean I am." It was when she was calm she was the most spectacular. Over dinner he'd hardly been able to concentrate on the meal especially when they'd gotten to talking about the ranch. Her love of it was obvious. He'd enjoyed listening to her more than he had anything in a long time.

"We know shes beautiful, but...it's Maddie." Dalton's eyes narrowed to slits. "You watch yourself with her."

"Yeah, she's off-limits," Chase snapped. He stepped up to Cliff. "She's no rodeo groupie."

The others quickly echoed his warning.

Cliff raised his hands to halt them. "Hold on. For one, I've never been into groupies. Second, I'm here scouting ranches to buy for a bull ranch, so relax."

Rafe's frown turned instantly to a smile. "You're serious?"

"I told you three weeks ago I was coming to do that."

"Yeah, but saying it and doing it are two entirely different things."

So that was why his brother hadn't said anything about him moving here. He didn't believe Cliff was going to do it.

"I'm doing it. I'm not getting any younger and it's time for me to get the ball rolling on my future." And I like Maddie, he almost said but caught himself. He wasn't ready to voice the interest their female partner had stirred in him. Especially after the warnings they'd issued.

"What *is* that smell?" Dalton lifted the lid on the pot sitting on the stove and breathed appreciatively letting the full saucy aroma fill the room.

That was all it took for the four of them to lay off him as they pounced on the dinner like a pack of coyotes to road-kill.

Which was exactly what Cliff had felt like there for a few minutes when they'd started warning him away from Maddie.

CHAPTER FIVE

"Ohhh, tell me I'm not dead," Maddie groaned the instant she woke. Sprawled on her bed she stared up at the ceiling, like she had for much of the endless night. She lifted an arm and the movement hurt all the way to her bellybutton.

Bed rest was not for her though. Pushing herself up from the mattress she groaned when her ribs and all the muscles in her back seized up. She bit her lip to hold back a cry of pain.

Today was not going to be fun. Gritting her teeth, she moved toward the bathroom and a really hot shower.

Twenty minutes or so later, her muscles more relaxed from the near-blazing hot water, she moved slowly down the hall toward the kitchen. Laughter and joking filled the house and the comforting sound of her friends eased her pain. She also knew working her sore muscles would help as much as the camaraderie she'd have out there with them. It would help take her mind off her pain and make her feel like she was doing her fair share of the work.

Suffering in her room alone was not for Maddie.

"Are you looking at land today?"

Maddie heard Rafe's question as she rounded the corner into the kitchen. Cliff had been on her mind all night—okay, so thinking about him helped ease her pain a few times.

Then her thoughts had crossed over into remembering how it had felt to be held in his arms and she'd slammed the door on those thoughts. They were too dangerous to contemplate; she was already in enough pain.

Though she'd expected to see him in the kitchen this

morning, she wasn't prepared for the way her pulse took off at a reckless gallop the moment those indigo eyes met hers. A sigh whispered through her looking at him.

Thankfully the kitchen was alive with activity even though it was only six in the morning and she was able to focus on the activity of eggs frying and bacon sizzling in the pans. Okay, so maybe not that, since she felt like she was in the frying pan herself.

"Good morning," she said.

Rafe and Cliff were working side by side at the stove as she passed them and went straight for the coffee.

"You look better," Cliff said, drawing her gaze. He smiled and for that brief unrealistic moment, all was wonderful in the world.

Maddie lost her voice. His eyes crinkled at the edges, the blue warming as if he could tell he affected her so strongly.

"I feel better." She hugged her insulated coffee mug between both hands and took a sip trying not to be affected.

She reached for a banana, ignoring the shooting pain the motion caused.

Immediately she was bombarded with questions. She lived in a huge house with four gorgeous men who were the brothers she never had. She had expected this. Still, she wasn't uncomfortable with it.

"I'm fine everyone. Yes my ribs are sore, but it's nothing I can't handle. Thanks to Cliff I sustained only bruising from the pen and not stomping from Buford." She headed for the door intent on getting her horse saddled and ready for the day before they all threw a fit and tried to stop her.

"Hang on, where are you going?" Dalton asked.

Rafe swung around with a spatula in his hand. "Sit down," he pointed the spatula at the chair and sounded far too much like his brother.

"I'm sure y'all already have your horses saddled and loaded for the branding today and I have a feeling mines been conveniently left in the barn."

"Nope, no way." Cliff's scowl could have fried the bacon

FIRST KISSES

without a burner—her too for that matter.

"Maybe you need to hang loose today, Maddie." Dalton looked from her to Cliff. "We'll get the branding done. From what Cliff said, you're bruised up pretty bad."

Maddie was in no mood for this. "I'm fine. I missed helping with the cattle yesterday."

"Yeah, but we needed Buford on the auction block and you were the one who pulled the short straw."

That was true. Taking the old bull to the auction hadn't been something any of them had wanted to do. But she'd been the one to pull the straw, literally. After what he'd done to her, she hadn't felt so bad selling him.

"I'm fine, y'all. And I'm helping with the cattle today."

She didn't wait for further protests. They wouldn't have let bruised ribs keep them from doing their job. And she wouldn't either.

Rafe and Cliff followed her onto the porch, their boots clomping hard behind her. She didn't look back but kept on going as fast as her ribs would let her.

"Hold on, would you?" Cliff called, easily catching up to her. "Why are you being so stubborn about this? You're in no shape to be out there on a horse much less working a branding iron. It's ridiculous."

Oh—she stopped and met his exasperated eyes with a warning glare. "Hold it, bucko, just because you helped me yesterday and then fixed me supper and we had a lovely meal--" and it was a really lovely meal. "It gives you no say in what I do or don't do." This close Maddie couldn't help noticing how good he looked in the morning sunlight. His scent wrapped around her. His dark brown hair picked up specks of gold in the slanting light. *Focus Maddie, focus.*

His lip twitched and then he laughed. *Laughed!*

"Maddie, c'mon. You're too stubborn for your own good. You would hurt yourself just to prove you're going to do things your way. I thought you were smarter than that." He shook his head, spun on his boot heel and strode back across the patio. "Have it your way."

Rafe hadn't said anything as he looked from her to Cliff. After Cliff stalked back inside the house he shot her a questioning eyebrow. "He's right you know. There is no reason you need to be out there today. As an owner there is plenty that you could do here if you had to do something. But honestly, Maddie, take a day off. Rest. Go shopping or get your hair done. Anything. You deserve it."

What was wrong with her hair? Why would he say that?

"Yeah," Chase agreed coming out onto the patio. "You've been getting a little crazy working ever since C.C. passed on and left us the ranch. He'd tell you straight up to take a rest."

Tears sprang to her eyes thinking about C.C. He would have demanded that she take time off and she knew it. Feeling foolish suddenly and not liking that at all she blinked the tears away. Crying would not solve anything. It never had.

"I need to check on my horse." They had no right trying to make her feel bad. Taking a swig of her coffee she fought through the pain that throbbed throughout her torso with each step she took. She didn't let herself think about how bad it was going to feel when she climbed into the saddle.

They were only trying to help you.

Inside the barn stall she spoke softly to her gelding when he stuck his head over the stall. "Hey buddy," she said, feeling a little tension ease from her as she placed her forehead against his. "What am I doing?" she asked as if he could help her.

She *was* being overly stubborn, she knew it but she couldn't seem to stop herself. What was it about Cliff that had her so uptight?

Setting her coffee mug on the bench beside the stall, she went to grab her saddle. Maddie reached to lift it from its rack—instantly splinters of pain shot through her. Crying out, tears flooded her eyes and she dropped the saddle on the concrete floor. Staring down at it she fought not to cry.

Was she being too stubborn?

Cliff entered the barn right as Maddie cried out and the saddle thudded to the concrete. Her shoulders slumped and the fight went out of her in a rush.

It hit him hard. She rubbed her forehead, her eyes closed—probably fighting back the need to cry. His heart cinched tight.

He liked her spunk. Her fire.

Liked that she stood her ground.

But this was unreasonable. What was going on in that pretty head of hers?

"Okay, that does it." He stalked across the fifteen feet to her. "You might be used to getting away with mistreating yourself today—not when I see how bad you're hurting."

That protective instinct he'd felt from the first moment he'd watched her slam into that pipe fence kicked into overdrive when he saw tears shimmering in her green eyes.

She quickly wiped them away with the back of her hands.

"I'm concerned about you, Maddie. Everyone is."

"I know." She sniffed and wrapped one arm protectively across her ribs. He knew from experience that the pressure helped the pain a little. She opened her mouth to say something more then shook her head and looked away.

He wanted to pull her close, comfort her, but he sensed she'd push him away.

He hadn't held a woman in months. Hadn't even been tempted as he'd struggled, running on empty. It was a blow when a man realized the dreams he'd been chasing weren't enough. And that was before he learned his dad was dead and the unexpected emotional toll that kicked him with.

What emotions drove this stubborn-kill-herself-with-work need in Maddie?

"Want to talk about it? About why you're doing this to yourself?"

She sniffed and looked away. He waited, giving her time to get a grip on her emotions, sensing she didn't let people see her cry. Why he knew that he wasn't sure but he felt like he'd known her for longer.

"You and I both know as much as I want to, I'm not going to make it onto that horse." A resigned sigh escaped her.

"Yeah, we know that. My question is why are you even

trying when there is no reason you need to push yourself like this? I asked the fellas and they said they had no idea. But that you've been pushing extra hard since your boss died. Since he named you a partner. Why are you doing that, Maddie?"

Cliff's earnest question tugged at Maddie. "Because there is so much to be done," she blurted out, as if she'd known Cliff all of her life and shared things with him all the time. She didn't share things with anyone. Didn't let people get close. Those walls of disappointment and loss she'd experienced too many times growing up had taught her to keep her emotions close and people on the outside.

She let those she called friends in only so far before the barriers slammed firmly into place. So what was different about Cliff? Other than he'd infuriated her half the time she'd known him.

And rescued her. And made her supper.

And now he's looking at you as if he genuinely cares.

"The way I see it, as big as this ranch is I'm sure there's been a lot to do from the day you first hired on. What's driving you now? Is it because you're an owner?"

She looked away, the truth eating at her. The strain of believing she shouldn't be an owner. That she hadn't done enough to deserve the honor. "In a way," she admitted. "Before I was employed by C.C., a hired hand. I gave a hundred percent to my job, but I didn't have to worry about whether the bills got paid or the ranch grew stronger. I could go to my little apartment at night with no worries."

His shoulders relaxed and his expression mellowed into understanding. "That makes sense. A *lot* of sense. Especially for a nomad like me who doesn't own anything other than my truck and riding gear. And a few bulls."

Relief eased some of the tension gripping her. "Exactly. It's not like I hadn't planned on settling down eventually. Like you're about to do. I had planned on it too, and soon. You know, buy a small place and make a payment..." She stopped herself from saying more. She certainly wasn't going to blurt out that she had planned to work on letting down the walls around herself in the hopes of finding a soul mate.

"Maddie, Rafe and I talked late into the night and one of the things we talked about was the ranch. He said y'all were a great team. He said Chase had been doing the books for several years and that the rest of y'all had different strengths that worked well to keep this ranch going strong."

How could she make him understand? "If we each do our part. I'm the weak link." *What are you doing? Why do you want him to understand?*

He laughed. "Yeah, right. No one believes that. Not even me and I've only known you for two days."

She bit her lip as he suddenly seemed to look even closer into her thoughts. She felt exposed in a way she'd never felt before. As if he could actually see her. Who she really was.

It wasn't realistic. He'd only just met her. But still...

"There's more to this," he said, knowingly.

He cupped her jaw gently, surprising her with his touch as much as with what he'd said. She couldn't breathe—and she hadn't been hit by a gate this time.

"I'm not going to press, but if you want to tell me I'm here and would like to help if you'll let me." His thumb brushed along her jaw.

Longing ached in Maddie's heart, startling her with the intensity of it. She realized that she was staring into Cliff's eyes like a school girl anticipating her first kiss.

She swallowed hard, shaken by the emotions this man had awakened in her.

It didn't make sense. It was too fast.

But right now, she didn't care because Cliff Masterson had just put a crack in the barrier around her emotions that she'd been trying to figure out how to break open for some time now. And he'd done it with no help from her.

She'd only known him two days. And while that should have scared her silly, it was what captivated her the most.

CHAPTER SIX

Cliff told himself to back off. He had never wanted to kiss a woman as badly or as completely as he wanted to kiss Maddie Rose. Impulsive as he tended to be he pulled back, this was not the time to let himself have free rein. Maddie was vulnerable and he knew it. There was something going on inside that beautiful head of hers and maybe even her heart that he didn't want to harm.

She was far more fragile than anyone realized. She had strength and a lot of it, but he'd glimpsed more. Giving into the need, momentarily, he traced her jaw once more with his thumb then took a step back. Electricity hummed in the air between them.

He gave a shaky chuckle. "You're a stunning, strong woman Maddie. You are far from a weak link. But your body needs a break today. Probably tomorrow, too."

Looking almost as dazed as he felt she frowned. "I'm not going to lie around and eat cupcakes all day though. I'll go bonkers."

He threw back his head and laughed. "I bet you would. Tell you what. Come help me look at property. I'll drive easy and if your ribs get to hurting too much then I'll bring you home to lie down and eat cupcakes."

A little laugh huffed from her. She hesitated, nibbling her lip like he'd seen her do so many times. He almost groaned, thinking about kissing her again. If she rode along, it might make for a rough day now that he had thoughts of kissing her had super glued themselves in his brain.

"I could use your knowledge of the area," he said. When she remained conflicted he used what he hoped was his ace in the hole. "*And* you do owe me for saving you yesterday."

Her shoulders sagged. "You're right, I owe you."

He felt a stab of disappointment that he'd had to toss out that she owed him in order for her to agree. She didn't owe him anything.

"Great." The important part was that she wouldn't be hurting herself trying to brand cattle or getting into any other trouble she might find for herself to do when she got bored sitting around. "I really appreciate it."

"It's the least that I can do after what you did for me." She sighed and stared at her dejected saddle sitting on its side. "Could you put my poor mistreated saddle back on that rack for me, please?"

"My pleasure." He winked at her, excitement flashing through him thinking about spending the day with her. "This is going to be a great day."

To his surprise she laughed—or started to—then grabbed her ribs and groaned. Laughter might be the best medicine for most things but not bruised or busted ribs.

"Ow," she croaked, but her gaze looked bright. Things were looking up.

Was she really doing this? Maddie wondered again as she walked beside Cliff toward Hailey Bell Sutton's real estate office. Of course that wasn't what had her feeling like she'd jumped off a cliff. It was that she was actually going to *try* and crack the shell around her emotions. Cliff had gotten past a boundary no one else ever had. Could she let him in further?

They'd called ahead to make sure Hailey was at the office. These days it was uncertain since Hailey was almost nine months pregnant and due any day. She was in and questioned Cliff over the phone and promised to have property suggestions ready when they arrived at her office on Main Street.

Hailey was a gorgeous blonde and one of the nicest people

in town—and that was saying a lot because Mule Hollow was loaded with a full deck of good people. She waved them in as soon as she spotted them through the window.

"Hey Maddie, y'all come in and have a seat. And please excuse me for not standing up." She rubbed her huge tummy and smiled widely. "Doctor's orders and he has my husband, Will, lined up as my bouncer should I not comply. I can come to work, but I have to sit. If I do more than waddle to the bathroom after I get here then I can't come to work anymore." She smiled looking extremely happy then held her hand out to Cliff.

"And you must be Cliff? It is so nice to meet you. And exciting that you're going to settle here." They shook and then she waved them to the chairs across from her. "You'll love it and from a real estate prospective, there's a lot to choose from hidden across the county. And at pretty fair prices."

When they were seated she handed him a stack of pages photos and property descriptions.

"Thanks," Cliff said, his smile had widened as the words had rolled from Hailey at a fast clip. He thumbed through them quickly. "These look great."

"I hope there's something in there you'll like." She looked from him to Maddie with interest. "I'm glad you're going with him since you're familiar with the area. I'll feel less like I'm abandoning him with you along."

"I'm glad to do it," Maddie said, still in shock that she was contemplating pushing the feelings Cliff stirred in her.

She and Hailey chatted about the baby while Cliff looked through the pages. Maddie couldn't help be a little envious of Hailey. She really wanted a baby. Not that she ever talked about it to anyone. If she talked about it then she'd have to explain to her friends why she was afraid she'd never have children of her own. Truth was, when a person was as afraid as she was of showing her heart to someone—well, it made falling in love pretty hard. And if she wasn't falling in love there wasn't a possibility of her having a baby. It was complicated.

When Cliff finished choosing the properties he wanted to see there were a total of six listings in his hand. None of them had an owner on the premises so they didn't have to set up any appointments and that made viewing easy.

"Hopefully, I'll still be around by the time you find something," Hailey said before they left. "But if I'm not, my friend, Sugar Rae will step in. She was my assistant for several years and is going to fill in part time, finishing up any deals that I leave dangling. So, you don't have to worry about that."

"I wasn't worried." Cliff shook her hand again. "You take care of yourself and don't worry about us, we'll be fine."

Easy for him to say, Maddie thought. If he could only see into the mass confusion inside her mind! If he could, then he'd know she had absolutely no idea whether she was going to be fine or not.

Within minutes they were heading out of town. Maddie told herself to relax and enjoy the day and the—she searched for the right word for what she was doing—*possibilities*. She was exploring possibilities.

The thought made her smile inside.

What was the worst thing that could happen? That by the end of the day her attraction to him wasn't strong enough to take a risk for what she wanted?

Or, was it that at the end of the day she'd realize his interest wasn't strong enough to break completely through her emotional shields?

Either of those scenarios would put her right back where she'd been before he'd shown up yesterday.

She could handle that. She could.

At least she'd be able to say she put herself out there.

She'd taken a risk.

She was calm by the time they reached the first property. It was a nice place. Not far from Horizon Ranch it had stock pens that sat off from the house and its location appealed to Cliff.

It was a nice morning, with the sun flirting with them through fluffy clouds as they pulled to a halt near the barn and the cattle pens.

"Nope," he said after a quick scan of the area. "This isn't it."

She laughed, shocked by his reaction. "But you didn't even get out of the truck."

"I didn't need to. What's the next one?"

He'd lined them up in order that he wanted to see them so she pulled the next one off the list. "Here it is. Are you sure you even want to bother driving out there?"

His eyes crinkled at the edges. "Yes, I want to drive out there. This one had points against it coming in. It's the smallest on the list with less than a two hundred acres, which is a little small for what I need. And the pens need a lot of work and they're too close to the house."

"I see what you're saying." She gave him directions to the next place. "At this rate we'll be home by noon," she joked and seriously hoped not.

He talked about what he was looking for as they drove to the next listing. She liked listening to the cadence in his voice and deep timbre of it. She'd been too upset and aggravated the day before when they'd been in the truck together to enjoy anything. She'd been too busy thinking about strangling him...

"You said you're going to raise rodeo stock? Right?" she asked.

"I'm going to raise bulls. The stock I raise will be strictly for my own cattle business and it won't be a large herd so this acreage would work."

He was standing with his hands on his hips taking in the house, pens and surrounding acreage of the second listing. He looked impossibly perfect in that moment. Impossibly appealing. She pushed the negative thought away and struggled to be positive.

"Are you giving up riding them?" She held her breath, knowing if he said yes that would mean he wouldn't be an absentee owner.

"I'm thinking about it." His eyes met hers and held before he headed across the yard to the house, a brick home with a large porch overlooking the pastures. There were some huge old oak trees shading the yard and though it wasn't as spectacular as the patio of the ranch house C.C. had built, it was homey and appealing.

The flare of attraction burned strong and bold as she followed him. And it had only grown stronger as the morning had progressed.

Hailey had warned them that the house had sat vacant for many years, and was in need of repair. While Cliff unlocked the door, she peeked in the windows. "Hailey wasn't kidding. The place is crying out for help."

She had to pass close to Cliff as she walked through the doorway. Her pulse hummed with his nearness—and she almost leaned in and inhaled.

Soap and aftershave had never smelled so good.

There was some kind of chemistry bubbling between she and Cliff...chemistry she'd never, *ever* experienced before. Rafe, Ty, Chase and Dalton were amazing, hunky, handsome cowboys. When they spruced up for one of their dates they smelled good too—but she'd never had the urge to tackle one of them!

Okay. So, her imagination was getting out of hand.

Time to put some space between her and this cowboy. Moving quickly, she headed to the far side of the room to study the fireplace and then the kitchen as if her life depended on it.

She forced her mind to the task of evaluating the property—*not* Cliff. It had been vacant for over ten years. Since the oil boom around the area had dried up and folks had been forced to move away for jobs. It was apparent that it had once been a nice place, but time and neglect had taken its toll.

Not a problem Cliff had—he was perfect.

"I don't know."

She jumped at Cliff's voice and focused. He was looking about skeptically.

"A buyer might be better off starting from scratch and building."

Maddie cringed when a rodent scurried down the hall and disappeared into a bedroom. "You might be right." She hadn't been able to get any good feelings going about the place. Of course that could very likely be because all of her feelings were preoccupied with Cliff. And now, the rodent.

"Then let's move on to the next place." He shot her a smile. "We have all day. I'm not feeling excited about the house. And I can see in your eyes that you aren't either."

Maddie hoped that was all he could see in her eyes. "Right. We have a lot of places to choose from." She was almost to the door when she realized that she'd said "we" as if it mattered if she liked the place...

Back off now. You'll only be hurt if you invest any more of yourself. And you are acting way too unlike yourself, sister.

Maddie knew she should listen to the voice of warning but she'd promised herself that she would push herself. And that was exactly what she planned to do.

Of course she wasn't getting crazy or anything and that meant not being reckless—there was no "we" in this equation. She was just a gal trying to get to know a guy.

There was nothing wrong with that. Nothing.

It was natural. Holing up with herself and her stinkin' fear of letting someone close—that was the thing that was wrong.

CHAPTER SEVEN

The scent of home cooking and the rowdy tones of Toby Keith playing on the Juke Box greeted them as Maddie and Cliff slid into a booth at Sam's Diner. The hub of the town, the rustic diner was where Mule Hollow folks congregated all through the day to eat and catch up on the latest goings on. Cliff liked the place.

"Hi, Sam," Maddie called across the room to the tiny man behind the counter.

Sam was short and small like a jockey, with a weather worn face and intelligent eyes. Cliff had been in the diner several times when his shoulder had been hurt. Had even played some checkers with App and Stanley, a couple of retired ranchers who had checker battles every morning over coffee and sunflower seeds.

"Hey, Cliff. Heard you were in town," Sam said coming their way.

Sam had a legendary, fierce grip and Cliff braced for it as Sam clamped down hard.

"I hear you're looking for land around here. You getting out of the PBR?" Sam asked.

The Professional Bull Riders circuit had been Cliff's world for years. *Was it now?* He had an event coming up in about two weeks. He hadn't decided what he was going to do about it.

Cliff was aware of Maddie watching him. He grinned at Sam. "News travels fast around here."

"Small town. You gotta be quick to get somethin' by all of them well-meaning busy bodies. Particularly App and Stanley,"

Sam chuckled, his entire face crinkling with laughter. "My wife, sweet as she is, included. They were all in here talkin' about you two round breakfast. One of them saw y'all over at Hailey Belle's this mornin' together. Stirred up quite a dither."

Maddie's eyes widened. "I was helping Cliff."

"That's reasonable. So are you done riding bulls professionally?" Sam asked again.

"No, taking a break is all. I'm making some changes." Cliff knew he was going to come across this question a lot, but he wasn't ready to talk about it. He was still trying to understand why things had been different since learning his dad was dead. He hadn't seen his dad in six years. And it had only been that one time since the day he'd left home. He pushed the thoughts away, now was not the time to contemplate that part of his life.

"The PBR has been good to me and I have some commitments. But I figure it's time to start looking past bull riding to raising them."

"Smart. We've got a few folks around here who do that."

More folks came in so Sam took their order of burgers then headed off in the direction of the kitchen.

"Where's App and Stanley?" Cliff asked glancing over at the table by the window where the two old checker players were usually hunched over their game.

"They start the day early and are usually back home before lunch." She chuckled. "You have to be early to catch them. Breakfast till brunch is their time."

"I forgot. I'll have to swing by one morning and say hello. I met them when I was here before. Really enjoyed my visit."

Maddie smiled. "It's a great town."

"Yeah, I haven't been by as often as I should to see Rafe."

"You've been busy, had commitments."

"Yeah, I did. But..." He rested his elbows on the table and cupped his hands as he glanced around. He knew it was more than that. He'd been running—he'd only just realized that was what he'd been doing. "Rafe is my only family. It will be nice to see him more."

Something shadowed in her eyes and he wondered what

she was thinking as she studied him. "It's nice to have family. You're right, you shouldn't take it lightly or for granted."

"What about your family, Maddie? Where do they live?" He'd realized that she talked less about her past than he did. And he was curious—he knew that just because someone didn't talk about their past it didn't mean that they'd lived with an abusive drunk like he and Rafe had. Some people didn't talk about their past because they were private people.

Not because thinking of the past made them angry.

"I," she hesitated as if weighing what she wanted to say. "I was raised in foster care. My parents gave me up when I was a baby."

Sam brought their tea and burgers and Cliff hardly even noticed. "I'm sorry." He felt like an oaf because he could see in Maddie's eyes, those expressive eyes, that damage had been done. He knew there were an abundance of good caring folks out there who opened up their homes for hurting and abandoned kids. He prayed Maddie's had been good. He also knew there were plenty of them who housed as many as allowed for the steady source of income it provided them. "You had good people, right?"

"They were fine." She took a bite of her burger. "Sam makes the best burgers."

It didn't take a kindergartner to recognize her evasion.

He was about to ask for more when a group of young wranglers entered the diner and took the table across from them.

"Hey man! That's Cliff Masterson," one of them declared.

"Wow, I watched you win the Bull Riding Championship down in Houston two years ago," another one added and within seconds Cliff was the one back in the hot seat, bombarded with questions about bulls and competition. Before he knew it lunch was over and they were heading outside an hour later.

"That was nice of you to agree to give them pointers," Maddie said as he held the door opened for her.

He took her elbow to help her step up on the running

board and then into the seat.

"I had some help when I started out. I recognize the fresh hungry look on their faces. Gotta give back sometimes."

She studied him as he held the door open for her. "You might irritate the fire out of me being bossy and all, but you're a nice guy." A smile hovered on her lips.

He leaned over her to buckle the seatbelt for her because he knew she would have trouble, holding her gaze as he did it. Her sweet scent and that smile had been driving him crazy all day. "You're rubbing off on me."

She laughed. "Did you forget how mad I got yesterday?"

"You're a woman with some fire to her that doesn't mean you're not sweet."

She was and he knew it. Instinctively he knew much of her spunk had probably come from defense from the background of being raised the way she had. He understood that his past had shaped him too.

They stared at each other. She swallowed hard and held his gaze. Before he could stop himself he'd leaned in and kissed her...and just like when he climbed on the back of a bull he realized this could go one of two ways.

It could go good or it could go bad.

And it would only take eight seconds or less to know.

Maddie was so startled when Cliff dipped his head and covered her lips with his. She froze, her mind reeling, her senses exploding as his warm breath mingled with hers. Everything blurred, her eyes drifted closed, and she found herself responding to his touch to the gentleness of the kiss. The tenderness of his fingertips lightly tracing her jawline, then cupping her head, drawing her closer as he deepened the kiss.

Maddie's heart thundered in her chest, she was lost in the feel of his firm lips moving over hers.

When he pulled back, his breathing ragged, his eyes probing he looked as dazed as she was.

What had just happened?

"I'm sorry," he said, and an instant later he closed the door and headed around the truck.

Maddie's heart hammered, she struggled to catch her breath as she gripped the door handle and let the world slowly stop spinning.

Let it gradually come back into focus.

Only then did she remember that it was right past lunch time and Cliff had just planted a smokin' hot kiss on her—*right smack in the middle of Main Street.*

Right where anyone who was looking would see.

Glancing around she groaned—because standing on the sidewalk two doors down stood Esther Mae Wilcox, Norma Sue Jenkins and Sam's wife, Adela Ledbetter Green.

Better known as the Match Makin' Posse of Mule Hollow.

CHAPTER EIGHT

Climbing into the truck Cliff's insides were all jangled up. He cranked the key, shifted to reverse and in a daze, backed out of the parking lot.

What had he been thinking?

He'd hauled off and let his impulsive nature take hold of him kissing Maddie right out of the blue like that.

Right there in front of Sam's Diner for the entire world to see.

The realization of what he'd done got lost in the euphoria of the kiss though. Man, had that been something.

He glanced over at Maddie hoping she wasn't as mad as he feared she might be. Her blistering gaze instantly shot that hope to pieces.

"What's wrong?" The truck was stopped and he hesitated, his hand on the shift ready to ram it into drive. He hadn't expected her to be *that* mad.

"What's wrong? That is." She lifted a hand in a hesitant wave.

His gazed followed hers.

He'd only been here two weeks when he'd visited Rafe, but he knew exactly who the ladies were waving at them from the sidewalk.

He groaned. Waved. And hit the gas.

Maggie woke before dawn and headed out to the barn. She was moving a little better and glad of it. It took a lot of struggling but she got her horse saddled.

The kiss, despite everything, remained on Maddie's mind all afternoon and through the night. She'd overreacted when she'd realized the matchmakers had witnessed the kiss.

Yes, they may have ideas now—okay, there was no doubt that when three known matchmakers witnessed a kiss in broad daylight on the main drag of town—they were going to get ideas.

All *kinds* of ideas and all of them were going to end with a matchmaking plan. Her sleepless night couldn't change that.

There was nothing to be done about it.

But that kiss. That amazing, gentle kiss that had whispered to the deepest dark corners of her wounded heart where dreams and fear clung together...

She'd lost her good sense yesterday.

These feelings he'd initiated inside of her could get out of hand. Spending time with him in large doses could be dangerous to her heart.

Maddie tightened her horses cinch and girded up her emotions at the same time and then she headed to the house. Everyone would be in the kitchen by now.

She prepared herself for their protest but as far as she was concerned she was working today. And that was final.

Cliff—his smile wide and welcoming was the first handsome face her wretched gaze sought out. Oh dear goodness but the man took her breath away.

How could anyone look so good leaning against the counter drinking a glass of orange juice?

But with lean, corded muscles honed from years of bull riding, his dark hair curling at his collar and his blue eyes gleaming like stained glass shot through with sunbeams he could have sold orange juice by the case. Her mouth went dry.

He was the epitome of every Prince Charming she'd ever dreamed of as a lonely young girl growing up.

No doubt about it, it was time for her to put some distance between her and Cliff.

"You were outside early. How are you feeling this morning?" he asked.

"Fine," she said, then, unable to lie added, "Sore, but better."

Rafe handed her a mug of coffee. "Second day is always the worst. You'd better take it easy again today."

"Thanks, but I've already saddled my horse. I'm going today."

"Told y'all. I win." Chase gave a triumphant laugh.

"Win what?" She looked about the room.

"Chase said you'd be going this morning." Dalton grinned.

Maddie wasn't sure how to take this information. "And y'all didn't think I would be."

"Now, don't go getting all riled up. We figured you'd be hurting worse today than yesterday."

Ty grabbed a pan of biscuits from the oven. "You need to heal up."

"You don't have to help on our account. You need to take care of yourself." Dalton flipped bacon in a pan.

Cliff's husky chuckle touched her from across the room and made her feel his kiss again. Her stomach clenched and she shot him a glare, not at all happy with the way every cell in her body was straining toward him.

"I'm coming, so end of story," she snapped, then headed back outside. "Hurry your breakfast, boys. Daylight's burnin'."

No sooner had she sat down on the patio chair to wait on the fellas to finish than Cliff followed her outside. "Don't even try to talk me out of this," she warned, shoring up her defenses against letting herself fall for him.

He pulled out a chair and sat down. "I figured this was what you'd do. Are you still mad about the kiss?"

Yes. The dull ache of her ribs was a reminder of how much more a broken heart could hurt. "This is not a good idea, Cliff."

His jaw tensed and he rubbed the back of his neck. "I shouldn't have kissed you. Not so soon and not like that where it could cause you trouble. That's the last thing I'd want to do."

She couldn't look at him.

"Make sure you've wrapped your ribs good. You have

wrapped them?" he asked, gently.

Completely surprised that he wasn't trying to tell her she didn't need to go, she stared at him. "Yes, I have."

He was looking out for her. Just like yesterday but in a completely different way. *How was she supposed to handle that?*

"I figured you'd wrapped them, but I wanted you to know I cared."

Her pulse skipped a beat at the sincerity in his voice. She needed that distance she'd decided on. She stood too quickly and her ribs let her know it. But she had to put some space between them. And she had to do it now.

The guys came out of the house at that moment and she wanted to hug them. Their timing was so perfect. No one had ever put this much effort into flustering her!

"Let's load up," Chase said, winking at Maddie.

"Y'all don't work her too hard," Cliff warned.

Maddie headed toward the trucks. "They don't determine how hard I work," Maddie tossed over her shoulder, feeling churlish. "I do. I'll do what I want out there." That said, she climbed into the cab of the truck and slammed the door.

She was startled to see him climb into one of the other trucks. "He's going with us?" she asked Chase when he got behind the wheel.

"Yup. He always helps us some when he comes down. He loves working cattle."

She bit back a groan. Well, if he thought he was going to be her nursemaid today, he was wrong.

She had been doing fine before he came along. She'd made it just fine without someone following her and bossing her around.

Worrying about her.

Doing nice things for her.

She didn't need any of that. She didn't.

"She'll slow down when she needs to, Cliff," Rafe warned, from the saddle of his horse. "You have to give a woman like Maddie her space. If you're thinking you like her—like I'm thinking you do, then you'd better lay low and get to know the real Maddie Rose. She doesn't take to coddling too well."

Cliff's movements were jerky as he pulled his rope, recoiling it after they finished with the calf he'd drug over to be branded. He'd been roping and dragging calves to the fire all morning while Maddie administered the meds and shots. Chase branded them and Ty tagged them. At the rate they were going they'd be finished by early afternoon. It felt good to be cowboy'n and he'd been glad Rafe had invited him along. Though honestly, he'd come because he wanted to be near Maddie.

He had to admit that Maddie wasn't slowing them down. The constant up and down had to be killing her ribs, but he could see the truth in his brother's words. He was going to have to give her room. After all, she'd only known him three days.

His downfall had always been that when he saw something he wanted he went after it with gusto. His determination had always been his strong suit. But, he did tend to steamroll his way into things. That, apparently wasn't the way to win Maddie's favor.

By noon, they were all filthy and the sun had them all beat down a bit. Maddie was moving more slowly, though she wasn't going to admit it. But why did she think she had to prove anything with her friends? Didn't she know that it was okay to slow down and show a little vulnerability?

Of course she was a woman in a male dominated world.

By one o'clock they had the last calf branded, tagged and vaccinated. Maddie pulled off her gloves and wiped the sweat out of her eyes as they gathered around the water cooler.

Cliff filled up a cup and handed it to her, their fingers brushed and that tsunami of awareness crashed through him. "Great job, today."

"Thanks," she said, her voice gritty from all the dusty air that hovered about them. She downed water in three gulps. Despite her sun kissed skin, there was a paleness to her.

He pulled his gaze away from her then moved over so others could get to the cooler. It was taking every ounce of

FIRST KISSES

determination he had not to ask Maddie how she felt.

What he wanted to do was scoop her into his arms and make her take it easy and rest her ribs. He wanted to take care of her.

"You still holding out okay?" Rafe asked her.

"Doing fine." She shot him a smile—*a smile!*

Cliff holstered his irritation. If he'd asked her that, she wouldn't have sent that dazzling smile his way.

"I've got business in town. I'll see y'all later," he practically growled. He stalked across to his truck and hauled out of there like an idiot. Jealousy had never been a problem of his...today, he was as green as it got. Frustration played a part in it. He was about as frustrated as a man could be.

He'd never had these kinds of reactions to a woman before.

He was in new territory. Maddie had turned his world upside down.

CHAPTER NINE

Maddie figured she'd made her point. Two days straight she'd helped work cattle like the rest of her partners. She'd worked hard and her body ached—but there were good signs that tomorrow would be better.

The first day when Cliff had come along she'd expected him to scowl and tell her to take it easy. Instead he'd backed off and it had been Rafe and the gang who'd watched her like hawks. If she didn't know any better—and she did—they were hoping Cliff would open his mouth and she'd explode. *The mud-grubbers*. But he hadn't—oh he wasn't happy and every time their gazes had met she knew it. But he kept his opinion to himself.

Today he hadn't come along, choosing instead to look at more properties. He'd seemed a little disgruntled at breakfast and headed off soon after she'd walked into the kitchen.

As odd as it was, she'd missed sparring with him today. It was actually fun. Did that make her weird?

She had obviously been kicked in the head by Buford.

Cliff remained on her mind Friday after work. She'd cleaned up and headed to town for a meeting about the festival coming up in a week. With all the Buford and Cliff shenanigans, she'd almost forgotten she'd gotten roped into helping them. Once she'd remembered her commitment she'd tried not to stress about it. She was doing pretty good too, considering the meeting involved the matchmakers. She was anticipating a lot of questions.

Three weeks ago Norma Sue had snookered her by saying

since Maddie was now a land owner, it would be good for her to get involved helping the town's economy. Maddie wasn't so sure she believed the matchmakers' reason, especially since she hadn't gone to the guys with the same request. But she *was* a land owner now. And the fellas had agreed to help her with the riding lesson pen she'd chosen to be involved with, so that was good.

"Yoo-hoo, Maddie, over here!" Esther Mae called, her bright red hair standing out like a beacon the moment Maddie walked into Sam's.

"Where is everyone?" she asked, assuming the other ladies who helped run the festivals would be here. Lacy the local hairstylist was a huge help and usually in on the meetings. There were several others too but the older ladies and Lacy, were the hub of the group.

Norman Sue shook her head. "Lacy's tied up trying to rescue Maureen Simpson from her self-inflicted color disaster. Poor woman has messed herself up but good."

Esther May harrumphed. "It's terrible. Looks like she dipped her head in a can of black tar. Every time she gets bored she does something different to her hair and poor Lacy has to fix the problem."

"Some people are restless that way," Adela said. Maddie had never heard the gentle lady utter a bad word about anyone.

"True." Norma Sue grinned wide, her plump cheeks shiny. "If Esther Mae had that notion, there is no telling *what* her hair would look like."

Esther Mae looked appalled. "Ha! I have other things that keep my attention. For one, Maddie and her cowboy. Tell us about that good-lookin' hunk you were kissing the other day?"

Maddie felt a headache coming on. She'd known this was coming.

Adela leaned toward her and squeezed her arm with her delicate hand. "We'd heard Rafe's twin brother, was back in town. Such a nice looking young man."

"Cliff. Yes, he is." It was true, he was nice. Maddening and bossy at times, but a nice guy. She thought about the way her pulse had skittered as she'd sneaked a peek at him while he was riding his horse and roping calves. Hunk described him perfectly. She realized all three ladies were watching her with big grins.

"I was showing him property," she added quickly. It was a lame evasive attempt. "I was only helping him out."

"Looked like he needed a lot of help." Norma Sue chuckled, her eyes twinkling.

Maddie had stepped right into that one.

Esther Mae tapped her packet of diet sweetener on the table top like a gavel. "Honey, there is nothing wrong with kissing a man. You need to be doing more of that. We've been worried about you, isn't that right, Norma Sue?"

"Absolutely." Her friend jumped in with both feet. "Kissing is great. Don't think because we're older than you that we don't enjoy our fair share. That Roy Don still turns my head every time he ambles into a room. But if you're always working like you are then you're never gonna find time to meet a man to smooch with."

Maddie almost choked on her water.

Adela bobbed her dewey, white haired head in agreement. "And that is exactly why we were so delighted to see you snuggled up to him on Tuesday."

"You need to get out more," Esther Mae said. "It's healthy, and honey you're supposed to have some fun. Go to the movies, out to eat. To a festival—which we happen to have a lot of."

Norma Sue was grinning widly again. "That's right. Festivals give our cowboys and cowgirls like you a chance to kick up your boots every once in a while."

"Okay, I'm helping at the festival." Maddie stared at the matchmakers, a little stuptified by their logic. She'd been afraid of this, but it wasn't so bad.

And what had Cliff really done?

Made her wake up?

Made her want to finally confront her fear of abandonment?

As if it had been planned before hand, Maddie heard a familiar, delicious laugh and shot a startled glance over her shoulder. Sure enough there was Cliff walking into the diner with the group of cowboys he'd promised to give bull riding tips too. His gaze locked onto hers like she was the only person in the crowded diner.

His laughter stalled and tension cracked between them like a bull whip. His eyes warmed, a slow smile tickled Maddie's insides as if he'd just traced the curve of her cheek with his fingertips. Or teased her lips with a brush of his lips on hers.

Oh goodness.

Esther Mae's sigh from across the table made Maddie jump and snap to.

She had a romantic movie moment. A boy-meets-girl-sigh-worthy moment that Maddie had never experienced before, not personally. She'd watched many a chick-flick over the years and experienced moments like that.

But this was a first.

"Yoo-hoo, Cliff. Over here," Esther Mae called.

Maddie's jaw dropped and it was crawl under the table time.

Cliff parted from his friends and came their way. His long legs had him to the table in three strides.

His smile continued to dazzle as he held out his hand to each of the ladies. "It's been a long time, ladies. Y'all look like you're doing well and having a good time."

"Oh, *we are*," Esther Mae cooed. "We were actually discussing our Maddie here."

Maddie went on full alert.

Norma Sue pushed back her white Stetson. "We've been thinking that our Maddie should get out more. You know date more, and we're just thrilled to pieces about the two of you."

Oh, no. Maddie had relaxed. Forgotten she'd let the ladies see her thoughts—they were good at reading signs of attraction. She almost rubbed the tension that had formed smack in the middle of her eyes but caught herself before doing it. Instead she willed her expression to relax as Cliff's amused gaze slid to hers.

"I can't imagine Maddie not having dates lined up from here to the next county," he said, sounding like he meant what he said.

Norma Sue frowned. "Oh, she could, but she works all the time. We're trying to pull her out of the pasture more."

"That's right," Esther Mae interrupted in a rush. "There's more to life than riding a horse and roping a bunch of cows."

Surely this wasn't happening.

"I couldn't agree more." Cliff grinned and Maddie scowled nervously at him. He knew exactly what he was doing adding fuel to the meddlesome posse's bonfire. They were eating it up.

"Matter of fact," he said, milking the whole ordeal for all it was worth. "I heard the theater on the outskirts of town is great and I was going to see if Maddie would go with me this weekend. Maybe y'all could help a cowboy out and put in a good word for me."

If she hadn't been so mad at him she would have laughed. He was really cute and having such a fun time teasing her. And that was what he was doing, she knew it. But still, *please-Louise*, he was about to make her life hard.

The problem was that he had no idea who he was dealing with. While the innocent looking posse knew *exactly* what they were doing.

At least she thought they did. Their matchmaking resume had blossomed into the high double digits in the last few years.

That lit their eyes up and if Cliff had been sitting down Maddie would have kicked him under the table for encouraging them!

"That's perfect, Maddie," Adela encouraged. "You should do that."

"But—"

"Maddie," Esther Mae joined in. "It's not healthy the way you work all the time."

"I like working," Maddie argued. "And no one says anything about it when a man works like that. Norma Sue, you're a ranch woman, you know what it's like." It was true. Norma Sue loved her work. The woman wore overalls or jeans all the time with boots and her white Stetson.

"She's got you on that, Norma," Esther Mae agreed.

"Hold on. I love ranch work, sure do. But when I met my Roy Don that man made my heart start thinking of other things. Believe me, I was more than ready to get out of the sun and make a life with that cowboy." She grinned. "Like we told you a few minutes ago, there is a *lot* more to life than cattle. Some really good stuff. Like that kissin' you and this good lookin' hunk of cowboy were doing the other day."

Maddie rubbed her suddenly clammy hands on her thighs, as heat suffused her cheeks, thoughts of that kiss she'd shared with Cliff instantly came to mind. No matter how much she tried not to think about it she wouldn't mind doing it again. Her gaze flicked to his and he smiled, as if he could read her mind!

Laughter crinkled the edges of Cliff's eyes. "Sounds good to me."

Maddie's mind reeled. She didn't ever remember the matchmakers ever, *ever,* being so blunt and to the point. Did they consider her that desperate—or that hard to find a match for?

If they only knew how badly she wanted a family. How she struggled with making ranching be enough fulfillment for her because she didn't think anyone could ever love her enough to stick around. Or that she'd let them close enough.

Sadly she knew that the way the ladies depicted her was exactly how it would be if she didn't make some changes.

Esther Mae patted the edge of her short red hair. "A woman has to show the fellas she's available. Why, Maddie you've got walls up a mile high and they need to be torn down. Cliff, don't you think that would be fun?"

Maddie gasped. "Esther Mae!" This was beyond okay.

Cliff's brows dipped.

"Oh, I didn't mean nothing mean about that," Esther Mae said, actually looking sheepish. "I—"

"She gets carried away sometimes," Adela apologized giving her friend a gentle warning look.

Cliff cocked his head and his eyes thoughtful. "The man who falls for Maddie needs to love her for the woman she is. Maddie, here, needs a partner with a vision for the same things she wants. I wouldn't change anything about her."

Maddie's stomach tumbled a few times and her heart followed. Humiliation burned her cheeks as she hated to think what Cliff might be thinking after all of this craziness.

Cliff's expression shifted with sincerity. "I'm serious, Maddie. I really would love to take you to the theater. But only if you want to go."

Maddie didn't have to see the other three pairs of eyes to know that they shared her focus on Cliff. Maddie could feel their matchmaking minds speed into overdrive.

Her heart raced out of control at his words and she didn't know whether to whack him with a menu for helping create this fiasco or thank him for the invitation.

Norma Sue elbowed her. "Say something, Maddie. He's good."

Maddie stood up. "Fine. I'll go." She looked about the table. "But, so you know—I understand exactly what just happened here. And y'all do not play fair." Zeroed in on the exit she didn't stop until she was at her truck.

Her life had just turned into a circus.

And she'd accepted a date with Cliff...

CHAPTER TEN

"I have a date with Maddie," Cliff told Rafe a few hours after the incident at the diner.

They had met at one of the neighboring ranch arenas to watch the group of young cowboys ride bulls like he'd promised.

Cliff was still reeling over what had happened in the diner. He wasn't real sure the posse wasn't a few cards short of a full deck. He hadn't appreciated them making Maddie feel bad about herself. Although he didn't think that was what they'd meant to do he'd seen it in her eyes. Some of the advice they'd offered could do her some good. But still...wow, they'd poured it on strong.

The truth was, he'd walked right into their little setup with his eyes wide open.

Sure he was teasing Maddie, and going along with them before it had gotten out of hand. But *only* because he could sense that they really cared about Maddie. They wanted good things for her. Still, they'd gotten a little carried away.

And Adela had completely blindsided him when she'd been the one who suggested the date.

He'd gotten serious when he realized Maddie thought he was having a good time toying with her.

"Really?" Rafe said.

"You don't have a problem with that do you?"

Rafe had his arms crossed and hanging over the edge of the arena. He cocked his head at Cliff. "None. Just treat her with respect."

"And you actually thought you had to tell me that." Cliff was no saint, but he wasn't some womanizing love'em and leave'em jerk.

"No that's not it. You need to know Maddie is special."

"I know that."

"I don't know if you do. She doesn't date and we've all noticed that. She's become like a little sister to us but we don't pry. She's private and the fact that she's accepted a date with you is a good thing. I'm thinking you need to know the full score though. I think she could be hurt real easy. She's not as tough as she wants us all to think."

"I had figured some of that out, but thanks for filling me in," Cliff said.

Rafe turned toward him. "Look, I know we had a crummy background and I know you've been running around the country trying to outrun it all these years."

He stared at Rafe in disbelief. "How do you know that? I didn't even realize it until I found out dad was dead." He laughed harsh, bitter. "It doesn't even make sense to me. I love riding bulls. But no matter how hard I tried to settle down I couldn't do it. The minute I heard the news, it was like some fist inside me unclenched."

"I know."

"How do you know that?"

"You're not the only one who was angry. I was just forced to deal with it before you. When my knee blew out, I couldn't run from the past any more. C.C. helped me understand it. That man had a way of looking at a people and knowing what they needed."

Cliff stared at his brother. "What did you need?"

"A place to be at peace. A place to belong and feel a sense of accomplishment. Ending up at the ranch grounded me like I'd never had before. Certainly not in our home growing up."

No, their home growing up had been as loud and dysfunctional as it got. "He was a piece of work wasn't he?" Cliff took a deep breath tension had coiled tight thinking about his father. It eased out of him, as he exhaled.

"Yeah, and then some," Rafe snorted. "If Mom hadn't gotten sick and died I guess she'd have stayed with him until the end."

They were silent for a moment, the sadness of that statement a deep gash of pain between them.

"I guess love is not always easy to understand." It was all Cliff could come up with. He'd stopped trying to figure out his mother a long time ago. "So why haven't you found me a nice sister in law and settled down and given me some nieces and nephews?" he asked, changing the subject.

Rafe's expression shadowed. "Hey, don't rush me and I won't rush you. Like you said, love's not always easy to understand and I sure don't have it figured out."

Had Rafe been in love?

"Me either." Cliff thought of Maddie and the date that couldn't get here soon enough.

"Show's about to start," Rafe said, changing the subject again. "You better get up there. These fellas are expecting you to turn them into champions. So get to work."

Cliff chuckled. "I'll do my best. It might be time to pass the torch."

Maddie was loading up calf feeding bottles and dealing with the shock of having said yes to a date with Cliff the day before.

Her mind still hadn't wrapped around the events of the diner episode and she'd tossed and turned with it all night long. Her pillow was probably sore from the workout she'd given it.

"Hey. Good morning."

The sound of Cliff's voice caused her insides to jumble nervously. It was both a dangerous and good feeling at the same time.

When she glanced at him the air felt alive with electricity.

"Good morning." She closed the tailgate and tried not to seem affected. *Yeah right.*

"Did you sleep good?"

She cut you've-got-to-be-kidding eyes at him. Getting mad and mortified all over again about the ambush.

"Look, about all of that yesterday. I'm sorry if it embarrassed you or made you uncomfortable."

"It was kind of hard not to be. Don't you think? You heard what they said. For goodness sakes, I didn't realize exactly how pitiful I was until they pointed it out to me." Okay, so she hadn't meant to let those feelings out of the bag. She felt bad enough knowing them herself.

He looked uncomfortable. "I don't think they meant it that way. I really don't."

She sighed and looked away. Studying Ty in the distance working with a horse in the early morning light. Finally she looked back at Cliff. Crossing her arms over ribs that barely hurt any more. "I know. But I hope you know that the posse has declared us their next matchmaking project. You do realize that, right?"

"Yeah, I might have started out with blinders on yesterday but I picked up on that."

Surprisingly that made her lips twitch with the need to smile. "Well I hope you're prepared."

He hitched a brow and his lips curved into a smirk. "I ain't scared. Are you?"

"I'm not scared of anything," she blurted, her pulse pounding at his words.

He sobered. "I believe that for the most part. But everyone's scared of something."

Maddie's hands tightened on her arms. "I'm going to feed a couple of orphaned calves, would you like to ride along?" The invitation was out before she could stop it or analyze it. Maybe she was trying to prove to him she wasn't scared.

But she was terrified and she knew it.

Cliff had jumped on the offer from Maddie like a man diving into the last lifeboat. The fact that she'd asked him to come along—especially after seeing how miffed she was meant a lot. He tried not to read too much into it but he knew he was. With everything he learned about Maddie he was more and more drawn to her. He wanted to see what she enjoyed.

Wanted to get to know the woman who held people at bay.

And he sensed with every yard of pasture they crossed that orphaned calves meant something.

It had rained sometime in the night and more was threatening as she showed him the barn and feedlot where they kept the orphans and their new "adoptive" mamas as she called them.

When she spoke of the program it was written all over her face and in the sound of her enthusiasm that it was close to her heart.

There were three fairly newborn calves in the pen and three heifers. The babies each wore a calf skin over their backs like a second skin. He knew how it worked, using the skin from a calf that died and using it to cover an orphan so that the mama that had lost her baby would accept the orphan because it carried the scent of her baby. He knew how it worked but when he watched Maddie talk about it, it hit him hard.

"This really means a lot to you doesn't it?" he asked. Maddie felt things deep. It was obvious.

She was standing beside him and looking at the babies and mamas. "I can't stand for anything to be without a mom, so I love matching up orphans with new mamas." She waved a hand toward the cattle in the surrounding pasture. "All of those are new families." She smiled. "Isn't it cool?"

He was mesmerized by the intensity of her devotion. "You're a good mama, you know."

Shock flashed over her expression.

"Hey, don't look so shocked. You are. These are your babies and you've matched them up and given them love and nurturing. You've taken a mama calf who longed for her baby and a baby who longed and needed a new mom to survive and you've put them together. But, they're still your babies."

"Hey, I'm a cattle woman, I'm not supposed to get so attached."

He nudged her arm and smiled. "But you do."

She nodded. "I do."

He couldn't help himself as he lifted his hand and traced

the profile of her face. "You have a big heart, Maddie."

She swallowed hard, drawing his gaze to her lips. His hand curled through her hair to gently cup the nape of her neck and he tugged lightly. She stepped close, her gaze locked with his. His pulse thundered and the need to kiss her was overwhelming.

This time they were alone in the middle of nowhere without an audience watching them. Other than Maddie's little bovine families.

He brushed his lips across hers, a driving need to taste the sweetness of her. An urgency he'd never felt before drove him as he realized he could kiss her forever. Almost instantly, a deep sigh whispered from her. She settled in his arms, her lips moving achingly soft against his, warm and answering as she took his breath away.

Cliff forgot everything but the feel of Maddie in his arms.

CHAPTER ELEVEN

Maddie hadn't forgotten the kiss in the truck. But it didn't compare to the tenderness of this kiss from the moment he pressed his lips to hers. "Maddie," he whispered, trailing kisses along her jaw then back to her mouth as if he couldn't stay away too long. She knew she should pull away, run, flee before her heart did something irrevocable. But she couldn't, just a little longer.

When he pulled away she was breathless. Dazed. And she had to stand very still while the world stopped spinning.

He raked a hand through his hair, his hat lying on the ground from where she must have knocked it off when she ran her fingers through his wavy hair.

"Maddie," he said, looking as stunned as her.

She had to find footing. "I have to feed the babies." She strode to the rear of her truck. He followed her and she could feel him watching her. Her hand trembled as she opened the cooler and though she tried to make them stop her hands trembled as she pulled the two large bottles from the ice.

"You can be daddy for a day," she said, pushing one into his chest and letting go too quickly as she started for the pen. Luckily he grabbed it before it fell.

She led the way back to the barn and out to the other side where two baby calves waited in a small pen. They started bawling the moment they spotted her.

"Hey, little girls," she cooed, her nerves calming with something else to think about than the feel of Cliff's kiss. She had to think. Had to calm down the chaos going on inside of her.

She reached into the pen to pet them, rubbing their ears as they tried to butt each other out of the way.

"Maddie that kiss was incredible."

She didn't look at him. She couldn't. If she looked at him he would see exactly how incredible she'd thought it was. He would be able to see every hidden longing of her soul if she looked at him. If she looked at him he would see the fear that gripped her. Could she risk that he wouldn't abandon her in the end too?

Think Cliff.

Cliff knew that was easier said than done after having experienced the kiss of a lifetime. From the moment Maddie had rolled over in that dirt that first day and looked up at him with those fathomless green eyes the fog he'd been moving in for days had started clearing out of his head. Every day he'd spent around her had brought him further out of any unresolved anger he'd felt toward his dad.

He was thinking only about what he wanted out of life now.

And he knew he wanted Maddie in his life. His agent had called telling him they needed him in Mesquite the following weekend, and he'd told him to do what he had to but that he wasn't coming back. Not full time and only when he wanted. He knew he'd lose his sponsors but it had been a long haul and he finally knew it was time. He trusted his agent to handle it with care and professionalism. He knew what was important in his life now and he was looking at her.

"Maddie, say something please."

She smiled over her shoulder, that vulnerable look still there behind her smile. "Poor things, they're twins. When their mother died, there wasn't a mama available and all the other newborns were alive and well—which is a good thing. Anyway, if you'll help we'll get these two rascals fed."

"Fine." He stepped up beside her, his arm brushing hers as he petted the one on her left and stuck the bottle through the gate. She was getting her emotions in check. The thought was like cheer in his heart.

He smiled as the twins latched onto the bottles and tried to yank them through the fence as they attacked the formula. He laughed, suddenly feeling like everything in the world was right.

"It's been a long time since I did this. I forgot how greedy they can be."

"It's an adventure."

"I have to agree."

She blushed.

The twins kicked each other again and he chuckled along with Maddie before looking away. It took everything he had not to say anything else about the kiss. They'd talk about it when she was ready. Maybe he was moving too fast. It wasn't as if he'd chosen the pace though.

She looked past the pen to the land beyond, a contented expression on her face. "I've always wanted my own land, my own place. Always."

"Well, I'd say you've accomplished that."

The breeze lifted the edges of her blonde hair. "If C.C. hadn't made me a partner I'd never have been able to afford anything near this size. But I'd have been content with something smaller. As long as I could feel like I owned a piece of Texas."

"We agree on that." He nudged her gently with his elbow, drawing her gaze to his again. "Texas is the place I knew I wanted to come back to. Rafe settling here helped me decide to try Mule Hollow."

The twins finished their bottles in that moment and immediately started head butting each other trying to reach the others bottle.

She took the bottles and headed toward the truck.

"Do you know why your parents gave you up and let you go into the foster system?" he asked, following her. Wanting more than ever to know more about her.

"No."

The sharp, dead way she said no red flagged it that it still hurt.

She moistened her lips. Her expression tightened.

"The truth, I was a very sick baby abandoned on the doorstep of the post office when I was just a few weeks old. Like my mom went to mail a letter and walked off and forgot me."

Cliff's throat squeezed tight and he hung his head, staring at his boots, hurting for Maddie. "Awe Maddie. I'm so sorry."

A too vivid picture of Maddie as an infant crying for her mama filled his mind and caused the back sides of his eyes to burn.

"What, what happened? Who found you?" he said, gravel in this throat.

"One of the mailmen. I was taken in by the state. I was a very sickly child. My immune system was compromised and almost non-existent. Because of that I was weak and pale and in and out of the hospital. Anyway, that's my story. I was raised in an orphanage the first part of my life and later different foster homes."

Cliff felt as if someone had kicked him in the gut. "Are you all right now? You work like a pack mule."

"See. That is exactly why I don't talk about myself. I don't like everyone looking at me and feeling sorry for me. I'm fine. I'm strong and I rarely get sick." She put distance between them. "I shouldn't have told you that." She headed to the truck cab. "Let's go back."

He stalked after her. "Maddie, no kid should have to go through what you went through. Yeah it upsets me for you."

"Don't look at me that way. I can't deal with it."

She climbed into her truck and slammed the door. Cliff was left standing on the outside looking in.

If he lived to be a hundred he'd never understand Maddie Rose.

He yanked open the door. "Get out of that truck."

"Don't you tell me what to do." She grabbed the steering wheel with both hands and stared straight ahead.

"Okay, that does it. I warned you." He reached into the

truck and scooped her into his arms. She held on to the steering wheel until her hands slipped off. She was no match for him.

"Let go of me," she snapped, kicking as he pulled her out and then slammed the door with his boot.

Not sure what he was doing but not caring. All he wanted to do was hold her.

"Let me down Cliff Masterson or I'll kick you. I will."

He set her on her feet and dragged her against him. Needing to feel her heartbeat against his. "Maddie, it's okay to let people get close." He rested his head on the top of hers and held her. She had gone still in his arms her heart was thundering he could feel every angry beat of it.

"It makes me angry. And yeah I'd be telling a bald-faced lie if I said I didn't feel bad for you for what you went through. I do." She pushed against his chest on that. "But I'm more impressed with what you've become. Maddie, you are amazing."

He wished he had the right words to say.

The pressure eased and he leaned his head back so he could see her. "Your past isn't you today." He'd come to terms with that for himself finally.

Looking into Maddie's beautiful face all he wanted to do now was help her realized that.

Maddie fought the raw ache of tears that threatened to spill over the edges of her eyes and roll down her cheeks.

She wouldn't cry. This too, was why she kept her mouth shut about her past. It wasn't good to drag her memories back there.

This was ridiculous. Why did talking about the past still affect her so? *Maybe because you don't talk about it. Ever.*

"Talk to me Maddie. I'm your friend. Right?"

"I'm not sure calling us friends is the right term," she said, a husky laugh surprising her.

"Hey, I totally disagree with that. If you remember, I pulled you out from under Buford's hooves. And we did just share the kiss of a lifetime." The reminder of that kiss filled her thoughts wiping everything else away.

She laughed and his eyes twinkled.

"See there," he said, gently. "I told you, we're friends. A friend does whatever it takes to make a friend feel better."

"Cliff, I don't know, this is all happening so fast."

He kissed her forehead. "You feel it as much as I do. You can deny it and back away from it, but just so you know, I'm not one to back away from something like that. I'm a bull rider. I like danger." He grinned, looking cocky and heart-stoppingly handsome.

Maddie knew she could fall in love with Cliff. And he had a way of making her so angry but so...reckless. This was too much.

She'd been hurt so much growing up. So very much. She backed up to the truck and he placed his hands on either side of her shoulders... he was going to kiss her again.

"Cliff, I don't really know what to do about you. I have trouble opening up. Trusting."

He smiled and dipped his head and stole a swift gentle kiss. "Be my friend, let me be there for you."

She nodded. Feeling overwhelmed.

He smiled. "And let me take you to the theater tomorrow night like we planned."

She couldn't say anything, just looked at him.

"And Maddie, don't be afraid of me. I wouldn't hurt you for the world."

He dipped in for another kiss and Maddie it didn't even occur to her to push him away. Instead she cupped his jaw with her hands and returned the kiss.

When he had kissed her breathless and pulled back she smiled shakily at him. "Okay, the theater is still on."

CHAPTER TWELVE

Maddie rolled over in bed and stuffed her face in the pillow. She'd agreed to a date with Cliff—after he'd curled her toes with a kiss that lingered on her lips even now.

She would never, never, *never* forget that kiss.

The feel of his arms, the taste of mint, the feel of a smile as it rippled through her hours afterward they'd parted.

She was petrified.

She was used to making herself be strong. To hide the fear.

Cliff didn't let her hide inside herself. He'd pushed her to open up because he cared. And then he'd refused to let her close him out after she'd told him her past.

For all the hard-working cowgirl she was, no one would guess how vulnerable she was on the inside. While she craved her own family, she couldn't help feel she wasn't worthy of one.

Yet just thinking about the gentle way he'd kissed her had her insides melting all over again. Looking into his eyes she'd believed him when he'd said he wouldn't hurt her. He'd been trying to keep her from hurting herself since the moment they'd met. So it was easy to believe him that he wouldn't hurt her.

Only problem, he had no idea how tender her heart was. For a girl who'd never known what love was, not from anyone...stepping out to risk her heart was hard. She'd prayed for God to send her someone ever since she was a fourteen-year-old romantic up in the attic of one of the foster homes she happened to live at that summer. Could God have finally answered her prayers?

And so, as scared and uncertain as she felt, Maddie found herself smiling most of the week.

Was she ready for this? She honestly didn't know, but she couldn't resist.

Cliff had decided to buy the second property that he and Maddie had looked at. It was perfect and he sensed Maddie liked it too. It would be a few weeks until the closing but Hailey had worked it out so that he could rent it until the contract went through. He spent the week cleaning it up.

Maddie came and helped him some but just because she'd given him a look into her past Maddie was still Maddie. She was still driven to push herself with her work and he knew when to back off. She had obligations and she was her own person.

He respected that about her.

Working at his new place gave him time away from her too. Gave him time to think. It also minimized the possibility that he'd do or say something that would cause her to shut him out again.

They'd made progress and he wasn't backtracking.

He was done with looking back and he planned to help Maddie do the same.

The big barn where the theater was set up sat a little ways off the road. On evenings when they held the play, cars and trucks would come from the surrounding counties in droves. It had become a small piece of Branson right there outside Mule Hollow.

"Hey, there," Applegate Thornton boomed as they walked up. Maddie loved ol' App and his buddy Stanley, both so hard of hearing, their conversations tended to carry to everyone. They played more checkers at Sam's than ranched, now that they were retired and spent their weekend evenings handing out flyers for the shows and running the spotlights because they enjoyed it.

Stanley came hustling over, his plump face a full-blown grin. "Hey Cliff, missed you at the checker game this mornin'." He sounded as if he were speaking through a megaphone.

Cliff mentioned that he'd played checkers a couple of mornings with App and Stanley and they'd both beat him.

The perpetual frown that normally dominated Applegate's expression lifted as he looked from Cliff to Maddie. "'Bout time this here date night has finally arrived," he boomed for the world to hear.

People turned to look and Maddie froze.

"It's a good night," Cliff said.

App shook his hand. "I figure you're one smart cookie to have this little gal on your arm."

"Yup." Stanley gave her a one-armed hug. "We were 'bout to decide she was gonna grow old and single because none of these cowpokes round here had sense enough to ask her out."

People were looking. Listening. Maddie tried to smile, as she grabbed Cliff by the arm. "Thanks, fellas. We'll seat ourselves." Not waiting for more to be said, she dragged Cliff toward the first seats available. Plunking herself down she yanked Cliff into the seat beside her.

He was chuckling and immediately draped his arm over the back of her chair, cupping her shoulder.

"Relax, Maddie, it's all right," he said, close to her ear.

She turned her head bumping her nose into his unexpectedly. His eyes sparkled. "And yes, they are all looking, but that's just fine with me."

Looking into his amazing, mischief filled eyes Maddie felt like the girl who was late to the party but won the door prize. Her insides trembled when he planted a kiss on the top of her nose and tugged her close as the lights began to dim.

In a daze, Maddie caught Esther Mae four rows up giving her a thumbs up signal.

"Your friends are eating this up," he whispered, giving her shoulder a gentle squeeze as the cowboy band began playing the introduction music.

"I'm glad you came with me," Cliff whispered in her ear.

In the darkness she inhaled his scent; rich spice and sun warmed leather. "I'm glad to be here."

He touched his forehead to hers, gently caressed her shoulder and turned to enjoy the show.

A door in Maddie's heart cracked open and she knew in that moment she could have sat that way for the rest of her life.

...And the voice of worry whispering she was getting in too deep—she ignored.

The next morning they had the horses and travel supplies they were taking to the festival loaded before breakfast.

It didn't take thirty minutes to transform their patch of the festival into a riding school. And Cliff was amazed how many people were milling around by nine o'clock.

He enjoyed the way Maddie greeted the kids who came by and the way she obviously enjoyed their excitement about getting on a horse. Now that he had more insight into her background he appreciated even more the connection she had toward these kids. Many of them probably hadn't ever been on a horse; it was only something they dreamed about, like she had. Thinking about that made him smile. Just as watching her now, made him smile. Made him feel like a whole big world was opening up and all they had to do was step into it together. His phone buzzed and he pulled it from his pocket and his smile faded when he saw his agent's name. As he hit the accept button a sense of unease settled over him.

"Don't tug on the reins too hard, it hurts his mouth," Maddie told a little boy with stars in his eyes at the very idea of being on the back of a horse.

Seeing the kids on the horses reminded her of how she'd longed to ride one growing up. The kids energized her, as did the hum of awareness she felt when she was near Cliff.

Crazy partners! She'd wanted to both hug the guys last night and throttle them when she'd found them waiting up after the date. She was a grown woman and she could take care of herself, and yet it had been touching to see them sitting there on the patio when Cliff took her home.

She had been quite certain that Cliff saw through their ruse of playing cards.

She glanced his way now, standing behind the pens he was talking on his cell phone, deep in conversation. Mule Hollow had terrible phone service, but there was a new tower, and reception was better than it used to be. The intense, long conversation he was engaged in would not have been happening too long ago.

What were they talking about?

Pulling her attention from Cliff pacing back and forth, she led the little boy whose name was Randy around the round pen delighting in the pure joy in his laughter. The laughter faded in to the background as she glanced at Cliff again and saw him pocket his phone and hang his head.

What had happened?

Something was wrong.

She knew it before he motioned for her to come over. Her stomach quivered as she handed the lead rope to Chase.

"What's wrong," she asked after she climbed through the rungs on the portable round pen and met him.

"Maddie, I hate this, but I have to leave town for a few days. There's a PBR event that I can't get out of. I thought it would be no big deal to miss, but I was wrong. My sponsor is up in arms about it and contractually, I'm bound."

"Wh, when do you leave?" she asked, forcing the words when they threatened to stick in the back of her throat.

"I have to grab my gear and head out now."

Her spirits deflated. "You have a career," she said, struggling not to overreact. But the voice of worry reared its ugly head—had this settling down idea been only a whim?

Was he really not done with the road? Did his sponsors have so much control over him that he couldn't stop?

He touched her cheek and the thrill of his touch skittered through her. Stiffening, she fought to harden her emotions to it.

"Go—I'll see you when I see you." Not that she had any hold on him. They'd been on one date. They'd only know each other two weeks.

Two weeks.

Two unbelievable, memorable, life changing weeks.

He wrapped her in his arms and brushed a quick kiss across her lips. "I'll be back as soon as I can. You stay safe and out from under bulls' feet."

"Sure, just for you." She laughed huskily to hide the emotion threatening to burst from her.

It wasn't until he'd disappeared among the trucks heading for his own that she realized she hadn't told him to do the same.

Riding bulls for a living, no matter how good you were, was a dangerous job. A job that he loved.

Cliff Masterson was a bull rider. One of the best and it was money made from surviving on the backs of those animals that was paying for the ranch he was buying. Could he really, truly turn his back on the career he loved and be satisfied to settle down away from the excitement of the ride?

Turning back to the round pen, she forced her nerves to settle and her mind away from Cliff.

She wasn't sure what she'd been thinking, but one thing was certain: she hadn't been using her head the last few days.

CHAPTER THIRTEEN

On Monday night, Cliff called. She hadn't heard from him either of the two nights after he left so quickly. When he finally did call she was miffed, not to mention hurt.

Maddie didn't mind the miffed part as much as she minded the hurt part. She did not like being hurt.

And that was what happened when you opened up your heart. You were vulnerable to hurt.

She hated being vulnerable. It brought back the helpless days of her childhood when she'd hoped and prayed that some family would come along and think she was worthy to be loved. When she'd see the hopeful couples come through the orphanage she'd remember the thrill of anticipation that this might be the couple.

That this might be her family...and then she'd feel the devastating hurt when they passed her by for the child they'd chosen.

Maddie had cried herself to sleep so many times, until finally she'd hardened her heart.

As an adult she'd shoved that pain to the furthest recess of her heart and slammed an iron grill around it.

She hadn't let anything penetrate that grill—until Cliff had blasted into her life, rescued her from Buford, then proceeded to knock down the barriers to her heart one by one—and stolen her heart.

What if he decided this had all been too fast?

That bulls were his life?

When he'd called, she hadn't talked to him long. The

loudspeakers had been in the background and he'd tried to explain over the noise that they were filming a show for one of the networks and that he'd been obligated to stay.

She tried to brush it off. After all she'd only known Cliff a short time...too short of a time to put any real merit in a relationship building between them.

And yet, she knew somehow during all the sweet talk and gentle ways he'd slipped past her barriers and captured her heart. Her hope. Made her start dreaming of a life with him.

That alone irritated the fire out of her.

But it was undeniable.

How had she been so stupid? He'd never settled down before, had she really believed that this time was different?

"I've got problems, girls," she confessed to the twins as they greedily attacked their bottles.

Memories of Cliff standing beside her helping feed them weren't helping.

Needing to talk she was glad she had the twins. "You gals are going to have to toughen up those hearts of yours. And don't let any young, good looking bull come along and talk you into turning soft. No ma'am, you stay strong or you'll get your heart broken."

Maddie knew it was easier to say than do. Because even though it had only been a two weeks, two irritating, fun, exciting weeks, she knew the moment he'd kissed her that she had stepped into unchartered waters. There was nothing she could do but suffer now.

Suffer the uncertainty of whether he was coming back to Mule Hollow to stay as he'd led her to believe. Or was he jumping back into bull riding with barely enough time to call?

Maddie was afraid that she'd been a fool. She'd known that no one in her life had ever believed she was worth sticking around for—why had she let herself hope that Cliff was different?

A fool. That was exactly what she was.

"Hey, Cliff, you're up."

"Yeah, be right there," Cliff called over his shoulder, but let the phone keep ringing. After their call yesterday he'd been increasingly worried about Maddie. "C'ome on Maddie, pick up."

He'd been calling all day and no answer. The answering machine clicked in and he left a message again. "Maddie, I'm worried. Give me a call and let me know that you're okay."

He ended the call and then stared at the screen, as if doing that would will her to call him back instantly. She'd sounded closed off and distant the last time he'd spoken with her, like she'd been when he'd first met her. Like she was shutting him out.

Unease gripped him. He needed to talk to her.

"Cliff. You gonna ride?"

"Yeah, I'm riding." Stuffing the phone in his gear bag he forced Maddie out of his mind and he strode toward the bull with his number.

He'd called Rafe earlier to find out if he'd seen Maddie and his brother had said she'd been acting kind of weird since he'd left.

Cliff hadn't liked that at all. He hadn't planned on being here for this three-day event. He'd tried to get out of it but there were certain things that, unless you were injured and unable to ride, you couldn't get out of. He jogged up the metal steps and strode toward the chute. He hardly hesitated as he climbed over the rail and planted his boots on the rails, straddling the bull but not lowering himself down to its back yet.

Cinnabar required full concentration if one was going to even attempt a six-second go, much less a full eight seconds without getting stomped.

"You okay, Cliff?" Brody Buchanan asked. Brody was a long-time friend from the circuit.

Cliff yanked at his gloves, making sure they were secure and gave a sharp nod.

"You don't look so good." Brody's piercing eyes searched his. "Come on man, you've got to have your head on straight for this freight train and you know it."

Cliff grunted then gave Brody no choice but to let him go. He waited for Cinnabar to settle down, then lowered himself down on top of the rusty red bull.

Cliff had to see Maddie. The best way to do that was to get this ride done so he could catch a flight home.

All he had to do was make this ride.

"Come on, girls, give a girl a break," Maddie said, playing tug-of-war with the twins on Monday evening. They were competing to see which one could yank off an arm first—or at least yank the bottle from her hand first.

"You are baby cows, not hogs," she said, feeling grumpy. She'd been unable to pull herself out of the low place she'd nosedived to since Cliff left town. Did the twins care that she felt lousy? Nope. They kept right on slobbering and yanking on the bottles like she'd done something to make them mad.

The overzealous calf gave a particularly hard tug and Maddie lost her hold on the bottle. The calf raced across the pen, the big bottle dangling from her teeth. Why, the baby was so excited, she did a little kick with her hind legs. Distracted watching the calf, Maddie fumbled the other bottle when the other one gave it a yank and watched in dismay as the little glutton pranced off with her prize too.

Hefting up a big sigh, Maddie climbed through the rails and chased after the duo. She would have to wrestle the bottles away from them and then finish the feeding, because it was certain that they weren't going to get fed as the bottle dragged along in the dirt.

Heading toward the nearest one she latched hold of the bottle but the calf was not giving up on her prize easily. She dug in her hooves, gritted her pearly whites and held on. One minute Maddie was standing and the next she was being yanked around, her foot slipped in the soft dirt and she found herself face first in the dirt. It was a good thing her ribs were feeling better, she thought as she pushed herself to a sitting position.

"I leave for four days and you're back swimming in the dirt."

At the husky drawl Maddie's heart slowed and then picked up speed. She spun in the dirt to see Cliff grinning at her from the other side of the pen.

He looked so good she almost forgot how mad she was. His jaw was covered in a five o'clock shadow that seemed to accentuate his dazzling smile and his twinkling eyes.

Goodness, she had to fight the urge to run over and throw her arms around him. She'd missed him more than she wanted to admit. More than she could believe.

She'd been as wary of letting a man wiggle past her defenses and here he'd gone and done it. And done it good.

And now, she was terrified she couldn't live without him.

She was sitting in the dirt, wanting to cry because she knew that falling in love with the twinkle-eyed cowboy grinning at her from across the arena fence had the ability to crush her world. And he'd done it in only two week's time!

What damage could he do given longer?

Cliff climbed over the fence and strode toward her. Her heart fluttered like a panicked parakeet.

She scrambled up finally, moving as the panic set in.

He stalked across the pen, his eyes turning serious as he came. "Maddie, why didn't you take my last calls? What's wrong? All I could think about was getting back here to see what was going on."

He was mere inches from her and she planted a hand in the middle of his chest to keep him from wrapping those strong arms of his around her. "Stop," she commanded, having already learned that she didn't think well when he did that. "This moved too fast, Cliff."

"Love moves at its own pace, darlin', and that is just the way it is."

She narrowed her eyes, as if narrowing them would narrow the gap trying to pull open in her heart. Her stinkin' heart lurched despite the battle she was putting up. "Don't sweet-talk me. You move too fast. How am I supposed to believe you haven't dipped into Mule Hollow like a whirlwind before spinning off to new places? Because I know your personality is too strong to settle for the quiet life we all live here."

His grin slashed cocky and crooked. "See there, already you know me like it's been forever. Believe me, darlin', there's going to be excitement in our lives. Don't you doubt it, and I'm not talkin' about the wild bulls we're going to raise. God didn't say when a man and woman got married that life lost its luster."

Her insides rolled over like a puppy begging for a belly rub at the look in his eyes. She knew life being married to Cliff wouldn't be dull or lackluster. It would be passionate and fun and there would be plenty of head butting too. If the matchmakers liked sparks, well Maddie had no doubt that she and Cliff could start a forest fire with the ones they'd raise. It was him she worried about. Would she be woman enough to hold him if she was strong enough to allow her heart to let him in?

"We need to slow down," she snapped, self-preservation kicking in when she felt the chink in her armor crack a little wider.

Cliff stepped up and took her in his arms. She knew if he kissed her—she'd melt like butter again.

He kissed the tip of her nose and her breath caught in her throat and her knees felt weak.

"I love you, Maddie Rose. I've told you before I'm a man who knows what he wants and I'm planning on spending the rest of my life proving to you that I'm a man of my word."

Maddie's world started spinning. "I'm afraid, Cliff. There, I've admitted it."

He lifted her chin to gaze into her eyes. "Then we'll slow down, take it slow—it'll be hard for me but I'll do it because you need time. I understand that." He kissed her forehead.

She could feel his heartbeat against her hand, so strong. She wanted to believe him so badly it hurt. She'd longed her whole life to be loved.

"Maddie, you changed my world from the moment I saw

you. And the moment I first kissed you I knew you were the woman for me. You knew it too. We'll take all the time you need. Just know I'm the man who is going to give you the family you've always wanted. I've been waiting my whole life to find you. And I'll wait my whole life to have you if that's what it takes."

He had looked into her soul and read exactly what she'd been thinking. Knew exactly what her hopes and dreams were. Did it really matter if he'd known her a week or fifty-two?

"You would do that? But your sponsors? Your contracts?"

His gaze gentled and shined with love. "This event fulfilled my contract and they offered me another one, but I told them thanks, but no thanks. I've got new dreams now, Maddie. And I'll do whatever it takes for you to know that I'm the man who loves you and who'll love you always with every breath I breathe. Whatever it takes to prove that I'll do."

Maddie stared into his beautiful eyes and believed him. He'd actually chosen to come back to her. She loved this man. Suddenly, spontaneously she shocked herself, springing to her tiptoes she planted her lips on his.

If she'd wanted to hold off and be cautious, this was not the way to do it. But Maddie had been cautious all her life and it hit her as he'd said he'd wait that for the first time in her life she didn't want to wait. Her lips melted to Cliff's and molded to his like they'd been made for each other and she was convinced they had been. God was one smart cookie.

Her arms wound themselves around Cliff's neck and she tugged him closer. He didn't hesitate to join in, kissing her with power and tenderness and promise of things to come.

"Maddie," he growled, pulling back finally, his heart thundering against her own. "What are you telling me with this kiss? Because I'm telling you, that this is powerful and I don't want to misunderstand."

"I'm *saying* that I've been waiting for love my entire life. Is this irresponsible? Some might say so, but I know that many happily-ever-after, true-life love stories have been love at first sight—"

"Or first fight," he chuckled.

"That is for certain." She grinned, her heart swelling with hope and love and dreams...new dreams of a ranch they'd build together and a family they'd raise.

Cupping her face between his hands, he stared with such loving intensity into hers. "Darlin', will you marry me? Now, or later, I simply want to know you're going to be mine."

She loved the sound of that. "Yes, I love you, Cliff with all my heart."

"Yes!" The smile that spread over his face filled every dark corner of her soul. "Maddie I promise to guard your precious heart with my love for the rest of my life."

With that, he lowered his lips to hers and, Maddie knew she was home at last...

ABOUT DEBRA CLOPTON

Bestselling author Debra Clopton has sold over 2.5 million books and her holiday story, OPERATION: MARRIED BY CHRISTMAS has been optioned for an ABC Family Movie starring LeAnn Rimes. Debra writes cowboy romances, inspirational, Christian romance, contemporary and western romances set in Texas. She is known for her snappy dialogue, cowboy heroes and spunky heroines. Her awards include: The Book Sellers Best, Romantic Times Magazine's Book of the Year. She's also a Romance Writers of America Golden Heart Finalist, and a triple finalist in the American Christian Fiction Writers Carol Award.

A sixth generation Texan, Debra lives on a ranch in central Texas with her husband Chuck. She loves to travel and spend time with her family. She is the author of the much loved Mule Hollow Matchmakers series where you never know what the Matchmaking "Posse" is going to do next! She writes for Harlequin Love Inspired and Thomas Nelson/Harper Collins Christian. She is currently working on her 25th novel surrounded by cows, dogs and even renegade donkey herds that keep her writing authentic and often find their way into her stories. She loves helping people smile with her fun, fast paced stories.

DEADLY HUNT

MARGARET DALEY

CHAPTER ONE

Tess Miller pivoted as something thumped against the door. An animal? With the cabin's isolation in the Arizona mountains, she couldn't take any chances. She crossed the distance to a combination-locked cabinet and quickly entered the numbers. After withdrawing the shotgun, she checked to make sure it was loaded then started toward the door to bolt it, adrenaline pumping through her veins.

Silence. Had she imagined the noise? Maybe her work was getting to her, making her paranoid. But as she crept toward the entrance, a faint scratching against the wood told her otherwise. Her senses sharpened like they would at work. Only this time, there was no client to protect. Just her own skin. Her heartbeat accelerated as she planted herself firmly. She reached toward the handle to throw the bolt.

The door crashed open before she touched the knob. She scrambled backwards and to the side at the same time steadying the weapon in her grasp. A large man tumbled into the cabin, collapsing face down at her feet. His head rolled to the side. His eyelids fluttered, then closed.

Stunned, Tess froze. She stared at the man's profile.

Who is he?

The stranger moaned. She knelt next to him to assess what was wrong. Her gaze traveled down his long length. Clotted blood matted his unruly black hair. A plaid flannel shirt, torn in a couple of places, exposed scratches and minor cuts. A rag that had been tied around his leg was soaked with blood. Laying her weapon at her side, she eased the piece of cloth

down an inch and discovered a hole in his thigh, still bleeding.
He's been shot.
Is he alone? She bolted to her feet. Sidestepping his prone body, she snatched up the shotgun again and surveyed the area outside her cabin. All she saw was the sparse, lonely terrain. With little vegetation, hiding places were limited in the immediate vicinity, and she had no time to check further away. She examined the ground to see which direction he'd come from. There weren't any visible red splotches and only one set of large footprints coming from around the side of the cabin. His fall must have started his bleeding again.

Another groan pierced the early morning quiet. She returned to the man, knelt, and pressed her two fingers into the side of his neck. His pulse was rapid, thready, and his skin was cold with a slight bluish tint.

He was going into shock. Her emergency-care training took over. She jumped to her feet, grabbed her backpack off the wooden table and found her first aid kit. After securing a knife from the shelf next to the fireplace, she hurried back to the man and moved his legs slightly so she could close the door and lock it. She yanked her sleeping bag off the bunk, spread it open, then rolled the stranger onto it. When she'd maneuvered his body face-up, she covered his torso.

For a few seconds she stared at him. He had a day's growth of beard covering his jaw. Was he running away from someone—the law? What happened to him? From his disheveled look, he'd been out in the elements all night. She patted him down for a wallet but found no identification. Her suspicion skyrocketed.

Her attention fixed again on the side of his head where blood had coagulated. The wound wasn't bleeding anymore. She would tend that injury later.

As her gaze quickly trekked toward his left leg, her mind registered his features—a strong, square jaw, a cleft in his chin, long, dark eyelashes that fanned the top of his cheeks in stark contrast to the pallor that tinged his tanned skin. Her attention focused on the blood-soaked cloth that had been used to stop the bleeding.

Tess snatched a pair of latex gloves from her first aid kit, then snapped them on and untied the cloth, removing it from his leg. There was a small bullet hole in the front part of his thigh. Was that an exit wound? She prayed it was and checked the back of his leg. She found a larger wound there, which meant the bullet had exited from the front.

Shot from behind. Was he ambushed? A shiver snaked down her spine.

At least she didn't have to deal with extracting a bullet. What she did have to cope with was bad enough. The very seclusion she'd craved this past week was her enemy now. The closest road was nearly a day's hike away.

First, stop the bleeding. Trying not to jostle him too much, she cut his left jean leg away to expose the injury more clearly.

She scanned the cabin for something to elevate his lower limbs. A footstool. She used that to raise his legs higher than his heart. Then she put pressure on his wounds to stop the renewed flow of blood from the bullet holes. She cleansed the areas, then bandaged them. After that, she cleaned the injury on his head and covered it with a gauze pad.

When she finished, she sat back and waited to see if indeed the bleeding from the two wounds in his thigh had stopped. From where the holes were, it looked as though the bullet had passed through muscles, missing bone and major blood vessels. But from the condition the man had been in when he'd arrived, he was lucky he'd survived this long. If the bullet had hit an inch over, he would have bled out.

She looked at his face again. "What happened to you?"

Even in his unconscious, unkempt state, his features gave an impression of authority and quiet power. In her line of work, she'd learned to think the worst and question everything. Was he a victim? Was there somebody else out there who'd been injured? Who had pulled the trigger—a criminal or the law?

Then it hit her. She was this man's lifeline. If she hadn't been here in this cabin at this time, he would have surely died in these mountains. Civilization was a ten-hour hike from here. From his appearance, he'd already pushed himself beyond most men's endurance.

Lord, I need Your help. I've been responsible for people's lives before, but this is different. I'm alone up here, except for You.

Her memories of her last assignment inundated Tess. Guarding an eight-year-old girl whose rich parents had received threats had mentally exhausted her. The child had nearly been kidnapped and so frightened when Tess had gone to protect her. It had been the longest month of her life, praying every day that nothing happened to Clare. By the end Tess had hated leaving the girl whose parents were usually too busy for her. This vacation had been paramount to her.

The stranger moaned. His eyelids fluttered, and his uninjured leg moved a few inches.

"Oh, no you don't. Stay still. I just got you stabilized." She anchored his shoulders to the floor and prayed even more. Even if he were a criminal, she wouldn't let him die.

Slowly the stranger's restlessness abated. Tess exhaled a deep, steadying breath through pursed lips, examining the white bandage for any sign of red. None. She sighed again.

When she'd done all she could, she covered him completely with a blanket and then made her way to the fireplace. The last log burned in the middle of a pile of ashes. Though the days were still warm in October, the temperature would drop into the forties come evening. She'd need more fuel.

Tess crossed the few steps to the kitchen, lifted the coffeepot and poured the last of it into her mug. Her hands shook as she lifted the drink to her lips. She dealt in life and death situations in her work as a bodyguard all the time, but this was different. How often did half-dead bodies crash through her front door? Worse than that, she was all alone up here. This man's survival depended on her. She was accustomed to protecting people, not doctoring them. The coffee in her stomach mixed with a healthy dose of fear, and she swallowed the sudden nausea.

Turning back, she studied the stranger.

Maybe it was a hunting accident. If so, why didn't he have identification on him? Where were the other hunters? How did he get shot? All over again, the questions flooded her mind with a pounding intensity, her natural curiosity not appeased.

The crude cabin, with its worn, wooden floor and its walls made of rough old logs, was suddenly no longer the retreat she'd been anticipating for months. Now it was a cage, trapping her here with a man who might not live.

No, he had to. She would make sure of it—somehow.

Through a haze Shane Burkhart saw a beautiful vision bending over him with concern clouding her face. Had he died? No, he hurt too much to be dead. Every muscle in his body ached. A razor-sharp pain spread throughout him until it consumed his sanity. It emanated from his leg and vied with the pounding in his head.

He tried to swallow, but his mouth and throat felt as if a soiled rag had been stuffed down there. He tasted dirt and dust. Forcing his eyelids to remain open, he licked his dry lips and whispered, "Water."

The woman stood and moved away from him. Where was he? He remembered ... Every effort—even to think—zapped what little energy he had.

He needed to ask something. What? His mind blanked as pain drove him toward a dark void.

Tess knelt next to the stranger with the cup of water on the floor beside her, disappointed she couldn't get some answers to her myriad questions. With her muscles stiff from sitting on the hard floor for so long, she rose and stretched. She would chop some much-needed wood for a fire later, and then she'd scout the terrain near the cabin to check for signs of others. She couldn't shake the feeling there might be others—criminals—nearby who were connected to the stranger.

She bent over and grazed the back of her hand across his forehead to make sure her patient wasn't feverish, combing away a lock of black hair. Neither she nor he needed that complication in these primitive conditions. The wounds were clean. The rest was in the Lord's hands.

After slipping on a light jacket, she grabbed her binoculars and shotgun, stuffed her handgun into her waistband and went outside, relishing the cool breeze that whipped her long hair around her shoulders.

She strode toward the cliff nearby and surveyed the area, taking in the rugged landscape, the granite spirals jutting up from the tan and moss green of the valley below. The path to the cabin was visible part of the way up the mountain, and she couldn't see any evidence of hunters or hikers. Close to the bottom a grove of sycamores and oaks, their leaves shades of green, yellow and brown, obstructed her view. But again, aside from a circling falcon, there was no movement. She watched the bird swoop into the valley and snatch something from the ground. She shuddered, knowing something had just become dinner.

Her uncle, who owned the cabin, had told her he'd chopped down a tree and hauled it to the summit, so there would be wood for her. Now, all she had to do was split some of the logs, a job she usually enjoyed.

Today, she didn't want to be gone long in case something happened to the stranger. She located the medium-size tree trunk, checked on her patient to make sure he was still sleeping and set about chopping enough wood for the evening and night. The temperature could plummet in this mountainous desert terrain.

The repetitive sound of the axe striking the wood lured Tess into a hypnotic state until a yelp pierced her mind. She dropped the axe and hurried toward the cabin. Shoving the door open wide, she crossed the threshold to find the stranger trying to rise from the sleeping bag. Pain carved lines deeper into his grimacing face. His groan propelled her forward.

"Leaving so soon." Her lighthearted tone didn't reflect the anxiety she felt at his condition. "You just got here." She knelt beside him, breathing in the antiseptic scent that tangled with the musky odor of the room.

Propping his body up with his elbows, he stared at her, trying to mask the effort that little movement had cost him. "Where ... am ... I?" His speech slow, he shifted, struggling to make himself more comfortable.

"You don't remember how you got here?" Tess placed her arm behind his back to support him.

"No."

"What happened to you?"

The man sagged wearily against her. "Water."

His nearness jolted her senses, as though she were the one who had been deprived of water and overwhelmed with thirst. She glanced over her shoulder to where she'd placed the tin cup. After lowering him onto the sleeping bag, she quickly retrieved the drink and helped him take a couple of sips.

"Why do I ... hurt?" he murmured, his eyelids fluttering.

He didn't remember what happened to him. Head wounds could lead to memory loss, but was it really that? Her suspicion continued to climb. "You were shot in the leg," she said, her gaze lifting to assess his reaction.

A blank stare looked back at her. "What?" He blinked, his eyelids sliding down.

"You were shot. Who are you? What happened?"

She waited for a moment, but when he didn't reply, she realized he'd drifted off to sleep. Or maybe he was faking it. Either way, he was only prolonging the moment when he would have to face her with answers to her questions. The mantle of tension she wore when she worked a job fell over her shoulders, and all the stress she'd shed the day before when she'd arrived at the cabin late in the afternoon returned and multiplied.

Rising, she dusted off the knees of her jeans, her attention fixed on his face. Some color tinted his features now, although they still remained pale beneath his bronzed skin. Noting his even breathing, she left the cabin and walked around studying the area before returning to chop the wood. She completed her task in less than an hour with enough logs to last a few days.

With her arms full of the fuel, she kicked the ajar door open wider and reentered the one-room, rustic abode. She found the stranger awake, more alert. He hadn't moved an inch.

"It's good to see you're up." She crossed to the fireplace and stacked the wood.

"I thought I might have imagined you."

"Nope." As she swept toward him, she smiled. "Before you decide to take another nap, what is your name?"

"Shane Burkhart, and you?"

"Tess Miller."

"Water please?"

"Sure." She hurried to him with the tin cup and lifted him a few inches from the floor.

"Where am I?"

"A nine to ten hour walk from any kind of help, depending on how fast you hike. That's what I've always loved about this place, its isolation. But right now I'd trade it for a phone or a neighbor with a medical degree."

"You're all I have?"

"At the moment."

Those words came out in a whisper as the air between them thickened, cementing a bond that Tess wanted to deny, to break. But she was his lifeline. And this was different from her job as a bodyguard. Maybe because he had invaded her personal alone time—time she needed to refill her well to allow her to do her best work.

She couldn't shake that feeling that perhaps it was something else.

"What happened to you?"

His forehead wrinkled in thought, his expression shadowed. "You said I was shot?"

"Yes. How? Who shot you?"

"I don't remember." He rubbed his temple. "All I remember is ... standing on a cliff." Frustration infused each word.

Okay, this wasn't going to be easy. Usually it wasn't. If she thought of him as an innocent, then hounding him for answers would only add to his confusion, making getting those answers harder.

She rose and peered toward the fireplace. "I thought about fixing some soup for lunch." Normally she wouldn't have chosen soup, but she didn't think he'd be able to eat much else and he needed his strength. "You should try,"—she returned her gaze to him and noticed his eyes were closed—"to eat."

He didn't respond. Leaning over him, she gently shook his arm. His face twitched, but he didn't open his eyes.

Restless, she made her way outside with her shotgun and binoculars, leaving the door open in case he needed her. She scoured anyplace within a hundred yards that could be a hiding place but found nothing. Then she perched on a crop of rocks that projected out from the cliff, giving her a majestic vista of the mountain range and ravines. Autumn crept over the landscape, adding touches of yellows, oranges and reds to her view. Twice a year she visited this cabin, and this was always her favorite spot.

With her binoculars, she studied the landscape around her. Still no sight of anyone else. All the questions she had concerning Shane Burkhart—if that was his name—continued to plague her. Until she got some answers, she'd keep watch on him and the area. She'd learned in her work that she needed to plan for trouble, so if it came she'd be ready. If it didn't, that was great. Often, however, it did. And a niggling sensation along her spine told her something was definitely wrong.

Although there were hunters in the fall in these mountains, she had a strong suspicion that Shane's wound was no accident. The feeling someone shot him deliberately took hold and grew, reinforcing her plan to be extra vigilant.

Mid-afternoon, when the sun was its strongest, Tess stood on her perch and worked the kinks out of her body. Her stranger needed sleep, but she needed to check on him every hour to make sure everything was all right. After one last scan of the terrain, she headed to the door. Inside, her gaze immediately flew to Shane who lay on the floor nearby.

He stared up at her, a smile fighting its way past the pain

reflected in his eyes. "I thought you'd deserted me."

"How long have you been awake?"

"Not long."

"I'll make us some soup." Although the desire to have answers was still strong, she'd forgotten to eat anything today except the energy bar she'd had before he'd arrived. But now her stomach grumbled with hunger.

He reached out for the tin cup a few feet from him. She quickly grabbed it and gave him a drink, this time placing it on the floor beside him.

"I have acetaminophen if you want some for the pain," she said as she straightened, noting the shadows in his eyes. "I imagine your leg and head are killing you."

"Don't use that word. I don't want to think about how close I came to dying. If it hadn't been for you ..."

Again that connection sprang up between them, and she wanted to deny it. She didn't want to be responsible for anyone in her personal life. She had enough of that in her professional life. Her trips to the cabin were the only time she was able to let go of the stress and tension that were so much a part of her life. She stifled a sigh. It wasn't like he'd asked to be shot. "Do you want some acetaminophen?"

"Acetaminophen? That's like throwing a glass of water on a forest fire." He cocked a grin that fell almost instantly. "But I guess I should try."

"Good."

She delved into her first aid kit and produced the bottle of painkillers. After shaking a few into her palm, she gave them to him and again helped him to sip some water. The continual close contact with him played havoc with her senses. Usually she managed to keep her distance—at least emotionally—from her clients and others, but this whole situation was forcing her out of her comfort zone and much closer to him than she was used to.

After he swallowed the pills, she stood and stepped back. "I'd better get started on that soup. It's a little harder up here to make it than at home."

"Are you from Phoenix?"

"Dallas. I come to this cabin every fall and spring, if possible." She crossed to the fireplace, squatted by the logs and began to build a fire. It would be cold once the sun set, so even if she weren't going to fix soup, she would've made a fire to keep them warm.

"Why? This isn't the Ritz."

"I like to get totally away from civilization."

"You've succeeded."

"Why were you hiking up here? Do you have a campsite nearby? Maybe someone's looking for you—someone I can search for tomorrow." Once the fire started going, she found the iron pot and slipped it on the hook that would swing over the blaze.

"No, I came alone. I like to get away from it all, too. Take photographs."

"Where's your camera?" *Where's your wallet and your driver's license?*

"It's all still fuzzy. I think my backpack with my satellite phone and camera went over the cliff when I fell. A ledge broke my fall."

He'd fallen from a cliff? That explanation sent all her alarms blaring. Tess filled the pot with purified water from the container she'd stocked yesterday and dumped some chicken noodle soup from a packet into it. "How did you get shot?" she asked, glancing back to make sure he was awake.

His dark eyebrows slashed downward. "I'm not sure. I think a hunter mistook me for a deer."

"A deer?" *Not likely.*

"I saw two hunters earlier yesterday. One minute I was standing near a cliff enjoying the gorgeous view of the sunset, the next minute ..." His frown deepened. "I woke up on a ledge a few feet from the cliff I had been standing on, so I guess I fell over the edge. It was getting dark, but I could still see the blood on the rock where I must have hit my head and my leg felt on fire."

"You dragged yourself up from the ledge and somehow

made it here?"

"Yes."

She whistled. "You're mighty determined."

"I have a teenage daughter at home. I'm a single dad. I had no choice." Determination glinted in his eyes, almost persuading her he was telling the truth. But what if it was all a lie? She couldn't risk believing him without proof. For all she knew, he was a criminal, and she was in danger.

"Okay, so you think a hunter mistakenly shot you. Are you sure about that? Why would he leave you to die?"

"Maybe he didn't realize what he'd done? Maybe his shot ricocheted off the rock and hit me? I don't know." He scrubbed his hand across his forehead. "What other explanation would there be?"

You're lying to me. She couldn't shake the thought.

"Someone wanted to kill you."

CHAPTER TWO

"Kill me?" Shane asked, his mind muddled by the question. The very thought was too much for him to take in. "Why?"

"Have you angered anyone lately?" The woman pushed her auburn hair away from her face and poked at the fire.

When he didn't say anything, she turned from the blaze and faced him.

"I run a company," he said, "so I suppose there are people who aren't too happy with some of my decisions. But to murder me?" He shook his head once and instantly realized his mistake when the room swirled before him. He closed his eyes and waited for the room to stop spinning, then asked, "Why do you say that?"

"What kind of business do you run?"

"Digital Drive, Inc."

Tess whistled. "A company? DDI is a big corporation, so I would say you could have definitely made some people unhappy. DDI is way ahead of its competition, and that might not set well with some of them."

His company was number one in its area, but there were three others not that far behind. He rubbed his forehead, wishing he could massage the pounding away as he tried to wrap his mind around the fact someone might have deliberately shot him and left him for dead. The realization escalated the hammering against his skull. When he reconnected visually with Tess, concern dulled her vibrant green eyes.

"You don't have to play Superman for my benefit. I do

know a gunshot wound hurts as does a concussion."

He blinked. "You sound like you've had personal experience."

"I was shot once and have suffered two concussions."

"You!"

"I got in the way of a bullet meant for someone else, but in my line of work, that can be a hazard of the job."

"What do you do?"

"I work for a security agency in Dallas. I'm a bodyguard—usually for people who don't want to call attention to the fact they need one. I have protected female clients, but guarding children is my specialty."

He looked her up and down, noting her small frame, and couldn't believe what she'd just said. She wasn't what most men would consider a beauty, but her mass of reddish brown hair that she had tamed enough to put into a ponytail and her crystal clear eyes that spoke of her straightforwardness were appealing. "I've never met a bodyguard."

"Not that I want a job, but you might need the services of one when you get back to Phoenix." She backhanded a wispy curl from her face. Her creamy complexion was dotted with a few freckles across the bridge of her nose.

"So you think someone is trying to murder me?"

"Yes." Tess swung toward the fireplace and removed the iron pot from the hook. "Mmm. This actually smells good, but then I haven't eaten much today."

The scent of chicken noodle soup spiced the air, laced with an earthy odor, but its aroma—or more likely the fact that he might have someone trying to kill him—roiled his stomach. "I'm not very hungry."

She ladled some liquid into another tin cup while steam wafted toward the ceiling. "Try to get some down. You need your strength. My uncle isn't supposed to join me for several days, and either you'll have to hike down the mountain with me or I'll have to leave you alone for most of the day to get you some help."

"I vote for the second option."

When she smiled at him, the warmth of it reached into the ice he'd packed around his heart years ago. He looked away, but she approached, and her steps eroded more than distance between them. "I agree, but I don't want to leave you alone until I know you can make it without me around." She sat cross-legged near him on the floor while he lay on the sleeping bag. "And I want to check out the area for your—hunters. You wouldn't want them paying you a visit here."

The more he thought about it the more he had to acknowledge Tess was probably right about someone wanting him dead. Although he didn't remember exactly what happened, it was unlikely a hunter had pulled the trigger. He'd rather be cautious than ignore her warnings and be murdered.

So who knew he was going hiking in the mountains? It had been a sudden decision. At work his executive assistant, Diane Flood, was the only one he'd told. She'd been with him from the beginning. It couldn't have been her. But perhaps she'd told someone. His whereabouts wasn't a state secret. Plus, he usually came to this area of wilderness when he wanted to be alone, and a lot of people knew that. And even if someone hadn't known where he was going, it would've been easy to follow him. It wasn't like he'd been looking for a tail.

And what was he even thinking, worried about having been *tailed*? This wasn't his life.

Which brought him back to the question: who wanted him dead? A few rivals popped into his mind. His business could be cutthroat at times, but would any of them resort to murdering the competition? He pictured two of them, Anthony Revell and Mark Collins. Anthony's main offices were in Phoenix. Mark worked out of Los Angeles but often visited his offices in Phoenix. He hadn't made an offer to merge with the company Shane wanted in order to expand DDI's share of the market, but Shane wouldn't be surprised if he did. Neither Anthony nor Mark wanted Shane to succeed with the merger with Virtual Technologies.

"I'm going to lift you up." Tess's husky voice pierced his thoughts. "That way you can drink your soup."

The softness of her touch belied the very idea she protected people for a living. A warm flush infused his face at her nearness. Ever since his wife had died four years ago, he'd kept his distance from women, wanting nothing to do with a casual relationship, while they had thrown themselves at him. They'd seen an unattached rich man, ripe for the picking. He was thankful that his work had given him the direction he'd needed at a terrible time in his life.

While Tess supported his back, he took the cup and tried to bring it to his lips. His arms trembled so much she reached around and stabilized his hands by covering them with hers. Her warmth against them sucked the breath from his lungs until he determinedly shut down his reaction to her.

I'm just grateful, tired and weak. She saved my life. That's all there is. All? He scuffed at the direction of his thoughts. This was a big deal. He made it a point not to depend on anyone. However now, he had no choice but to depend on Tess Miller.

If she hadn't been holding the cup, too, he would have dropped it and scalded himself. Frustration burned a hole into his gut. "I should be able to feed myself," he muttered and let her lift the tin cup to his lips.

"And you will as soon as you get your strength back. This will help."

After several cautious sips, Shane sagged back against her completely, but she still supported his weight. Exhaustion hovered at the edges of his mind, tugging at him. "I appreciate...what you've done for me."

"You're welcome. More?"

He gave a slight nod and drank the soup, the warm liquid sliding down his throat as his eyelids closed. "I think...that's all."

Sleep descended quickly and whisked him into the blackness.

After Tess finished eating her own soup, she strode outside with her binoculars and both weapons. Nothing he'd told her had calmed the alarm bells going off in her mind. She didn't like unsolved gunshot wounds, and she couldn't shake the feeling someone was out there watching them waiting for the right moment. But all she saw were oaks, junipers and pinion pines blanketing the landscape, their scent hanging on the light breeze that blew wisps of her hair about her face.

She'd learned in her line of work to be cautious and slightly paranoid. She circled the cabin and the small area where it perched on a cliff at one end of a high country ridge then headed back to the cabin. The sun behind her started its descent toward the horizon. When she reached the door, the hairs on her nape tingled. Again, the feeling of being watched crawled up her spine. She swept one last look over the landscape before going inside.

With a glance toward the sleeping Shane, she quickly crossed the room and withdrew extra ammunition from the locked cabinet and stuffed it into her jeans pocket. If someone were out there, she would be ready for him. After talking with Shane, she had no doubt she needed to carry both of her weapons at all times.

There had been a time when she'd been passive, waiting for life to happen around her. Not anymore, thanks to Uncle Jack. She no longer ran from life or any type of situation, whether dangerous or not.

"Going hunting?"

She whirled around at the sound of Shane's voice, the shotgun grasped in front of her like a shield. "No."

"Then why that?" His gaze veered to the gun, a frown wrinkling his forehead. "Is there some kind of trouble outside?"

I think we're being watched. "Just getting prepared."

"Because you think someone's after me?"

She nodded, seeing the realization in his eyes. "And I think you see the possibility now, too."

"I want to believe it was a careless hunter, but I just can't any longer. Don't you think they're long gone by now? I did go over a cliff when I was shot."

"What if the shooter had been where he couldn't get to you

easily? You said it was late when it happened yesterday. Maybe he came back to make sure you were dead. Maybe he followed your trail. It was easy enough for me to find which direction you came from."

"I guess that's a possibility. DDI is close to introducing a revolutionary microchip as well as merging with another company. Let's just say a couple of my competitors would like to beat me to the punch and stop me from strengthening my position in the marketplace."

"How did you find this cabin?"

"I saw smoke. I followed it." He shifted in the sleeping bag and winced.

If he did, so could the person after him, even if some of the rocky terrain obscured Shane's path part of the way. "Do you want some more pain medicine?"

"No, but I could use a drink of water."

She poured some into the tin cup and gave it to him. His hand shook as he drank, but she let him do it by himself. She sensed he needed to feel he could do it himself.

"Thanks." He again adjusted his body, trying to make himself more comfortable on the hard floor.

"I think it's safe enough to move you to the cot if we take it slow and easy." Tess took the cup from him and set it on the table next to the shotgun.

He glanced at the cot a few feet away against the wall. "I'm in your hands."

Tess didn't respond. What she wanted to tell him was that she wasn't responsible for him or anybody. And yet, she was, and there was no way she could deny it.

She positioned herself behind him, squatted and locked her arms around his chest. "Okay. On the count of three help me as much as you can. One. Two. Three."

Aware of the gunshot wound, she carefully hoisted him from the floor. A groan escaped his lips. When he stood, she supported his weight while he slung his arm over her shoulder. She clasped him from his left side so he wouldn't use that leg.

When he lay on the bunk, he trembled. She covered him

with an extra blanket that Uncle Jack kept at the cabin. But before she could straighten and step away from Shane, he captured her wrist and held her close in a surprisingly tight clasp for someone in such a weakened state.

"Thanks. I've been saying that a lot lately, but I would have probably died if you hadn't been here."

Again, wanting to deny his words, she looked at his face and saw red tinting his cheeks. Listening to him panting after that small exertion, she knew he wouldn't be walking out of the mountains anytime soon. "It was nothing," she finally said and pulled away, his grasp loosening immediately.

He let go of her wrist. "Nothing? I could argue that with you, but it would take too much effort."

"I'm doing what has to be done. Anyone would have."

"Perhaps." His slate gray gaze fused with hers. "Do you always have such a hard time accepting a compliment?" He swiped away the beads of sweat on his forehead, his arm thumping against the canvas of the cot as it dropped back to his side.

"I couldn't let you die." She put a few feet between them. She needed to think of this man as a client, someone to protect. Or a criminal evading the police or other criminals. She only had his word that he was who he said he was. She didn't know what Shane Burkhart looked like. Either way, she needed to don her professional façade.

"Don't shortchange yourself, and I'll ignore the fact you didn't answer my question." He licked his lips. "Can I have some more water?"

When she scooped some out of the container, she noticed she was running low. She frowned as she stared at the few inches of water left in the pot.

"What's wrong, Tess?"

When he said her name, it felt almost like a caress, and her heartbeat accelerated. She quickly squashed any kind of reaction to his smoky timbre. "I'll need to go get some more water at the spring. I think we have enough for this evening, but first thing tomorrow morning, we'll need more."

When she gave him the cup, his fingers, warm against her skin, brushed over hers and sent goose bumps zipping up her arm. She quickly withdrew a few feet.

He downed the liquid. "I never drink this much water." He lost his grasp of the empty cup, and it clanged against the floor.

"Obviously, your body needs it." She stooped to pick the cup up. Her gaze connected to his for a moment before his eyelids closed. He seemed to be fighting to stay awake.

When she studied his face, she glimpsed the paleness beneath the flush to his cheeks. She neared him and grazed her fingertips across his forehead. His skin was on fire, and she snatched her hand back, fear taking hold.

He had a fever, a complication she had hoped to avoid. But she realized that had been a pipe dream. When she'd cleaned his wounds, they'd been filled with dirt matted in the blood around the edges as well as embedded in the injuries.

With a glance at the container of water on the table, she sighed and grabbed her shotgun and flashlight then the handle on the plastic jug. She had to go to the spring. She needed to get water now.

She gave him one quick look, then left, heading behind the cabin and down the slope. The temperature had dropped at least ten degrees as dusk settled over the landscape. She needed to hurry. Even with a flashlight, it wasn't safe traversing out here in the dark. The uneven terrain and sheer cliffs heightened the danger she felt. This far from civilization, there were bears and mountain lions. And most likely a murderer.

At the spring, she clicked on her flashlight to illuminate the path back to the cabin, dark from the overhanging branches of the trees around the area. She quickly scooped up enough water to fill the plastic gallon jug, twisted the cap on tight, and then turned to make her way back. Her foot caught on a rock, and she fell onto her knees. Pain shot up her legs from the hard impact with the ground. She took two breaths and tried to exhale her fear.

She started to push herself to a standing position but stopped when her gaze locked onto a couple of cigarette butts—two to be exact—near the base of a large bush next to the spring. She picked one up and scrutinized it. From the looks of it, the butt hadn't been there long. It certainly hadn't been there yesterday when she'd come for water. The implication escalated her concern they weren't alone.

Using her flashlight, she studied the ground and noticed the footprints. Hiking boots. Only one person. That thought should've relieved her, but it didn't. She knew the damage one person could do to another.

She stepped behind a large bush and looked back at Uncle Jack's cabin. She could see part of the front door. The vegetation was trampled here. The perfect place to stand if someone wanted to watch the door without being seen. Another three cigarette butts lay in the dust near her feet.

Clutching the shotgun in one hand and the water container and flashlight in the other, Tess hurried toward the cabin a hundred yards away. Her heart pounded against her ribcage with each step she took. Someone had been watching her and the cabin. She'd checked the spring out earlier but from the rise twenty yards away. He'd probably hidden behind the bush, out of sight of her survey.

But when she'd circled the cabin earlier and checked hiding places, he hadn't been there. Had he retreated? Come after that? She'd been armed. Maybe that had scared him off—for the time being.

I won't be caught off guard again. On her job she'd always listened to her intuition. She should have scoured the area more closely until she'd found the intruder, but she hadn't wanted to wander too far from the cabin in case her patient had needed her. Now she didn't know where the assailant was, and she'd be busy and distracted fighting to save Shane's life.

As she approached the door, all her instincts were on high alert. She scanned the terrain one last time before opening the door. At least she could engage the deadbolt tonight while she tried to keep Shane alive.

Just inside the entrance, she froze. She dropped the jug and flashlight, raised the shotgun, and aimed.

CHAPTER THREE

"Step away from him. I have a gun pointed at you." Tess braced her feet apart, prepared to use the weapon.

The intruder slowly straightened, giving her a glimpse of his battered old navy blue ball cap. She sagged with relief. "Uncle Jack! You're not supposed to be here for two days. You just dropped me off in the parking area yesterday. You should have come up then with me."

Her uncle swung around, his bushy eyebrows slashing downward. "Miles from civilization and you still manage to find trouble."

"In this case, trouble came knocking." She eased the shotgun down and placed the weapon on the table. "And it looks like it could get worse." Snatching up her first aid kit and the water she had already purified, she approached Uncle Jack and gave him a hug. "I'm glad you're here."

"So am I."

Tess turned toward her patient. "He's got a fever."

"Yeah, I noticed. How did he get shot?"

"Good question. He doesn't know. He was on a cliff one second, the next tumbling over the edge. But after what I found at the spring—"

"What did you find?"

"A couple of cigarette butts and a set of footprints behind that big bush by the spring. I'd checked that area earlier and they weren't there then. Someone's after him, and he was watching the cabin. The trouble is, I don't know if I believe his story."

"Which is?"

"He says he's Shane Burkhart, but I didn't find a wallet or any kind of ID on him. So he could be anyone."

Her uncle again examined the man lying on the cot. "I thought I recognized him. He's Shane Burkhart. I saw his photo in the business section of the newspaper a few weeks back about a possible merger. What does he think?"

"He thought it was a hunter until I convinced him otherwise. He doesn't know who's after him." She moved to the side of the bunk and knelt. "I dropped the water jug in the doorway. Can you boil it for me? I have a feeling we may need it."

"Sure." He grabbed the container and unscrewed its cap as he made his way to the fireplace. "I'll put it on the fire then take a look around. See if I can follow the man's tracks."

"Be careful."

"Tessa, I'm always careful." Uncle Jack winked at her and left the cabin.

She turned her attention to Shane, relieved she didn't have to worry about who he was anymore. One less problem she had to deal with. Shane's groan brought her gaze to his face. He was covered in sweat, heat radiating off him.

"You can't die. I won't let you," Tess whispered.

Think. What more could she do in this primitive environment? Liquids and acetaminophen were all she had to fight a fever. Taking out the bottle of medicine, she mashed three tablets and put them into a cup of water. Somehow she had to get him to drink this.

Sitting on the edge of the cot, she lifted his dead weight, supporting him with one arm while holding the cup in the other hand. At least he wasn't delirious and fighting her. *Thank you, Lord. I need all the help I can get.*

"Come on, Shane. You need this." She prayed her words would reach into his fever-racked mind and make sense to him.

"Elena." He moaned and shook his head, pushing her hand away.

Elena? His wife? No, he'd shared he was a single parent. *Then ex-wife or daughter? Girlfriend?*

Shoving her curiosity to the background, Tess put the tin cup on the floor and tried to secure Shane more firmly against her. When he settled down, she picked up the drink and lifted it to his lips, forcing them open with its rim. At first the water dribbled out of his mouth, but finally, with a lot of gentle coercion and then dire threats of further bodily harm, she managed to get some down him. The front of his shirt and her arm were wet, but she estimated she'd gotten almost half of the doctored liquid in him. She could give him more acetaminophen in a few hours.

After examining the wounds again and finding to her relief that they weren't bleeding, she took a cloth, dipped it into the last of the purified water and bathed his face and neck. She refused to give into the fear building inside. She would not let him die. She would not.

"You listen up, Shane. You'll get well, hear me? You have to."

When Uncle Jack returned, a scowl lined his craggy features. "I didn't see any signs of his assailant." He gestured toward Shane. "The footprints I found at the spring led away from here. But I don't think we should let down our guard."

As much as she didn't like depending on anyone, Tess was glad to hear her uncle say "our guard."

She checked the pot on the fire, removed it and let the boiling water cool on the table. "Why did you come two days early?"

He shrugged. "Last spring we didn't get to spend as much time together as I wished. I'm getting old. I don't put off things like I used to so I told my buddies we would have to reschedule."

Tess sighed. "I came a week early. I should have waited, but I didn't want my boss to give me a long-term assignment and miss this good weather and healing time. There are only so many perfect weeks up here."

"It seems the Lord conspired for us to help this young man."

Tess dragged a chair to the bunk and sat. "I guess so, but I was really looking forward to peace and quiet. I get enough tension at work. I prefer my vacations to be relaxing."

"I know, Tessa." Her uncle clasped her shoulder. "I sometimes miss that life. Mine is too quiet."

She glanced toward him as he shuffled to the table and eased into the other chair. Tired lines cut deep into his tanned face. His blue eyes didn't hold the sparkle they usually did. Retirement wasn't treating him kindly. "Have you thought of doing something with your expertise? Look what you did for me."

He swept his arm down his body. "What? The NYPD didn't need my services any longer. I was forced to retire when I didn't want to. I'm only sixty-three."

"That's my point. You still have a lot of time to do whatever you want. You have a black belt in karate and knowledge in all kinds of ways to protect yourself. You were in law enforcement for forty years. Uncle Jack, you were a captain when you retired. You have lots of information and abilities stored up there." Tess pointed toward his head. "Do something with it besides playing chess and golf. You used to make fun of people who spent half their day at the golf course."

"I'm into bowling now. Golf and I didn't mix. Besides, it gets hot as—let's just say very hot here in Arizona."

"Go back to New York then. You have buddies there."

"Too cold in winter."

She laughed. Her uncle had grown up in Arizona and his heart had always been here, even during the years he'd lived in New York City. He'd been a grump during the winter months when the temperature got below freezing, but his late wife, Patricia, was a New Yorker through and through. She never wanted to leave Manhattan. "I was glad you lived in the city. I owe you so much."

"You're family. What's an uncle for if not to teach his niece how to defend herself?"

"Not all uncles can do that. When I was beat up and left for dead, I decided I wasn't ever going to be defenseless again, and you gave me a way to protect myself—and now others. I make a pretty good living out of all you taught me. I know I've told you thanks before, but I'm telling you again. You gave me a second chance." As she had Shane, at least she hoped.

Uncle Jack snorted and scanned the room. "Where's the coffee, girl?"

"I haven't fixed any since my guest arrived. I was kinda busy today."

"Well, I guess we better get a pot on because it may be a long night." He pushed to his feet and walked to the fireplace's mantle where the necessary items to prepare what he lived on most of the day were stored.

"Great. Your coffee is much better than mine. I was just waiting for you to show up."

He gave her another snort and finished the task, then took a seat at the table. "So what's your plan concerning our patient?"

Again the word *our*. Although her father was still alive, the very thought of him brought a chill washing through her. He had retired and now lived in a small town outside of Phoenix, but she hadn't seen him on her trips to visit Uncle Jack, and that was the way it would stay if she had anything to say about it. Her dad had bullied her verbally most of her life. As a teenager she'd been timid until a home invasion had left her badly hurt. That was when her uncle had shown up. He'd taken her back to live with him and Aunt Patricia in Manhattan. Her father had been glad to be rid of her.

"Earth to moon."

"Sorry. Just thinking about how much I love you." She knew that would fluster him, and he wouldn't probe too much into why she had been in deep thought. He was the dad she should have had, except her uncle was always trying to reconcile her and her biological father, his brother. But she'd lived under that man's iron rule for too long. Never again. "Tomorrow as soon as Shane is out of trouble, I'll be hiking down the mountain to get help."

"And leave me with him?"

"He won't bite, but our little friend by the spring might. Think you can baby-sit Shane for the day until I can get a helicopter to airlift him out of here? Maybe you can catch a ride home since you're such an *old* man."

The dare, she knew, would rile his temper. With a sharp look toward her, he grumbled something under his breath as he covered the short distance to the fireplace. The only thing Tess heard was "the things I do for you."

"Will you pour me some? It's gonna be a long night."

He poured the coffee and handed her the cup. "I'm going back outside to keep watch. Be useful."

"Don't drink too much coffee. One of us should get some sleep."

"Girl, it isn't going to be me. I don't sleep much anyway, and there's no way I would with someone after him. So I guess you'd better."

She took a long sip, relishing the scent and taste, strong and rich. Then she lifted her chin and stared at her uncle. "Not until his fever breaks. So I guess we'll both be up."

He retrieved the shotgun from the table and with his coffee headed outside, muttering something about how the patient better be worth all the trouble he was causing.

Tess chuckled when the door closed. Her uncle would have been the first person to help Shane. He was always rescuing people and animals. Since he had returned to the Phoenix area three years ago, he'd filled his house and barn with adopted pets. He'd told her the Lord had put him on this earth for that very reason.

She took another sip of her drink, then turned her attention to her patient. She surveyed Shane's tensed features, her fingers combing his dark, wet hair back from his face. Taking the cloth, she mopped away the sweat, only to have it coat his skin almost instantly again. The bond she'd felt earlier strengthened. She'd never forget this man—her stranger. Although she'd had other lives in her hands, protecting someone against a possible threat was nothing like nursing someone back to health. Shane was completely dependent on her. The feeling terrified her, but there was something different, too. Something she couldn't quite name.

After propping him halfway up against the pillow, she poured some water into a tin cup and tried to coax the liquid down his throat, using her fingertips to lightly massage the sides of his neck. His eyes blinked open.

"Come on, drink this," Tess whispered, her gaze locked with his fevered one. "I'm not going to let you dehydrate."

He took several swallows, and then he frowned and knocked the cup away. "I don't know you!" His voice rose louder with each word. His body stiffened.

Although some liquid spilled from the cup, Tess managed to save a little. "Shane, drink," she said in her most commanding tone.

She brought the cup to his lips, but his eyelids slid down and the tension siphoned from him. With the little water left, she got another few gulps down his throat between groans. Then she ran a cool cloth over his face. He batted at her arm, twisting away.

Afraid he would reopen his wounds, she held his limb against his side. "I will not let you die. I will not let you ruin my vacation."

His eyes popped open, and he looked straight through her. "Elena, you came back." A smile graced his lips for a few seconds before he surrendered to sleep.

Do I look like Elena?

Before she could ponder that question, she heard Shane mumbling, "Don't leave me. Rachel needs you."

Now Rachel? Who is that? The daughter?

More questions drenched her thoughts, all involving this man. She needed to get back to Dallas to her simple life where she knew the rules and her boundaries.

Lord, I need You to heal Shane. I've done all I can. Now he's in Your hands.

After Tess spent hours forcing water, some laced with

acetaminophen, down Shane's throat, bathing his face with a cold cloth, and praying like crazy, his fever broke. She sat exhausted, her head dropping toward her chest. Fighting sleep, she jerked up and spied the pot on the fire. Coffee. She needed some if she was going to stay awake and get him the medical and police help he needed.

She headed for the fireplace and filled her mug. When she turned back toward Shane, his dull gaze captured hers. She went still, waiting to see if he was coherent and aware of his surroundings. He eased his eyelids closed for a moment, then looked at her again.

"Just checking I'm not dreaming," he said, swallowing hard. He lifted his hand and touched his chest. "I'm wet."

"It's a combination of sweat and water. You weren't always as willing to take your sips as I'd hoped."

"Is there someone else here? I thought I remembered seeing a man standing over me." His forehead creased as his gaze scanned the cabin. "I guess I dreamed that."

She shook her head. "My uncle is around somewhere. He comes in every once in a while to let me know that all's well outside."

Shane's attention strayed to an oblong window, set high near the ceiling for privacy. "It's night."

Tess cut the space between them, took a seat, and drank several sips of her coffee. After glancing at her watch, she said, "It's almost dawn."

"Your uncle's been outside all night?"

"Part of it."

"Why?"

"I found footprints by the spring. Somebody was watching the cabin yesterday."

"So he's been on guard?"

"Something like that." She smiled for the first time in hours. "Truthfully my uncle likes the solitude. When he's up here, he spends a good deal of time outside even at night." She was a lot like that, too.

Shane swiped his hand across his forehead. "So I'm not

only indebted to you but now to your uncle as well."

"Don't make it sound like a dose of awful tasting medicine."

"I'm not used to depending on others."

Neither am I. Another link formed between them, deepening their bond.

"You don't owe me a thing. When dawn breaks, I'll hike out of here while Uncle Jack watches over you. By evening, you should be enjoying a nice visit to a hospital."

Shane flinched. "Not something I'm looking forward to. I make a habit of avoiding hospitals."

"I don't think you can this time. Would you like anything to drink?"

He shook his head, but immediately winced at the action. "I forgot my head was split open."

The memories of the two times she'd suffered a concussion crept into her mind. She shoved them away before the doubts took hold. She wouldn't allow those doubts in her life anymore. "How could you forget that? I've had a concussion, and I know how painful it can be."

"My leg hurts even more." He studied her for a long moment. "You've had a concussion as well as a shotgun wound. I remember you telling me that." A shadow entered his eyes. "Your life is full of danger."

She stood and strode toward the door, purposefully ignoring his last statement. Her life before she'd become a bodyguard had been full of a different kind of peril—a peril that threatened the type of person she was. Not only had Uncle Jack and his wife taken her in as a teenager, but also they had taught her about the Lord. Through Him she'd gained an inner strength. "I hope your injuries won't keep you in the hospital long." Stepping outside, she surveyed the area and found her uncle sitting on an outcropping, as though announcing to whomever was watching that Shane had people protecting him. "Uncle Jack, you're a sitting duck."

"I'm fine. I can survey the area better up here."

Tess shook her head. Her uncle had once told her that the

Lord looked out for him and he wouldn't die until God wanted him to join Him in heaven. "Shane's awake."

"Coherent?"

"Yep."

Her uncle swung around and came toward her. "Good. It should be dawn in another half an hour. Then you can boogie on down the mountain."

Although he'd tried to hide it behind a flippant comment, concern laced his statement. "What are you not saying?"

He rubbed the back of his neck. "I've just got that feeling I get when things aren't right. We don't know who we're dealing with, and that always bothers me."

Over the years she'd learned to respect her instinctive feelings. "I'm heading out as soon as it's light enough."

"Great. I'll fix some breakfast." He passed her at the door and went to the food supplies he'd brought. "I'll make some oatmeal and fry bacon. We have to eat it before it goes bad."

"Aren't you supposed to be watching your fat intake?" Tess asked, downing the last swig of her coffee before pouring another cup. Her uncle always brought items to the cabin like bacon even though it meant keeping it cold on the hike up the mountain. He told her once it was a luxury he insisted on having at least for a meal or two.

"Tessa—" Uncle Jack shook his head, tsking, "Tessa, I'm on vacation. Haven't you heard calories and fat content don't count then?"

"I missed that bulletin." She faced Shane, who had been following their bantering. "Would you like some water?"

"No, coffee. The smell is driving me crazy."

"Caffeine probably isn't the best thing for you at the moment. You need rest."

"Didn't you hear your uncle? When you're on vacation, it doesn't count what you eat and, as far as I'm concerned, drink." Slowly, he inched up to a half sitting position.

"Humph." She poured the last of the coffee into his mug, and then handed it to Shane.

As he lifted his drink to his lips, his hand shook, sloshing some of the liquid. He drew in a deep breath. "I think I dreamed about this last night."

"I suppose it's mostly water, so it shouldn't do too much harm."

"After a crack on my head and a gunshot wound, I think a cup of coffee is the least of my worries. Especially with someone out to kill me."

"Which brings me back to, who would want you dead? Any ideas?"

Shane sipped his drink, staring at the far wall. "I've got two competitors who don't play by the book and are ruthless in some of their practices, especially Anthony Revell. He lives in Phoenix. But the other, Mark Collins, isn't too far away—Los Angeles."

"Okay. How about people who have worked for you? Have you made anyone mad lately?"

"Four hundred people work at my office in Phoenix, not to mention the thousands worldwide. The odds are there are a few who aren't happy with me."

"Anyone threatened you?"

Shane cocked his head to the side, staring off into space for a long moment. "Six months ago, I personally fired one of my researchers. He was stealing information and selling it to the highest bidder."

"He could be the one. Who is he?"

"He's in Mexico. Fled prosecution and disappeared."

"When you get back to town, you need to have the police look into it. And get some protection until you know who shot you."

"You're the only bodyguard I know." While taking a sip, he watched her over the rim of the cup.

She felt the silent question. No, she couldn't guard Shane. This personal connection they had between them was exactly the kind of thing she tried to avoid with her clients. She needed a level of detachment to do her job. Tess barely knew him, but she already knew there was no way she could be objective. After sitting by his bed, struggling to save him, she'd forged a bond with him that could threaten her peace of mind if she allowed him in her life. "I don't think I'm the person for you. You have a security team at the company?"

"Yes."

"Ask your head guy. He should be able to find a person who would work for you."

"I'm a private person. I don't want a stranger guarding me. You aren't a stranger. And right now isn't the best time to let people know someone is after me. I'm in the middle of some delicate negotiations that could fall apart if they knew."

"Your life may depend on it." Even after she said that, from the doubt in his eyes, she wasn't sure if he would pursue her suggestion. She would talk to her uncle about trying to persuade Shane to get protection.

"Breakfast is ready." Uncle Jack brought the pot of oatmeal to the table.

Tess dished up some hot cereal with honey, minus the milk, for herself and Shane. She took him his bowl and assisted him so he could feed himself, then she went back and grabbed a couple of slices of bacon.

When she was finished with her breakfast, she quickly gathered her possessions and backpack for the hike. "I've got to get a move on it if you're to be rescued today. A helicopter would have trouble landing up here at night."

Shane set his spoon in his bowl. "You're going now? Will I see you later?"

"I'll make sure you get the help you need. Uncle Jack will take care of you until the rescuers arrive." She headed toward the door, hurrying before Shane asked another question she didn't want to answer.

She would make sure he was all right before she left, but she needed to cut her ties to him. She motioned for her uncle to follow her outside and waited by the door for him to join her.

During the long night, she'd contemplated what Shane's life was like. When she guarded a person, she made it her business to know all she could about her client. With him, she didn't know much, so she'd filled in the blank spaces. She'd often do that when she people watched. It helped her hone her skills, reading someone's body language—something she'd become quite good at. That had saved her life on several occasions. But in Shane's case, the spaces she'd filled in became more personal. She still couldn't shake the questions—who were Elena and Rachel? Probably his wife and daughter, but she wanted to know for sure.

The fact that she wanted to know bothered her.

"You aren't going to see him again?" Uncle Jack asked when he closed the door.

"I can't. You need to make sure he understands the gravity of his situation."

"Oh, I will. I have the whole day to work on him."

"Maybe you could even help him find someone to be his bodyguard."

"I'll do some checking when I get home."

"I'll be at your house until I can make arrangements to fly back to Dallas."

"I thought you had the week?"

Tess looked at the closed door and shook her head. "I think I'd better go now. I'll take your car, so you won't have to worry. Call me on my cell, and I'll come pick you up at the hospital."

Her uncle studied her. After a moment, she broke eye contact, but she realized it was useless. He knew her too well. "But you won't even go in to see him again?"

"No."

"Chicken." He dug his set of keys out of his jeans pocket and handed them to her.

"When it comes to relationships and men, yes, I am. Like you, I've seen the darker side of life with our jobs." She cared for Shane, and that was the problem. She waved and started toward the trail that led down the mountain.

Hours later near the bottom of the mountain, Tess paused and took her binoculars out to scan the area below where her uncle's car was parked. Another one was parked nearby—a black truck. Hunters? Hikers? Or a killer? Although there was only one decent trail that led to the cabin on this side of the mountain, and she hadn't encountered anyone on the path, the assailant might have gone another way. She would check the truck and get the license plate number before she left.

Finally, she neared the end of the trail. Uncle Jack's Jeep was in the lot thirty yards away, just around a bend. She hurried her pace as she turned on her cell phone. She'd tried several times on her hike down, but there hadn't been any reception. She probably would have to drive to the main highway–an hour's drive on a dirt road—before she'd get service.

She reached her uncle's Jeep and scanned the area for the black truck. It was gone. The hairs on her nape lifted. Something wasn't right. She inspected the ground where it had been parked and found cigarette butts littering the earth. The same brand of cigarettes as the ones found at the spring.

CHAPTER FOUR

Tess half leaned, half sat on the deck railing at Uncle Jack's ranch house south of Phoenix, enjoying a cup of coffee and watching birds fly into a twenty-foot saguaro ten yards away. A Gila woodpecker poked its head out of a hole in the cactus, the bright red splotch on the top of it instantly reminding her of Shane's gunshot wound at the cabin only three days before. She knew he would be all right. Her uncle had kept her informed, not just about his progress, but about the number of times he'd asked about her.

It was a good thing she'd cut her ties to the man. Even days later, Shane Burkhart dominated her thoughts more than she wished. She kept telling herself it was because she'd saved his life, but in her line of work, she'd saved plenty of lives, and that hadn't caused her to dwell on their image or go over the words they'd exchanged. But Shane . . . she couldn't forget the steel gray of his eyes, his muscular build, his unruly dark hair ...

The blare of a police siren startled her, pulling her mind from her memories of a man she needed to forget. She answered the special ring tone on her cell phone that indicated it was Uncle Jack. "I thought you'd be out of cell range by now."

"Nope. Almost to the bottom of my mountain, though. Turned off the main highway five minutes ago. Did you decide to stay longer? There's no reason to go back to Dallas so soon. You still have vacation time, and you could always come back to the cabin."

It might never be the quiet, peaceful retreat it used to be.

"Not this time, but I'm staying at your ranch until it's time to go home." She nearly stumbled over the word *home*, because she really didn't have one. The apartment she shared with another female bodyguard was hardly more than a place to sleep and warm up a can of soup. They rarely saw each other, since their schedules were so different. "I'll keep Charlie in line," she said in reference to the only cowhand her uncle employed.

"Your dad's place isn't too far away. You ought to pay him a visit. Find some resolution with him."

She shivered at the thought of seeing her father, the memories of his angry, wounding words. "Not gonna happen. And you know why."

"You need to forgive him, so you can move on."

Tess released a long breath. Deep down, she knew he was right. "I don't know if I can. You should have been my dad. In every way that matters, you are."

"There's a reason the Lord wants us to forgive."

She was desperate to change the subject. "When's Shane leaving the hospital?"

"Why don't you go see him and find out?"

Tess rolled her eyes and looked skyward to see a hawk overhead. Brilliant. She'd changed the topic to another one she needed to avoid. Her uncle had tried to get her to see Shane for two days.

"Still there, Tessa?"

"You wouldn't return to the cabin if he wasn't going to be okay, and I'm sure he's got plenty of family and friends looking in on him. Why do I need to visit him?"

"I didn't save his life. Don't you want to see how well he's doing?"

"My job is over. I saved him. I'm letting the doctors take care of him now."

"Not every marriage ends like your parents' did."

Suddenly Tess felt twelve again, watching the gurney being rolled out of her home. The sheet flapped in the wind, covering the body that used to be her mother. Tears pricked

Tess's eyes. She blinked and tried to push the mental picture away, but the memory of her father's insults bombarded her.

"I don't want to talk about my parents." Her mother committed suicide, leaving her alone with a father who didn't want to be one.

"I was happily married for thirty years."

"Patricia died, and you shut down. I wasn't sure you'd ever come out of your depression. So no, thank you. The divorce rate is sky high. I don't want to add another number to it." *How in the world had they gotten on the subject of marriage?*

Uncle Jack snorted. "Chicken. I didn't think you feared anything. Now, I know you do."

"Nice try. It isn't going to work. Enjoy your time at the cabin for me. I'm going to kick back here and relax. Maybe go riding. See a few friends who still live here."

His robust laughter filled her ear, and she pulled her phone away until he quieted. "I have friends here and in Dallas."

"You're in Phoenix maybe twice a year, if I'm lucky. I suppose you're in Dallas a little more, but not much."

"I go where the job takes me. Will you be back before I leave?"

"Yes, I've got to spend a couple of days with my gal."

Although she knew her uncle loved to hunt at this time of year, she wondered if he was giving her a chance to reconsider helping Shane. "Love you, Uncle Jack. See you in a week."

When she disconnected, she stuffed her cell phone in her front jeans pocket, took a deep breath of the fresh air—its scent different from Dallas—and went back into the kitchen. She headed for the coffeepot, refilled her mug and started for the deck again.

The doorbell rang. She changed directions and made her way to the foyer. Wondering who was at the door, she checked out the peephole and frowned.

Why is he *here?*

She stepped away and debated whether to open the door or not. Uncle Jack's earlier taunt about being afraid of Shane mocked her, and she reached for the knob. When she opened the door, her gaze locked with Shane's, a gleam in his eyes as if he'd seen her hesitation. She remembered those beautiful eyes—hard to forget that steel gray—but nothing could've prepared her for his mesmerizing look.

She stared, dumbfounded, until he broke the silence. "May I come in?"

She mentally shook herself and opened the door wider. Every instinct shouted for her to slam it in his face and lock him out. Too much idle time on this vacation—it was messing with her nerves. And this was why she worked more cases than any other bodyguard at the agency—she needed to stay busy. To stay detached. Alone.

He entered, leaning heavily against a cane, and brushed past her. One of his hands clutched a brown paper bag.

When he paused, scanning the foyer, she gestured toward the sack. "What's in there?"

"Lunch."

"What if I've already eaten?"

"Then I wasted my money. Have you?"

A *yes* was on the tip of her tongue, but she couldn't lie, especially not to him. "No."

"Good. I brought your favorite sandwich from your favorite Phoenix café."

Surprise widened her eyes. "What?"

"A spicy taco sandwich from Pete's Deli."

"How did you know?"

"Jack."

Suspicion pinched her mouth as she narrowed her gaze on him. "What else did you ask him?"

"Why you didn't come to the hospital to see me?"

She was going to wring Uncle Jack's neck when she saw him. "What did he say?"

"That I needed to ask you. Then he gave me directions to his ranch and told me I should bring you that sandwich. I happen to like Pete's Deli too, so I also got us both something."

She poked her head outside and surveyed the front yard,

noting a Lexus but nobody else. "You came all this way by yourself?"

"I'm a big boy, and the doc okayed me to drive."

She huffed. "Somehow I get the feeling even if he didn't, you'd do what you wanted. You do realize there's a killer out there after you?"

"Yes." He glanced down at his leg and the cane, then met her eyes with a smile. "Now, where do you want to eat?"

His determination reminded her of herself. No wonder he was the head of a multi-million dollar corporation.

"Out on the back deck. Would you like coffee?" She moved toward the kitchen, her stomach rumbling with hunger at the mention of her favorite sandwich. She decided she would hear him out, and then send him on his way.

"That's fine. I like mine black."

Just like me. What other similarities did they have? She filled a mug for him, then held the back door open for him to maneuver through the exit to the wraparound deck. "The table and chairs are this way. The eastern view is better." Her attention latched onto the mountains in the distance, and she thought back to when she'd met Shane. Who was after him? Why? And why wasn't he more concerned? Did the police have a lead? She intended to find out.

After Shane settled into a chair at the round glass table, he placed his cane on the deck and opened the bag. "I brought you two of them."

She'd kill her uncle, telling Shane she always ate two. But how often did she get Pete's? "Uncle Jack ratted me out, huh?"

"No, it was just a hunch."

"Really? Do I look like I overeat?" She slid his mug across the table to him. "Wait. Don't answer that."

"Don't be ridiculous. I'm not sure why, but it felt right to get you two. I always have seconds of something I really enjoy."

After blessing her food, she took a bite of her sandwich, savoring the spicy flavor of the taco meat mixed with lettuce, tomatoes and cheese. "No one makes it better than Pete. I've been going to his deli since I was a kid."

"So, you grew up here?"

Give her a taste of one of her favorite foods, and she might just tell him her whole life story. His question put her on guard, though. She didn't go down memory lane, even with Uncle Jack when she could avoid it. "Yes. Where did you grow up?"

"Back East. That's where I sent my daughter yesterday—to stay at my parents' estate."

"You mentioned her at the cabin? How old is she?"

"Fifteen. She wasn't too happy, but I didn't want her here in Phoenix until the police discover who shot me. I hired a bodyguard from your agency to guard her. Although the security at my parents' estate is excellent, I'm not taking any chances."

"Is her name Elena or Rachel?"

His brow furrowed. "Rachel. How did you know?"

"You said both of those names in your delirium. Is Elena your wife?" She cringed, horrified she'd asked the question that had been plaguing her for days. Did she really want to know?

"She was. She died four years ago." Neither his expression nor his tone revealed what he was thinking.

"I'm sorry." She took another bite of her sandwich, and then washed it down with a swallow of her coffee.

"So am I." He stared off toward the mountains to the east. "She's with the Lord now."

A moment of silence fell between them, but it wasn't uncomfortable. The urge to console him swamped Tess, and she gripped the arms of her chair to keep from reaching across the table and covering his hand. "Why are you here?" she finally asked, needing to end this meal and send him on his way.

"I need your help. When I arranged a bodyguard for Rachel, I checked to see if I could hire you to be my bodyguard. Your employer said you were on vacation and that she wouldn't force you to end your vacation early. So I'm here asking. Will you?"

This time of year the temperature was cool and only in the seventies with a light breeze blowing, but perspiration coated her upper lip and palms. The idea of guarding him set her nerves on edge. She'd always felt safe at Uncle Jack's ranch, but with Shane here, knowing someone wanted to kill him, she felt very exposed. He'd finished his food, and she couldn't stomach another bite. "Let's go inside."

As he hobbled toward the back door, Tess cleaned up the trash and then hurried after him. Before entering, she paused and glanced over her shoulder. The hairs on her nape prickled, and a shiver snaked down her spine.

"Let's go into the office." Probably the safest room downstairs, with its one window. Funny. A few minutes ago, she'd been a gal on vacation. Now, her bodyguard persona had taken over. She pulled the blinds while Shane sank onto a chair in front of the desk. She sat beside him. "I can't do it. I'm not on top of my game. I need a rest."

"Your employer said that if you take the assignment, she'll extend your vacation after the job. I'll pay for an extra week, too."

"Why me?"

"Because I saw you in action, so to speak. You saved my life. I wouldn't be here if I hadn't stumbled upon that cabin. You and I both know that. I had my head of security at DDI check into you, and you have an excellent reputation."

"Don't you have security at DDI who can help you?"

"They aren't bodyguards, and I don't want anyone at the company to know I have one. I'm in the middle of some important negotiations, and if word got out that someone is trying to kill me, everything could fall through. I don't want to risk that."

"So how are you going to explain me?"

"Since I'm injured, I'm going to work from my house. Everyone will think you're the woman I'm dating. I have a few engagements I must attend, and that way you can go as my date."

"And the other times?" Why was she asking questions,

when she knew she should say no?

"A concerned girlfriend taking care of me. The head of my security, Neil Compton, has made sure my security is topnotch at my home."

"You don't have staff at your house?"

"Yes. A housekeeper and a groundskeeper. They're a couple."

"Then it might be strange that I'm staying at your place."

"There might be speculation, but it won't affect the negotiations. When the person who is after me is caught, it won't make any difference. The police are working the case quietly."

"What have the police learned?"

"Not much. Both Anthony Revell and Mark Collins have an alibi for the time of the shooting."

"But they could have hired someone, so that doesn't mean much."

"I'm pushing to get these negotiations completed. I'm hoping DDI will merge with Virtual Technologies, but the VT's board has been stalling since my *accident*. I'm going to a dinner at the VT's president's house in three days. We should close the deal shortly after that. But first, I have to prove to them that I'm on top of my game, despite ..." He indicated his bandaged leg and the cane, leaning against Uncle Jack's desk.

"Are you?"

"I'm healing, and except for a dull ache in my leg I can tolerate, I'm fine. Nothing vital was damaged. I'm even hoping to give up the cane by then." He tilted his head to the left. "So will you help me? I'm asking for four or five days until the deal is finalized, then I'll hire a different bodyguard to follow me around, if I still need one."

She rose and crossed to the window to peek out between the slats in the blinds. Charlie exited the barn leading a chestnut horse. Uncle Jack's cowhand wasn't much younger than her uncle. She'd always enjoyed the time she'd spent with him riding over the rugged terrain checking on the fences and the couple of hundred head of cattle. If she took the job, she'd miss that this vacation.

The scrape of a chair against the tile floor sounded behind her. She sensed Shane bridging the distance between them, but she didn't look at him. Part of her wanted to help him. Heaven knows he needed it. But the other part demanded she refuse—and not because she couldn't do it. She didn't understand this hesitation. She rarely turned down work, but ...

Only inches away from her, Shane leaned toward her and said, "Please. I'll make it worth your time."

It wasn't about money. No, it was about the way her heartbeat sped up even now. How was she going to keep this relationship professional when her body went all haywire at his very nearness? She breathed in his scent of sandalwood, and was filled with a sudden fear for this man. Her mouth went dry. He needed to be protected, and she didn't know if she could do it. She had to swallow several times before she could deny him.

But she made the mistake of sweeping around and stepping back to allow more room between them. Their gazes fused, and she felt bound to him, responsible for his safety. He was only there now because she'd saved his life.

The corner of his mouth quirked. "Will you, Tess?"

Her name on his lips was like the comfort of a soft, warm blanket. Chills raced up and down her arms, leaving goose bumps.

"Yes."

His grin weakened her knees. She sank against the windowsill, drinking in his smile.

"Can you start right now?"

Right. Work. She shook off the feelings and gathered her professional façade. This was a mistake, but if anything happened to him, she wouldn't be able to forgive herself. *God, I'm going to need You on this assignment.*

"I'll wait for you to pack something. You can follow me, if you want."

"No, I'll be going in your car."

"But—"

She held up her hand, palm toward him. "If I'm going to guard you, you have to agree to do everything I say. No questions. There may come a time when there won't be any time for debate."

"Okay."

"You driving here by yourself was a stupid thing to do. You exposed yourself, and for all you know, your killer is right outside, waiting for you to walk out."

"You didn't give me a choice, Tess. You never came to the hospital."

"I hate hospitals." *And I was avoiding you.*

"Like me."

Another thing they had in common. She hated them because, as a teenager, she'd spent four days in one after those thugs had broken into her home and beaten her senseless. What was his reason? No, she didn't want to know. Business only—nothing personal. "Remember, you do as I say," she said in her no-nonsense voice.

"I've already agreed to that."

She wasn't totally convinced she should take this job, and she wouldn't continue if he didn't listen to her. She'd dealt with men like Shane, men who were leaders, not followers, and they always felt capable of protecting themselves. Their arrogance made them vulnerable. "Wait in here. I'll be back in a little bit, and then we can leave."

Shane watched her walk away, finally letting down the pretense that he was all right. His wounded leg throbbed, and this excursion had exhausted him. A little blood loss and he felt woozy. Okay, it was more than a little blood loss, but he'd never been a good patient.

The only reason he'd agreed to this arrangement was because his head of security had insisted that he have a bodyguard and that he curtail his activities. Rachel had concurred and said she would behave if he hired a bodyguard, too. He couldn't take a risk with his daughter. He'd lost his wife to a reaction to an antibiotic that caused her body to dump her sodium. Rachel was his whole world.

After Elena died four years earlier, he'd thrown his energy into his company. But in the past few days, with his near death, he'd realized he had a lot to make up for with Rachel. And he would, once the person trying to kill him was caught.

"Are you ready?" Tess asked from the doorway into the office. She clutched a bag in her hand.

"That was fast."

"Clothes, weapons, ammo. I've got all I need."

"Weapons?"

"I carry several in case I need them. I always have two with me. Right now, one's in my holster. The other's in my purse. Do you know how to shoot?"

"Yes."

"Do you have a gun?"

"I lost my rifle when I fell from the cliff."

She started toward the foyer. "Do you hunt? Was that why you were in the mountains?"

"No. My daughter would disown me. I carry it for protection in case I come upon a mountain lion or a bear."

"Or a person trying to kill you."

He reached around her and opened the front door. "Or that."

"You're taking this pretty calmly." She held up her hand to halt him from coming outside, then she scanned the area before motioning him to leave her uncle's house.

"In the business world, especially when conducting negotiations, I've learned to keep my feelings private." *Probably too much.* Elena had complained she didn't know what he was thinking half the time, even though they'd been married twelve years when she died.

He stored her duffel bag in the trunk of his Lexus. While Tess slid into the front passenger seat, he climbed behind the steering wheel and slanted a look toward Tess. She surveyed the landscape, and by the alert expression on her face, she had slipped into her protective mode while packing—actually even before that. In that second, he knew he was in capable hands, and that thought relaxed him.

As he drove away from the ranch, he played through what he'd discovered about Tess when he asked his head of security to investigate her and Jack Miller. Her credentials were impeccable, and her uncle had been a police officer in New York for decades before he retired. As far as he could tell, Tess devoted herself to work. He could identify with that. Actually, there was something about Tess that made him feel comfortable—the same as he had with Elena when he'd first met her at college.

"Do the police have any idea who is after you?"

Her question dragged him away from the past. "I gave them all the names I could think of. Until this happened, I never thought there could be someone who'd want me dead. But I have to be honest with myself. I've made a few enemies in my work. I've taken over companies that resented it, although they are better off under my management."

"Some people can't stand not to be in control. Anyone in particular or connected to this most recent merger?"

"There's one guy on the board of Virtual Technologies who has been vocal. He's trying to get the votes to stop the merger."

"Who?"

"Chase Temple and he has a few allies supporting him." Shane turned onto the curvy part of the two-lane road between the ranch and the outskirts of Phoenix. "I don't know that I would like to travel this road at night. It must be pitch black except for your headlights."

"Yeah, I've told Uncle Jack that a couple of times, especially the time I encountered a deer leaping across the highway. I swerved to miss it and ran off the road into the cacti. But my uncle loves the quiet and isolation."

"And he lived in New York City for years?"

"I think he loves the isolation because he did live there."

As Shane took another sharp curve, he saw something on the side of the highway.

Tess held up her hand. "There's something across the

road."

CHAPTER FIVE

Shane stomped on the brakes while Tess swiveled her attention to the roadside. Tension whipped down her body as she drew her gun from the holster at her side. Two men dressed in black, faces covered with ski masks, ducked into the brush on the left. But not before she glimpsed their weapons.

The tires thumped as the Lexus drove over a barbed chain that had been thrown across the road. The car slowed, coming to a stop a few yards away from the spiked roadblock.

Tess yelled, "Get down," as a shot hit the driver side window. "Stay put and call 911."

Tess, hunkered down below the window, opened her door and slipped out of the car. Adrenaline surged through her as she low walked toward the front of the hood. When another shot blasted the air, she popped up and returned fired, sending the masked thugs into a ditch. Tess scrambled toward the rear of the Lexus to keep the two assailants guessing.

As she got off another round, in the car Shane poked his head up and squeezed off a shot. He must've grabbed the spare weapon in her purse. Tess gritted her teeth. What part of *stay put* did he not understand?

A bullet whizzed by her head, then another shattered the side window behind Shane. Their assailants continued raining bullets down on them as though they had an endless supply of ammunition. Tess didn't. On her, she had one extra clip while the rest of her ammo was in the duffel bag in the trunk.

She heard a distant siren coming from the south and thanked God that help had been close by. Suddenly, the two men burst from their hiding place and, with guns firing repeatedly, made a mad dash toward a dirt road a hundred feet north of their position. Tess wanted to go after them and put an end to this, but her primary job was to protect Shane. After getting off a couple more shots, she squatted by the hood of the Lexus until finally, silence reigned.

The sound of another siren, further away, came from the north. She peered around the front and saw a black pickup truck. It looked like the one that had been parked next to Uncle Jack's Jeep when she'd hiked down from the cabin. The truck zoomed out of the dirt road and sped north. She tried to read the license number, but mud obscured it. All she could see was that it was a New Mexico plate. As the pickup disappeared from view, she checked on Shane. When she climbed into the front seat of the Lexus, her heartbeat pulsated against her skull from the gunfire exchange.

Shane slowly straightened from a slouch, her Glock still in his hand, shattered glass sliding off him. He looked at her, his face pale. She took her gun from him and stuffed it back in her open purse.

She had a few words for Shane, but she clamped her lips together as one of the sheriff's cars arrived from the south. She stepped out of the Lexus, holstered her weapon, and walked around the car. All four tires were flat. Bullet holes riddled the white finish. If there'd been any doubt about someone wanting Shane dead, it was gone now.

Shane exited his Lexus as a deputy walked toward them. Tess relaxed for the first time. She knew the man.

"Are you Mr. Burkhart?" the officer asked as he took in the Lexus as if it had been in a war zone.

"Yes." Shane took out his wallet and showed the deputy his license.

"You called 911?" When Shane nodded, the deputy continued. "What happened?"

Shane pointed at the spiked roadblock stretched across the pavement. "I couldn't stop in time. Two men over there," he indicated the area, "fired on us. When they heard your siren, they ran off that way." He pointed north to the dirt road, obscured partially by the vegetation. "Got into a black pickup and took off north."

"Good thing I was nearby when I received the call." The deputy, a friend from high school named Brady, shifted his attention to Tess and smiled. "Are you on a job?"

"Yes. He hired me today. We were leaving Uncle Jack's and going to his house."

"Is Jack at the ranch? You aren't going anywhere in that car." Brady blew out a slow whistle as he inspected the Lexus again.

"No, he's in the mountains."

A second patrol car from the north pulled up, and Captain Paul Daniels exited his vehicle. He was a good friend of Uncle Jack's, but then he knew a lot of the law enforcement officers in the area, especially Maricopa County's District Six.

"Maybe you or Paul could give us a ride back to the ranch. I can use my uncle's truck." She nodded toward the captain, who stopped next to her.

"I'll do that, Brady, while you process the crime scene." Paul pushed his cowboy hat up on his forehead and examined the Lexus. "Tess Miller, trouble follows you everywhere. It's good to see no harm was done to you two. Not from lack of trying, from the looks of this car."

"Tess, did you or Mr. Burkhart get a look at the assailants?" Brady moved toward the area where the attackers had hidden.

"They had ski masks on, but one was about six feet and the other five nine or ten. Both had a stocky build. Paul, you should have passed the black truck as you came down the road."

The captain squinted north. "Nope, but there are several other dirt roads they could have turned onto. I'll have another deputy check them out. Did you get a license number?"

"No, but it was a New Mexico plate. The numbers were covered except"—Tess visualized the speeding truck—"the last number was nine, I think."

"At least that's something to go on." The captain pulled out his cell phone and placed a call.

Brady continued his trek toward the area where the two assailants had hunkered down in a ditch that had offered them some protection from Tess's return fire.

While Shane talked with Captain Daniels, giving him more details of what went down, Tess followed Brady. Her friend examined the ground, careful not to disturb any evidence, while Tess stood back on the pavement.

Brady crouched down even further. "Looks like blood. Did you hit one?"

"I don't know. Everything happened fast. Most of the time I was pinned down. But if that's human blood, it's most likely one of the assailants."

Brady grinned up at her. "Then we may be able to track him down. *If* he's in the system."

Tess looked to where the two thugs had first hidden before she exchanged fire with them. A cigarette butt, leaning against a bush and partially in the dirt caught Tess's attention. "Look at that, Brady. It might belong to one of the assailants. This isn't the first time someone tried to kill Shane." Brady sat back on his heels and looked at her, his eyebrows raised. She told him the story of what had happened on the mountain.

When she was finished, Brady nodded toward the cigarette butt. "Good. Another piece of evidence we might be able to use. From the looks of that Lexus, these scumbags meant business. I'm glad Mr. Burkhart hired you."

She glanced back at the shot up Lexus. When she thought of what could have happened if Shane had been alone returning to his house, Tess shivered.

Late that afternoon, Tess entered Shane's mansion. Just the foyer of his house was the size of half her apartment in Dallas. Straight ahead, a grand staircase of rich mahogany swept to the second floor. A matching round mahogany table stood in the center of the marble floor near the entrance. A large bouquet of fresh flowers, various varieties in many colors, drew Tess's gaze. Their sweet fragrance sprinkled the air, making her forget for a few seconds why she was here.

She circled the entry, peering into an elongated living room, decorated in an elegance that complemented the dining room, which lay across the foyer. Twelve people could sit at a massive table and enjoy a meal together.

"My wife decorated this area to entertain business associates. I rarely use these rooms. Come on. I'll show you around before I take you to your bedroom."

Tess looked at the rooms one more time. "Your wife had good taste."

"Yes, Elena did."

She followed him past the staircase, down a long hall, and into the den.

The first thing Tess saw was a beautifully carved dark mantel with a portrait of a stunning woman with auburn hair. Elena. "How did she die?"

He stared at his wife's portrait. "A drug reaction. All my money, and I couldn't do a thing to help her. Her sodium level plummeted, and the doctors couldn't turn it around. I was on a business trip. As soon as I heard she'd been taken to the hospital, I came home as fast as I could." He swallowed hard. "I didn't make it in time. I should have been there for her. The housekeeper found her delirious. If I'd been here, I might have been able to get her help in time." He blinked several times and wrenched his gaze away. "I don't usually share that story, but with all that has happened in the past days . . . "

"I guess getting shot at would bring a lot of things to the surface."

"You were in danger today because of me. Maybe this isn't such a good idea."

She held up her hand. "It's my job to protect you."

"I know, and I'm alive today because you did, but I can't take another person's life in my hands."

"Is this because I'm a female? Would you have said that if I were a man?"

He studied her for a long moment. "Elena had the same color hair as you do." His attention swiveled to the portrait. "I didn't think about it until now. I—"

Tess stood in front of Shane. "We look nothing alike except for that. There are a lot of people with auburn hair, but if you want to get another bodyguard, I understand. I won't leave, though, until the replacement shows up."

Shane shook his head. "No. I just think what happened this afternoon is finally catching up with me. I learned two things today. First, someone definitely wants me dead. Second, you're certainly capable of protecting me."

Tess nodded her acknowledgement. "Where's your housekeeper? I want to meet her and then finish the tour."

"Probably in the kitchen, fixing dinner. She and her husband have a suite of rooms off the kitchen. C'mon. I'll introduce you, then show you where you'll be staying."

"I want to be in the bedroom next to yours."

"That's fine. I thought you might and had Anna prepare it for you."

"You were that sure I would accept?"

Using his cane, he limped toward the hallway. "No, but I did a lot of praying that you would. I know when I need help. My expertise is in computers, not protection. That's why I promised to do what you say."

Staying where she was, Tess pressed her lips together. When he turned at the entrance and saw her standing there, one of his eyebrows arched.

"This is what it looks like to stay put. Earlier today, you returned fire. That was my job, not yours. I know what I'm doing."

He strode back to her, his arm stiff at his side while his fingers curled then uncurled. "I know how to shoot, and if a gun is available, I'm capable of helping. If you need a demonstration of my abilities with a weapon, I'll be glad to give you one. I often hike in remote places, and I always carry a gun as protection and hope I never have to use it." His bearing gave off waves of self-assurance as though he were in a boardroom issuing orders to his employees.

"Then why do you need me?"

"I'm no expert, just because I can fire a gun. I will do as you say unless I don't see the logic in it. I respect your abilities, but that doesn't mean I can't *help* defend myself. I won't be a passive client. Do you have a problem with that?"

Her first impulse was to head for the door and return to Uncle Jack's ranch. She scanned the den while trying to calm the anger bubbling to the surface. Her attention landed on a photo of Shane with a teenage girl who had his coloring but looked like Elena. The picture of him with his daughter melted her irritation. She'd dealt with worse clients, people who continually got in her way. She could deal with him. She wouldn't let anything happen to him, because Shane was the only parent Rachel had. That was motivation, if nothing else, but after what happened on the highway earlier, she wouldn't have walked away, even if he were childless.

She returned her focus to him. "Then I suggest we get to know each other, because this won't work if we're second guessing each other."

"Agreed. And you are the expert, but I'm not helpless."

She smiled. "Even when you were in the cabin, I knew you weren't helpless."

A sparkle gleamed in his gray eyes. "If a wounded man stumbled into my cabin with cuts and bruises and torn clothes, that wouldn't be the first thing that would come to mind for me. I bet there was a time you thought I was probably a criminal."

"It was that dark stubble of a beard, a couple of days old, that cautioned me. I certainly didn't think you were the CEO of a big corporation." She winked, then sauntered into the hallway and waited for him to show her where the kitchen was.

Shane passed her in the corridor. "Anna and Kevin think you're a special friend visiting. The only person who knows who you really are is my head of security."

"Don't you think they'll wonder why I roam around the house in the middle of night, checking doors and windows?"

"They'll just have to wonder. I love both of them, and they've been with me for many years, but Anna can't keep a secret, and I'm afraid she'd let something slip, especially when my executive assistant is here tomorrow." He paused near a door, closed the space between them and leaned in to whisper, "If you roam the house in the middle of the night, when are you going to sleep?"

Her pulse rate spiked from his nearness, but she didn't step away. "That depends on your security system, which I need to see in this tour."

"I bring a woman home, and the first thing she looks at is my security system. What do you think Anna and Kevin will think then?"

Tess chuckled. "Tell them anything you want. Tell them I have this thing about staying in a house that doesn't have a good security system, that I feel better after I see how safe a place is."

He tossed back his head and laughed, a deep belly kind. "They'll think you're strange, and I'm just as strange for falling for you."

The sound of his merriment urged her to join in, but she had to focus on business, not pleasure. "I figure they already think you're strange, bringing a woman home right after your daughter leaves, especially one they haven't heard about."

He sobered. "They'll be tickled. Anna has been trying to get me to date again. She's taken me to task for working twenty-four/seven and was the one who was happy when I decided to go for the hike that led to this." He swept his hand toward his injured leg.

Suspicion pricked her. "She was? How long have she and Kevin been working for you?"

"Since I married Elena."

"How about your executive assistant?"

"Ten years."

"And Nick Compton?"

"Five years. He started right after he left the army."

"Interesting."

"I know that tone. You think one of them could be involved. I think I know the employees who work closely with me better than that. Next, you're going to ask about my daughter."

Her eyes widened at the fierceness in his voice. "I have to suspect everyone. You don't."

The door behind Shane opened, and a petite woman no more than five feet tall with salt and pepper hair pulled in a tight bun at her nape fixed her gaze on them. "What's taking you so long to bring her in to meet me? You two have been out here for five minutes. I thought I raised you better than that, Shane."

"Raised you?" Tess murmured as she came around from behind Shane to greet the housekeeper.

"Yes, she was my nanny years ago, and later, I convinced her to come work for me. Anna, this is . . . my lady friend, Tess Miller."

The way he said *lady friend* as though it were true made her face heat. Tess shook the older woman's hand. "He's been telling me all about you."

"That's good, because until this morning, I didn't know you existed." Anna eyed Tess as though the housekeeper was inspecting the vegetables at the market. "And just so you know, I'm not ancient. He has been responsible for my gray hairs. He was the first and only child I was ever a nanny for." She swung her attention to him. "And what happened to you this week put a few more gray hairs on my head." As she turned and disappeared into the room, she added, "Come in and have some tea with me before I start dinner."

"She rules the house, not me," he whispered.

"Really? I would never have known that. You can run along. I'll probably get your life history by the time I finish my tea."

"You're supposed to be guarding me, so that's best done by my side."

That declaration heightened the heat of her blush. She shouldn't have taken this job. Only a few more days until the merger went through, and then he could have two big burly bodyguards plastered to his sides.

"The tea is getting cold." Anna carried the tray with the cups and the teapot on it to the kitchen table.

Tess entered the kitchen with Shane slightly behind her, almost touching. He could be clear across the room, and she'd be aware of his location—even if she weren't his bodyguard.

"Just so you know, Anna loves to embellish some of my childhood."

"Thanks for the warning. This should be interesting." Tess turned a smile on Anna, intending to discover as much as she could about the man who piqued her interest far beyond the job.

Early the next morning, before anyone was up, Tess prowled the ground floor, checking doors and windows, more as something to do than thinking they might be unlocked. Shane's security system was excellent. He had said his head of security was responsible for making sure his house was protected. She would thank Neil Compton when she met him. He and Diane Flood, Shane's executive assistant, were coming out today.

Tess paused at the large window that overlooked the front of his estate. It had a high wall around it and a sturdy gate, requiring visitors to call the main house to be buzzed in. Although no place was totally secure, it would be easier to guard him at his home. If Shane never left until the merger was announced, he should be safe. In two days, though, he had to attend the big party at the VT's president's house. That might present a problem. She'd have to glue herself to Shane's side and pretend for a whole room full of people they were a couple while watching for someone to make a move against him.

"You're up early."

The husky voice of the man who'd haunted her dreams last night cut into her thoughts. She turned toward him, hidden in the shadows by the entrance into the living room. But she felt the intensity pouring off of him and the drill of his gaze. She sucked in a deep breath and held it for seconds longer than usual.

"Is everything okay? Did something disturb your sleep?" Shane moved into the muted glow of the lamplight. Dressed in jeans and a long sleeve navy blue pullover, he looked comfortable and casual in the midst of the elegant room. His hair was tousled, as if he'd finger-combed it, and he was barefooted.

"It's four. I got five hours of sleep. That's all I need."

"That's about all I require, too."

Another thing they had in common. After her conversation with Anna yesterday, she'd learned she and Shane liked a lot of the same things: hiking, roughing it in the wilds, photography, coffee, pecan pie. She'd seen some of his photos as she'd toured the house and was impressed with how he could capture a scene at its essence. She'd recently taken up photography, because she traveled so much and saw some beautiful places. So she often took a couple of days to tour wherever she'd been working after her job was over.

Tess realized she'd been staring at Shane. What had he said? Oh, yeah. Sleep. "When I work, I sometimes sleep less," Tess finally said when she realized she was staring at him and a long silence had fallen between them. "I see your daughter likes to ride horses."

He came to her side. "Likes? Oh, no. *Love* is a better word. And at my parents' she'll get to ride a lot."

Tess shut the drapes and edged away from the window, so Shane wasn't exposed. "I got that feeling when I saw all the riding trophies in her bedroom."

"Do you like to ride?"

"Love is a better word for me, too. Every time I go to Uncle Jack's, I ride a couple of times a day, often with my uncle. That's one of the things I miss the most when I'm working, so I probably overdo it when I'm back in Phoenix."

"I have a small stable where I keep four horses. We could—"

"As much as I'd love to, I'd rather you not leave this house until we have to." It wasn't just about his security. If they rode together, it would just give them another thing in common.

"You think someone is out there?"

"Could be."

"I'd never thought of my home being anything but a safe haven."

"That's what I thought about the cabin. A retreat for me."

One of his eyebrows arched. "But not now?"

"Nowhere is completely safe. It's hard not to realize that in my line of work, but with the cabin, I put the outside world behind me. It was me, nature and sometimes Uncle Jack."

"And I ruined that for you." He reached out and touched her arm. "I'm sorry."

"I wouldn't have wanted it any other way. That's the only cabin around for several miles. You needed ..." She couldn't finish that. This job was more than just bodyguard and client. *Lord, what are You doing? I've never had this much trouble separating my professional and personal lives.*

"I know I needed you. I'm just lucky I didn't fall over a cliff to the valley below." He stepped closer and took her hand. "No words can express my gratitude to you and your uncle. My daughter has already lost her mother. I couldn't let her lose her dad, too. She took Elena's death so hard."

The sadness in his voice made her think about her mother. She knew how he felt.

His hands framed her face. "You okay? Have you lost someone close to you? You never talk about your parents. Just your uncle."

She needed to back away, but the look of concern in his eyes touched a chord deep inside her, strengthening a bond that had begun forming from the moment he stumbled into the cabin. "My mother killed herself. She drank too much and mixed alcohol with pills. I couldn't do anything to save her."

"Is that why you protect people now?"

Is it? "I was attacked in my home when I was sixteen. I think that's what really made me want to protect others. I couldn't defend myself. It took months to recover. That's when Uncle Jack insisted I come live with him and Patricia in

New York. Then he started teaching me to defend myself."

"Where was your father when all this happened?"

She stiffened and pulled away from him. "Drunk."

CHAPTER SIX

That one word. *Drunk*. It was so full of suppressed anger, it hung in the air between them. Shane realized the physical wounds from Tess's attack had healed, but not the emotional ones, especially the feelings concerning her father.

He took her hand. "I need some coffee. Want some?"

She looked away but nodded. The hard line of her jaw attested to her battle for control. He wanted to know much more about her. The pain emanating from her pierced his heart and made him feel what she must have gone through. Since Elena's death, he'd thought his feelings had been suspended, locked away in a block of ice. But not now.

Their hands still clasped, Shane made his way into the foyer, then the hallway that led to the kitchen. He slanted a look toward Tess, and a tic jerked in her cheek. He wanted to say something to comfort her, but he was at a loss. The house was so quiet that he heard his heart pounding in his ears.

He flipped the overhead light on as he entered the room.

She disconnected their link and crossed her arms.

He headed for the counter and the pot, giving her time to compose herself while he prepared the coffee.

"Will we wake up Kevin and Anna?" Tess asked as she prowled the perimeter, trying the back door, glancing out the windows. She wouldn't be able to see much because of the bright lights in the kitchen.

He watched her moving restlessly, as if she were struggling with something. "Anna is used to me coming in here early and fixing coffee. After it perks, we can go into the den and drink it. I usually go to my home office and work."

At the bay window in the breakfast nook, Tess spun around. "Listen. About what I said . . . I didn't mean to bring my personal life into this."

"I started it by telling you about Elena." He took down some mugs and filled them with hot, fragrant coffee, then handed her one. "Let's sit in the den."

A minute later when he settled on the couch next to her, he continued. "I didn't intend to tell you about Elena, either. It isn't something I share. My life was going along nicely, and then suddenly, everything changed. I felt as though I was put in a blender and the off button was missing. I kept going around and around."

"I know that feeling. I told Uncle Jack about the attack once. I've never discussed it again. I wanted to put it behind me and move forward."

"Did you?"

"I thought I had, but Uncle Jack keeps expecting me to forgive my dad. He thinks I need to do it to move on completely."

"Like I have to accept Elena is gone?"

"I suppose. I know God wants me to forgive him, but it's so hard. I was in the hospital for almost a day before the police found my dad, drunk and passed out in his car. As far as I was concerned, he shouldn't have come to visit me. He made me feel like the attack was my fault. He complained about having to clean up the mess at home and deal with the insurance company and the police."

"Did they ever find who did it?"

"Two young guys high on drugs, looking for money. I interrupted them, and they went crazy. Strangely, I've been able to forgive them. What they did led to me moving to New York to live with Uncle Jack. That changed my life for the better."

The urge to draw her into his embrace overwhelmed Shane, but he didn't want to stop her from talking. She needed to, just like he did. "What about your father?"

"The day I went to Uncle Jack's was the day he dismissed

me from his life. My uncle says he's still drinking."

"Did he always drink?"

"No. He started after my mother committed suicide. I tried to get him to stop, but he just got angrier and meaner."

"Suicide is hard for the people left behind." The thought of what Tess went through contracted his chest, and he inhaled a deep breath then slowly released it.

Her eyes glistened, and she swallowed hard. "I know. I was twelve. She got hooked on pain meds." Tess stared down at her lap, cradling the mug in her hands. "I don't think she meant to kill herself, but she began mixing alcohol and her pills, and one day, she didn't wake up. I didn't understand at the time."

"Maybe your dad blames himself and couldn't deal with the guilt."

She glanced at Shane. "So you think I should forgive him, too." Her words held a hard edge.

"I can't tell you what you need to do, but I do think your uncle is a smart man." Shane took a long sip of his coffee.

"I shouldn't have left you alone with Uncle Jack." She studied the dark liquid in her mug. "I'm surprised he didn't tell you my life story. He can be nosey. Must be the detective in him." She grumbled, but a smile flirted with the corners of her mouth.

"My childhood was pretty normal and uneventful. When Elena died unexpectedly, it really knocked my legs out from under me. If I hadn't had Rachel and the Lord, I might have gone down that path. There were times I wanted to escape the pain any way I could."

"I know what you mean. If it wasn't for the Lord, I'm not sure how I would have made it. My dad didn't believe in God, and I wasn't enough for him. Uncle Jack is the one who taught me about God's love. Uncle Jack is so different from my father."

"We are the sum of our experiences. After this is over, you can bet I will be looking at things differently. I have always realized having money could put a target on my back, but whoever is after me isn't doing it for a ransom. The second attempt proved that."

"Speaking of that, besides the party tomorrow night, will you need to leave here before you make your announcement about the merger?"

"No. Diane and Nick are coming here today, and Diane will come over tomorrow. We're making arrangements for the announcement, assuming the deal goes through. I'll meet with the board the day after the party, and a decision will be made then."

"What's the party for?" Tess swallowed a sip of coffee.

"To persuade a few who are against the merger. The vote may be close. From what the president of Virtual Technologies, Dale Mason, said yesterday there are two men who don't want this, and they're trying to influence the rest of the board members."

"Could they be behind the attempts on your life?"

"I've done several mergers over the past few years. I've had a couple that met opposition, but no one ever resorted to trying to kill me."

"Who are the men? I have told my boss about Anthony Revell, Mark Collins and Chase Temple. She's running a background check on them. I think I should have her run one on the men opposing the merger."

"Ben Smith. Together with Chase Temple, they own thirty-eight percent of the company."

"I like to know what I can about who might be behind the attempts on your life, but also have a photo of what they look like. All the information I can gather helps me be prepared while guarding you."

"In the latest development, Anthony Revell is making a play for Virtual Technologies. I won't be surprise if he's at the party. Should be an interesting evening."

"That depends on how you look at it. For me, I'd rather you passed on the party. It exposes you to whoever is after you."

"VT needs an infusion of money, whether it comes from

my company or Revell's. I have my supporters on the board, and Revell has his." Just thinking about tomorrow evening made his neck muscles tighten like fists. The pain spread out from there. "Mark Collins was invited and probably will show up, too, although he hasn't made a formal move to merge with VT. There are one or two swing votes, which could shift everything toward Revell or even Collins. That's why I can't let the board know about the threats to my life."

"Then you think it will be over in a few days, and I can return to Dallas?"

"Yes." He wouldn't see Tess again, and he realized in that moment that he was bothered by that fact. He wanted to get to know her. He hadn't felt that way about a woman since he dated Elena. That surge of emotion—that surprised him.

"Are you okay?"

Tess's voice penetrated his stunned mind. He'd never considered becoming involved with another woman. To him, Elena had been his one true love.

"Shane?"

He blinked and focused on Tess's beautiful face, the one he saw when he'd first opened his eyes at the cabin. "There's nothing wrong."

"You paled. I thought you might have remembered something."

Yes, the way you looked when I recovered consciousness. Like an angel—my guardian angel. "I hope you'll give me some time to hire another bodyguard."

"Of course, but you might contact my agency and talk with your head of security when he comes out today. I can give you some suggestions, if you want."

"Are you sure you won't stay?"

Her mouth twisted in a thoughtful look, and he waited, filled with hope.

"I really shouldn't. If you're going back and forth to work, you'll need more than one person. You might need to look at a full detail."

"You could be part of that."

She sighed, peered away for a long moment, and then met his gaze. "No. We need to stick to the agreement we made yesterday." She rose. "I'm going to refill my cup then continue my walk through the house."

Shane watched her leave, thinking about the wall that had gone up when he'd suggested she stay and guard him. Her professional façade, as he'd come to think of that persona, was firmly in place now. For a while, she'd let down her guard and been herself. He'd glimpsed the true woman behind the front she presented to others.

As he finished the last of his coffee, he decided he needed to stop these thoughts about more with Tess. Her life wasn't suited to a relationship. Even if she weren't protecting him, she must travel all over the world, guarding others. These feelings developing for her were momentarily spurred by the fact she'd saved his life twice. Nothing more.

Shane sat at the dining room table with his work spread out as Diane Flood and he went through the business that needed to be done. Tess watched him from the living room across the foyer. His executive assistant hadn't questioned working at his house, but Tess had seen a puzzled look in her eyes when Diane had walked into the house. Shane and Diane, though, soon fell into a work pattern that included Shane taking occasional breaks to check on her. Tess was pretending to read a book on her electronic device a good part of the morning while perched in a rather uncomfortable wingback. Shane had even moved the large round table in the entry hall so she could see him. She checked her emails frequently, as her employer sent updated information on the men she was investigating. On the surface, all four men appeared to be upstanding members of the community, which didn't really mean anything. But at least Tess had their photos and now knew what they looked like.

At noon instead of eating the meal Anna had prepared, Diane left to run some errands for Shane. Nick, the head of security at DDI, arrived to join her and Shane for lunch at the game table in the den. Tess's stomach rumbled at the delicious scent of a Mexican casserole. After last night's dinner and this morning's breakfast, she couldn't wait to eat something else cooked by Anna. Definitely a perk of the job.

"Everything set up for the party tomorrow night?" Shane asked Nick as his security chief took his seat across from Tess.

"Yes. Dale Mason's staff has everything covered. I and a few of my top men will be at the party. I'm the only one who knows about the threats, per your instructions, but they know keeping an eye on you is their priority."

"Good. Tess, do you have any concerns or questions?" Shane asked as he picked up his fork.

"I would like photos of each DDI security man at the party, as well as a diagram of where the party is taking place."

"I'll have them to you by the end of the day so you can familiarize yourself with the layout. I understand from Shane you've been a bodyguard for seven years."

Although not a question, Tess said, "It gives me an opportunity to see the world. I always wanted to travel."

Shane's forehead crinkled, and he lowered his head while he forked some of the Mexican casserole and ate it.

For the next ten minutes, Shane and Nick discussed a few issues at the corporation's headquarters in Phoenix. Tess heard the words, but they didn't really register. Instead she watched each one, cataloguing their mannerisms. She learned so much by studying a person's body language. Shane talked with his hands while Nick's movements were controlled and reserved.

When something bothered Shane, he would rub his nape while keeping his expression neutral. Some people might notice the look on his face at best, but most concentrated on what was said, not how it was spoken.

By the time the lunch was over, Tess was convinced she could trust Nick. He was a no-nonsense man who knew his job. But what had intrigued her most today was how Shane worked with his staff. He treated them as associates with valuable input. He respected his employees' opinions and let them know it. Much like her employer at the agency.

Shane and Nick relaxed back in their chairs and discussed the upcoming Phoenix Suns' season. Tess's mind was elsewhere, though, remembering the conversation she and Shane had shared in this room in the wee hours of the morning. She still couldn't believe she'd told Shane about her mother and father. She'd finally discussed the kind of childhood she'd had before going to live with her uncle and his wife. She'd held it inside so long, it felt good to share with Shane.

All morning while staring at the ebook she was supposed to be reading, she'd thought about what Shane had said about forgiving her father. She didn't know if she could. Even today, she felt the sting of her dad's words and the consequences of his drinking problem. Those things had affected every aspect of her life. How could she forgive that?

One step at a time.

The words flowed through her mind as though the Lord had spoken them directly to her. Was that possible? Could she let the hurt and anger go enough to forgive her father and move on?

Nick stood and turned toward Tess. "I'll be back by the end of the day with the information you need. I hope you can give us some good suggestions for a couple of bodyguards to replace you when we make the merger announcement."

Shane rose. "I tried to get her to reconsider. She promised to stay until we find some good replacements."

Nick smiled. "Good." With a nod, he headed toward the foyer.

Shane came behind Tess's chair and pulled it out for her, leaning down to say, "I'll double your pay if you stay."

How could she? He knew more about her than most people, and that was only after a few days. She was managing to keep herself professionally focused, but she didn't know how long she could maintain that. She was beginning to care about him, and if it went any further, it might distract her from her work.

She pushed to her feet and turned, keeping the chair

between them. "I haven't had a man pull a chair out for me in ages."

"You're just not hanging around with the right guys. Stay, and I'll pull your chair out all the time."

She started for the hallway. "I'm at a particularly fascinating part of the book I'm reading. I can't wait to get back to it."

Shane chuckled. "What's it about? Maybe I should read it."

"It's a romance. Nothing you would like."

"Try me."

"A woman meets a man, and they fall in love." She hurried her step.

He kept pace with her. "Interesting you like to read romances."

She halted in the foyer and faced him. "What's that mean?"

"I would have pegged you for a thriller reader."

"Too close to my job. I prefer a change of pace."

Nick stood in the entrance talking with Diane who carried a big white box. Nick glanced at Shane and Tess, said something else to Diane, then left.

Tess nodded to Shane's executive assistant. "I'll leave you to your work." She headed for the living room.

But Shane clasped her arm. "Wait. She went to pick up something for you."

The feel of his fingers sent her heartbeat racing. She needed space. She needed to leave before he had her whole life history. And her heart. Two, three at the most, days left. *I can do this.*

"It's in the white box?" Tess eyed Diane as she and Shane covered the distance to the woman.

"Yes." Then to Diane Shane said, "Thanks for picking this up. I'll be in the dining room soon."

His executive assistant handed him the box, gave Tess a quick once-over, and walked away.

"C'mon. I want to see you open it." Shane placed his hand on the small of her back and started for the living room.

Heat seared Tess's face. The only person she exchanged gifts with was Uncle Jack.

Shane presented her with the box. "Open it."

When she did, her eyes widened on a beautiful, emerald green cocktail dress nestled in the white tissue paper. "I can't accept this." She looked up. "Why did you buy me this?"

"For tomorrow night. Surely, you didn't already have a dress in that duffel bag you brought with you."

"But I was going to wear..." What? Had she really thought that black slacks and a white blouse would be appropriate for a fancy cocktail party? "Frankly, I didn't think about what I was going to wear, and you're right. I didn't bring anything appropriate." This was what he did to her—flustered her to the point she didn't think of every contingency.

She lifted the dress out of the box and checked its size. Six. How did he know?

"And I had Diane pick up some shoes and a purse to match. If something doesn't fit, she can take it back and get the right size. Go try it on." A smile spread across his mouth.

"I'll try the dress on later, but I'll see if the shoes fit." Tess sat in a chair and slipped on the matching emerald green two-inch heels. She felt like Cinderella with Prince Charming standing in front of her, waiting to see if she was the one he'd danced with at the ball. "They fit."

"And this purse is plenty big enough for your gun." He held the evening bag up, his smile infectious.

She couldn't resist grinning back at Shane. "Thank you. Now I'll fit in at the"—she almost said ball—"cocktail party."

He set the box on the couch nearby. "Well, I'd better go work."

As he left, Tess murmured, "Thank you. I love it."

He glanced over his shoulder. "It's perfect for you."

His intense look caused butterflies to flutter in her stomach. *Only a few more days. Why aren't I happier about that?*

Tess put the finishing touches to her make-up, which she rarely wore. Then she stepped back to check her reflection in the full-length mirror. Diane had told her that Shane had personally picked the cocktail dress out for her, using a Phoenix high-end store that had a large online presence. Tess couldn't believe how well it fit her. Its shimmering satin fell in soft folds below her knees.

This wasn't her first time to dress up on the job, but as she turned from side to side, she felt like Cinderella again. Like yesterday when he presented her with the dress, she realized how emotionally invested she was becoming with Shane. It scared her. What if something happened to him? She would blame herself, always wondering if she'd blown it because she was becoming more focused on him instead of the job.

"Show time," she whispered to her image in the mirror.

She snatched up her purse and snapped it open to check her weapon inside. It was loaded and ready. She wouldn't let Shane down. He was her only concern tonight. Soon this assignment would be over, and she could get back to her normal life.

Shane waited for her at the bottom of the staircase. As she descended the steps, he moved forward, hardly limping, and watched her. The sight of him in his black tuxedo, so different from the day she'd met him, stole her breath. She had to force herself to breathe.

"You clean up nicely" A smile flirted with the corners of her mouth as if he were her date to the senior prom. She stopped on the first step.

His gray eyes lit like polished silver. "I could say the same for you, but it wouldn't be an adequate description." One of his hands cupped her face.

Standing on the bottom step, still having to look up slightly into his gaze, she needed to end the warm touch of his palm against her cheek, but she felt paralyzed by the mesmerizing expression in those gray depths. For a few seconds while he bent his head toward hers, she forgot she was his bodyguard. He made her feel special, as though she were the only woman in his life. The anticipation of his lips brushing against hers spurred her heartbeat. She swayed toward him.

CHAPTER SEVEN

Shane wrapped his arms around Tess, tugging her until she pressed against him. His mouth came down to claim hers completely. He hadn't kissed a woman since Elena, and the sensations Tess created in him rocked him to his core. Suddenly, he didn't want to go to the party. He wanted to spend the evening alone with Tess, getting to know her even better. Her embrace enveloped him, and he imagined their hearts beating as one.

Someone cleared a throat. The sound irritated him, and he wanted whoever was in the foyer with them to leave, but reality intruded. Tess pulled away. She straightened and stepped to the side as if nothing had happened between them. Only the flush of her cheeks remained to indicate she'd enjoyed the kiss as much as he had.

He didn't want her to leave after the decision on the merger was announced, but Nick had told him today he'd found two excellent bodyguards who could take over as soon as he was ready. He'd been working on this merger for almost a year, and now he wished he could delay the decision a few more days.

Turning slowly, he composed himself and faced his head of security, who was their driver to the party. "You're right on time. We're ready. Let's get this over with."

He offered Tess his arm and escorted her to the double front doors. He saw the puzzled look Nick had tossed at him and thought about saying he was preparing for his role as Tess's date. Nick knew him better than that.

When Shane settled into the back of the limousine, he slid a glance toward Tess who had slipped into her bodyguard mode—alert, assessing her environment, focused on her job. He should be happy about that. One part of him was, but another part wished this was a normal date and that he and Tess could enjoy the evening as a true couple.

She shifted toward him, her purse in her lap with her hand covering her bag. He studied her expression in the soft lighting. It revealed nothing of what she was thinking. Not anything like when she'd been on the staircase. He released a long breath.

"In a few hours this will be over," she said, all business now. "I'll be right beside you the whole evening. I'm not going to let anything happen to you."

Although her tone was businesslike, there was a hint of something beneath her words. Concern? Regret? "I know. But you'll have to relax and play the part of my date."

"Don't worry. I will."

An hour later on the edge of a small ballroom, Tess watched the crowd and Shane. It reminded her of a jammed marketplace she'd visited in Spain where her client was nearly kidnapped. Too many people, too much noise. And while being vigilant about her surroundings, she had to act like she was in love with Shane. Truth was, that last part wasn't that difficult. Watching Shane was easy. Tearing her eyes away to focus on the crowd—that was the hard part. But Shane's life was in the balance, and she wouldn't risk him by giving into the feelings churning her stomach.

Lord, help me do what needs to be done.

Shane leaned toward her ear and whispered, "Here comes Dale Mason, the president, and Chase Temple, one of the board members who doesn't want to merge with DDI."

She'd memorized the looks of the main players in this merger. She'd already seen and met Mark Collins. Anthony Revell was across the room, occasionally throwing a glance Shane's way. No love lost there.

"I haven't seen Ben Smith yet," he continued. "Surely he'll

be here."

Tess curled her arm around Shane and pressed close to him as if she were enthralled with every word he said. She was playing her part.

Not true. I am enthralled, and that's the problem.

"Ah, I see Ben in the entrance with his wife," Shane said.

Chase and Dale stopped in front of them, and Shane smiled at them. Tess was impressed at how well he carried his façade. Most people couldn't smile at a man they suspected might've been trying to kill them.

Chase Temple was a large man, built like a linebacker, and he blocked Tess's view of the rest of the guests.

A frown marred the president of Virtual Technologies' face. "We need to talk to you." He looked at Tess, then back at Shane. "In *private*. Something has come to our attention."

When Shane stiffened, Tess squeezed his arm then slipped her hand away. "I can leave you three alone right now." Then she leaned close and whispered, "I won't be far away, keeping my eye on you."

Shane turned partly away from the two gentlemen and gave Tess a quick kiss on her cheek near her ear. "Dale is the one person on DDI's side."

Before she moved away, Dale Mason said, "We'll go into my library, Shane. I don't want anyone overhearing us."

Shane threw her a glance then smiled at the two men. Tess could tell it was forced, because his eyes didn't light up as they usually did when he genuinely grinned.

"Gentlemen, I'm at your disposal."

Tess forged her way through the fifty guests toward the entrance, so she could watch which room the trio entered. The layout of the house Nick had given her indicated a study, but not a library. Were they the same room?

Near the doorway into the corridor, Chase said something to Shane and Dale, then excused himself and made his way toward Ben Smith about ten feet off to the side. Strange. With the absence of Chase, Tess relaxed a little. She exited the ballroom and hurried across the hall, where she entered the powder room. She immediately spun around and cracked the door open to watch the president and Shane head down the hallway. When they disappeared, around the corner, she came out of the restroom and quickened her step after the pair. She rounded the corner as a door closed at the end of the corridor.

Nick came up behind her. "I saw you take off. What's happening?"

"Shane went with Dale Mason. The man wants to talk with him about a concern. My first impulse is to barge into the room, but that wouldn't put Dale's mind at peace. I wonder what he'd think if he found me standing guard in the hallway."

"I've got an idea. We could be talking right here." He stepped across from her and propped his shoulder against the wall on the other side. "Now you can keep an eye on the door. There's only one way into that room. Shane will be safe with Dale."

"What do you want to talk about? The weather?"

Nick smiled. "It's been perfect the last few days. Not too hot."

Tess chuckled. "What did you do before this?"

"I was in the military."

"I noticed you wear a wedding ring. Tell me about your wife."

"She's the love of my life."

As he said it, the shadow in his eyes didn't coincide with his words. She wondered if they were having marital problems. According to Shane, Nick kept long hours at DDI. Tess started to say something when the door opened and Shane and Mr. Mason came out. Shane's smile reached deep into his eyes, and Tess's tensed shoulders sagged.

"It looks like they cleared it up," she murmured to Nick. She stepped toward the pair coming down the hall. "I hope the business portion of the evening is over with, darling." With what she hoped was an adoring look, she approached Shane and fell into step next to him.

"Yes, Dale and I have come to agreement, and it should become official tomorrow after the board meeting."

"It was nice meeting you, Ms. Miller. You do a good job watching over Shane." Mr. Mason shook Tess's hand. "If you all will excuse me, I'd better get back to my guests." He nodded toward Shane and Nick before he sauntered toward the ballroom.

"Nick, we're leaving. There's no reason for us to stay, and I'm sure Tess would prefer if I were at home rather than out in the open."

"I'll bring the car around."

As Nick left, Shane faced her. "Chase Temple informed Dale that the hunting accident was really an attempt on my life."

"How did he find out?"

"Anthony Revell told Chase, who immediately ran to Dale and everyone else on the board he could find."

"Mr. Mason didn't seem to be concerned about it."

"I assured him that my corporation is his best bet to revive his own, whether I was at the head or not. I also told him I have taken precautions. Our two companies will make a powerful team."

"You told him about me?"

Shane nodded. "As well as what security measures would be put in place when the merger was announced. I'm not taking the threats to my life lightly."

"This is one . . . bodyguard who is glad you aren't. You're right. I'll feel better when we're back at your house."

When the limousine pulled up to the door, Tess exited the house first and scanned her surroundings before giving Shane the signal to follow. The valet opened the car door, and Shane and Tess slid into the luxurious car. The limo pulled away from the entrance.

Shane took her hand. "I'm glad that's over with. I hate working a party, and I can imagine you were bored."

"No, not bored. I was too busy watching all the people, hoping we could leave when you persuaded that board member to vote for DDI tomorrow. From what you said, that would cinch your merger."

"I'm glad I stayed around. I knew Chase Temple wasn't in favor of my company merging with Virtual Technologies, but I didn't know exactly who he wanted, because the corporation needed an influx of money. Now I believe he's working with Anthony Revell."

In two days she'd be gone, and none of this would be her problem, but she wished the person behind the attempts on Shane's life would be caught before she left Phoenix.

"We need to talk about what happened on the staircase, Tess. You can't deny there are feelings between us."

She closed her eyes for a few seconds and fortified herself with a deep inhalation, then let it go slowly. "We live in two different worlds. When I stop long enough to be home, I live in Dallas. I don't think it's a good idea for ..." Her words came to a halt as the limousine did at an intersection.

Nick turned to face them. The locks clicked, and the door next to Shane flew open. Tess had her hand in her purse when Nick pointed a weapon at her.

"Don't even think about it." Shane's head of security's voice was lethally quiet. "Give your purse to my associate."

The man in the doorway had a revolver aimed at Shane's chest. Reluctantly, Tess handed him her purse while noting two things about the man: the scent of tobacco emanating from him and a white bandage around his forearm. One of the men in the ditch?

"Good girl," Nick said.

The man in the doorway set her purse on top of the limo, never taking his gaze off of them. A moment later, he yanked a pair of handcuffs from his back pocket.

Nick spoke again. "Shane, take the handcuffs and put them on Tess, arms behind her back."

The soft interior light cast a shadow across Nick's face, but Tess spied the fierce determination in his eyes and shivered. "So Nick, was that you shooting at us that day when Shane came to my uncle's ranch?"

"Yes. I didn't think he'd convince you to guard him." Nick returned his attention to Shane. "Now lean forward. Your turn to be handcuffed. I don't want you two to run away before I get the ransom."

"The ransom?" Shane asked.

"My friend here will be taking you two away, leaving me beside the road for dead. He'll knock me out and shoot me in the chest, not realizing that I have a bullet proof vest, like any security guy would wear when there has been a threat against the employer he's protecting."

"What do you think that will accomplish?" Shane asked. "You know I've made arrangements that no ransom can be paid for my kidnapping from company funds."

"Maybe not, but I bet your parents won't let their only granddaughter be without her father. I'll make sure of that when I talk with them tomorrow."

"Why are you doing this?" Shane bit out the last word between clenched teeth.

"Money, of course."

While Shane occupied Nick's attention, Tess slowly worked her hands down behind the back of the seat. Thank God she'd hidden her second weapon there earlier. She also had a knife strapped to her thigh, but with her hands behind her back, that would be harder to get.

"Don't do this, Nick," Shane said, a nerve jerking in his jaw line.

"Too late. I was committed when Mark Collins approached me about taking you out. With his money and your parents' money, I can get lost and live the kind of life I should've."

"What about your wife?" Tess asked as she worked the handle of the gun into her right palm.

"She walked out on me three months ago. I have nothing to lose. I'm gonna start over in a place the authorities will never find me, assuming they even figure out I'm behind it. Let's go, Cal. You know what to do."

After Cal shut the door and the locks clicked closed, Nick left the front seat and rounded the rear of the limousine.

"Keep an eye on them, I stashed a gun in here earlier." Tess had to get her cuffed hands around to the front.

"Cal hit Nick," Shane said, his voice not betraying any emotion. "He went down."

The sound of the gunshot shuddered down Tess's spine as she brought her arms under her backside and wiggled her legs through the tight loop formed by her bound hands. "It's a good thing I have long arms, or this wouldn't work."

"Cal's coming around to the driver's side."

Tess stopped moving and buried her hands in the folds of her dress, praying the thug didn't look back at them until he got into the limousine. "Good thing Nick left the glass partition open. It gives me a good shot when Cal gets in."

Right on cue, the assailant unlocked the driver's door and opened it. The interior lights popped on. As the man climbed in, he turned toward them. Tess raised her gun and leveled it at the man's head.

"I'm an expert shot, and before you get your weapon up, you'll have a bullet in your brain."

The thug paled.

"Lift your gun up slowly by the barrel then drop it on the backseat floor. I won't hesitate to kill you if you try anything." A steel thread wove through her voice with the last sentence emphasized.

Cal did as instructed.

"Now toss me the key to the handcuffs. I will be watching."

While she talked, Shane contorted himself until his hands were in front of him, too. A few grunts peppered the air, but Tess didn't take her eyes off Cal. When he threw the key into the back, Shane caught it with his bound hands and began working on his lock. Freed, he took Cal's weapon from the floor and aimed it at him.

"Unlock your cuffs, Tess. I've got him." He turned his attention to Cal. "And just so you know, I know how to use this weapon."

Tess hurried to free herself. "Unlock the back doors."

When she heard the click, she slipped out. "I'll be greeting Nick when he awakens. Hand me your cell. I'll call the police."

Standing behind the limousine watching Nick slowly wake

up, Tess placed a 911 call then waited. It was over, all except rounding up Mark Collins.

The next day after the police left, Tess finally allowed herself to relax. She and Shane were sitting in his den. He'd been on the phone a number of times that morning, but she'd stayed in her comfortable place. Her job was over. Mark Collins had been arrested, along with Nick and Cal. Seemed they'd planned for the suspicion to fall on Anthony Revell. Shane was the driving force behind DDI, and with him gone, Mark planned to offer Virtual Technologies a merger that would make them competitive with what was left of Shane's company for the majority share of the marketplace. It was unthinkable the things people would do for money.

Her packed duffel bag was in Uncle Jack's truck, and she would leave as soon as Shane heard if the Virtual Technologies' board approved the merger. He'd been on the phone an hour earlier talking with Dale Mason about what had happened. She'd heard his voice as they'd spoken about the new prospects for both companies as they blended their technology together. Listening to Shane's excitement made her wish she felt that way about her work. Never before had she been dissatisfied with her job. Where had these feelings come from? And why? Because her vacation had been disrupted? It didn't matter. When she returned to Dallas and her life, she'd be fine.

The phone rang, and Shane snatched up the receiver. A smile transformed his whole bearing. When he hung up, he said, "It's official. We're merging with Virtual Technologies."

"I'm glad it worked out. I'm not surprised, though. They'd be foolish to work with anyone but you."

That was her cue. It was time to go.

"The new gaming system they're developing will be fantastic, and with our capabilities, we'll be unstoppable." He rounded his desk and came toward her. "A week ago, I didn't know if I'd see this happen. It wasn't that long ago I was in Jack's cabin, fighting for my life."

Tess stood. "Speaking about your life, I need to get back to mine." She straightened her clothes and pushed back her shoulders, pushing away her feelings for him at the same time. Those feelings should never have developed in the first place. His world was so different from hers.

He bridged the few feet between them and took her hands. "Can't you stay a while and finally have the vacation I interrupted?"

"No, I need to get back to Dallas." *Then I can start forgetting you.*

"Why? You have an apartment there you stay in only because of your job." He tugged her nearer, wrapping his arms around her. "I want us to get to know each other even better."

She felt as though she already knew Shane better than a lot of people. She'd seen him in tough situations, the kinds of situations that could bring out both the best and the worst in people. She loved what she'd discovered—his best. But this ... this falling in love thing? This lifestyle? It wasn't her. She relished living simply, relying only on herself. Having servants didn't fit her lifestyle. Neither did having a man in her life.

"I have to make a living. My job isn't here."

"What if I offered you Nick's position? I need a new head of security, and I've seen you at work. Nothing gets past you."

She stepped away, breaking his embrace. "No. Uncle Jack would be better suited to that job. Ask him."

"What are you afraid of? Remember the kiss on the staircase? I want to see where it leads."

It leads to heartache. She remembered her parents' marriage. Uncle Jack's was good, but most weren't like his. And even his led to heartache. "That kiss should never have happened. You're mistaking gratitude for something more. We both need to forget the kiss and move on. I'm leaving." She pivoted and marched toward the front door, berating herself for ever letting down her professional guard and getting close to Shane.

As she drove toward Uncle Jack's ranch, she made plans to be on a plane for Dallas first thing in the morning. His daughter would be coming back home, and before long, Shane's life would return to normal. And so would hers.

#

Shane stared at the closed door a long moment after Tess left. His chest constricted him, making breathing difficult. *Forget the kiss.* He didn't know if he could. He'd felt as if he'd come home in her arms. Raking his hand through his hair, he began pacing, his thoughts racing.

Maybe she was right. What had transpired between them was all built on the fact that she'd saved his life. He was grateful, not falling in love. If that were the case, once he threw himself into his work he'd forget her.

CHAPTER EIGHT

Three months later

Tess was in her tiny living room in the middle of her exercise routine when her cell phone rang. She wanted to ignore it, but what if it was her boss calling with a new assignment? Her last one had ended a few days ago, and she was ready for another job. Anything to keep herself from thinking about Shane.

She grabbed her cell phone off the coffee table and frowned when she saw the number. She almost didn't answer. But she'd made the first move, writing him a letter. Seemed wrong to ignore him now.

Her finger hovered over the button as she fought her fear. She'd finally forgiven him for the past and had told him that in her letter. She hadn't been able to bring herself to call him and say the words, although she'd meant them. Bitterness and anger that she'd been carrying had only pulled her down and hurt her. Shane and her uncle had been right about forgiveness.

She punched the answer button. "Hello."

"I didn't do anything wrong. I don't need your *forgiveness*." Her father spat the word. "Your mother killed herself. That wasn't my fault. And you wanted to leave me. I didn't send you away."

For a few seconds her dad's raspy voice chilled her as if he were right in front of her, belittling her for something she'd done. Then she thought of God and the peace she'd experienced when she'd written the letter last week. She wouldn't let her father rob her of that peace anymore.

"I'm sorry you feel that way, but it doesn't change how I feel. I forgive you for what happened all those years ago. I wish you the best. Please take care of yourself." *And I really mean that.*

"How . . . dare ...?" His words sputtered to a stop.

Dead silence followed.

"Good bye, Dad."

The sound of his phone slamming filled her ear before she had a chance to disconnect her cell phone. She bowed her head and said, "Please, Lord, help him. He's in Your hands."

When she began her next exercise, she lost herself in it, clearing her mind.

Until five minutes later when the doorbell interrupted her.

Grasping a hand towel, she wiped her sweaty face and neck as she headed toward the door. Through the peephole, she checked to see whom her visitor was.

Shane.

She rested her forehead against the cool wood. What was he doing here? She'd managed today only to think about him once, so far. Of course, she'd only been awake for two hours. No matter what she did, even work, she couldn't get him out of her mind.

And why did she have to be hot and sweaty. What timing! She looked at the ceiling. *Really, if this is Your idea of a joke, I don't think it's very funny.* But then she couldn't deny that rush of feelings. Shane. Here.

She looked through the peephole again and saw Shane start to walk away. She needed to let him go. But before she could stop herself, she unlocked her door and opened it.

He stopped and slowly turned around. His smile melted her insides. She clutched the doorjamb before her legs gave out. She'd missed him so much. Her dreams every night hadn't done him justice.

"Why are you here?" she finally asked. "Uncle Jack would have told me if someone else was after you." Her uncle was working temporarily for Shane until he found the perfect head of security. Uncle Jack didn't want to work full-time, but he didn't mind helping Shane out for a short time.

"May I come in?"

She stepped to the side and allowed him into her apartment, glad her roommate was gone. She didn't want to explain Shane to her. "I was exercising. I'd change, but I haven't finished yet." She was babbling. What she really wanted to do was throw her arms around his neck and kiss him.

"I've tried to stay away, but I can't do it any longer. Ever since you've left, all I think about is you. Instead of time making it better, it's getting worse with you gone. Please reconsider moving to Phoenix. If you don't want to be the head of security at DDI, then work from Phoenix. Jack tells me you really don't have to be in the same town as your agency."

"My uncle has a big mouth."

"Is it true?"

"Yes. But us working together probably wouldn't be a good idea. My parents did, and it was disastrous."

"We aren't your parents. You can still be a bodyguard. You can do whatever you want to do. I don't care. I just know I want you in my life. I love you, Tess."

His declaration zapped her as if she'd held a live electrical wire and survived the shock. "But we were only together a week." She could hardly contain the urge to hold him, but she had to be sensible.

"A very intense week. We skipped the casual dating part of a relationship."

She nodded slowly. "Our feelings are probably not based on anything normal for a couple."

His eyebrows lifted. "*Our* feelings?"

She shrugged, heat filling her face.

"So what if we started differently than other couples? What's wrong with that? I never thought of myself as *normal* anyway. Tell me one thing. How do you feel about me?"

Her throat tightened, locking inside the words she'd wanted to tell him so many times over the past few months.

His earnest expression fell.

"I care about you." No, no. She couldn't lie to him. "That's not quite all. I guess . . . you're always in my thoughts. I've gone over our short time together so many times, trying to understand. A relationship takes months, years to develop. How can I feel like this after just a week?"

"Like . . . this?" he prompted.

"How can I have fallen in love so quickly?"

He gathered her into his arms. "I don't know, and I don't care how we got here. The important part is how we feel. Please, give us a chance. Come to Phoenix. We can become a normal couple and date for months if you want."

She buried her face into his chest, suddenly dying to confess everything. "Can I tell you one of the dreams I had? I dreamed I was having your baby. A child. Me. I mean, I love kids, but I never thought . . ."

He cupped her face. "I think that's a beautiful dream. I know my daughter would love to have a little brother or sister."

"But I haven't even met Rachel."

"That's easy to remedy. Come back to Phoenix with me. Stay at my house or at your uncle's. Whatever you want, but just give us a chance. You can continue to work as a bodyguard or at DDI in security. Or" —he brushed his lips across hers— "you can marry me and have that baby you dreamed about."

It was sweet that he gave her the option to keep working, but she couldn't imagine keeping her job. How could she go on all those trips away when she had him at home, waiting for her?

"Okay. If we promise to take it slow. I want to get to know Rachel. Mostly, I want to be with you." Locking her arms around him, she stood on her tiptoes and kissed him with all her love. Here in his embrace, this was where she belonged.

ABOUT MARGARET DALEY

Bestselling author, Margaret Daley, is multi-published with 94 books. She has written for Harlequin, Abingdon, Kensington, Dell, and Simon and Schuster. She has won multiple awards, including the prestigious Carol Award, Holt Medallion and Inspirational Readers' Choice Contest.

NECESSARY PROOF

CAMY TANG

CHAPTER ONE

For the second time in his life, Alex Villa was accused of a crime. Except that this time, he didn't do it.

He crept through the underbrush, trying not to crunch the dry grass under his work boots, with his eyes on the figure of the lean man in a dirty T-shirt and torn jeans who strode confidently through the trees thirty yards ahead.

It was difficult to stay hidden from the man because the trees here on Harman Ridge in Sonoma County were scraggly, and even the hardy oaks and laurels looked a little shriveled after the dry winter. Soon, the spring rains would turn the California foothills green again, but today the sun beat hot, and the dry undergrowth threatened to give away Alex's presence to the man he was following.

At first glance, the man had looked like a Hispanic migrant worker, with darkly tanned skin and straight midnight hair. But every so often, his shirt would hike up and reveal tattoos across his lower back of strange writing. The letters weren't the standard English alphabet, and certainly not Spanish. The swirling symbols twisted with the movement of the man's torso as he clambered over manzanita and slithered between juniper bushes.

This man had started the stories about the meth lab near Graves Peak, the stories that had begun Alex's recent troubles. This man was the one who had framed him. This man was the reason Alex was facing prison. Again.

He had to pause to take a deep, sharp breath. Prison had been a brutal place, and the memories were like dark ghosts that hovered at the edges of his vision. But prison had also been a place where his life had taken a drastic turn and he'd found peace for the first time in years. He'd found love. He'd found Christ.

The memory calmed the churning in his stomach, and he hunched lower and crept after the man. He'd been feeling mildly nauseated since Detective Carter had reluctantly revealed the "evidence" against Alex. He'd been released, but he wasn't about to wait around to see what other planted evidence would surface that would enable the Sonoma police to convict him.

The trees grew thicker here, and he hung back even more. If this was a second meth lab site, there would be more people around guarding it.

But there weren't other guards. The man headed directly for a mobile home that seemed sunken deep into the scrub brush. A narrow, deeply rutted trail ran from the building back down the other side of the ridge, where the distance to the nearest road was several miles. In contrast, he and the man had been walking cross country from the opposite direction for only about twenty minutes.

With no guards and only a few people aware of this remote location, this lab site would be difficult for law enforcement to find.

Not anymore. He would inform Detective Carter about this meth lab, too, just as soon as ...

He clenched his jaw. Just as soon as he cleared his name. He'd forgotten about his predicament for a pitiful moment. He was no longer a trusted confidential informant for the Sonoma PD. Instead, he was implicated in a police officer's murder.

He circled the mobile home. An acrid toxic gas burned his nostrils, and he gagged at a combination of cat urine and rotten egg smells that wafted over him, emanating from the chemicals in the lab. The drone of a generator almost drowned out the sound of voices, and he crept toward the other side of the trailer. He lay on his stomach and peered through the weeds.

The man he had followed was talking rapidly to two other

men. After a few minutes, Alex recognized the language as Filipino. He'd known several Filipino gang members in prison, and after he came to Christ, he was still friends with some of them, visiting the two still in prison and doing what he could to help the others stay out of jail. Two of them had come to church with Alex once.

He had suspected the language of the man's tattoos were Filipino. It looked like a Filipino gang was involved. Not a big surprise. Alex was friends with many of the local farm workers, who had mentioned seeing more and more Filipino strangers in the area in the past couple years. It matched what Detective Carter had told him about the Tumibay Filipino gang, based in San Francisco, who had been ramping up meth production in the rural areas outside of Sonoma.

The two men he talked to were a study of opposites. One was taller, dressed in a dirty, long-sleeved shirt and jeans despite the heat, sweat running down his shaved head. He was lean, and some wicked knife wound scars running across his left cheek made him look as if he had a permanent one-sided sneer.

The other man was shorter and even more slender, but with paler skin and long black hair pulled into a ponytail. His polo shirt and shorts, while casual, were expensive, as was his watch. He wore glasses, although they couldn't have been very strong because they barely distorted his heavy-lidded black eyes.

Both men responded in Filipino, and the shorter one gestured to a nearby folding table and chair set up several feet away from the mobile home, near the generator that powered the meth lab. A laptop stood open on the table.

The men argued for a few minutes more, then the one he had followed turned and stomped away, back the way he'd come. Alex flattened himself further into the grass, glad he hadn't remained behind the man. He'd have been spotted in a heartbeat.

The two men stood and talked in low voices. From their body language, they appeared to be equals in authority, despite the differences in dress. Another man's voice called from inside the trailer, and the taller one went back into the lab.

The shorter man pulled out a cell phone and frowned at it. He then lifted it up, still staring, and walked in a widening circle.

Straight toward Alex.

God, don't let him find me. He stilled, hearing his heartbeat in his ears. His dark shirt and khaki pants made him hard to spot against the undergrowth, but it wouldn't matter if the man simply stumbled over him.

The man stopped, then backtracked, still staring at his phone. He moved around the trailer and away from Alex while dialing someone. His voice carried over the sound of the generator as he seemed to be giving instructions to someone in rapid Filipino.

Alex made his decision in the space of time between one breath and another.

He leaped to his feet and sprinted to the table. He closed the laptop as quietly as he could and unplugged the power cord, which tangled among some other electrical equipment under the table which he hadn't noticed. One looked like an external hard drive, snarled in a mass of wires. He reached for it, but the man's voice grew louder again.

No time to unplug the external hard drive. Alex took the laptop and ran. He didn't bother to hide the noise as he crashed through bushes and circled around the other side of the trailer. He picked up speed as he headed back the direction he'd come, jumping over bushes and dodging trees.

Shouts sounded behind him, but he didn't look back. There was the crack of a gunshot, and he ducked his head but tried not to slow his speed. More gunshots, but he heard the bullets hit trees several yards behind him. They stopped firing, probably since the trees made him a more difficult target to hit.

He sprinted past the tattooed man that he had followed. The man was several yards away, but apparently unarmed. All he could do was shout as Alex dashed by.

On the way to the meth lab, they'd taken a straight route through the wilderness, about a mile or a little more. The man had parked on the remote access road at the back of old Mr. Rivers's farm, but Alex, trying not to be seen tailing him, had parked on an unused farm track on Mr. Rivers's property, hidden from the road by rows of dead grape vines.

Once out of the trees, he raced for his truck. He stumbled over some clods of dirt from the unused track and nearly dropped the laptop, but he was used to keeping his balance in uneven dirt thanks to his hours working in the fields of his mama's farm and in his brother's greenhouses, and he was able to right himself quickly. He scrounged in his pocket for his car keys and hit the unlock button only a second before he yanked the door open.

As he turned over the engine, the three men he'd seen exploded from the tree line and dashed toward him. The tallest man was in front, and he now pulled out his gun and fired again. Alex ducked low as his window exploded in a cloudy spiderweb of cracks around the bullet hole. He slammed his foot on the accelerator and the truck leaped forward.

More shots, but these hit the frame of his truck. He bumped and jolted down the farm track, but quickly skidded to turn onto the access road. He looked in his rearview mirror and saw the men running toward the tattooed man's car, but he was far down the road before they even reached it. He slid onto the curvy highway that wound through the foothills, and after a few turns, pulled into the long driveway belonging to the farm of a family he knew. He parked behind a stand of trees a little ways back from the road and waited.

The tattooed man's car soon passed by the driveway.

Alex leaned back against the seat. He'd wait to make sure they didn't double back, then he'd find his way to the main highway to Sonoma.

He laid his hand on the laptop on the passenger seat. He was comfortable with electronics, but he was a hardware guy. He understood enough software to know he was a bull in a china shop, so he didn't want to fiddle with the computer in case it had a security feature.

He needed help. He needed to clear his name. His race for

his life couldn't have been for nothing.

Jane Lawton nearly dropped her steaming pot of Mac-N-Cheese at the sound of a powerful fist knocking at her apartment door. "Coming!" She spooned the gooey, bad-for-you goodness into a bowl, then ran some water in the pot in the sink.

The urgent knocking sounded again. Somehow it didn't sound like one of her neighbors, wanting Jane's help with a computer problem. She looked through the peephole.

She felt a sharp pulse at the base of her throat. "Alex?" She opened the door.

Normally a walking Calvin Klein ad, he now had a grim, serious cast to his face as he hurriedly entered her apartment with a messenger bag slung across one broad shoulder. "Quick, close the door."

"What's going on?" She locked the deadbolt.

It frightened her that he looked so different now, lacking his usual smile and dimples. "I need your help, Jane."

She couldn't control the bitterness that burned the back of her throat. It seemed that was the only thing she was good for, helping the men in her life so they could leave her and move on. She swallowed and said carefully, "Doing what?"

He pulled a laptop from his messenger bag. "There's information on this that I need, but I'm not sure if there's any type of security protecting it."

"Whoa." Jane took a step back. "You're saying that's not your laptop, and you want me to get into it? What's going on?" She knew he had been in prison for a few years, but she thought he'd put his illegal past behind him.

He scrubbed his hand over his high forehead. "It's not what it looks like."

"That makes it sound even worse."

He exhaled and seemed to study her. His intent, dark eyes made her squirm. She knew she'd changed a lot in the past year. She'd only spoken to him once in all that time, a few months ago at the party celebrating his brother's engagement to Rachel, Jane's second cousin but as close as a sister. After a minute or two of chit-chat, he had been quick to leave her to speak to Detective Carter, which had given her a pang even though she hadn't been in a sociable mood. What a difference from when she and Alex had first met years ago. He had seemed interested in her, but she'd been ...

She shoved the memories aside. "I'm only going to ask this one more time. What's going on?"

"I just ... I can trust you, right?"

"Trust me with what?"

"Could I sit down? Have some coffee?" He sniffed. "Is that Mac-N-Cheese?"

"Did you want some?"

He gave her a smile that caused that sharp pulse at the base of her throat again. "I haven't eaten since breakfast."

And it was already past seven. "But it's Mac-N-Cheese. From a box."

"So?"

"You eat Mac-N-Cheese? Isn't your mother good enough to be on Iron Chef or something like that?"

The smile disappeared, and long lines were drawn on either side of his mouth. "I haven't been home all day."

The wooden tone of his voice made Jane wonder if he hadn't gone home because he couldn't, not because he chose not to. Unlike Jane, Alex and his brother had a solid relationship with their mother and would do anything to protect her.

The combination living room/dining room in her one-bedroom apartment was currently her office, so she hastily swept aside some electrical equipment and notes from the dining table and set them in a neat stack on the floor. "Have a seat. I don't have decaf coffee."

He sank into a wooden chair with a sigh. "I need leaded right now, anyway."

As she retrieved her bowl of food from the kitchen, she eyed his six-foot-plus frame, at least two hundred pounds of solid muscle. She set the entire thing in front of him. "Go ahead."

"No—" he began.

"I'll cook some eggs."

His eyes softened. "Thanks, Jane."

She tried not to think of those eyes as she started the coffee maker and whisked eggs with soy sauce. He made her feel ... special, and she couldn't trust her own feelings anymore. Rachel had accused her of becoming too cynical this past year, but could anyone blame her after what had happened?

So in her frying pan, she scrambled the eggs mixed with soy sauce and served it on some rice she'd heated in the microwave. "Shoyu-egg-rice," as her Japanese mother called it, and it was Jane's comfort food. She needed comfort right now, in preparing to deal with the handsome man at her dining table and whatever trouble he'd brought into her home.

When she returned to the dining table, he had just finished the Mac-N-Cheese, but she had anticipated that. She served him some of the eggs and rice. "Here."

He frowned at the brown-colored scrambled eggs. "What's this?"

"Japanese-style breakfast. Try it."

She bowed her head to say grace, but she felt self-conscious. Not because he wasn't Christian, because she knew he was, but she only said grace these days out of habit. She'd been feeling like a chasm had opened between her and God. She couldn't understand why He'd allowed her to be so hurt, and maybe her distrust of men had extended to Him, too.

She took a bite of salty egg, hot rice, and remembered breakfasts at home with her mom and her brother, a peaceful and innocent time before she'd been aware of how little her father had cared for her.

Of how little anyone cared for her, apparently.

"This is good." He paused from shoveling food into his mouth. "What's wrong?"

She realized she'd been frowning into her bowl. "Nothing." She stabbed at the rice with her fork. "That should be my question."

He grimaced and slowed his eating. "Look, Jane ..."

"I want the full version. Not the version you'd tell your mama."

The glance he sent her could almost have been playful, but Jane steeled herself against the dimples that appeared briefly in his cheeks. "It's a little unnerving how you can read me, Jane."

"You're stalling." She could hear the coffeemaker burbling. "You don't get coffee until you explain yourself."

He took the last bite of eggs and rice and pushed the bowl away from him. "I'm being set up, Jane, and I have to clear my name. You heard about the police officer who died in that shoot-out at a meth lab in the foothills last week?"

She nodded.

His face tightened and he stared at her wooden tabletop. "That man is dead because of me."

CHAPTER TWO

After a beat of shock, Jane said, "Aren't you being a little melodramatic? The paper said it was a gang member who shot him."

"I gave the police the location of that meth lab, but it was a trap."

"How did you know about the lab?"

He ran a tanned hand through his short, dark hair. "I know a lot of the farm workers around Sonoma, and some of them found out about the lab and told me."

"How'd they find it?"

"A meth lab smells pretty potent."

"Oh."

"I told Detective Carter, but there were gang members waiting for the Sonoma PD to arrive."

She could see how he might feel it was his fault. "There's no way you could have known that would happen."

"Then the next day, five thousand dollars were deposited into my bank account from an offshore account."

"From who?"

He shook his head. "I don't know. I told Detective Carter about the deposit right away, but it looks like I was paid to tell the Sonoma PD about the lab so they'd get gunned down. I'm under investigation."

"But you help Detective Carter all the time. Doesn't that count for something?" When Jane had first met Alex, she'd overheard the detective asking to speak to him about helping the police with a case. Alex's brother, Edward, had explained to her that Alex was a confidential informant for the Sonoma PD. Alex was friends with many of the farm workers in Sonoma, and if they had a concern, they told him, who would tell the detective. This roundabout way to get information to the police protected the identities of people who weren't comfortable going to the police directly.

"Detective Carter knows I'm innocent, but it looks bad." A muscle in his jaw flexed. "I'm being set up. I'm thinking that it's only a matter of time before the police find planted evidence that will get me convicted."

He must feel trapped. Suffocating. It would be intolerable to someone like him, who was full of life, full of energy, and always transparent. "I'm sorry." She touched his forearm.

She didn't feel a jolt, but something about touching him made her feel ... different. As if he'd flipped on some switch inside her.

She snatched her hand back and stood up. "I'll get the coffee."

She had to remember this was Alex, for goodness' sake. She'd known him for a few years already. What was more, when they'd first met, he'd asked her out to dinner, and she'd turned him down, admitting that she was interested in someone else.

And she had been, at the time. She'd had grand hopes of a lasting, meaningful relationship built on respect.

What a colossal idiot she'd been to think there was anything about herself that would attract anyone.

But Alex had been attracted to you, a small voice whispered.

Except she was no longer that woman he'd asked out on a date. And she never would be again.

She needed to focus on the issue right now. She put his coffee in front of him, black, the way he liked it. "Who's setting you up? Although if people know you help the police, that list might be long."

"I know exactly who it is. The Tumibays."

The Filipino gang who had meth labs scattered in the wilderness areas around Sonoma. "The police raided a few of their labs in the past few months. You told the police about them?"

He nodded. "I found out from some day laborers. Lots of people are worried about the meth. Kids are getting addicted, especially in the poorer areas."

"I know," Jane said in a low voice. "Monica was telling me that there have been more and more meth overdose cases at her free children's clinic."

"I've been following up on any leads I can ferret out about the Tumibays. They threatened me a few times." He shrugged. "They soon figured out it wouldn't work. But then they tried to attack Mama."

"When did this happen?" Jane sat up in her chair. "Is she all right?"

"She's fine. It was a month ago. I was at the greenhouses, but three of the farmhands live with us at the house, and they held the gang off until the police arrived. They arrested the gang captain in charge of the meth operation here in Sonoma."

"So shouldn't that have ended it all?"

"There's a new captain the Tumibays sent to take over the operation."

Jane finally saw what was happening. "The new captain is trying to ruin your reputation with the police. He saw that threatening you or your family wasn't effective."

"After the officer was killed, I went to talk to the farm workers who told me about the meth lab in the first place. They had heard about it from a day laborer who spoke Spanish with a strange accent. I have a couple Filipino friends who speak Spanish with an accent, and I thought he might have been planted by the Tumibays. I found the guy and followed him to Graves Peak." He told her about the meth lab and the three men he'd seen.

"So you stole the laptop from the new Tumibay captain?"

"No, it wasn't the captain. I know what Talaba looks like. These were just his men."

"Still." Jane stared at the innocuous-looking laptop. "You should turn this in to the police."

"And tell them I found another meth lab? How convenient. If they were on the fence about if I'm involved with the Tumibays, I'm sure that wouldn't change their minds *at all*."

"But they're the *police*—"

"And they think I gave them information that got one of their own killed. I'm not their favorite person at this moment. If I hand this laptop to them, they're going to view it with suspicion. They're not going to be careful about any kind of data it might have, because I could be feeding them more false leads. If it were my laptop, I'd set up security protocols in case it was taken, some program to erase sensitive data. That means we only get one shot at this, and the data on this computer might be the only thing to clear my name." He reached out to cover her hand with his. "Jane, you're the only one I know who can find a way to bypass any security protocols."

His palm was large and warm. Derek used to touch her like this, and it had made her stomach flutter like it did right now with Alex.

She pulled her hand away from him.

Could she trust him? She'd trusted Derek and look how that had gone.

But she knew Alex. She trusted his brother, Edward. And the fact he was being set up, that people who knew him were no longer believing him, must feel like a spear to the gut. She knew, because it had felt that way when her father hadn't believed her.

She wanted to help him because she couldn't let someone else feel he was being abandoned by his friends.

At that moment, her neighbor's dog began barking. "That's strange," Jane murmured before she could stop herself.

"What's strange?" He had grown tense.

She shook her head. "I'm being paranoid after what you've been talking about."

He gave her a hard look. "Just tell me, Jane."

"Well, Wiley—the dog—hardly ever barks. Sarah's a dog trainer, and her well-behaved pets are a point of professional pride for her."

His eyes narrowed. "Now that I think about it, the dog didn't bark when I came to your apartment."

"The last time Wiley barked was when some kids were fooling around on the fire escape."

There was a heartbeat of silence, then he shot to his feet. "Jane, get down."

To her credit, Jane didn't ask why or demand to know what was happening. She stared at him with her wide, gold-flecked brown eyes for a moment, then she dropped to her knees.

"Where's the fire escape?" he asked.

"Bedroom window."

He snapped off the lights as he made his way to the dark bedroom. The dog's yapping pierced through several apartment walls to reach his ears, but he hoped it masked the sound as he eased open the sliding glass window. He grabbed a small facial mirror propped up on Jane's dressing table and stuck a corner out the window. It took him a bit of tilting to find the right angle to see the fire escape balcony.

There was a man on the fire escape, heading his way.

He had to get Jane out of here. He'd guess there was also a man heading down the hallway toward Jane's apartment. It's what he would do, in this situation.

Thank You, Father God. If the dog hadn't barked, or Jane hadn't noticed, they might have been trapped. He'd figure out later how they'd found him.

He weighed his options. The fire escape was narrow and difficult fighting terrain, but he didn't know how many men were nearing the front door, whereas there was only one outside Jane's window.

He hurried to the bedroom door and gestured to Jane. "Grab the laptop," he said in a quiet voice.

She scurried toward him, shoving the laptop into the messenger bag he'd brought with him.

"Stay down," he told her, "but be ready to follow me."

She nodded. Her face was even paler in the dimness of her bedroom, and he saw the trembling in her hands, but she had a firm determination to her chin.

He hesitated beside the open window. He had only one shot at this. He took a deep breath, then lightly leaped over the sill onto the fire escape.

His boots hit the metal with a clang. He immediately sprinted toward the man, who was only a few feet away now.

The man had stiffened when Alex appeared out of the window, and he hadn't yet recovered when Alex barreled into him. The man was shorter but still taller than average, and even though Alex had had the element of surprise when he attacked, the man was faster. His elbow snapped out, and although Alex ducked his head, the blow grazed his temple.

The two of them hit the floor of the balcony with a thundering shudder from the metal. The narrow width of the fire escape and Alex's broad shoulders made his punches awkward, and his blows were weaker than his sparring sessions at the gym with his buddies. But he only needed to incapacitate the man until he and Jane could get away.

Alex grabbed a fistful of shirt and slammed the frontal bone of his own skull into the man's face. He felt rather than heard the man's nose break, and blood spurted across his cheek. The man gave a sharp groan of pain, and Alex followed with a jab to the jaw.

The man's body stiffened, then fell back. He wasn't completely out because his arms waved feebly, but Alex yelled, "Jane!"

She was already climbing out the window with the messenger bag thrown over her shoulder. Her eyes slid over the man as she leaped over his body on the fire escape, but she didn't glance back as she followed Alex down the stairs.

They were on the ground in seconds since Jane was only on the third floor. He had his truck keys, but realized the men probably knew the make and model of his pickup. "Do you have your car keys?"

Jane pulled the keys from her slacks pocket. "Over here." Luckily, her parking slot was near the fire escape.

Of course, her car was practical and sensible, like her. The hybrid would be uncomfortable for him to sit in, much less drive. He shook his head when she offered him the keys.

She stared for a quick moment. "Really? Not what I would have expected from a guy." She scrambled into the driver's seat.

"I'm secure in my masculinity," he couldn't resist teasing. As they buckled up, he added, "Besides, I'm probably better than you at spotting a tail."

She backed out of the parking slot like a rocket, slamming his body against the seatbelt. He thought her driving might be attributed to nerves, until she got onto the street.

The woman drove like a maniac. Who knew that lurking under Jane's neutral colored, professional clothing was a *Grand Theft Auto* leaderboard winner?

"Where to?" The tires screeched a little as she took a corner onto the expressway.

"Into traffic." He searched the cars behind them. "If we're being followed, it won't hurt to be somewhere we can try to lose them."

She wove between cars, darting left and right without warning and without hitting the brakes. He had to grab the door handle so he wouldn't fly out of his seat.

"See anyone?" She finally had to brake hard when she cut in front of a minivan and behind a convertible who had just moved into the lane.

"I think we're safe," he said.

She eased up on the gas a minuscule amount. "Now where to?"

He nodded toward the backseat, where she'd tossed the messenger bag containing the laptop. "Anywhere you can get the information off of that computer."

"You're kidding, right?"

"What do you mean?"

Jane turned exasperated eyes to his. "All the equipment I needed to examine that laptop is in a place currently crawling with Filipino gang members—my apartment."

CHAPTER THREE

Even though it looked like they'd lost anyone trying to follow them, Alex closely observed the cars around them as he directed Jane outside of Sonoma toward Jorge's tavern. It was in a remote area, he had a lot of friends there, and more importantly, he'd left his computer toolbox there last week.

Jane turned into the tiny dirt parking lot in front of the brown building. It stood in a small lot between two orchards, both in bud with new fruits soon to appear as spring swept into the county. His expert gardening nose smelled cherry blossoms as he unfolded himself from Jane's car and stretched.

"Does Jorge have wireless internet?" Jane grabbed the laptop from the backseat.

"No, he's hard-wired."

"How close is the nearest house?"

"A couple miles in either direction." He nodded toward the narrow road that fronted the tavern. "There's only farms and orchards in this area. Why?"

"I'm probably being overly cautious, but I don't know what kind of security this computer has. The security program might be instructed to find the nearest wireless network and broadcast data so the owner can find it again."

"And you don't want there to be a wireless network it can find."

"Exactly. And you said you don't know anything about software." Jane's tone was almost teasing, although her eyes were still somber from the events of only an hour ago.

"I know only enough to make me dangerous." He led the

way up to the narrow front porch, then opened one of the two swinging double doors to the tavern.

It had been an old farmhouse before Jorge bought it for his tavern, useless because the farmland had been sold around it. He'd torn down most of the walls on the first floor in order to put in scarred, mismatched tables and chairs, but there was still the stairs to the second floor living quarters on one side of the front hallway. There was no one inside except the deeply tanned, old Hispanic man standing behind the counter at the back of the front room, near the kitchen door.

"Alejandro!" Jorge raised his hands in greeting and waved them toward the counter.

In Spanish, Alex said, "Thanks for letting us come so late, Jorge."

"For you, anything, my friend."

Alex turned to Jane and said in English, "This is Jorge."

Jane shook Jorge's hand and surprised them both by answering in Spanish. "I'm Jane Lawton. Nice to meet you."

"You speak Spanish?" Alex asked her.

"I took it in high school." She shrugged. "And a couple of my neighbors are Hispanic, so I use it often enough."

"Are you hungry? Adelita should be almost done cooking." Jorge disappeared behind the kitchen door.

"Where's your toolbox?" Jane asked.

"Later. Adelita and Jorge rarely cook this late. They're doing it just for us."

Jane looked around the empty tavern. "Why aren't they open for dinner?"

"Jorge and Adelita started their business by making burritos and selling them cheaply to the farm hands in the fields. They got so popular that they opened this tavern, but it's for breakfast and lunch only because they still send the lunch wagon out to the fields every day. They're usually in bed by now because they get up so early."

Jane's delicate cheeks colored a strawberry pink that reminded him of some of the rare roses his brother cultivated for clients at the greenhouses. "They shouldn't have cooked for us."

"They enjoy being hospitable."

A silence fell between them that was more awkward than the silence in the car. Then, Jane had been concentrating on driving and he had been keeping an eye out for anyone following them. Here, in the quiet of the tavern, he became aware again of how beautiful she was, with her slightly slanted eyes and high cheekbones, the graceful neck exposed by her dark straight hair swept up into a twist at the back of her head. It had been perfectly smooth when he'd arrived at her apartment, but now wisps fell, probably from their mad dash down the fire escape.

Every time he saw her was like a kick in his gut, no matter how many times they happened to meet. He had been eager to ask her out when they first met, but she'd shyly confessed she was interested in someone else. He had been jealous of the guy who could put the glow in her cheeks and the golden glitter in her brown eyes.

But when he'd seen her at his brother's engagement party, he'd been surprised at the faint lines alongside her pink mouth, the deadness in her eyes. Someone had hurt her, badly. He'd wanted to ask, but hesitated because it was obvious she was still in pain. And in the end, Detective Carter had waved urgently to him, and he'd had to leave her to speak to him.

"How have you been lately?" The question seemed a bit lame, considering they'd spent the better part of the last two hours together. "The last time we met, you said you had a new job."

There was a flash of pain that tightened the skin around her eyes, and he wanted to kick himself. But she answered in a quiet voice, "It's fine. It pays the bills."

What a change from when they'd first met, and she'd talked excitedly about the startup she worked for and the voice recognition software she was helping to write. "Are you still writing voice software?"

Her jaw flexed before she answered him. "No. I'm doing IT support for an insurance company."

"Oh," he said faintly. Jane was brilliant. Why was she doing routine IT work rather than shining like a star at a tech startup?

She obviously didn't want to talk about it. "You're still helping to run your mama's farm?"

"And helping Edward with his greenhouse business."

"And being a CI for Sonoma PD. When do you sleep?" Her attempt at a joke didn't quite lighten the brittleness in her voice.

"All I do is talk to people, be friendly. It's not work." He liked feeling that he was helping the community. He could take risks others couldn't, like fighting against the Tumibays' meth production. What if he couldn't do it anymore? What would happen to him?

He didn't want to think about it. He *would* clear his name. He had to.

"Are you still dating that one guy?" He tried to sound casual, to hide the fact he wanted to know.

She stiffened, all her muscles rigid. "What guy?"

He just couldn't stop making things worse. "You, uh, told me about that guy at work ..."

She turned her face away from him. "It didn't work out," she said in a wooden voice.

"I'm sorry." He wasn't. How long ago had it been? What kind of a loser didn't appreciate the jewel she was?

Thankfully, Jorge and his wife, Adelita, entered with steaming plates of food. Adelita laid the plate she carried in front of Alex, then reached across the counter to grasp his face and kiss his cheek. "So good to see you, Alejandro."

"You smell like cinnamon." He grinned at her. "Does that mean you made me *sopapillas?*"

She rolled her eyes. "You and your bottomless stomach."

"I just like your cooking."

Adelita then turned and kissed Jane, too, which made her cheeks flush with pleasure. "Call me Adelita."

"I'm Jane."

"Eat, eat." Adelita gestured to the plates of food.

"I'll pray for us," Alex said to Jane.

Before he bowed his head to say grace, he saw the bleakness that shuttered over Jane's eyes for a brief moment. She had always been a strong Christian. Had whatever gave her that brittle, fragile quality struck a blow against her faith in God, too?

He glanced at her as he finished saying grace, but her face was a polite mask. However, that slipped to reveal awe as she took her first bite of the bean burrito Jorge and Adelita had made.

"That's amazing," Jane said to Adelita. "You make your own tortillas?"

"Of course." Jorge seemed offended she would think he'd serve anything else.

Alex hid his smile as he wolfed down a burrito. The flour tortilla was soft and slightly crispy on the outside from being lightly pan-seared, while the beans were silky and flavorful with Adelita's secret spice mix.

Jorge set two bottles of Mexican orange soda in front of them. "Now, you tell me what kind of trouble you're in."

Alex hesitated.

"Alejandro, you must let me help you," Jorge said quietly.

So he told them about the shootout at the meth lab, about the money appearing in his bank account, about following the tattooed man to the second meth lab on Graves Peak.

Jorge's dark eyes narrowed, making the lines deepen on his broad forehead. "I know the man you speak of. The tattoo, the accent. His name is Rodrigo."

"You don't know his last name?"

"No. I saw him in the fields once, last week or the week before, but never again. He never came here with the regulars."

Many of the Filipinos Alex had known had Spanish names, so that didn't help him much. The man had probably been working in the fields in order to spread the information about the meth lab trap.

He told them about the laptop and the men at Jane's apartment. Adelita's chocolate colored eyes grew large, and she covered Jane's forearm with her hand. "You are all right?"

"I'm fine." Jane smiled and it transformed her, revealing a radiance that made his chest tighten.

"You stay here and rest tonight," Jorge said. "We have extra bedrooms."

"No, too many people will come for breakfast in the morning," he said.

"Leave before then," Adelita said. "No one will know you were here."

"Thank you."

"We must go to bed," Jorge said. "We wake at four to start breakfast."

"You know where the bedrooms are upstairs?" Adelita said, and Alex nodded. "There are fresh sheets in the hall closet."

She kissed his cheek again, then also kissed Jane. Her hands lingered on the girl's smooth hair. "Alejandro is a good man. He will take care of you."

Jane's neck turned scarlet, and her gaze dropped.

Adelita's words only reinforced his protective instinct toward Jane. He wouldn't let anything happen to her. He wanted to make sure no one hurt her ever again.

Jorge and Adelita said their goodnights, then headed up the stairs.

Jane and Alex picked at their food in silence for a while. Her neck was still red with embarrassment, and he didn't know what to say to smooth over the moment. He cleared his throat. "They're good people."

"They trust you, which makes me feel better about trusting you, too. I don't want to put them in danger."

The way he had put her in danger. "I'm sorry to drag you into this. I didn't think. I just knew I needed your help."

"Don't feel bad. I would never refuse to help you." She sipped her soda. "To help anyone," she added.

Ouch. But a part of him suspected that she was pushing him away as a defense mechanism, due to whatever had changed her so much in the past year.

He wanted to put his arms around her, to surround her with his strength so she wouldn't have anything to fear, but she had a quality of barbed self-sufficiency emanating from her body language that kept him in his seat.

She had always been quiet, serious, even geeky in her conversation, but she'd never before looked so ... desolate. What had happened to her? He knew she wouldn't tell him.

"How did those guys find you?" Jane asked. "You ditched your cell phone, right?"

He nodded. Jane had done the same within minutes of escaping her apartment.

"Did they follow you to my apartment?"

"I know they didn't, because I was looking out for them and I drove in circles for a while to make sure no one was behind me. They saw my truck, but the only way they could have tracked that was through traffic cameras."

Jane gave him a sidelong look. "If they have someone in Sonoma PD, they could have."

He hadn't thought of that. "They may not have been able to track your car here. There aren't many traffic cameras out near these farmlands."

"We probably shouldn't stay here, regardless. But they might spot my car when we leave the area."

"I know a way back to Sonoma through back roads." Before he had spoken to Jane, he had agonized about simply turning the laptop over to the police, but he'd been desperate and he knew the police hadn't trusted him, not after the death of that officer. Now he was glad he hadn't turned in the laptop. What might have happened to it if the Tumibays did indeed have a mole in the Sonoma police department?

He suddenly realized, "I didn't check the laptop for a GPS tracker."

"I'll check, but I doubt it. An installed GPS tracker requires a continuous connection to a cellular network or satellite, and I can't see a gang member who's doing illegal things on a laptop signing up for a GPS subscription that the FBI can trace back to them. Plus it's a major drain on the battery. Tracking software is more practical than GPS." She picked up the messenger bag and pulled out the laptop. "Where's your toolbox? I want to look under this baby's hood."

"Jorge said he'd leave it behind the counter for me." He slid off his stool and went behind the pitted wooden counter. His toolbox lay on the floor, and he hefted it up to set it before Jane.

"Why is your toolbox here?" She opened it and sifted through the small gauge screwdrivers.

"One of Jorge's kids gave him a larger memory card for his computer, so I came over to install it for him. Then I started playing soccer with Jorge's grandkids and stayed for dinner. After dinner, I left and forgot my toolbox here."

"You didn't need it at home?" She started unscrewing the back of the laptop.

"This is my computer toolbox. I have other toolboxes at home for the cars and the farming equipment." He was comfortable around computers, but Jane began unscrewing components left and right. "You're taking it apart without booting it up first?"

"I'm removing the wireless adapter and bluetooth card." She attacked something with a pair of tweezers. "I don't know what kind of security software it has, but if he was paranoid, he'd have installed a LoJack type of software in the UEFI that would connect to the internet as soon as it had a chance. It could even be programmed to delete sensitive data. I don't want this laptop to phone home and give our location away."

He winced as something snapped, but Jane wasn't unduly worried as she removed an electrical piece from the vicinity of the motherboard. "Hardware isn't my specialty, but if I can get the hard drive out, I might be able to use another computer to hack the information off of it."

He thought of her computer at her apartment. "What kind of computer?"

"I can't use just any computer." Jane stared at the hard drive in the laptop, chewing her bottom lip as she thought. "But there's one at my workplace."

"Those guys were at your apartment. They'll know by now where you work and they might be looking out for you."

"This late at night? And this soon after they raided my apartment?"

"You want to go tonight?"

She shrugged. "Part of the job is being on call for emergencies. I've had to go into work late at night lots of times."

"They still might be watching the building. They know you're with me and that we have the laptop, so they're not going to leave any stone unturned. At least, that's what I would do if I were a desperate drug gang captain."

Jane leaned forward over the countertop toward him, and there was a calculating light in her eyes. "What if we could get into the building without being seen?"

CHAPTER FOUR

Jane shivered as she and Alex hiked across the manicured lawns of the Magnolia Scott Business Complex campus, but not from the cold. There were occasional lampposts along the cement walkways that cut between the shadowy buildings, but most of the campus was in darkness that had a deathly stillness to it. No night birds, no cicadas at this time of year, just a wet coldness to the air that seemed to make their footsteps echo even louder.

He had indeed known back roads back to Sonoma, although the potholes had made her teeth rattle. But they avoided traffic cameras, and luckily Jane's workplace was in a business complex that nestled next to the rolling foothills, not in the middle of a busy urban area. They'd driven as close as they could, then parked along the far edge of the campus to walk to the building where her company lay.

She shivered again in her cardigan, the only outerwear she'd been wearing when they ran from her apartment. He noticed.

"Are you cold?" He wrapped a large arm around her shoulders, his hand rubbing her shoulders.

She had never been this close to him before. She caught the green sweetness of basil, the woody tang of rosemary, and overlying it all was the sharp, earthy scent of his musk. It made the tension across her shoulders release, while at the same time a fluttering started in her ribcage.

She could almost pretend that she was protected, that she was cherished by someone.

"You'll be warmer when we get inside," he whispered to

her, his breath tickling her ear. "How far is it?"

"Building G is right there." She pointed to the looming hulk of the four-story office building at the west-most corner of the business complex, which sat next to Building H.

"That's J. Callaway Insurance?"

"No, my workplace is Building H. Building G is empty right now, but both buildings used to be used by the Jorden Corporation. My card key will get us into Building G, and there's a walkway on the fourth floor that will get us into Building H."

"They won't see us entering Building G?"

"We'll use the back entrance, which can't be seen from the parking lot."

"Let's start avoiding the lampposts." He steered her onto the grass, wet and sharp with cold dew.

They melted into the shadows as they approached the entrance doors, which were lighted by an overhead floodlight. The light couldn't be avoided, but Jane swiped her card key quickly through the card reader and the bolts for the door snapped open. She yanked at the glass door and they slipped inside.

He headed to the elevator doors in the foyer, but Jane pulled him to the stairwell. "The elevators are really slow. It's faster to walk up."

They climbed to the fourth floor, their steps echoing loudly in the spartan stairwell. She led him through a large area empty of anything but shabby looking cubicles to the far corridor that ended at another locked door. She swiped her card and got them access to the enclosed walkway to Building H.

They walked quickly, but Jane glanced down to where she could see a corner of the parking lot. There were no cars, but anyone after them could have parked in a dark corner of the lot that she couldn't see.

Building H had more carpeting than empty Building G, but it created a muffled pall that made Jane nervous. Anyone could sneak up on them.

"Where to?" he asked.

"Second floor."

They took the stairwell down two flights to the IT department, one room filled with servers and another office area where her cubicle sat against a wall. The air was cold and dry from the air conditioning keeping the equipment from overheating in the server room, and she could hear the whir of the fans. She didn't turn on the lights, however, as she made her way to her desk.

Like her dining room table at home, her desk was piled with papers as well as equipment and cables, almost burying her desktop computer. She picked up the phone. "I have to call Security to let them know I'm here."

"Aren't they in the building?"

"No, Security is across campus in Building A, but they'll have seen my card key entry already on their computer monitors."

He nodded, but his eyes were moving around the quiet room at her coworkers' desks.

Jane dialed Security, and a friendly man's voice answered immediately. "Hi, Miss Lawton. I saw your card key entry through Building G."

"Hi, James." She always chatted with James and it would look strange if she didn't, so she said, "You got the night shift again this week?"

He gave a long-suffering sigh. "Yup. Jesse's got the flu. But the overtime will pay for a new bike for my daughter."

"How's Rosa's broken arm? Did she get her cast off yet?"

"It comes off next week."

"Bet she can't wait." She saw Alex's wary expression. "James, I'm not sure how long I'll be here tonight."

"No problem, Miss Lawton. When you do leave, just to warn you, a couple hours ago, I got an error message from the card key reader for the front door of Building G. I went to check it, and it looked okay, but let me know if you have problems."

"All right. Thanks, James."

As she hung up the phone, a chill passed through her that

had nothing to do with the darkness, or the air conditioning. An error message for the card key reader ... and they'd made noise walking down the stairwell ... and she'd spent time chatting with James ...

The air in her lungs suddenly felt thin.

"Alex—"

He turned toward her.

The gunshot was deafening, even with the carpet and cloth-covered cubicle walls absorbing some of the sound. His entire body jerked. "Jane, get down!"

Her scream lodged in her throat. She fell to her knees beside him, her shaking hands pressing to the dark, wet stain on his arm. It felt hot to the touch, or maybe her hands were cold.

If he hadn't turned toward her at that moment, where would he have been shot instead?

His body jolted at the pressure of her hands on his wound. "They're coming for you," he said through gritted teeth.

No, they were coming for the computer. She had an idea.

"Put pressure on it." She guided his hand to the wound, then moved to her desk. She reached for a hammer and an extra laptop hard drive. She hadn't removed the hard drive from the laptop yet, but they didn't know that.

"Stay back or I'll destroy the hard drive!"

She peeked around the edge of her cubicle wall and saw two men in the shadows of the door to the office room. One was the man who had been on the fire escape balcony. She got a better look at him this time, noting his dark hair, dark skin, wiry build, and the gun he held in his hand. His nose had been broken in his fight with Alex, and there was already dark purple bruising beneath his eye.

The second man was a stranger to her, but she remembered Alex's description of the finely dressed man at the meth lab. This man wore a polo shirt and slacks, and he didn't have a gun. When he turned his head, she saw he was wearing glasses.

"You're being ridiculous, Jane," the Glasses Man called to her, but he didn't come any closer. "You're trapped."

After tracking Alex to her apartment, he must have gone through it to find out who she was. "Trapped animals are the most vicious," she shot back. "I have a hammer and your hard drive here on my desk."

"Well, that's convenient," he drawled. He even stuck his hands in his pants pockets. "You work in IT, Jane. Of course you'd have extra hard drives lying around. That one isn't mine."

"Are you so sure about that? The hard drive was a breeze compared to when I removed your bluetooth card and wireless adapter." She rattled off the specs of the pieces she had removed earlier this evening. "Those are yours, aren't they?"

She could see that the Glasses Man had stiffened. "Jane, you can't win. As soon as I saw your apartment, as soon as I found out what you do for a living, I knew you'd come here, to your workplace, to utilize your computers here."

"He's just trying to rattle you. Don't listen to him." Alex's whisper was right next to her ear, and she jumped. He had gotten up and was crouched next to her, blood still slowly soaking into his shirtsleeves.

"Your arm—"

"I'm fine. I have an idea. Keep him talking." He grabbed the fire extinguisher she kept under her desk and silently moved away, staying low and under the edge of the cubicles so the two men couldn't see him. The thick carpet muffled his footsteps.

"Jane, I got into a locked building just to wait for you. And no one will be able to find any evidence at the card key reader that we were here. They might even think you let us into the building. Do you see? There's nothing I can't do." Glasses Man nodded to his associate, who started moving toward the far wall.

Her heart rate picked up. Would he be able to see Alex? "One more step, and I'm going to start whaling on this hard drive."

The man didn't stop walking.

"You can't blame me for knowing Alex is somewhere

planning something," Glasses Man said, "gunshot wound or not."

"I'm sure you could retrieve *some* data from isolated sectors in a broken platter," Jane said, "but not much."

Glasses Man's face became an ugly sneer, then he hissed at his associate, who finally stopped moving.

After a moment, Glasses Man regained his confident, almost-bored tone. "What are we doing to do, Jane? Sit here all night?"

Maybe she could play the stupid female role. "Your friend is going to drop his gun, and then I'm going to throw the hard drive to you."

Even in the darkness of the office, she could see Glasses Man smile. "Fine. And then we'll let you both go. No harm, no foul."

Yeah, right. "Okay." She tried not to let her sarcasm show.

Glasses Man nodded to his associate, who reluctantly set his gun on the floor close to his foot.

"Kick it away from you," Jane said.

The man frowned, but nudged the gun away a few inches with his foot. If she told him to kick it farther, he might take a step and see Alex, wherever he was.

Jane slowly stood up so the two men could see her over the top of the cubicle walls. She raised the hard drive in her left hand, while her right still clenched tightly around the hammer. "Here it is."

"Just throw it to me nice and easy," Glasses Man said.

Jane stepped out so that she had a clear line of sight to Glasses Man. She made as if to throw the hard drive, then hurled the hammer straight at his knees.

At that moment, Alex leaped up and shot the other man with a blast from the fire extinguisher. The sound roared in Jane's ears.

Her hammer struck Glasses Man's left kneecap. He crumpled, but his shout of pain was drowned by the report from the other man's gun.

Alex! Was he all right?

Jane dropped to the ground. She hesitated, but knew what Alex would want her to do. She began crawling frantically toward the door. She was tempted to get to her feet, but didn't want to become a target for the other man and his gun.

Glasses Man lay rolling on the floor and she had to circle wide around him. However, he lunged for her and grabbed her ankle. His face was contorted with rage and pain, and his fingers bit into her tendons and bones.

She pulled her other foot back and kicked at him, but his head was too far away, so she began aiming for his elbow. She slammed into it once, then twice. Finally his hand loosened and she yanked her ankle free.

He swore at her and lunged for her again, both hands scrabbling at her legs.

God, help me!

At that moment, she spotted a dark shape on the beige carpet. The hammer, where it had fallen after it ricocheted off of the man's knee. She dove for it, her fingers curling around the smooth wooden handle. She twisted around and swung it wildly at the man's hands.

He jerked his hands back, but the hammer knocked at a finger or knuckle, and he winced.

And then suddenly a huge figure crashed on top of Glasses Man, rolling them away.

"Alex!"

Alex swung a fist at the man's jaw, and his eyes rolled back, showing the whites. His body immediately became a rag doll.

Jane crawled to him at the same moment he looked up at her. "Are you all right?" they both asked at the same time.

And then Jane's hands were around his waist, her head tucked under his chin, his arms tight around her. His heartbeat galloped under her cheek, and she felt the *whoosh* of his hard breathing. The scent of his musk wrapped around her like a cape.

It was only for a few seconds, a handful of heartbeats. He released her. "I knocked the other one out, but it won't be long before they come to."

She nodded, and forced herself to her shaky legs. She stumbled back to her desk to grab the messenger bag with the laptop, then followed him out of the building.

They ran back to the car, slipping over the cold grass, their breaths faint white puffs in the air. Once inside, she gunned the engine and shot back down the residential street they'd followed to get to the business complex.

Her hands shook, and she tightened them against the steering wheel. It took her a while to realize Alex was calling her name.

"Jane. Jane, slow down."

Her jaw was clamped shut, so she inhaled sharply through her nose. As she exhaled, she eased up on the accelerator, then finally stepped on the brakes. They stopped in the middle of a lonely stretch of road under a large oak tree. Shadows enveloped the car.

His hand covered hers on the steering wheel. His palm was tacky. It took her a moment to realize it was his blood.

"We need to take you to a hospital," she said.

He shook his head. "It's only a flesh wound."

"Men always say that in the movies."

She saw the gleam of his teeth as he smiled. "This time, it really is. Trust me, I've been shot before. Besides, the hospital will have to report the gunshot wound."

"We have to clean it." She considered her cousin Monica Grant, who was a nurse by profession, but she didn't want to involve her family in something so dangerous. Besides which, Monica still lived at home with their Aunt Becca, who happened to be dating Detective Carter. It wouldn't be the best thing to run into him with a man bleeding from a gunshot wound.

And she couldn't forget the laptop. There was only one option she could think of, and it caused a violent twisting in her gut. She screwed her eyes shut, leaning her head back against the headrest. It couldn't be avoided. He needed help, and she needed that computer equipment.

She put the car in motion again.

"Where are we going?"

"The only place I know where we can clean your wound and find a computer to analyze the hard drive." She swallowed the bitter bile that rose up in her throat. "We're going to my parents' house."

CHAPTER FIVE

Jane hadn't spoken to her father since that day, over a year ago. Even worse than what Derek and done to her had been the carelessness of her father's words, which had cut like her grandfather's *katana* sword thrust into her heart.

Taking back roads all the way, Jane and Alex drove into her parents' neighborhood just as the sun turned the sky to pale orange. Jane knew they'd already be awake.

Just go in, use her dad's computer. He wouldn't refuse her, especially not with a guest present. If he said anything to her, she could just ignore it.

She no longer cared about earning his good opinion.

They didn't drive right up to her parents' house, just in case the Tumibays were watching the front. Instead, she took a different street that wound its way through some foothills before curving back around to edge the property behind her parents' home. They parked along the side of the road next to a ditch and a fence.

When she got out of her car, a ray of morning sun kissed her cheek, and she paused, closing her eyes and feeling the gentle warmth. A lot had happened to her in the past year, and she'd spent time dealing with it. But now, she wondered if maybe she was ready to move on, for new beginnings.

Her gaze slid to Alex, who had climbed out of the tiny car and was stretching his long body. Just a few hours in his company, and she was starting to release her pain. How did he do that?

They hopped the fence, then crossed the pasture, smelling

strongly of cow, to a second fence that bordered the backyard of the Lawton family home. The wide swatch of manicured grass had a flagstone border along the sides, and Jane walked slowly, noticing that the leaves of her mother's miniature rose bushes, lining the walkway, were a pale, mottled green because of the cold weather. She climbed the two short steps to the covered back porch. With a quick indrawn breath, she knocked on the back door.

Her mother answered, dressed in an apron. Rather than being surprised that her daughter knocked on the back instead of the front door, she had a slightly vague smile on her face. "Jane, what a surprise."

"Hi, Mom." Jane had to bend almost double to kiss her tiny mother's cheek.

"You're just in time for breakfast." Her mother's dark eyes drifted onto Alex, standing behind Jane, his head almost brushing the roof of the porch. He'd draped his jacket in such a way that it hid the bloody stain on his shirt.

"Mom, you remember Alex Villa? Edward's brother."

He smiled at her mother as if Jane's introduction had not been as stiff as a dead tree. "We met at Edward and Rachel's engagement party, Mrs. Lawton."

"Yes, now I remember. Well, I suppose you should come in." She turned and led the way inside.

Jane steeled herself before she crossed the threshold, as if there were some invisible barrier she had to fight through. She felt Alex's hand touching the small of her back, and turned to look at him.

His face registered more concern than curiosity. He didn't ask meaningless questions like if she was all right, because he could see that she wasn't, but he said in a low voice, "I'm right here."

The words rumbled beneath her breastbone, an oasis of calmness, a source of strength.

The back door opened into the laundry room, which in turn led to the kitchen. Her father sat at the breakfast table, reading the morning paper.

"Hi, Dad," Jane said neutrally. She knew he'd heard their conversation when Mom answered the door.

He grunted but didn't look at her, continuing to read his paper.

"Dad, this is Alex Villa."

He treated her friend like an extension of Jane, simply frowning and nodding curtly to Alex, before returning to his paper.

Yes, he was still upset at the words she'd flung at him the last time they'd spoken, over a year ago. Maybe she was more like him than she realized, because wasn't she still holding a grudge, too?

"Mrs. Lawton, could I use your bathroom?" Alex asked.

"Oh, certainly." She waved toward the hallway.

"I'll show you." Jane led the way out of the kitchen, but she detoured into the extra bedroom that had used to belong to her. She knew her mom still kept some of her brother's old clothes in the dresser, and she grabbed a knit polo shirt that would stretch to fit Alex. She gestured toward the hallway bathroom and whispered, "First Aid kit is under the sink."

He nodded and went to clean his wound.

"Scrambled eggs okay?" Her mom was at the stove, melting butter. It sizzled, and Jane realized how hungry she was.

Years of habit made her look to her father's face for signs of his opinion. He wasn't looking at her, but he wasn't frowning, so she said, "Yes. Thanks, Mom."

"Did you want some coffee?" Her mother nodded toward the coffeemaker on the counter.

Jane retrieved mugs from the cabinet and poured coffee for herself and Alex. By the time she finished, the toast had popped up in the toaster, so she put them on a plate and buttered them for her mom. She took the toast to the kitchen table along with some plates for everyone just as Alex returned from the bathroom. Neither of her parents seemed to notice the different shirt, which was a little snug on his large frame.

She and Alex sat at the table to sip coffee and munch on toast, and her father finally spoke up, without putting down his paper. "You don't have food at your own house?" Implied was the criticism that she had to come to her parents' house to get fed.

Or was she reading more into it than was there? She wasn't about to address her parental issues with Alex here. "Dad, could I use your computer? I have a hard drive I want to access."

"Where's yours?"

"Inaccessible," she replied in the same clipped tone he had used.

The paper lowered so he could regard her with a pale blue eye beneath his bushy gray brows. "What's that supposed to mean?"

"Exactly that, Dad."

"Please." Mom laid a plate of scrambled eggs on the table. "Don't fight."

Jane backed down, and her father went back to reading his paper. She spooned eggs on her toast and finished eating it before saying, "May I please use your computer, Dad?"

He didn't reply.

Jane took a last sip of coffee. "If you'd rather I didn't, we'll just go." She stood up, and Alex followed suit.

"I didn't say that," her father said irritably. He jerked his head toward his office. "Go ahead. You know the password."

Jane suspected that he'd only agreed so he wouldn't look quite so churlish in front of Alex, but she didn't care. She headed to the living room, followed by Alex's silent form, and went through to the hallway. At the end of the short corridor was the open door to his office.

Jane was struck by how much it resembled her dining room table. She'd never noticed before. She and Alex sat at two chairs in front of her father's computer, and she took out the laptop. She shoved some papers and equipment aside to have room to set it on the desk.

He surprised her with a warm hand gently massaging the tight muscles at the base of her neck. He didn't say anything, but his touch was reassuring, pouring cold water on her sizzling temper.

She paused to take a deep breath. She didn't look at him, but she touched his hand with her fingers once. Then she went to work.

She knew where to rummage in her father's desk for his screwdrivers and other small instruments she needed to open up the laptop and remove the hard drive. It was a bit tricky because a few components had been taped down, and she had to remove the tape carefully.

She was just finishing when her father wandered into his office, coffee cup in hand. He peered over her shoulder at the laptop on the desk. "Whose is that?"

"No one you know." Jane lifted the drive from the casing.

"Why are *you* fiddling with it?"

"Alex knew I could handle the security software measures."

He grunted. He'd been in IT until he retired, and his company had often looked to him for computer security questions. "Someone locked themselves out of their computer?"

"I have to bypass the security software or this data will be as good as lost."

"You didn't do something stupid like try to turn it on, did you?"

"No, Dad," Jane said through a clenched jaw.

"Because if there's security software loaded directly into the UEFI, the computer could just connect to the internet to receive instructions. It might erase everything before you get a chance to try to get in."

Which was exactly what she'd told Alex, back in Jorge's tavern. "That's why I removed the wireless adapter, Dad. And the Bluetooth card for good measure."

He peered at the open laptop casing. "You did a messy job removing that Bluetooth card."

Was it her imagination, or was he more critical of her since their argument? For most of her life, she'd have done anything to prove herself to him, to win the same kind of approval that he doled out to her older brother so freely.

But now, more than ever, she was aware of how his criticism felt like hammer blows, knocking her down.

Alex interrupted him. "Mr. Lawton, how's your son doing?" His voice was tight, but polite.

One of Dad's favorite topics. That should keep him off of Jane's back for a little while. She flashed Alex a grateful look for distracting her father.

Dad's voice took on a brighter note. "Jason's company went IPO last year, you heard about that? He and his wife bought a new house in Cupertino."

She hooked up the hard drive to her father's computer and wasn't surprised to see full-disk encryption. However, she had probably bypassed the laptop's tracking software.

Her father listed the specs of a new tablet computer that Jason's company had just released, which probably bored Alex to tears, but to his credit, he kept a politely interested expression on his face as her father talked.

Jane worked steadily. She'd heard about all this from Jason himself. Her brother truly was brilliant, if arrogant, and Jane's relationship with him hadn't been altered by her tension with their father. Jason and his wife had Jane over for dinner once a month or so, and he kept urging Jane to quit her low-paying IT job to write software for his company. Jane had considered it, but the idea of working for her brother had seemed suffocating, as if she were still working for Derek's company, EMRY. Jason would demand everything he could from her— he would use her, like Derek had.

She made a working copy of the hard drive and then started attacking the encryption with various programs and scripts. She didn't look at Alex very often. He mostly sat beside her and listened to her father. But she started to sense the tension in his muscles. His hands clenched and unclenched once or twice. His leg jiggled every so often. When she did glance at him, she noticed the hard line of his jaw.

Was he frustrated at her lack of progress? She couldn't help it. This wasn't a run-of-the-mill laptop used for emails and web surfing. Or was he trying not to be bored to death by her dad's going on about his perfect son?

"You must be proud at how successful Jason has become," Alex said to her father. There was a strange, hard edge to his voice that Jane didn't understand. She glanced at him, but beyond a glitter in his dark eyes and the rigid set of his shoulders, nothing seemed amiss.

Her father chuckled. "He's smart, but he's worked hard, too—"

"Both your children are pretty smart."

Jane winced. Her vertebrae fused together as she tried not to anticipate her father's reply. They were only words.

Dad snorted. "This one doesn't have what it takes to make it in the high tech business." He then noticed when she opened a program she'd written specifically for her work at EMRY. "What are you doing? That program is trying to force a volume to mount."

"I've looked through the visible volume, but I think there's a hidden partition."

"Why aren't you just breaking the encryption?"

"I might lose some data."

"Sure, but the hidden partition will be fine. *If* there is one."

Jane's temper flared. "There's nothing there. If it were me, I would have at least one hidden partition unmounted at all times for my most sensitive data. We need to get everything off this hard drive."

"Why do you ... Wait a minute."

Oh, no. She had said too much.

"What exactly are you doing?" His voice rose. "I thought you were just trying to help someone who locked themselves out of their computer."

"Dad, I don't have time to explain—"

"You better find time to explain."

"All I can tell you is that it's important." Jane's typing grew harder and faster on the keyboard.

"Important? What kind of trouble have you gotten yourself into?"

"I'm not in trouble."

"No? Then why are you breaking into someone's hard drive?" he roared.

She squeezed her eyes shut in frustration. "There's more to it than that—"

"This is rich, coming from you." His voice had grown hard and vicious. "After all the stuff you spouted about Derek and EMRY. I bet you're regretting your bad decision now."

"It wasn't a bad decision," she said hoarsely.

"Your problem is you think nobody knows better than yourself."

She wanted to laugh and scream at the same time. He'd exactly described himself.

"Blayne," her mother's voice called from the living room. "Your blood pressure ..."

"I'm just telling my daughter what she needs to hear. She's never going to learn if she doesn't hear it straight from someone."

There was an almost audible *snap!* in her head. Never going to learn. It was true. She had been denying it her entire life. She'd thought she could learn how to please him. But the reality was that she would never have his approval. *That* was the lesson she'd needed to learn.

The words shot out of her mouth. "I am not your daughter. I'm some puppy you like to kick around."

There was a horrible moment of silence.

Then her mother's wheedling voice, "Blayne ..."

Jane kept typing, but she heard her father leave his office.

Then the soft words from her mother reached her ears. "Leave her alone. You need to let her make her own mistakes."

Something squeezed hard inside of her. It choked her. She couldn't breathe, but she didn't care.

The slamming of her father's office door made her jerk in her seat. She gasped in a breath, and her heartbeat roared hard and fast in her ears. She twisted around to see Alex locking the door.

"You can't lock my dad out of his own office," she said feebly.

"I just did." He began pacing—more like prowling—in front of the door, his mouth hard and his eyes fierce. "Are you almost done?"

She turned back to the computer. "Sort of. The program did find a hidden partition and I'm running another piece of software to retrieve data from the exposed sectors." Her voice was rising as she babbled. "I'm working as fast as—"

"Jane." His gentle voice and the soft pressure of his hands on her shoulders made her feel as if her heart had cracked open. She swallowed.

And then he was sitting beside her, taking her hands in his. "Jane, I wasn't rushing you. I want to leave because I can't stand listening to him talk to you that way."

She began to tremble, and his fingers pressed harder against her palms.

No one had ever protected her against her father.

"He's not always this caustic," she was forced to admit. "It's only been in the last year that he's gotten like this." Before that, she had always responded eagerly to his instructions, so he had no need to be scornful. But after quitting her job at EMRY, she had become the arrogant, foolish daughter, and so was treated as such. "And I couldn't explain to him about the hard drive, so that frustrated him."

"Don't defend him," he said fiercely, which surprised her. "He's your father. He shouldn't speak to you that way."

Jane realized that Alex's hands were trembling now, too.

The computer beeped, and she pulled her hands away to get back to her work. She blinked at the screen. "I don't understand."

"What?"

"It's done."

"Isn't that a good thing?"

"Sort of ... It took less time than I thought it would." She frowned and double-checked that the software had done its job. "Let's go. I sent the data packets to my secure cloud drive." She started packing up, including the copy of the hard drive that she had made. She spotted a laptop made by her brother's company and grabbed it.

He unlocked the door and they exited the office. Jane said stiffly, "Dad, I'm going to borrow this laptop, if you're not using it?" She held it up.

He barely looked at her. He sat on the living room couch, frowning fiercely, his face a splotchy red. "Fine."

"Thanks. I'll return it."

Neither of her parents said anything as she and Alex crossed the living room to the open doorway into the kitchen.

"Thanks for breakfast, Mr. and Mrs. Lawton." Alex strode into the kitchen and out the back door as if escaping from jail.

Jane hesitated in the doorway, as she had when she first entered the threshold. Her head bowed. She opened her mouth, then closed it. What was there to say? "Bye." She left.

They crossed the field again in silence. Cows were grazing at a distance, and the animals gave them uninterested looks as they climbed over the fence.

She always felt ... efficient when she got into her hybrid car. But today, she remembered her father convincing her to buy it.

She was done pleasing her father.

She should have felt empowered, free. Instead she felt weighted down and unwieldy, like when she'd had to move an old-fashioned tube computer monitor and the large, heavy thing had nearly taken her arms off at the sockets.

As she drove back down the road, he asked, "Are you all right?"

"As fine as I can be." That wasn't true. She felt alone. She felt as if she'd always been alone.

And what had all that gotten for them? "I think there's something wrong with the hard drive."

A vein in his temple pulsed. "Wrong, how?"

"The security on the drive was relatively minimal."

"Maybe he got lazy about security. No one ever expects their computer to go missing."

"Maybe. Or maybe the information on the hard drive isn't as important as we thought." She glanced at him, nervous about conveying her fears. "What if there isn't any proof that the Tumibays set you up? What if there's nothing to convict the Tumibays of any crimes?" She swallowed. "What if all this was for nothing?"

"It's not for nothing." He put strong emphasis on his words, but Jane heard a thread of determination. Or desperation. "What do we need now?"

"I need internet access so we can look at the files on my cloud drive. I thought maybe we could go back to Jorge's tavern to use his internet." She turned onto the main road that led out of her parents' neighborhood.

"No, there will be lots of people at the tavern by now, and we don't know who might belong to the Tumibays." He was silent a moment, then he heaved a sigh. "I know where we can get wireless internet easily. The only problem is that ..."

They were passing a blue Dodge Challenger heading in the opposite direction, and it wasn't until they were almost next to each other that Jane recognized the driver.

The man from the fire escape balcony. And in the passenger seat, the polo shirt man.

CHAPTER SIX

Jane slammed on the gas.

The Challenger's tires squealed as the two men turned to follow them.

Jane's heart was drumming, her hands on the steering wheel trembled. The hybrid car had no chance against the Challenger. It was only a matter of time before the more powerful car caught up to them.

She had to even the odds.

"Jane, traffic." Alex's voice was tight, his hands white knuckled as he gripped the dashboard. "You need traffic."

There was a large shopping mall nearby. This main road led toward it, but there was also Barclay Road, a narrow, winding road that led to the southeast side of the mall. And she knew a shortcut to it.

Jane made a sudden left turn into a long dirt driveway. The Challenger had been too close, and they overshot the driveway. In the time it took them to swerve and follow them, Jane was nearly at the end of the driveway, coming up to the farmhouse. The car skidded sideways on the dirt as she turned right onto a farm road that would cut her through the farm property to Barclay Road.

The Challenger's engine roared. The men were within a car's length of her back bumper when Jane flew out of the farm road, jouncing up onto the asphalt as she turned onto Barclay Road.

As a teen, she had often loved driving this winding road at dangerous speeds, and she pulled out all the stops now. The road was narrower than a residential street, with sharp turns that rolled up and down. The hybrid caught air as she drove over the top of a rise, crashing down with a bounce that made her teeth clack together.

She didn't want to take her eyes off the road. "Are they gaining on us?"

He had twisted around. "No. But they're not falling behind."

Jane went faster.

Barclay Road finally T-junctioned with Lewis Expressway, a broad road that would take them past the mall and eventually onto the freeway. Jane took a hard right onto the expressway, directly in front of an oncoming minivan. She left the sound of the minivan's horns behind them as she accelerated as fast as the hybrid could handle.

As she had during the escape from her apartment, she wove in between cars aggressively. The expressway didn't have a wide enough shoulder for the Challenger to drive on it to catch up to them. But she needed to lose their pursuers, not just get ahead of them.

She cut sharply across two lanes into a left turn lane, then jammed in front of the oncoming cars. Tires squealed. Car horns blared in a cacophony directly into her ears as they shot down a side road.

"Did they follow us?"

"No, they couldn't. But they'll be trying to find a way back to find us again."

This road led to another residential area, with farms. She remembered that there was one family who had horses—and a large barn.

She took a few turns, including a shortcut through a small orchard, following the dirt tractor trail. She finally saw the barn coming up on her left, and turned into the driveway. The house of the family who owned the property was far enough away from the barn that they wouldn't notice if she parked behind it, which would hide their car from view of the road.

When Jane turned off the engine, she gasped as if she

hadn't taken a breath the entire frightening time.

"You're okay." He clenched her hand in his. "You did great. They weren't behind us from the moment you made that left turn."

His touch was hot, spreading warmth down her hands, into her wrists. She unclamped her fingers from around the steering wheel, and he let go.

She massaged her cramped fingers. "How did they find us?"

"I think this was by accident. They were heading toward your parent's house."

"But I thought they might have already been watching the house."

"Maybe we gave them too much credit. It might have taken them this long to guess you might go to your parents' place. Or maybe they did have someone in front of their house, and those two were coming to relieve them."

Jane heaved a sigh and leaned her head back against the head rest. "We need a new car."

"We need to look through the data you pulled from the hard drive. And I think I know where we can do both."

Alex looked around, making sure there was no one in sight as he and Jane crossed the strip of forested land between the neighboring farm's access road and the east edge of his brother's property. The nearest greenhouse lay only a few yards from the treeline.

They approached the frosted door, and he gasped the handle. It turned easily in his hand.

"You said this was dangerous?" Jane asked him as they entered the greenhouse.

"Not for us, for me." He sighed heavily. "My brother is going to kill me."

Edward stood leaning against a stainless steel gardening table, arms crossed, his face like thunder. Luckily, Mama was nowhere to be seen.

Edward noticed him looking around. "Don't worry, I didn't tell Mama."

"Praise God for small blessings."

Edward spotted Jane, and his grim expression softened. He came forward to kiss her cheek. "Hi, Jane. Are you all right?"

"I'm fine." Even with little sleep, her smile for his brother was wide, and her eyes turned to amber in the sunlight slanting through the glass panes on the roof. She was still a little pale from her ordeal with her father.

While at her parents' house, Alex had had to fight to keep his big mouth shut in order to be respectful, but he'd wanted to jump up to defend her every time the man grated out yet another harsh observation of his daughter, another worshipful tidbit about his son. The man was toxic, and while he might have gotten worse only in the last year, as Jane had said, there was something about his manner to Jane that made it obvious that he was rarely complimentary.

Alex's father had not been kind, and he had been stubborn, but he had rarely been cruel. Alex couldn't imagine what that kind of relationship had done to Jane's self-esteem. Maybe that was also why her faith had seemed to have become lukewarm lately.

"You're lucky I don't give you a thrashing," Edward said to him.

"What do you mean? I left a message on your phone yesterday."

"'I don't know how long I'll be gone, don't freak out if I don't answer my cell phone, and protect Mama'? You call that a message?"

Jane bit her lip to hide her smile, and the shadow of a dimple appeared in her left cheek.

"All this after you'd been arrested a few days ago," Edward continued. "Your communication skills suck, bro."

"I was distracted," he said. "I was trying to lose a tail."

Edward's dark brows slammed down over his eyes. "You better explain that."

He told him everything, which only made his brother more and more alarmed.

"You got shot? Why didn't you tell me that when you

called?" Edward stepped forward, scanning Alex's body. "Where?"

He winced as he eased off his jacket, then rolled up the sleeve of the borrowed shirt. "Grazed me."

Edward wasn't so blasé. "You idiot. That needs to be taken care of. Stitches, or—"

"I will." He'd been shot before on more than one occasion, and although his arm hurt, this wasn't as bad as some other wounds he'd had. He needed stitches, but he also knew he could get away with waiting before he had it looked at. He'd used butterfly bandages to close the wound, which had stopped bleeding, at least.

Jane said, "I just realized there are at least two bullet holes in the walls of the IT office at my workplace."

"Maybe your coworkers won't notice?" Alex said.

"You're going to tell Detective Carter all about it," Edward said firmly. "I don't understand why you didn't speak to him about this first."

"His superiors are not happy that he defended me," he said. "I didn't want to involve him until I had proof that I was innocent."

"Because everything you've done so far has made you seem above suspicion?"

"Alex wasn't the one coming after us with guns," Jane said quietly.

Edward sighed, then tapped the computer lying on the table next to him. "I brought my laptop, as you asked."

"Good. Jane has another one, so we can both look through the data from that hard drive."

"There's WiFi here?" Jane looked around the greenhouse. It was only partially filled at the moment with the last of the latest Malaysian basil crop that Edward and Alex were growing for Rachel Grant. It certainly didn't look like an internet cafe.

"All the greenhouses have WiFi," Edward said. "The buildings have security and sensors, and Alex helped me install soil sensors for the plants. We needed WiFi to be able to monitor them all with our computers." Edward hesitated, then said, "Is there anything else I can do?"

"Do me a favor," he said, "and don't tell—"

"I won't tell Mama," Edward said. "But just ..." His mouth tightened, and his expression was anguished. "... Just fix this. Soon."

He nodded.

Edward cleared his throat and clumsily waved a hand toward a paper sack on the table. "I made you sandwiches, and there's bottled water and a thermos of coffee."

"Thanks." His head was starting to whirl from lack of sleep. He'd be glad for food and more caffeine. He hadn't been able to eat much at Jane's parents' house.

"Have you slept at all?"

"After the car chase, since we were out of sight of the road, we napped in the car for a couple hours." Then they'd been awakened by the farmer whose land they were parked on, demanding they leave his property.

Edward's cell phone beeped once, and he glanced at it. "I have to get back to work." Edward gave him a long, steady look, then left the greenhouse.

He grabbed two stools and set them at the gardening table. The greenhouses were all equipped with electrical outlets which had covers to protect them from water when there wasn't anything plugged in, so they had power for the laptops. After he had connected them to the WiFi, Jane told him how to access her cloud drive, and divided up the data she'd retrieved from the hard drive.

They worked in silence for a few minutes. He glanced at her intent face a few times. Finally he said, "Did you want to talk about it?"

"No." Her jaw tightened briefly.

"Jane, you can't pretend you don't feel anything." He had learned that lesson very well.

"It's none of your business. You shouldn't have witnessed that in the first place."

"I think I witnessed that for a reason. I think I understand better than you realize."

She sighed, bowing her head and rubbing her forehead with her fingers. "He's not normally like that. It's only been for the past year."

She had mentioned that before. "What happened last year?"

Her face hardened, and her voice was hollow as she said, "I quit my job, and Dad thought it was a bad idea."

"Why did you quit? You loved your job."

"It didn't love me." There was something odd in her tone as she said that. Something bruised.

"Jane—"

"Alex, just leave it alone."

"Look, I get it. I get not living up to your father's expectations." He couldn't stop his hands from clenching as he said it. After all these years, it still stabbed at him like a broken bone that wouldn't heal properly.

Jane had stilled. The silence hung between them like the heavy chill at the bottom of a canyon. Finally she whispered, "It never occurred to me that you and Edward never talk about him."

"The last time I spoke to my father, was an argument the week before I got arrested."

"But ... he died after you got out of prison."

"Don't get me wrong, he had every reason to yell at me. I ran with a bad crowd. I'd been bullied in grade school, so when I filled out, I vowed to protect anyone else who got bullied, but some of them were into things I should have avoided. After high school, I got even worse. That's what Papa and I argued about."

He could still hear the thundering of his father's voice, shuddering off the walls of the low-ceilinged living room. He heard Mama's pleas. Papa's normally immaculate work suit had become rumpled with the force of his anger.

"But when you became a Christian in prison ..." Jane's face was utterly confused.

"I went to him. I apologized. I told him I was a different person." His father's face had been stone. He hadn't looked at Alex. The silence had been unbearable, and Alex had finally left. "But he couldn't forgive me for the shame I'd brought on the family. On *him*."

Her small hand reached out to cover his. The feather-light touch was like the striking of a gong, causing a deep hum throughout his body.

"When he was in the hospital, he still wouldn't speak to me. And then he died."

Jane didn't try to tell him that his father had loved him. She understood how impossible that could be to believe.

"He was disappointed in me. He simply didn't care about Edward," he said. "He abandoned both of us emotionally. So Edward and I found a father's love in God, instead."

Jane withdrew her hand and turned her face away from him. "I feel like God has abandoned me. And don't try to tell me that He hasn't, because it really feels like He has."

She sat stiffly on the stool, self-contained, brittle, and alone. He wanted to reach out to her, but he could sense that if he did, she might shatter. And he'd lose any chance at helping her.

Then words tumbled out of his mouth, and he didn't understand why he said them. "Sometimes when we feel alone, we're really not. We just can't see Him behind us."

She wrapped her arms around herself and didn't answer.

"Jane, I'll be here for you." He realized how deeply he meant it. He had always liked her, always been attracted to her, but seeing her strength in the face of stress and danger made him see how amazing she really was. "And I know you don't want to hear this, but God is here for you, too. He won't turn away from you."

"He already did." She heaved a long breath that sounded like dry leaves rattling in the orchard. "I don't want to talk about it."

He had to be content with that. *Lord, only You can convince her of how intensely You love her, of how she's not alone.*

Jane turned back to her computer. "Let's just get back to work."

It was true, he needed to clear his name. He needed to stop the Tumibays from gaining a foothold here in Sonoma. But now, repairing his reputation was no longer as important as repairing the pain he'd seen in Jane's eyes. When this was over, he had to show her how her father was wrong.

Nothing. There was no evidence that the Tumibays had set Alex up.

He had been so sure there would be something. It might not have been front and center, but it would be there. But the hard drive didn't mention anything about Alex or even the Sonoma operation. It was all banking information and shipping records. "This is everything from the hard drive?" he asked her.

"I think so." Jane rested her forehead in her hand as she stared at her laptop. "I found that hidden partition. I thought for sure there would be something in it about the money they wired to your bank account."

"There's plenty of bank accounts here, although they're all in code. Can you crack it?"

"It's not my forte. You'd need a forensic accountant to analyze all this banking information in the hidden partition, to see if it's enough to convict anyone. "

"Did you find anything else?"

"He uses a secure cloud server for his email, so I don't have the actual messages on this computer, but I can see notes he's made to himself about messages he's sent. He doesn't email many people at all, and the ones he does email, he refers to by code names."

"What names?" He moved toward her and looked over her shoulder.

"Emeril is the one he emails the most."

He gave a bark of laughter. "Not very original. I'll bet that's the bald guy I saw at the meth lab, the one cooking the drugs."

"How can you be sure?"

"I've known lots of different drug gang members. A lot of them call their chemists 'Emeril.'"

"Then there's this one, Oyster."

He felt a bubbling in his chest, like a pot about to boil over. "That's the Tumibay captain in charge of the drug operations here in Sonoma. He's referred to as Talaba, although I'm not sure if that's his real name. It means oyster in Tagalog. Any other names? Maybe this accountant emailed Tumibay officers in San Francisco."

"He emailed four other people, and he refers to them as Sleepy, Dopey, Happy, and Doc."

He groaned. "Practically every gang on the planet has members with names from the Seven Dwarves."

"There's one other name." She clicked a few folders. "It wasn't in the hidden partition, it was a memo in the outer volume. I didn't pay much attention at first because the accountant wrote it all in code words, and since it was in the outer volume, there's a good chance it's not very important. But it's the only memo with a first and last name mentioned."

She pulled up a document. "It's about payment for delivery—he refers to it as a shipment of Thighbusters."

He had to swallow a laugh. "Seriously?"

Jane shrugged. "At the bottom is a bunch of notes to himself. One is to remind himself to ask Jejomar Babingao about delivery schedules."

He straightened. "That's not a nickname or a code name. That's a real name."

"It is?" Jane clicked through and started searching for it online. "Filipino?"

"Yes."

"For everything else he used code names. He must have overlooked this one. That's probably also why it was in the unprotected outer volume."

They actually found the man on Facebook. His page was in Filipino, but Jane put it through a translation program. He worked as a customs officer for a small shipping port in the Philippines.

Shipping from the Philippines. "Jane, you hit the jackpot."

"I did?"

"The main ingredient for meth production is ephedrine. It comes from the *ma huang* plant. Most gangs get ephedrine from Mexico, but some still smuggle it in from the Philippines."

"So this man might be involved in supplying the ephedrine for the Tumibays?"

"The FBI can follow him back to the ephedrine supply in the Philippines. We could cut off the Tumibays' drug production at the knees."

Jane frowned at him. "But even if we give this information to the FBI, this Tumibay captain has already destroyed your relationship with the Sonoma police. This information won't necessarily change that."

He hadn't realized how much he enjoyed working with Detective Carter until it was gone. He had always been friendly with people, but with Detective Carter's support, he had been able to use his friendships to help the community. To protect people. He liked doing that.

He enjoyed working with his brother and on his mother's farm. He enjoyed the physical work, even though it was tiring, and they were fortunate that they made enough of a profit to be able to hire help so the work wasn't so backbreaking.

But his work with the Sonoma PD had slowly become as much a part of his life as his other jobs.

Except that it didn't define who he was. And if he had to give up his work with Detective Carter in order to keep firm in his own personal integrity, that's what he'd do.

"My reputation isn't worth anything to me if I don't do what I can to protect this community," he said slowly. "But we're still in danger. The Tumibay captain—the oyster guy—and the accountant will still be after us because of what we know. They might have a mole in the Sonoma PD. They'll threaten our families to get to us."

She studied him, and seemed to know what he was thinking, because she said, "It's not your fault that my family and I are in danger."

But it was.

"So what do we do?" she asked.

"If that guy in the polo shirt and glasses is the accountant, he doesn't strike me as being very loyal. If we get to him, he might flip on the Tumibay captain in charge of the meth operation in Sonoma, the Oyster."

Jane shook her head. "From what he said to me at my workplace last night, he's not stupid. He reminds me ..." She gave a small sigh. "He reminds me of my brother, actually. Smart and arrogant. I don't think we should assume he'll turn on his captain. We need something that'll bring both of them in."

"Then let's play to the weaknesses of a smart but arrogant man. He still wants the hard drive."

Jane started clicking on windows on her computer. "I looked at the coding for the tracking software he had on the hard drive. I think I can alter it so that if he hooks the hard drive up to another one of his computers, it will alert one of our laptops with its location."

"But that doesn't help us also get the Oyster."

She looked up at him, speculation shining in her eyes. "I think I know how to get them both."

CHAPTER SEVEN

In the end, it wasn't very dramatic. Jane walked up to a car parked outside her apartment and knocked on the window. She leaned against the car frame to hide her trembling knees and told the startled Filipino man who sat inside, "I want to talk to your boss."

Alex hadn't wanted her to do this, but she'd convinced him. What choice did they have? They had reached the point where their backs were to the wall. The accountant wanted three things—the hard drive, Jane, and Alex.

Jane would guess that he'd be happy to take two out of three.

The two men took the messenger bag from her before they shoved her into the back seat of the car. The smell of garlic and onions made her gag. One of them telephoned someone, speaking rapidly in Filipino, as the driver headed out of Sonoma.

They didn't bother to blindfold her. They apparently didn't care that she saw where they were taking her. Jane closed her eyes and tried not to panic at the implications of that.

It seemed they drove for a long time, past vineyards and fields, and finally down a deep gully. The only people they saw on the road were a few bikers in black leather and a lunch wagon on its way back from the midday business.

As they drove down a deeply rutted dirt track into the foothills, the wind in their faces carried the acrid scent of ammonia. Jane coughed and breathed through her mouth. Soon the road ended next to a mobile trailer. Several yards away from the trailer sat a generator and a folding table with computer equipment.

Glasses Man sat at the table, typing at another laptop, but he stopped when he saw the car. And when he spotted Jane, he smiled.

Jane shivered.

As she got out of the car, she said, "I want to make a deal." The chemical odors from the meth lab made her cough again.

"Of course you do."

The driver handed Glasses Man the messenger bag, and he dug out the laptop casing. "You did quite a hack job on this." He set it on the table.

He next removed the laptop Jane had borrowed from her father, flipping it back and forth in his hands. "This looks like it's one made by your brother's company. I think I'll keep this."

In the side pocket of the messenger bag, he found the hard drive and the wireless adapter and Bluetooth card Jane had removed from his laptop. There was nothing else.

He stared hard at Jane with black eyes glittering. "I know you made a copy of the hard drive. It's what I would do."

Jane stared back at him, and her jaw grew tight.

"I'm sure you don't want me to ask one of these men to search you for it."

She couldn't stop the shudder that passed through her. She reached under her shirt and pulled it out from where it had been lying between her waistband and lower back. "I want to meet with your captain. I want to work for him."

"And why would he want to hire you?" The man nodded to the two who had brought Jane there, and they got back in the car. In a swirl of dust and dead leaves, they executed a three point turn and left.

The grit and heat were starting to make Jane sweat even more. She moved from the patch of direct sunlight into the shade of a bedraggled oak tree, near the folding table. "Look and see what I did. Your full-disk encryption wasn't very encrypted."

He gave her a long look. For the first time, she noticed how young he was—her age, perhaps. He had thick dark lashes that made his eyes look like they had on eyeliner.

"Why not?" He called something guttural to the trailer, and a skinny young man—barely more than a teenager—exited the lab. His dark eyes fell on Jane with a sort of hunger that had her involuntarily taking a step back. "Happy, keep an eye on her while I work."

The young man gave Jane a feral smile, and he casually pulled a handgun from the back of his jeans. He didn't point it at her. It hung almost carelessly from his twitching fingers.

Glasses Man sat at the folding table and plugged the copied hard drive into his computer.

"What's your name? Let me guess. Doc?"

"Farmboy." He gave her a bland smile. "I bring home the bacon."

Alex had probably been right. This was an accountant for the gang.

Farmboy studied the computer, and his smile widened. "I see you didn't find the second hidden partition."

She couldn't stop the surprised twitch of her shoulders.

"You're really not as smart as you think you are. Why are you even bothering trying to play with the big boys?"

Different voice, same words. But this man wasn't her father, and she no longer cared about trying to please her dad, or any man, because none of them would ever be pleased with her. It seemed she tried so hard, and she always fell short. Why bother?

But wasn't that just fulfilling what her father had always said about her?

Farmboy laughed as he looked at the code on his screen. "Oh, that's cute. You altered the tracking software. No wonder you wanted me to look at this hard drive. Too bad there isn't a random wireless internet signal out here." He swept a hand at the twisted trees and scrub brush of the wilderness around them. "Meth labs tend to annoy the neighbors, so we had to go out a little far from civilization."

She clenched her jaw at his tone.

He feigned surprise. "Did you really think that would work? While I do have wireless internet, it has security to prevent computers from hopping on. Duh. And you really thought you could work for my boss?"

The sound of a car—no, two cars coming up the pitted road drew her attention. And then she recognized the truck in front.

Oh, no. It wasn't supposed to happen like this.

The man from the fire escape balcony drove Edward's truck, which Alex had been using. Behind him was the Challenger, driven by another man. Where was Alex?

The driver got out of the truck and lifted a hand in greeting, and Happy returned the gesture.

"Where is he?" Farmboy demanded.

The driver opened the back door to the truck cab and hauled on something heavy. Alex slid off the back seat and fell into a heap on the ground. He grunted and stirred, and Jane saw the purple bruising already starting to form around his eye. His hands had been duct-taped together.

"He was trying to follow her." The driver nodded toward Jane.

Farmboy nodded. "Thought he might."

"Let me talk to your captain," Jane said. "We can still make a deal." She had to stall. This was not going the way they had planned it.

"What do you possibly have that I would want?" Farmboy gave a short laugh. "You delivered yourself to me like a Thanksgiving turkey."

"Can I eat her?" Happy leered at her.

"Go ahead and try," Jane shot at him acidly.

A growl came from Alex's form, and he sat up with a wince. "Didn't expect that to happen," he muttered.

"You're not as good a driver as your girlfriend," jeered the driver of the Challenger.

"But you're just as stupid," Farmboy said. "I looked up the make and model of your brother's truck as soon as I figured out who you were. We've been watching for it."

Jane eyed Happy's gun, then Alex's slumped figure. Nothing was going the way Alex said it would.

Alex looked up at her from where he still sat in the dirt. "Just do it."

Farmboy spun to face her. "Do what?"

Jane glared at Alex. What was he doing?

Farmboy grabbed her shoulders and shoved her back against a tree trunk. The sharp edges dug into her spine. "Do. What."

Jane closed her eyes and exhaled. Fine. She'd do it. "It's already done."

Farmboy slammed her against the tree again, blowing the air out of her lungs. Her heart was racing like an engine.

She had to gasp a few breaths before she could speak. "The laptop."

He stared at his laptop, which sat there innocuously.

"Mine," she said.

Farmboy strode to the table and flipped open her brother's laptop. The screen was flashing, while code scrolled up the screen.

"What?" He slapped the keys. "What's it doing?"

Then the code scrolling on the screen abruptly ended, and a cursor blinked next to the words, "BAILE cloud server hacked. You lose."

Within a few seconds of him opening the laptop, it suddenly went dark.

Farmboy rushed at Jane, his fingers biting into her shoulders. Happy grinned and raised his gun, and then there was the sound of guns being drawn by the other two gang members, as well. "Hey, hey!" Alex said.

From the mobile trailer, a tall man with a shaved head emerged, also holding a gun.

"Calm down or you'll never know what happened." Alex had risen to his knees, his hands still taped together, which contrasted with the ring of authority in his voice.

Farmboy's face was close to Jane's. Anger had drawn harsh lines against his mouth, alongside his nose. His breath was hot and foul in her face.

"If you hurt her, you'll never find out what she did." Alex's voice sounded reasonable and confident. "And I sure couldn't tell you."

If they got out of this alive, Jane was going to kill him. Or even worse, tell everything to his mama, and let *her* kill him.

Farmboy shoved Jane once more, but stepped back. Happy sighed and dropped his gun, and the others did, as well.

"I hacked your cloud server." Jane's throat was dry, and she swallowed.

"I know that," Farmboy bit out. "What did you do to it? How did you do it?"

"I knew you had secure WiFi at the other meth lab, because I saw the network connection on the laptop Alex stole, although I figured you'd change the password. But your second laptop would be connected to the internet, and if I could get your guys to bring me to you ..."

Farmboy paled. His lips barely moved as he said, "What did you do?"

"I uploaded a virus that hit my workplace a few weeks ago. They're all insurance guys so they weren't very cautious about spammy emails. I altered the virus." Jane licked her lips. "It's being sent specifically to your captain."

Farmboy backhanded her across the mouth. Pain shot up her jaw as if it had been disconnected, and she tasted blood. She'd bitten her tongue.

"Hey!" Alex had climbed to his feet.

The driver of the Challenger shoved his gun in Alex's face. "Get back."

"The virus," Farmboy said to her.

Jane spat out some blood. "It'll email everyone in your captain's address book, except I altered this one to carbon copy the Sonoma police department on all those emails. So the Sonoma PD will see every person your captain has ever contacted." It hurt for her to talk.

Farmboy whipped out his cell phone, and within seconds he was talking to someone in Filipino. He repeated himself earnestly a few times, then his brow clouded in confusion.

Was it enough time? Had her program worked?

Finally he hung up the phone, then stalked to Jane. "He didn't get an email. You didn't do anything."

"Of course not—"

He drew back his hand. Alex yelled, "Hey!"

Jane cringed and quickly said, "Of course I can't hack into your cloud server ... But I can make it look like I can."

"What?"

"I didn't need to meet with your captain. I just needed you to call him." She nodded toward his hand, holding his cell phone. "I noticed your wireless was secure, but your bluetooth wasn't. My computer just hacked your phone and got your captain's cell number. The police will track him in a few minutes."

Farmboy's lips pulled back in a snarl. He strode to Happy, grabbing his gun, but suddenly stopped at the sound of a shotgun being primed.

"Drop the guns," said a deep voice with a Hispanic accent.

Jane hadn't expected them to have gotten so close to the camp. She turned to see Alex's friends with rifles and shotguns closing in on them. One had snuck up on the driver of the Challenger. With the man's rifle pressed to the back of his head, the driver dropped his gun away from Alex.

Farmboy circled around, his mouth open. "What the—"

"There's exactly twelve of us," said a tall man with a cowboy hat who had appeared from behind the mobile trailer. "Counting you five and the two guards you stationed on that ridge behind us, we've got you outnumbered."

Within seconds, all of them were disarmed and Alex's friends began tying them up with the zip ties they'd brought with them. Farmboy started cussing in Filipino as he was tied.

Jane's hands began to shake, and she clenched them together.

It was over.

"Are you all right?" Alex was in front of her, his hand not quite touching her face.

Her cheek felt hot, and it throbbed. "What were you thinking?"

"What do you mean? It went off without a hitch. Sort of." He winced.

"You weren't supposed to get caught." Her legs were starting to shake, too. She sank down onto a chair by the folding table.

His hands closed over her shoulders. His look was serious. "I wasn't about to let you walk in here by yourself."

"I was afraid for you."

He touched the puffiness at the side of her face. "If I hadn't been here, they might have hurt you even worse."

"But I knew your friends were here."

The truth hit her with a thud of her heartbeat. She'd been nervous. She'd been afraid for Alex. And she certainly hadn't liked being knocked around. But she hadn't felt alone. Because the entire time, she'd never been alone.

She knew there was something there that she would need to think about later.

"Detective Carter's on his way," said a voice in Spanish.

Jane saw Jorge clambering over brush and rocks from behind where the Challenger was parked on the pitted road.

"Jorge, you were supposed to stay in your lunch wagon," Alex said to him in Spanish. "Adelita's going to kill us."

"So is Detective Carter. I think he didn't like us cowboys doing his job."

"His job?" The man with the cowboy hat, a rancher named Emory Valdez, had an innocent expression. "We saw our good friend Alex being kidnapped by these guys and followed him to rescue him. Not our fault they drove up to a meth lab."

Meth lab. Funny how she couldn't smell the fumes anymore. Her head felt as big as a basketball. Stars began to crowd the edges of her vision.

She didn't remember hitting the ground.

CHAPTER EIGHT

Jane was alone again. She really shouldn't be surprised.

The rest of the day was a blur. She had woken up lying on the ground with Alex yelling at her. So she'd yelled back—or more like whispered back—for him to keep his voice down.

Detective Carter arrived within minutes. Paramedics arrived half an hour later, but by then Jane had moved to sit on a rock far away from the toxic gases of the meth lab and was feeling better. She was relieved when the paramedics dressed Alex's gunshot wound.

At the police station, Alex's mama had yelled and cried and hugged him and scolded him. She also spent a lot of time alternately poking at and then crying over his gunshot wound. His mama had cried and hugged Jane, too, and her embrace had smelled like apricots and pies. Jane hadn't wanted to let her go.

Detective Carter was dating Jane's Aunt Becca, and so all of Jane's cousins came to the station to make sure she was all right. Maybe to make up for the fact that her own parents were absent.

But Alex and his family had gone back to their farmhouse. Jorge and Adelina and Alex's friends—neighboring ranchers, farmhands, and farmers—had gone home after giving their statements. The Grants had gone back to their mansion outside of Sonoma.

Jane entered her empty apartment and began to cry.

She shut the door quickly, but her legs failed her and she slid to the floor. It was just the shock. She was responding to the stress of the past two days.

No. She was crying because Alex had been trying to tell her something, and she'd turned away. God had been trying to tell her something, and she hadn't wanted to hear.

Hadn't God failed her? Hadn't He allowed Derek and then her father to rip gigantic holes in her chest?

Why had He allowed these people to hurt her?

But He hadn't allowed Farmboy to kill her. Their desperate plan had worked. Detective Carter had said they had picked up the Tumibay captain, the Oyster, within an hour of the accountant's phone call to him.

Jane and Alex were safe.

She rubbed her cheek and jaw, still sore from the blow Farmboy had given to her. Safe, but not unscathed.

They had done a good thing today. That was worth a blow to the jaw.

She grudgingly admitted there was good that had come out of her pain from a year ago. She had broken the chains of her father's disapproval. She had discovered Derek's lies and left EMRY.

With all these things that should free her, why did she feel so alone?

She was cried out. She crawled across the floor to the living room couch, shoved some books and cables off the cushions, and climbed into it.

One of the things that dropped to the floor was her Bible.

It lay in a forlorn heap, pages rippling. She immediately picked it up and smoothed the wrinkles.

Her bookmark was still in place. She'd been reading the Bible in a year when everything happened with Derek and her father, and she hadn't opened it since. It was in Jeremiah, a book she hadn't understood very well at all.

The Lord appeared to us in the past, saying:
"I have loved you with an everlasting love;
I have drawn you with loving-kindness.
I will build you up again
and you will be rebuilt, O Virgin Israel.

*Again you will take up your tambourines
and go out to dance with the joyful."*

She couldn't stop reading these two verses as she lay curled up on the couch. She was loved. Derek's betrayal and her father's rejection had devastated her because it made her feel so unloveable. But she was loved with a love she was starting to realize she couldn't comprehend.

And that love could heal her. Rebuild her life.

She crushed the Bible to her chest. It was as if she were hiding in a closet and there was a gentle whisper at the closed door. *I am here for you.*

She hesitated, then said, *Come in.*

The Villa farmhouse was loud and warm from the people crowded into it. Jane would normally have felt claustrophobic, but she was happy.

One reason was because she'd finally tasted Alex's mama's cooking, and she wanted to move in so she could have that amazing food every single day. At the moment, everyone was waiting for the apricot *empanada* pies to come out of the oven, and the buttery scent of their crusts was filling the house.

Another reason was because she had a chance to thank each of Alex's friends, his own personal cavalry, who had helped last week to take down Farmboy and his associates. Some of them had known Alex in prison. Some were friends of the Villa family. They all had been glad for the chance to help stop the Tumibays.

And a third reason was because she'd had her last day at work today. As of tomorrow, she was making a go of her own business, and the party tonight was an appropriate send-off.

Throughout the evening, she hadn't had much time to speak to Alex, but now he pulled her away from staring at the oven. "The *empanadas* will come out soon. I want to show you something." He grabbed a quilt from the couch before leading her out the back door.

The motion-sensing floodlights turned on as soon as they stepped off the back porch into the yard. Fruit trees lined the yard on three sides, and half the yard was taken up by his mama's vegetable garden, where the shapes of kale and leeks were gilded by the light.

He led her to a trellised bench set in the far corner. Grape vines had been trained into the lattice, and they were just starting to mist with green from new leaves.

They sat, and he draped the quilt over them both. "Edward built this for Mama. I trained the grape vines."

"Do you get grapes?"

"Yes, but they're sour." He made a face, and she laughed. "I have great news. Detective Carter said that they managed to unmount that second hidden partition on the laptop, and it had all the information on how the accountant was going to set me up. I am officially cleared of suspicion."

She squeezed him tight. "I know that was bothering you."

"They also found the name of a police officer who was on the Tumibays' payroll."

Her mouth dropped open. "I know we speculated about the gang having someone at the station who would search traffic cam footage for my car, but it seems so much more awful to find out it was true."

"Detective Carter also said that customs official we found led the FBI to the Tumibays' ephedrine supplier in the Philippines. The gang won't be getting any more of it shipped to the Port of San Francisco."

"That'll stop the meth production?"

"I'd like to think so, but ..." He grimaced. "At the very least, it'll slow things down for them while they search for a new supplier."

"Hopefully Detective Carter will get a bit of break."

"He might try to talk to you later."

"About what?"

"I mentioned how you could have found that second hidden partition in the hard drive so much faster, and that now that you're starting your own contracting business, maybe the Sonoma PD could hire you once in a while."

"I'll take any work I can get. Uncle Aggie has hired me to

write new software to integrate the reservations for both the Joy Luck Life Spa and the hotel."

"How was your last day at work today?"

"I said goodbye to everyone, which was sad, but turning in my security badge was ... great." She smiled. "I'm glad they let me give only a week's notice rather than two."

"Are you going to like writing software all the time?"

"It's what I'm best at."

He leaned closer to her. "But is it what you enjoy doing?"

"It used to be. That's why I think it can be, again."

The floodlights switched off, and he said, "Look up."

The clear night sky unfolded over them. It wasn't black, but a deep, deep blue, and the stars looked like they were hanging just over the top of the trellis. She felt his chest expand as he breathed in the night air.

"It reminds me that God is bigger than any of my problems," he said.

"It makes me feel loved," Jane said.

His arm tightened around her.

"I wrote software for EMRY up until a year ago."

"You don't have to tell me," he said.

"Do you want to know?"

He hesitated only a second. "Yes," he whispered.

"My boss was Derek Wallace, and I thought I loved him."

"Is he the one you were dating when we first met?"

"I told you I was interested in him, but we weren't dating. But he gave every indication that he was interested in me. EMRY was a startup, and we worked sixty hours a week together. We wrote a powerful voice recognition software program. Whenever I wrote a piece of code that was especially brilliant, he was affectionate and appreciative. And I kept wanting to please him. You probably know why."

In answer, his hand rubbed her arm.

"We were having a problem with the program, and I had lunch with an old college girlfriend working for a company who makes bluetooth headsets. After I explained what I was working on, she told me about a software engineer at her company who's been working on vocal optimization for their headsets, and how this engineer has found a way to adjust for slurring and incidental throat and lip noise. I told Derek I'd talk to the engineer to ask for any ideas he could give me that wouldn't violate his non-disclosure agreement with his company, but Derek ..." She swallowed. This was still difficult to talk about. "Derek wanted me to offer the engineer money to steal his software from his company and give it to EMRY."

Alex's expression was shocked. "He actually asked you to do that?"

"I refused. Derek was livid. I had thought he ... cared for me, but he said that he only pretended to like me because I was 'smarter' when he paid attention to me."

Alex's muscles had turned rigid. "So he just strung you along like that?"

"It doesn't hurt anymore. That's why I can tell you this. I think it actually hasn't hurt in a long time, but I was in pain for other reasons, and so I didn't notice."

"At least he didn't get the software, did he?"

"Derek went to the engineer himself and got it from him. He used the code to finish EMRY's voice recognition program."

"That's why you left EMRY?"

"I knew it was only a matter of time before Derek fired me, but he wanted to keep using me for my software skills as long as I stayed. Dad didn't want me to quit. That's why we argued. I couldn't stay, because that would be like pretending Derek's behavior was okay. Dad told me essentially to just suck it up. That I was exaggerating. That EMRY was going IPO soon and I'd be stupid to throw away all that money. Dad and I had a huge shouting match, and I walked out and quit EMRY the next day. A few months later, EMRY was bought by Google and my father was livid that I'd been so stupid."

"You weren't stupid," he said.

"I know, but at the time, I doubted myself. Derek wasn't done—I had signed an NDA, so he knew I couldn't say anything about what he'd told me to do, but maybe he was afraid I'd find a way around that. He spread rumors about me to other companies I might have worked for, and the only job I could find was working IT at half what I had been making. I felt so betrayed by everyone, including God. I thought God should have protected me for doing the right thing." Jane took a deep breath, and smelled rosemary and basil. "But it was right for me to leave EMRY, and if I'd gone to another software company, I would still be working for them rather than starting my own business."

She turned her head, rested her brow in the curve of his neck. His skin was warm. "Derek hadn't really loved me, and my father had showed how little he regarded me. This past year, I felt unloveable. And very alone."

"Derek is scum. And your father shouldn't have made you feel that way."

"I'm starting to realize that maybe he did. Because otherwise, I'd still be striving after his approval rather than discovering what God's love really is. I didn't understand God's love, because I'd thought it was like my father's love. But the way God loves me is different. It's real, and it's nonjudgmental, and it's unfailing."

There was a heartbeat of silence, then he whispered, "I love you, too."

She smiled.

He dipped his head and kissed her. His lips were cold, but his kiss was fervent. His hand tilted her face up, then caressed her cheek, her jaw, her neck. He kissed her as if there was nothing else in the world he wanted more, and yet there was also a tenderness as if she was more precious to him than breath.

He pulled back, but his face was still close enough that she could feel the warmth coming off his skin.

"I've never been kissed before," she said.

His smile was bright white, his dimples dark against his tanned cheeks. He kissed her again.

Much, much later, she said, "I want you to come car shopping with me tomorrow."

He gave her a curious look. "Okay ... Why the sudden urge?"

"It was Dad who convinced me to get the hybrid."

Alex grinned at her. "What car did you really want?"

"What I'm going to get tomorrow. A Mustang. Cherry red."

He leaned in for another kiss. "Why am I not surprised?"

ABOUT CAMY TANG

Camy Tang grew up in Hawaii and now lives in northern California with her engineer husband and rambunctious dog. She graduated from Stanford University and was a biologist researcher, but now she writes full-time. She is a staff worker for her church youth group and leads one of the Sunday worship teams. Visit her website at http://www.camytang.com to read free short stories and subscribe to her quarterly newsletter.

KISSED BY A COWBOY

LACY WILLIAMS

PROLOGUE

Prom night – twelve years ago.
This was a mistake.

The words reverberated through seventeen-year-old Haley Carston's head. Pulsed painfully through her heart.

They even trembled in her hands.

The pale pink princess-style prom dress poufed around her. There was no other word to describe it other than *poufed*. She looked like a strawberry cupcake.

The girl staring back at her in Katie's full-length mirror looked like a stranger. Too much blush, too much mascara. Dark pink lipstick. How had she let her new friend talk her into this much makeup?

Because everyone *let* Katie. Katie was that kind of person. The shining star.

Nothing like *tag-along Haley*.

But that girl in the mirror—she was a stranger.

Except for the scared eyes. Those were all Haley.

After Katie had found out she wasn't planning to go to the senior prom, she'd promised to find Haley a date. And no one said no to Katie.

But who could she have found?

Haley's dad had dragged her to Redbud Trails, Oklahoma in the middle of her senior year, after a job he'd been chasing hadn't panned out. They'd planned to leave after a few weeks, but Haley's Aunt Matilda had seen how unhappy she was at the prospect of moving again and offered to let her stay until her first semester of college.

Haley had expected to hate the minuscule high school, graduating class of a whole dozen. She'd never imagined she'd fit in, figuring she'd stick out like the outsider she was.

Instead, she'd found an immediate friend in Katie, who'd taken Haley under her wing and drawn her into her circle of friends—the popular kids—and made Haley forget that she hadn't been born and raised in small-town Oklahoma.

Most of the time.

Tonight, she felt like a silk flower in a room full of hothouse roses. Pretending she was one of the crowd but woefully inadequate.

The three-inch pumps that matched the dress were already pinching her toes. She wobbled into the hallway and hesitated outside Katie's bedroom doorway. How in the world was she going to get to the first floor without tumbling down them?

"What are we waiting for?" Haley recognized the complaining male voice wafting up from the living room—Katie's boyfriend-of-the-month, Ronald Walker. Katie had commented more than once about how fine they would look in their prom pictures together. Haley thought maybe that was the only reason her friend was dating the jock and half-expected a breakup soon after tonight.

"Haley will be down in a minute," Katie said.

Showtime.

There were other voices laughing and talking. Katie had convinced the group to meet up at the Michaels' farm and carpool. Which meant more people to see Haley descend and face whatever sap Katie had found for her, some guy who felt sorry enough for Haley to be her date.

Her feet didn't want to move. But she was afraid Katie would come upstairs looking for her if she didn't go. She took the first step and let her momentum carry her down, down...

Voices got louder. It sounded like Katie had a crowd of friends in the living room.

"Maddox, heads up!"

When she heard the name, Haley lifted her gaze from the stairs, and she stumbled on the last step. She barely registered the projectile flying toward her until it *whacked* the back of her shoulder. Her foot caught in the long dress, and she tilted precariously.

A strong pair of hands caught her waist and steadied her.

And a kid-sized play football fell to the floor.

"Sorry," Katie's younger brother Justin, a freshman, muttered from somewhere off to the side.

Haley looked up . . . and up . . . and up into the strong-jawed face of Maddox Michaels, Katie's older brother.

Who should've been in jeans and a Stetson but instead was wearing a smart black suit and white shirt and black tie...

No. Oh no.

"Great, we're all here!" Katie sang out. "Let's have mom do her three hundred pictures so we can go."

Maddox let go of Haley's waist, but only after he made sure she was steady in the uncomfortable heels. "All right?" he asked easily.

She nodded dumbly, her cheeks burning hotter than the face of the sun. She'd only met Maddox twice before, and she'd found herself tongue-tied both times.

He was *handsome*. A *college guy*.

And she couldn't even stutter out a sentence!

"I think this belongs to you." He presented her with a simple wrist corsage of white roses. His fingers were hot on her wrist as he slipped it over her hand.

"Oh, um..." *Thank you.* How hard would that have been to say? But she only had one thought blaring through her brain. *Find Katie!*

She excused herself—had she even said *pardon me?*—and moved faster than the shoes should have allowed, pushing through the other bodies crowding the room. There Katie was, coming out of the kitchen. Haley took her friend's arm and ducked back into the brightly-lit room.

"I can't go to *prom* with *your brother*," she hissed.

Katie patted her hand, looking over Haley's shoulder back into the other room. "Look, I know he's an old curmudgeon..."

Curmudgeon? Was Katie insane? Her brother was...was

amazing. Sure, he occasionally got irritated with Katie's wild schemes, but then, who wouldn't?

He'd just finished his freshman year on a football scholarship—quarterback, no less. And there was talk that a Division I team wanted to recruit him. He was that good.

And that far out of her league. What would she even say to him? Had Katie lost her ever-lovin' mind?

Katie's smile turned apologetic. "But he was the only one..."

...who would go with you.

Her friend didn't have the finish the sentence. The words Katie didn't say hurt just the same.

"Look, I don't have to go to prom," Haley whispered frantically. "I can just go home, and then he won't have to pretend to be my date."

"Quit worrying." Katie waved her hand like she was brushing away a gnat. "Everything will be fine. Everyone will be so focused on him, they won't even notice you."

Great.

And Katie was right.

Against her better judgment, Haley squeezed into the suburban Ronald had borrowed from his mom. She would've pressed up against the window but her voluminous skirt prevented her from scooting far enough in. Her face burned as Maddox calmly settled his lanky body beside her, one long leg pressing into the pink layers.

His shoulders were so wide he had to rest his arm behind her on the seat.

It took all her energy to keep from falling into him as Ronald showed off for the guys, speeding around corners until Haley thought she might get carsick. By the time they got to the banquet hall, her whole body ached from tension, and she hadn't danced a single song yet.

Maddox helped her out of the vehicle, and within seconds, they found themselves surrounded by guys offering high-fives and talking about the last games of the season. Girls flirted with him as if Haley weren't even there.

She couldn't believe Katie had done this to her.

#

Maddox wanted to kill his sister.

Not for the date. He'd met Haley a couple times before, and she seemed all right. Maybe a little shy, but not starstruck like a lot of the other high school kids.

Tonight was supposed to be three or four hours hanging out with Haley and his sister's friends. Home by midnight. No big deal.

But he hadn't counted on the other kids. They followed him around all night until he felt like a celebrity trying to avoid the paparazzi.

About halfway through the evening, he finally spotted a patch of daylight in the crowd and broke into the open field. Out of the decorated banquet room. All the way outside. There was a little church next door with a small playground and he made a beeline for it like he had a linebacker on his tail.

He probably shouldn't have pulled his date out with him. It had been sheer reflex to grab her hand when he'd made his escape.

But now that they were alone, he had second thoughts and dropped her hand. Maybe he should've left her in there with her friends. She was so quiet—it made her seem more mature or something—he kept forgetting she was a year younger than him.

The cool night air felt good against his hot face, but he still couldn't breathe. He loosened his tie, sticking a finger down his collar to try and alleviate the choking sensation.

Everyone's expectations were stifling. Even his mother! He remembered her whispered words before he'd left the house that night. *"Just don't get her pregnant—you don't want to ruin your life."* How embarrassing, and really, did his own mother not know him better than that? And what about ruining *Haley's life*? His mom didn't seem to have spared a thought for Haley at all.

He should be used to the pressure. After his dad drank himself to death when Maddox had been fourteen, she'd started calling him *man of the house*. He'd worked early mornings before practice and into the night, keeping the farm out of bankruptcy after his dad had almost lost it all.

And now that there was a hint of fame on the horizon, his mom had become obsessed with Maddox's football career.

The expectations wore on him.

Football season didn't start for months, but he already felt like he was about to be blitzed.

Even so, he should probably suck it up and be sociable for another hour or so, until they could get out of here. He looked up.

It was full dark out, but an outside light on the corner of the building illuminated Haley. She was watching him, her lower lip caught between her teeth.

"Sorry," he said.

She folded her arms around her middle and shrugged. Her dress was pretty, but she seemed uncomfortable. With him, or with the situation?

He nodded toward the banquet hall they'd come from. "I didn't realize it was going to turn into such a zoo."

She shrugged again. She was so *quiet*, he couldn't get a read on her.

"You're not having fun," he guessed. He turned slightly away and ran a hand through his hair. "This was a bad idea." He gave the empty merry-go-round a shove, sending it spinning. "This is probably a nightmare compared to how you imagined your senior prom."

"I never imagined it," she whispered.

He barely heard her over the metal squeaking as the merry-go-round wound down.

"Why not?" He glanced back at her.

She looked into the distance, still clutching her elbows with both hands. "My dad and I move around a lot. This is my fifth school in three years."

"So...?"

"So it's hard for me to make friends. I never planned on *going* to senior prom, but Katie..."

"Katie," he agreed, trying for lighthearted.

Instead of smiling, she turned her face to the side. "Sorry

you got stuck with me," she muttered.

"I'm not." He probably surprised them both with the statement. "Unlike most everybody else, I know how to say *no* to Katie."

In the dim light he could see her luminous hazel eyes. Maybe they were filled with hope, with expectations, but somehow, she didn't make his chest tighten up like all the other kids did.

"We didn't get to dance," he said. When he reached for her, she stepped into his arms. He'd expected her to be hesitant, and maybe she was, but somehow, she fit there, in his arms. His heart pounded like he was about to throw a fourth and goal. He shuffled his feet, barely moving to the muffled notes audible even though they were outdoors and away from the dance.

What was going on here?

"I'm sorry about all of...them," he finished lamely. All the fanfare, the kids following him around all night. They'd all heard about State sniffing around after the season wrapped. If he was recruited, there was a chance he'd been seen by the pro scouts.

His mother, his friends—heck, the whole town had stars in their eyes.

"I don't think they get it," she said softly, her words a puff of warmth against his neck. "Only like one percent of all college players get drafted to the NFL."

She peered up at him, biting her lip again like maybe she shouldn't have said that.

"You're a football fan?"

"Not really. My dad."

He was having a hard time concentrating on talking. He didn't want to think about all those *expectations*. Not right now.

She said softly, "It's a lot of hard work."

Looking down on her, he thought about the kind of work it would take to get to know someone like Haley. She wasn't the typical girl, falling all over herself to get him to like her. She was...real, somehow.

"I'm not afraid of hard work."

He saw goosebumps rise along the slope of her shoulders, felt her shiver through his hands at her waist.

"Do you have a backup plan?" she asked. "In case the football thing doesn't pan out?"

Here was another reason to like Haley. Her smarts. Once, he'd overheard her coaching Katie before a big test. Now that he knew she had moved from school to school, it was even more impressive that she could keep up with the assigned work.

He pulled her to his chest, and her face tipped up to his.

He thought he should probably kiss her.

When their lips were only an inch apart, she leaned back. "I don't want you to kiss me, just because Katie forced you to be my date."

And that's the moment he fell a little bit in love with Haley Carston.

"All right."

And he bent his head to kiss her anyway.

CHAPTER ONE

Present day.
Haley Carston walked out of the bank and into the mid-June day. Summer was coming to western Oklahoma, and she knew better than to expect this mild weather to last.

She clutched the manila folder in one hand. The power of attorney for her aunt was a sign that everything was changing—and Haley didn't want it to. But she didn't get a choice. Life was like that sometimes—which she knew better than anyone.

The gilded glass door locked behind her with a decisive click. Haley had been the last customer of the day, and her business had taken longer than she'd wanted. No doubt the bank employees were in a rush to get home.

It shouldn't have taken nearly so long, but several of the employees had wandered into the bank manager's office to greet her like the old friend that she wasn't.

She'd only been back in Redbud Trails, Oklahoma, for a week, but the small town seemed to have a long memory. Everyone remembered her as *Katie Michaels' tag-along,* even though it had been over a decade since she'd left for college and stayed in Oklahoma City. She'd already lost count of the times she'd heard someone say, *"You used to run around with the Michaels girl."*

She squinted in the afternoon sunlight. Her memories of Katie were like a giant fist squeezing her insides and twisting. Haley had worked hard during college to shed the perpetual shyness that had followed her to the state university. But she'd never forgotten her best friend. Katie was a light that had shone too brightly—and burned out too quickly.

Just like Aunt Matilda. Haley's aunt had been diagnosed with inoperable cancer and wouldn't last the summer. One thing Haley had learned from growing up the way she had was you didn't get that time back. Her boss had granted her a leave of absence, and she arrived in Redbud Trails the next day.

Aunt Matilda needed her. And her aunt had been there for Haley through the dark days after Paul had walked away. Haley would stay by her aunt's side until the end.

Even if it was hard.

She paused to take a breath and admire the picturesque square in front of the bank. It had always been her favorite place in this own. Just as she was turning away, a small voice cried out, "Wait!"

A young girl rode up on a bicycle, dark pigtails flying out behind her, red-faced and huffing, her forehead slick with sweat. She hopped off the bike before it had even stopped rolling. She didn't even glance at Haley but ran up to the glass door and banged on it. Her purple backpack bounced with the force of her whacking.

"Please—" the girl gasped. She sounded near tears.

And the bank was most definitely closed.

"Honey," Haley said, "I don't think they're going to open for you."

The girl just banged harder. Stubborn.

"They c-can't be closed. I need to talk to a loan officer. I have to show them!"

What was the girl so upset about? Haley looked for a parent, figuring that *someone* must be responsible for her. The girl looked about ten, but that was still too young to be in town, alone.

But no one was around.

"Hey." Haley approached the girl and put her hand on her shoulder.

The insistent banging finally stopped. The girl's head and shoulders drooped. She sniffled and rubbed a hand beneath her eyes, still looking down.

"Can I help you, hon?" Haley asked.

The little girl looked up, giving Haley her first good look at the turned-up tip of her nose, splash of freckles, and blue eyes. Her heart nearly stopped. The girl was a near-carbon copy of Katie. Down to the thick, curling eyelashes that Haley had been so jealous of back then.

She might've been the image of her mother, but the hesitant wariness in her gaze was all her Uncle Maddox. Haley's insides dipped at the single thought of the man she hadn't seen in over a decade.

"You're Livy, right? Livy Michaels?" Haley asked. "I'm Haley Carston."

The girl didn't react to Haley's name. Haley had rarely visited Redbud Trails after she'd entered college. Aunt Matilda had mostly opted to come down to the city. And Haley doubted Livy's uncle had ever mentioned her.

"Nobody calls me that," the girl said, pulling away and crossing her arms.

"Oh. Sorry. Olivia." Haley smiled, trying to show that she was a friend. She'd heard Katie call her the nickname once, right after Olivia had been born. Maybe the pet name hadn't stuck. Because Katie hadn't been around to use it.

"You look like your mother."

The softly-spoken statement did not gain Haley any points with Olivia, who watched her with slightly-narrowed eyes.

And there was still no parental figure in sight. "Is your uncle...?"

Olivia's expression changed to slightly-chagrined. "Um... I told Uncle Justin I was riding my bike."

To town? Haley's suspicions rose. She knew Maddox's mother had passed and had heard Maddox had custody of the little girl. Maybe Justin was watching her this afternoon.

"I really need to talk to a banker," Olivia said again, voice gone tiny. "It's important."

No one had even come to the door to see what all the banging was about. If Haley had to guess, the bank tellers and manager might've already left by a back exit.

"I don't think that's going to happen tonight. What about your uncle?"

Olivia looked away. "He's...um...he's on his way."

A likely story. "Can I give you a ride somewhere? Or walk with you...?"

Olivia's face scrunched. "I'm not supposed to ride with people I don't know."

Haley bit the inside of her lip, thinking. She couldn't just leave an eleven-year-old alone here, not knowing when one of Olivia's uncles might appear.

"Hmm. Well, you might not know me, but you probably know my aunt. Matilda Patterson."

The girl's face brightened. "Everyone knows Mrs. Matilda."

It was so bittersweet. Not many knew about her aunt's illness, and Haley's voice was soft when she answered the girl. "I know Aunt Matilda would love to see you. We can call your uncle and make sure it's all right. He can pick you up there."

The tip of Olivia's ears went pink. She turned her face to the ground.

Haley hated to be the bad guy but, "He's probably worried sick. I assume he has a cell phone...?" She fished her phone out of her purse and waited for Olivia to give her the number.

"Honey?"

Finally, Olivia rattled off a number, but when a gruff male voice answered with a curt, "Yeah?" Haley's heart pounded in her throat and ears.

The man on the line wasn't Justin.

It was Maddox.

"M-Maddox?" Oh, Haley hated the stutter that slipped into her voice.

There was a pause. Then a gruff, "Who is this?"

Looking up with an expression so like her mother's, Olivia's lower lip stuck out the slightest bit, her eyes pleading for Haley's understanding. Or help. How many times had Katie used that very look on Haley?

And apparently, it still worked.

Haley forced a polite, cheerful note into her voice, the same note she reserved for her coworkers back in Oklahoma City. "This is Haley Carston."

She didn't exactly expect a warm welcome, maybe more of a *what do you want,* given how they'd left things, but he was completely silent. She could hear the rumble of an engine, muffled like he was in the cab of a truck. Maybe he really was on his way.

"I'm in town for awhile, and I ran into your niece outside the Redbud Trails Bank. I wanted to see if she could come over to Aunt Matilda's with me until you or Justin can come pick her up."

"She's in town? Alone?" he barked. And she recognized the worry beneath the gruffness.

Olivia watched, clutching her hands together in front of her.

"Mmhmm," Haley said, her tone unnaturally bright.

He muttered under his breath. She thought it might've been something derogatory toward his brother, but she couldn't be sure.

"Justin can't drive," he said. "And I'm on my way home, but I'm probably an hour out of town."

"Well, Aunt Matilda and I would love to have Olivia over," Haley said.

He hesitated. "Are you sure?"

"Of course."

"I'll be there as soon as I can."

Maddox Michaels stood on the porch of the little Patterson cottage and braced his hand on the doorframe, letting his head hang low.

One of the large dining room windows was open a few inches, and he could hear Olivia chattering from somewhere in the house. Relief swamped him. She was okay.

He was going to kill his brother. Justin was supposed to have been *watching* her.

It was probably an act of mercy that Haley had found his

niece. Maddox was working for a custom harvester, trading shifts with another guy who had a new baby at home. The crew would travel all summer, running combines and a grain cart. Dave needed the extra income but didn't want to miss time with his new baby, and with Justin incapacitated, Maddox needed to be home more, too. Right now, they were working in southern Oklahoma, but they would also travel up through Kansas and Colorado and who knew where else. Maddox didn't like the travel, but he needed the money, and splitting the time on the crew seemed to be working for both of them.

Until now.

Coming face-to-face with Haley was the last thing he wanted to do when he was feeling exhausted and beat-down. How in the world had Olivia gotten to town?

In his peripheral vision, he caught sight of the dusty pink bike leaning against the front of the truck parked beneath the carport, and the muscles in his neck and shoulders tightened. His hand slipped down the doorframe.

No. Olivia wouldn't have ridden her bike into town alone. It was three and a quarter miles to the bank.

Justin was a dead man.

The door opened before he was ready, and he looked up. Slowly. His Stetson moved with his head, revealing her inch-by-inch.

But it didn't soften the blow of seeing her.

Her feet were bare beneath hip-hugging jeans, and she wore some kind of soft, flowy blouse. Her auburn hair was shorter, curling around her face.

And her brown eyes were as soft as he remembered.

She reached out and touched his forearm, and that's when he realized he'd leaned his palm against the doorbell. The buzzer had been sounding consistently. Annoyingly.

"Sorry."

"It's okay," she said. "Hi."

"Hi."

She was the same as she had been. That smile. Half shy and half knowing, and his gut twisted like he was nineteen again.

"You look good," she said softly.

He knew what he looked like. Older. Worry creases around his eyes. Covered in dust and wrinkled, like he'd slept in his truck. Which he had.

"You too." It was such an inane comment, and *good* didn't even come close to describing her. He needed to get out of here before he made more of a fool of himself.

"Can you send Olivia out? Is she okay?"

Haley's expression softened. "She's amazing. She's helping me cook supper. C'mon in."

He shouldn't. She must've seen his hesitation, because she paused on the threshold. "If you want to stay, Matilda and I would love to have you for supper. Either way, there's something I'd like to talk to you about."

He nodded. He swung his tired body into motion and stepped inside. Ahead and off to the left was the quaint, antiquey living room.

"Are you limping?" she asked.

He took off his hat, ran a hand through his brown curls, damp from sweating beneath the hat brim. The A/C on his pickup wasn't the best, but there was no money to fix it right now.

"Just tired. I've been out of town." His joints had gotten stiff sitting in his truck for hours. "I've picked up a job working with a harvest crew."

"Oh. So you have to travel a lot?"

"Yeah, a few days at a time. The farm's doing good though." If he could just keep ahead of his creditors. "Since Katie and my mom passed, it's just been me, Justin, and Olivia."

He tapped his hat against his leg. Nervous. And rambling. But seeing her again, after all this time... all his feelings came rushing back, like they'd been jostled loose by the vibrations of the combine.

He rubbed the back of his neck as he followed her through the dining room, where papers were strewn across the worn, wooden table. Past the dining room, he could see into a small kitchen.

That last summer, after Haley's senior prom, he'd followed Katie and Haley around like a safety chasing a wide receiver. He'd tried to be nonchalant about it, just show up wherever they were. He was pretty sure Katie had seen through him, but he didn't know if Haley had ever figured out how he felt about her.

And then Katie's pregnancy changed everything. Derailed his plans.

And heaped on another responsibility. Not that he regretted having charge of Olivia, but he'd only been twenty-one.

And speaking of.

"I should check on..." He nodded to the kitchen.

He passed by Haley, getting a whiff of something flowery.

Olivia caught sight of him and sent him a chagrined smile, not letting go of the spoon she held in one hand. "Hey, Uncle M."

Her subdued greeting was not lost on him, nothing like the chattering he'd heard before, through the open window.

She was safe. Thank God. He swallowed the emotion that tightened his throat. "You're in trouble, you know that?"

"I'm sorry," Olivia whispered.

"What exactly were you thinking?"

"I needed to go to the bank."

He shook his head, didn't even know what to say. What she'd done was dangerous. Then he got a whiff and a glimpse of the pan she was tending. "What is that?"

She said something he didn't understand, her voice still soft and subdued.

"What?" he asked warily.

"Duck," answered Haley. "It's French."

He wasn't sure what to think about that, and it must've shown in his face, because Olivia giggled hesitantly.

"Uncle M is more of a steak and potatoes kind of guy," his niece offered.

He shrugged. It was true.

"Well, maybe it's a good thing you and I met," Haley told Olivia. "We can both appreciate the finer culinary arts."

He watched Olivia repeatedly scoop up the sauce in the pan and drizzle it over the duck. He'd never seen her do anything like that before. "Where did you learn to do that?"

"Food Network," Olivia said at the same time that Haley said, "Cooking classes."

The girls shared a smile, and the sight of it was like getting socked in the solar plexus. How long had it been since Olivia had smiled at him like that? How had his niece formed a connection with Haley in just an hour? Was it the cooking together? Or was it because they were both female?

He didn't know, and he wasn't sure he wanted to find out. "We've gotta head home, kid."

Olivia and Haley shared a glance, and he braced himself for the upcoming battle.

But it wasn't Olivia who begged him to stay.

"I know you've got places to be," Haley said. "But I want to talk to you for a minute."

This was a little surreal.

Haley couldn't believe that Maddox was really here. The first man who'd kissed her.

The man she'd dreamed would fall in love with her and want to marry her. At least she'd dreamed it until Katie's death had changed everything.

He followed her back into the dining room. She stepped on one side of the table and turned to see he'd paused on the opposite side. He faced her like she was the opposing team. His broad shoulders—football shoulders—filled out the plain blue t-shirt, and his hair clung to his head after being under his cowboy hat all day.

But it was the shadows in his coffee-colored eyes that had her breath catching in her chest. This wasn't the confident *all of life ahead of him* Maddox that she remembered so vividly from that summer.

"Where's Matilda?" he asked with a glance toward the living

room.

Tears rose in the back of her throat, but she coughed them away. "Napping," she said.

His eyes questioned her, and she shook her head. "She's been diagnosed with...cancer." The word was a knife in her throat. "The doctors say..." She took a breath. And still couldn't say it. "So I'm here."

She'd tried to keep the tears back, but the diagnosis and her aunt's impending decline were too close. She wrapped her arms around her waist and squeezed her eyes tightly closed.

Aunt Matilda's diagnosis had given Haley focus. Her aunt had been there when Haley had moved to Redbud Trails during senior year. She'd offered her niece a home when Haley's footloose father had been ready to move on. They'd talked on the phone every week since Haley had gone off to college. And she'd offered Haley emotional support when Haley's serious boyfriend Paul had broken things off.

Until now, the breakup and the distance in her relationship with her father had been the biggest problems in Haley's life. But they were minor compared to what Matilda was facing now. Haley was done wallowing in self-pity. When she got back to her life in Oklahoma City, she was moving on.

She held her breath until the impulse to cry passed.

"I'm real sorry to hear that," he said, and his voice was a little gruff. "Your aunt's a classy lady."

She half-laughed, half-hiccuped. "Yes, she is. Anyway"—she waved off the grief—"that's not what I want to talk to you about. Have you seen this?" She tapped the three-ring binder that Livy had been carrying in her backpack.

He came closer, caddy-corner to her at the edge of the table, and looked down at the computer-printed pages. He flipped one, then another, reading over the information slowly.

"What is this?" he asked.

"It's a business plan. It's Livy's."

He looked up sharply. Haley flushed a little, but wouldn't take the nickname back. Katie's daughter had wanted to be called Livy after they'd bonded over their love of cooking.

He looked toward the kitchen, where they could hear Livy humming a little tune.

"For what?" he asked, still looking toward his niece.

"Ice cream."

"She makes a lot of ice cream at home, different flavors, but... She wants to start a business?"

He looked at her with those unfathomable eyes. For a brief moment, an awareness swelled between them. A memory, a connection. Then he blinked, and it dissolved, leaving nothing in its place.

Haley shook away a tic of sadness. "She was trying to get to the bank to ask for a loan. She made up this business plan—it's actually very detailed. I'm surprised at how much work she's put into it. It's impressive for someone her age."

He furrowed his brow. "Shouldn't she want to be a cheerleader or play basketball? You know, do normal kid things?"

Haley winced but tried to cover it with a smile. "She is a normal little girl," she said softly, glancing over her shoulder to make sure Livy wasn't listening. How many times in her own childhood had Haley wanted to fit in with the other kids? And she hardly ever had.

"Some kids want those things," Haley said. "I think some kids know what they want to do with their lives. What did you want to do when you were Livy's age?"

"Play football." By the clenched jaw, she figured he regretted that statement. "I just don't get why she wants to make ice cream. There's already a chain in town."

"Not just ice cream. *Gourmet* ice cream."

He shook his head. "I don't get it."

"It's a different market than fast food," she explained gently.

He exhaled a long, slow sigh, shifting his feet. "How much?"

"Fifteen hundred dollars."

He ran his fingers through his hair. "You've got to be—"

"She's got a restaurant willing to sell her a used blast freezer at a great deal."

"A what?"

"It's a commercial-grade ice-cream maker."

He shook his head, looking down at the papers in the binder.

"I know it's a lot of money." Haley tapped the folder. "She's done some research. She's got great ideas, I think we could work up a marketing plan—"

"Thanks for encouraging her, but I can't afford something like this." He sounded sincere in his thanks, but also discouraged. He ran one hand against the back of his neck, fluffing the bottom of his slightly-too-long brown curls.

"I'd like to do more than encourage her."

He narrowed his eyes. "You want to give my niece fifteen hundred dollars?" he asked slowly. "Why?"

She shrugged. "I'm here for"—she drew a breath—"the summer, probably. I'd kind of like to go into business with her. Be her partner."

"Why?" he repeated.

For Katie, she wanted to say. And for him. For the dreams that had been lost to Katie's pregnancy and untimely death.

But mostly for Livy. When they'd been talking this afternoon, Haley had seen a glimpse of herself in the younger girl—a little girl hungry for love, for someone to believe in her.

"What if she fails? What if you lose all that money?"

"It's just money."

He looked at her like she'd said something crazy.

"Anyway, that's my problem, mine and Livy's."

He was softening. She could see it in the minute drop of his shoulders.

"Whatever happens, it'll be a learning experience for her," she offered.

"Teach her that life's hard," he muttered, looking back down at the table again.

"What if she doesn't fail?"

When he looked up at her, she saw the truth in his gaze. This wasn't the same confident football star she'd known before. Maybe he didn't believe in his own dreams, anymore.

But Livy deserved her chance.

He glanced toward the kitchen again. From where she stood, Haley couldn't see Livy, but knew the girl could probably hear them. He seemed to have the same thought, because he lowered his voice. "If we do this, I'm not letting you take on the whole expense."

Her heart thumped loudly as she heard what he didn't say. "If...?"

He smiled. A sad little half-smile. More a turning up of one side of his mouth. "I shouldn't. This is crazy."

Maybe it *was* a little crazy. It felt more like one of Katie's old schemes than something the responsible, college-educated Haley would do.

But being here for her aunt, coming back to the place where Katie's life had ended too suddenly—both were reminders that sometimes, life didn't give you second chances.

Livy deserved to chase her dreams. Life was too short to waste it.

And Haley was determined Katie's daughter would have the chance. Even if it meant bumping into this handsome cowboy a few more times.

CHAPTER TWO

A week later, Maddox still couldn't quite believe he'd agreed to Haley's wild scheme. Or that Haley had agreed to give his niece that kind of money.

He'd been gone on the harvest crew for four days, arriving home late last night. While he'd been gone, he'd relied on his cousin Ryan to help out and keep Justin in line. At least Olivia hadn't run away again.

After a short night's sleep, Maddox had been out with the cattle since dawn, starting with a headcount and checking fences. Since high school, he'd spent years building the farm back up after his old man had let things get so bad. Maddox had vowed he would never give up on life like his father had.

He'd just ridden his horse into the barn after cooling the animal down when he heard a car pull up in the drive between the house and the barn. Haley had promised to deliver the machine this evening. Olivia had mentioned it about ten times when he'd gone in for lunch earlier.

He stayed with his horse. He wasn't going to rush out to greet her like a high schooler on a first date. Hadn't he behaved like that enough that last summer? He'd stay here in the barn, even if his heart started pounding and his palms slicked with sweat.

Haley was here for Olivia. Maddox was in no shape to be getting interested in a woman. End of story.

Maddox brushed down the horse, keeping his feet planted right where they were. He thought about how she might smile if he went to greet her, how her curls would look in the fading light. He ground his teeth and ran the brush through the horse hair.

"Hey, Mad!" Ryan's voice rang out. His cousin had been over this afternoon, trying for the thousandth time to cheer up Justin. Or get his butt out of that recliner. Or both.

"Your new girlfriend is here!" Ryan called as Maddox tucked his horse back into its stall.

Maddox gave his horse one last pat. "She's not my girl—" He turned and stopped short. "Howdy, Haley."

Ryan jerked a thumb at her. "Followed me out here."

She peeked at him over Ryan's shoulder, grinning.

Something inside him responded, like his insides broke open or something equally corny. Really? He wasn't nineteen anymore.

"You're early," he groused.

She seemed to see right through him, her smile widening. "I couldn't wait any longer. I love ice cream."

"Livy's in the house."

She nodded but didn't seem in any kind of hurry to head that way. She glanced around the interior of the barn, and he followed her gaze, seeing it through her eyes. Ryan boarded a few horses here, and Maddox's four had stuck their heads over the stall doors, craning to see the owner of that female voice. Or maybe it just seemed that way to him.

He was proud of the place. It wasn't new, not by any stretch, but he'd replaced the roof a couple years ago, and it was clean and the animals were well-cared-for.

"You know, I think I only ever came out here once when I knew..." She paused and seemed to shake off the words "Back in high school. The place looks totally different."

"Good." He ran a much tighter ship than his father ever had, and it showed.

"Uh, the junior high principal called again," Ryan said as they headed toward the barn door.

"Something about Livy?" Haley asked.

Maddox shook his head. The man wanted Maddox to teach a class and coach the junior high football team. Mostly coach.

And Maddox might have considered it if he had the college degree everyone in Redbud Trails thought he did. The job wouldn't make him rich, but it would be better than traveling all summer, and it would be a steady supplement to the income they got from the cattle and small crops they were able to raise.

They left the barn behind and crossed the short field toward the house. He noticed the fifteen-year-old Ford she'd parked in the drive, her aunt's truck.

"How big is this ice cream thing?" he asked. He'd cleared a spot on the counter, but maybe he should have asked for dimensions before he agreed to house it in his kitchen.

"Well, it took three college guys to load it in my aunt's truck."

"Sounds like you need me, too." Ryan winked and flexed a bicep.

Maddox rolled his eyes. He might have been worried about Ryan moving in on Haley, except he knew his cousin was hung up on his high school crush. She'd joined the military and had been stationed overseas when she was injured. Now she was in a military hospital stateside. Ryan had been in love with her since high school. Never really looked at another woman.

Haley rounded the truck on the opposite side and threw back a brown tarp, revealing a plastic-wrapped stainless steel box about the size of an ice chest.

"That's it?" he asked. "The magic machine?" *Which cost so much money...*

"Yep. You guys got it?" She didn't wait for an answer. She opened the cab door and stuck her head inside the truck.

The machine was heavier than he thought it would be, and Ryan hopped in the truck bed to push it toward the edge.

When they hefted it between them, she met them carrying a cardboard box.

"What's that?" he asked.

"Early birthday gift for Olivia."

He opened his mouth to protest, but Ryan shifted the machine, jiggling it. "Mad, c'mon. This is heavy. Let's move."

He ground his back teeth and headed for the house.

She trailed them toward the porch steps, a couple steps behind.

"Do you really call him that?" she asked.

"Everyone else calls him Mad Dog. High school football nickname," Ryan grunted. "Why?"

"It seems like it would be a self-fulfilling prophecy. Like if you expect him to be *Mad*, he will be. Why not something like Joy or Sunshine?"

She said it with such a straight face that at first Maddox didn't catch that she was joking.

Ryan burst out laughing.

She quirked a smile at Maddox, and he almost missed the first step. He bobbled but caught himself with only a knock of one knee on the porch post.

"I suppose it is kind of a natural evolution from *Maddox*. But still...what's your middle name?"

Maddox wasn't saying.

"William," Ryan offered.

They finally cleared the stairs, and Maddox realized she would have to open the door for them. He moved forward, shoving the machine into his cousin's chest in retaliation for making fun of him.

Ryan's eyes danced.

"Hmm...you could've been a Will. Not a Billy," she said as they carried the machine past her and through the living room and on into the kitchen.

"Why not shorten it to *Ox*?" he muttered. "That's what I feel like right now.".

Ryan froze, bringing the two of them up short, and looked at him over the top of the machine with an odd look on his face. Olivia, who was sitting on the far side of the counter, dropped her jaw.

Then his cousin laughed, a surprised burst of sound. "Did you just crack a joke?" Ryan asked.

Maddox ignored him as they maneuvered around the island to the space he'd cleared on the back counter. Finally, he put the machine down, arms aching, and turned to see Haley smiling down at the countertop.

"Who told a joke?" Justin asked, limping into the room, one crutch under his arm. He'd actually come out of his seclusion to watch the spectacle?

"Uncle M, I think," Olivia piped, her face scrunched in confusion.

The tips of Maddox's ears got hot. Had it really been such a long time since he'd made a wisecrack?

Luckily, Olivia's excitement seemed to distract his brother and cousin. She rushed to the machine, bumping past Maddox's elbow in the process. He overheard Haley murmur a soft 'hello' to his brother as she set her box down on the island counter.

Olivia started tugging at the plastic, but it wasn't coming off easy.

"Do you have some scissors? A box knife?" Haley asked.

"I'll do it," Ryan said cheerfully, digging in his jeans' pocket and coming up with a pocketknife. "Then I've got to get to the Reynolds'."

In moments, the plastic was shredded around the stainless steel box.

"It's awesome," Olivia breathed.

"It's a hunk of metal," Maddox argued. It pretty much was, with a small door on top and some buttons and a dispenser on the front.

Haley wrinkled her nose at him. "Just wait 'til you taste the magic that comes out of this baby." She started removing the plastic wrapping and crumpling the pieces between her hands.

"I'm out," said Ryan with a wave. He slipped through the back door, the girls chorusing "Bye," behind him.

Maddox leaned against the far counter and watched as Haley and Olivia made over the machine, Haley focusing as much on the girl as on the machine in front of them. Maddox wondered if she even remembered he and Justin were in the room. "We'll need to clean it first," she said.

Maddox was surprised his brother was still here. Justin had been a bull rider until that accident. It was one thing to get thrown from a bull, but to be trampled by one, too? It had resulted in a career-ending injury—a fractured pelvis. Now, Justin was all but a hermit, limping around the house and battling depression.

But here he was, easing himself down into a kitchen chair and watching the two girls as they disassembled the guts of the machine and dunked them in a sinkful of hot, sudsy water.

"What flavor are you going to try first?" Haley asked.

"I was thinking about something fun, like this recipe I created for banana split." Olivia's voice sounded metallic as she leaned in close, her arm inside the machine as she extracted its guts.

"But then I thought for the first try, maybe I should go with something standard, like vanilla."

"Can't go wrong with a longstanding favorite," Haley said. She scrubbed one of the parts, then rinsed it and set it on a dishtowel to one side of the sink. She'd made herself right at home. She and Olivia were two of a kind, Olivia's dark curls at Haley's auburn shoulder, both of them washing up.

He'd thought she would drop off the machine and be in a hurry to leave. Apparently he'd been wrong.

And then she looked over her shoulder, right at him. "So what's for supper, boys?"

He hadn't thought she would stay. But Olivia's face was all lit up, and he found himself saying, "I can fire up the grill..."

"Uncle Justin makes a mean barbecued chicken," Olivia said, then sent an uncertain look over her shoulder, as if she might've blundered by saying so.

Justin had been so closed in his own little world since his injury, temper close to the surface and frequently boiling over.

Maddox had shouted louder than a coach from the sidelines after he'd let Olivia ride off to town the other day. The younger man hadn't even noticed she'd been gone, too dazed and drugged on pain meds.

But now Justin met Olivia's gaze squarely, his expression clear-eyed for the first time in a long time.

"If I can get a pretty girl to hold the platter for me, I'll give it a shot."

Haley laughed, drying her hands. She threw her arm around Livy's shoulders. "Do you think he was talking about you or me?"

She wasn't quite the shy girl he remembered. She'd matured, but her gentle spirit was still there. He watched as the girls shifted from the now drying equipment to Olivia's notebook and bent over it.

He could almost feel himself falling for her again.

But that was dangerous.

He wasn't the same boy he'd been back then, either. He was a college dropout whose dreams had been put on hold forever.

He didn't know how to dream anymore.

Even though Justin flirted with Haley under the guise of teasing Livy, she knew he was harmless. There was something broken behind his eyes.

It was Maddox's sometimes-hot, sometimes-angsty gaze that she couldn't ignore.

It sent prickles up the back of her neck and made her fidgety as she and Olivia reassembled the blast freezer. At least she could pretend her fumbling was because the machine was new to them.

Finally, they got it back together.

"This is a great spot for it," she told Olivia. It really was. A wide swath of bare cabinet halfway between the stovetop and sink, with access to the island in the middle of the kitchen.

"Uncle Maddox moved some stuff around so it would fit."

"Oh, he did?"

Now that Olivia had mentioned it, the microwave was a newer model that didn't match the rest of the worn appliances. The microwave had been mounted above the stove, and freshly cut wood showed on the cabinets where he might've cut them to make it fit.

Haley flicked a gaze to Maddox. The tips of his ears had gone pink, just like Olivia's had the other day. An adorable shared family trait.

"Kitchen needed updating," he muttered beneath his breath. "Got to start the grill." He moved away, slipping out the back door.

Justin stayed, pushing himself slowly out of the chair and shuffling around the counter on his crutch. "Outta my way, cuties."

"But we have to start our base," Olivia protested. She was practically vibrating with excitement, bouncing on the balls of her feet.

"If you want my special chicken you've got to let me marinate it for a few minutes, Livy-Skivvy."

"Uncle Justin!" Olivia's token protest and giggle showed she wasn't too old yet for the silly nickname.

"I've got something for you first anyway," Haley said, drawing Olivia away.

A small alcove made a nice breakfast nook, and Haley well remembered sitting at the small, round table with Katie in the wee hours of the night, talking about boys. Dreaming about Maddox.

She shook away the memories and moved her box from the island to the table.

"You brought me something?" The hesitant hope in Olivia's voice pinched Haley's heart.

She sat down and motioned the girl next to her. Olivia stepped up to the table.

"The restaurant was liquidating, so I grabbed them for a great price. You've got to have the right tools, don't you?"

Olivia exclaimed over the stainless steel pans they could use to make an ice bath, the industrial whisk and strainer, and the two pots, all of which Haley had tucked into the cardboard box.

The restaurant owner had given it to Haley for a steep discount, happy to be rid of them.

"Here's the best part," Haley said. She took out the small white gift box she'd tucked in the bottom of the bigger cardboard box.

Olivia unfolded the lid almost reverently. "Is this...what I think it is?"

She took out the child-sized apron that Haley had sewn for her. White with vibrant red flowers all over, ruffled on the edges. Similar to the adult-sized one Olivia had worn at Aunt Matilda's last week, when they'd first bonded over their shared love of food.

And the most important part, in the center of the midsection, an embroidered logo. Olivia's ice cream logo.

The little girl was silent for a long moment, and Haley wondered if something was wrong, until Livy spun and threw her arms around Haley, burying her face against Haley's shoulder.

Haley blinked back the hot moisture that wanted to pool in her eyes. She hadn't meant to get emotional.

"Happy birthday," she whispered.

"Thank you, thank you!" Olivia came away, slipping the apron over her head and reaching behind to tie the bow. She danced over to her uncle at the counter. "Uncle Justin, look!"

He smiled his approval.

Olivia ran outside, calling, "Uncle Maddox..." her voice faded as the screen door slammed behind her.

And Haley was left alone with Maddox's younger brother.

She let her eyes skim around the room. It was much the same as she remembered, the pale green walls, the same cabinets and countertops. The womanly touches were gone. There was still a dishtowel hanging from a towel rack where Katie's mother had always kept it, but all of her knickknacks were gone.

It was plain, but homey, too. Comfortable.

And then she had nothing else to look at but Justin. He continued working with the raw chicken breasts on the cutting board, but he must've sensed her perusal.

"Nice gift," he said. "Nice of you to give her the machine, too."

She couldn't tell from the sound of his voice whether he really thought it was nice, or he was being sarcastic.

She'd asked Aunt Matilda about him after Maddox's

mention of his injury. But she didn't know if she should ask about his recovery or leave it alone.

"I'm excited to work with Livy," she said simply.

"It's not exactly a lemonade stand."

"You sound like Maddox," she said before she'd really thought about the words. The other night, Maddox had been more than concerned about Livy's venture. He'd been negative, though at least he hadn't said anything to the girl.

"I was sorry to hear about your accident."

"Wasn't an accident," he drawled. "Bull knew what it was doing when it stepped on me."

"Oh." What else to say to a remark like that? She listened to the scraping of the knife against the cutting board, the ticking of the clock on the far wall. What was taking Olivia so long?

She brightened her voice. "So what're you doing these days?"

His kept his focus on the chicken, but she saw his face crinkle in a smile. It wasn't a nice smile, more like a fierce baring of his teeth.

"That's the question, isn't it? And the answer is *nothing*. I sit around all day in my pop's old recliner and watch soap operas."

"Um..."

The waves of anger radiating off of him were almost palpable. But there was something deeper underneath. Desperation.

"Livy said you helped her with a school project. So that's something."

"Hmm. Well, maybe I could have a career tutoring kids. Oh, except I barely graduated high school."

She didn't know how to handle his anger and sarcasm. If he was one of her friends back in the city, she would be comfortable enough to offer an alternative. To say *something*.

"They have adult education scholarships," she said softly.

"What?" he barked.

She cleared her throat. "Scholarships," she forced the word out louder. "You could go back to school. The state university isn't too far from here."

"Did you hear me say I barely made it out of high school?"

She shrugged. "Doesn't mean you wouldn't do all right now. Especially as an older student."

"I'm not *that* much older," he muttered to the chicken.

Finally, Maddox and Livy returned, the girl wearing her apron and chattering excitedly.

Maddox looked between Justin and Haley. Thankfully, he didn't say anything.

But she wasn't sure how long that could last.

"So...thanks for bringing the freezer blaster thing out," Maddox said.

Haley laughed. "Blast freezer. You're welcome." She slipped out the Michaels' front door and down the porch steps, Maddox following.

The last bit of white light hung on the horizon as twilight deepened around them.

"The ice cream was...good," he said.

She glanced over at him, incredulous. She'd seen him palm a lightswitch as they exited the house, and now the porch light illuminated his faint smile and the day's growth of beard.

"Okay." His lips twitched. "It was better than good."

"It's incredible," she said. "And so is Livy."

She thought they had a real shot at making Livy's business a success. With Haley's education and her job as a marketing assistant back in Oklahoma City, and Livy's ingenuity, especially when it came to flavors, they had a chance.

He followed her to the truck, their shoes crunching in the gravel. She breathed in the cool country night air, nothing like the urban scents she was accustomed to in Oklahoma City.

"It must be hard to be away from her, traveling so much."

It must be difficult, period, for a man raising a young girl and trying to be an emotional support for his brother.

Maddox said nothing.

He'd been friendly enough over supper, asking about Haley's job and life back in Oklahoma City. But now he was quiet, pensive.

Haley had seen Livy's breathless hope when she'd presented the ice cream to her uncle. She remembered having that same gut-clenching feeling toward her own father. Whether she'd been handing him her report card or a cookie she'd baked herself, she'd wanted her father's approval, needed the emotional connection.

Maddox had praised the ice cream. But Haley also remembered that Livy hadn't gone to her uncle with the business plan.

And Haley wanted Livy to have that special connection with her uncle.

"I would have loved a childhood like this," she said, too vulnerable to look him in the face. She stared instead at the stars above the roof of the barn.

He snorted. "What, growing up with two bachelors?"

"Growing up with roots," she said softly.

He rested one palm on the top of the truck bed, and she leaned against the side and continued staring into the heavens. Another thing she missed living in the city—the bountiful stars.

"My dad and I moved around so much when I was growing up, I never felt like I belonged anywhere. You can give that to Livy. Roots."

"How come your dad didn't settle down?"

She shrugged. "He was always chasing...something. The next promotion. A different job..."

She breathed in deeply. "At first, I let myself get too attached to places. Found best friends. Settled into school. But I was never enough to make him stay. Or, my needs weren't..."

She felt it when he turned his head to look at her. A flare of heat hit her face.

"And I don't know why I'm telling you all this." She dusted off her hand on her jeans nervously and glanced at him. "I'm over it now. I have friends, good friends in Oklahoma City. I'm happy there. I'll be going back once Aunt Matilda..." She still couldn't finish the sentence.

"Good for you," he said. "I'm glad."

But he didn't say the same about himself. Why did he work so hard? Was he really happy on the farm, or did he think he didn't have options?

Instead of voicing those questions, Haley asked, "Why do you call her Olivia? In the hospital, I remember Katie calling her Livy."

He moved one arm, palm sliding along the side of the truck. "We don't talk about Katie much."

Why not? The words were on the tip of her tongue, but something zinged inside her. A warning, maybe?

His feet shifted, like he was uncomfortable. "Whatever your reason for doing this...helping Olivia... Just remember, she's a little girl who will still be here when you go back to the city."

He sounded like he thought Haley's presence was going to hurt the girl, but all she wanted was to help.

"If this is some kind of...I don't know...call back to Katie's memory—"

"It's not."

He shook his head, gripping the top of the truck bed. "I can't help remembering how you two were thick as thieves..."

Tag-along. His words doused ice water on her. She'd had a wonderful evening with Livy, cooking the first ice cream base and teasing Maddox...

And he still thought of her as Katie's tag-along, after all these years.

She didn't know what to say.

He seemed to understand her sudden uncertainty, because he went on. "Look, I'm just trying to protect my niece. I appreciate that you're trying to do something nice for her."

She waited for the *but*. And it came.

"But giving her that money...building up her dreams..."

"I'm not doing it for Katie. I'm doing it for Livy. We're partners."

Nearby, something rustled in the darkness against the side of the house. It moved, but she couldn't make out the form in the darkness. Whatever it was, it was big.

She thought Maddox was arguing with her, but her

thundering heartbeat drowned out anything he might've said. The Thing padded closer, quiet in the darkness. Were those fangs, glimmering in the dim porch light?

She grabbed his arm, ducking between him and the truck, turning her shoulder away from the animal's hot breath against her side. Was it a Rottweiler? Or just a huge mutt?

"Maddox," she hissed. Her breath came in gasps, fear overpowering her sense of propriety and personal space.

He brought his other arm down, caging her in. "What's the matter?"

"P-please tell me that's a friend."

He looked down, over the side of his arm, then tilted his chin back to her, the light from the corner of the house shining behind him and leaving his face in shadow. "You're still afraid of dogs?"

"I'm n-not afraid. Terrified."

He snorted.

"Git on, Emmie," he said softly.

The huge black dog sat, tail swishing audibly over the gravel of the drive. Its lips parted in a panting, doggie grin. The dim porch light showed that it lifted one paw in a polite shake.

"Git on," Maddox said again, his voice laced with humor.

The dog closed its mouth with a *huff* of air, stood, and sauntered off, fading into the darkness.

And then the man turned his gaze back on her. She looked up at Maddox in the moonlight, and her stomach swooped low, the same way it had when he'd held her on prom night all those years ago.

She could see the dark stubble of his days' growth of beard. His eyes were unreadable in the darkness.

If she wanted to, she could reach up and put her arms around his neck, stand on tiptoe...and claim the second kiss she'd been dreaming about for a dozen years.

But she wasn't seventeen anymore.

And he probably didn't think about her that way. They both had Olivia's best interests at heart.

And Haley wanted to protect her own heart, too.

His hands came to rest gently on her waist, but before he could push her away, Haley stepped out of the circle of his personal space. Her heart beat and pulsed in her throat, and it sounded a little like the taunt she always heard in her head. *Tagalong.*

"Thanks for supper. I had a fun time."

She thought he said *me too*, but she tucked herself in the cab of her truck and started the engine. She waved, smiling out the window into the dark so he wouldn't know how shaken the moment had left her.

She wasn't a little sheep any longer. She had her own friends back in Oklahoma City. She wasn't *desperate* for company, no matter what he thought.

She would do what she said. She would see him peripherally while helping Olivia with her ice cream business. She would care for her aunt and mind her own business.

And they could both pretend that the near-embrace never happened.

Maddox stood staring after Haley's taillights long after they'd disappeared down the dirt drive, hands fisted loosely at his sides.

What had he been thinking? He'd *touched* her. She'd been so close, and he'd wanted her closer—wanted to find out if her lips still tasted like the ice cream they'd shared.

But the moment he'd given in to the urge and reached for her, she'd backed away.

He knew better than to reach. Hadn't his past taught him anything?

He didn't have time for any kind of relationship and didn't need Haley nosing into his business.

She wanted him to give Olivia roots. How was he supposed to do that, when he could barely keep them afloat? He wasn't doing that good a job keeping Justin from sinking further into depression, and had a hard time keeping ahead of the medical bills.

He didn't know how to be a father to a little girl.

What did he have to give to Olivia? He was on the road or working dawn-to-dusk, just to make ends meet.

The expectations were too heavy. They had been ever since his teen years, when his mom had turned him into the man of the family. As if he could handle it, because no one else was there to do it. He'd just been a kid when his dad had died in a drunken stupor. He'd been a kid when they'd all expected him to become some kind of football star, and a kid when Katie had left him with a tiny bundle of pink. If love had been enough, he'd have been the best uncle in the world.

But what he'd learned was that his love and his desire to do the right thing weren't enough. He had to be better.

He was a mess, his thoughts churning with the burn in his gut, but no antacid would repair this mess. The last thing he needed was Haley around, tempting him to dream. If he had any brains at all, he'd tell Haley not to come to the house again, but...

She was good for Olivia. That was easy to see. She'd had all three of them, him, Olivia, and even Justin for a few minutes, laughing in the kitchen like a real family.

And Olivia had soaked it up like a parched field in a rainstorm.

He was afraid he had, too.

When was the last time they'd felt like a family, not just individuals living in the same house?

He'd promised himself never to end up like his dad, always stuck in the could-have-beens. Maddox was making a life for Olivia, doing what he could.

It would have to be enough.

But what if it wasn't?

CHAPTER THREE

Three weeks later, Maddox turned down the dirt lane toward home, fresh off of another four-day-stint on the harvest crew. He'd gotten up in the middle of the night and driven all morning to make it here by lunchtime.

The more he'd thought about the things Haley had revealed about her own childhood that night after supper, the more he'd been determined to prove that he could be the father-figure Olivia needed. He could do better than he had been doing. And being here today was a part of that.

Olivia and Haley had planned some elaborate birthday celebration. He thought they might've invited the entire elementary school. They were calling it a *business expense*, planning to do something with all the ice cream they'd made over the last few weeks.

Maddox had never seen so much of the sweet treat in his life. Olivia had been furiously mixing up batches, trying out new flavors with her old personal-sized ice cream maker, and hand-packing quart after quart in cardboard containers.

She'd even appropriated a deep freezer from a neighbor who wasn't using it any more. She already had that sucker half-full.

On one of his at-home breaks, he'd sat down with Olivia and talked about the three books her school had assigned as suggested summer reading. He'd asked about her friends, expecting her to duck his question. Instead, she'd chatted with him for almost an hour. Opened up to him, and all it had taken was him asking.

Haley had been at the house two Saturdays in a row, according to Justin. Maddox had been out with the crew both times.

During those long rides on the combine, he'd imagined his brother spending time with Haley. Justin had been known for his charming ways on the rodeo circuit. Unfortunately, thinking about the two together made Maddox need to pop an antacid. And he knew why.

Haley was special. Maddox had known it when she was seventeen, and he knew it now.

Knowing he was going to see her again today had him antsy and uncomfortable. And he had no business thinking about her like he was. He was barely keeping the farm afloat. Barely avoiding the creditors calling about the overdue medical bills.

Where he'd given up on his dreams, Haley had a fancy degree and no doubt fancy friends in the city. She even cooked fancy.

Even if he did find the guts to pursue her, what would she want with a farmer like him?

She was too good for him. The smartest thing to do would be to forget about her.

But Justin had seemed more grounded after her visits. Less stuck inside his own head. Maddox couldn't help wondering what passed between them.

He turned into the drive to see five farm trucks already parked in a snaking line.

"What the—?" He guided his truck around the outside, half-driving in the ditch so he could get to the house.

He would have sworn Olivia had told him the party would begin in the afternoon.

He parked his truck on the side of the barn, since apparently they were going to need most of the yard for guests.

"Mad, you're here!" Ryan's voice rang out, quickly followed by Olivia's, "Uncle Maddox!"

He braced one hand on his truck and caught Olivia with the other arm when she launched at him. She rubbed her face against his chest. "You made it!"

"I promised, didn't I?"

When she moved back, squealing with excitement, her face was shining. He was stiff and exhausted from driving most of the night, but it was worth it.

When she ran off, he looked up to see Haley standing right there, her eyes showing her surprise.

"Didn't think I'd make it, huh?" he asked.

"I'm glad you did." She seemed sincere, and his heart thumped once hard beneath his breastbone.

She led him to a picnic table that hadn't been in the yard before, beneath a tree that would shade him from some of the hot June sun. "Where'd this come from?" he asked.

"Neighbors," she answered. "Borrowed them."

That's when he saw there were ten tables arranged in a horseshoe.

And the yard had been mowed. "Who mowed?"

"Your brother." She nodded toward the row of trucks, where not only was Justin outdoors, he was leaning on his crutch, talking to old man Simpson. The grocer had been a friend of their mom's and Maddox guessed he had delivered one of the picnic tables.

It was the first time Maddox had seen Justin willingly engage with someone outside their family circle since his fall.

Haley was still talking. "He said, and I quote, *'I can drag along behind the push-mower just as well as I can drag behind my crutch.'*"

He could imagine his brother saying that. Somehow, Haley had gotten him to mow the yard. He hated to think how, but the image of the two flirting with each other came unwelcome into his mind.

"I'm so glad you're here," Haley said, interrupting his thoughts. "I need your help. Have a seat."

In the next few minutes, Haley showed him how she wanted him to slice about thirty watermelons. It seemed like they were planning for a horde—he hoped Haley and Olivia weren't disappointed.

Haley tilted her head to the side, looking at him for a long moment. "You good?" Haley asked.

"Fine."

He didn't like the hot knot that had settled behind his sternum, thinking about her and Justin together. As he watched under the guise of cutting into one of the melons, she got some kind of magazine out of her aunt's truck. Haley marched up to his brother and slapped the book into his stomach.

His brother hugged her briefly around the shoulders, like he would've hugged Katie or their mom, and just kept on talking.

"They're just friends," Ryan said, voice low. Maddox hadn't heard him walk up.

He clapped a hand on Maddox's shoulder. "At first, I thought the same thing you were thinking, but she doesn't look at him the way she looks at you."

Maddox's stomach swooped at that thought. He'd been half in love with Haley when he'd known her as Katie's friend—and the woman she was now affected him just as powerfully.

Ryan had been checking on Justin and Olivia on the weekends Maddox had to be gone, so he must have known what he was talking about.

But it didn't make Maddox feel that much better.

Haley dashed by his table a little later and left a sampler plate of the ice cream. This had been their plan all along. Invite people for free ice cream.

He grabbed Olivia when she tried to skip by. After he'd complimented her on the ice cream, which was delicious, he asked. "How much is this costing?"

"Haley says you have to spend money to make money."

He just hoped they weren't spending too much.

He'd barely gotten started slicing the watermelons when cars began arriving. He smiled and greeted Olivia's guests, shocked at how many came. And kept coming. They seemed to arrive by the van-load. A lot of people he knew from church but hardly greeted on Sundays. People he'd gone to high school with that now had children in elementary school.

Olivia and Haley were in their element, whirling through the crowd, dispensing ice cream and chatting with everyone.

He'd never seen either of them like this before. Haley had always been so shy. Apparently, she'd overcome that. And Olivia...watching Olivia was like seeing Katie alive again. It made his heart thump painfully.

Just a month before, his niece had been a sad little girl, defensive and lonely. Then she met Haley, and everything changed. Haley seemed to be exactly what Olivia needed. His little girl was blooming with Haley around. But how long was she going to stay?

Haley couldn't believe it. When Maddox had promised to be there, she'd envisioned comforting a very disappointed Olivia. Instead, Maddox had driven all night to be at Livy's party.

Her own father would never have done something like that.

She couldn't help it that her gaze kept straying to him during the hot afternoon. She saw plenty of folks greet him, many slapping him on the shoulder while he shook their hand.

She also saw the lines of stress around his mouth. But she didn't know why. Was it the money? Trying to run the farm while he supported Justin and Livy?

She'd barely seen him since their dinner together, but Livy had told her all about how they'd spent extra time together recently. The way Olivia talked about him, it was obvious the girl thought he hung the moon. And Justin had a grudging respect for him, even through his pain and depression.

Haley's high school crush had never completely gone away—and now it was back with a vengeance. She'd buried it under her busyness and college life. And that doomed relationship with Paul. Paul, who'd always made her feel like she wasn't good enough for him.

Watching Maddox now, she could see that he was still the same popular jock, but beneath that hard exterior lurked something darker. And she couldn't help wondering what it was.

By midafternoon, Haley needed a break. She'd been on her feet since this morning. She spotted a chance and plopped down on the bench beside Maddox, bumping his shoulder with hers. "Hey."

"Hey," he responded.

The top of the picnic table was covered with sticky juice from the watermelons and Haley was careful to keep clear of it.

Olivia showed no signs of fading. She spun from one person to the next, bubbly and grinning.

The little girl had been keeping count of the number of samples they'd handed out. They'd come up with the idea of purchasing small disposable condiment bowls and scooping samples into them. Each partygoer got a sampler plate, so they could try several different flavors.

And they'd printed quarter-sheet flyers listing the flavors and ordering instructions, which they'd handed out with each sample.

The response had been wonderful. People had marveled at all Livy had done, at the wonderful ice cream, and at the girl's ingenuity. Haley couldn't have been more pleased.

"She seems happy," Maddox said, voice low. "And I can't believe Justin was out here for awhile. What did you give him earlier?"

"Hmm?" She was so tired, she couldn't think straight.

"Earlier, I watched you hand him something. Looked like a magazine or—"

"College catalog. I've almost convinced him to enroll for the fall."

Maddox shifted to look into her face. "You're kidding."

He didn't seem particularly happy about it. The lines around his mouth had tightened even more.

"Hey, Katie's friend!" The voice came from a little cluster of folks near the back porch, and then a woman walked up to their table, waving off one of the last slices of watermelon that Maddox tried to slide across to her.

Haley froze, then forced a smile to her face. She recognized the woman from high school but couldn't remember her name, either. She shouldn't have been surprised to be called, "Katie's friend," even after all these years. Apparently, Haley would always be the *tag-along* in this town.

"Can I buy a quart today?" the woman asked.

"We hadn't planned to sell any until next week."

Maddox snorted. "Olivia's been running that machine night and day. I bet I could find a quart for you to take home. How much are you willing to pay for it?"

"You gonna auction off some ice cream, Mad Dog?" a man Haley didn't know asked, wandering closer from the crowd around the porch.

Maddox looked at Haley, something brewing behind his eyes.

He stood up, using the table for leverage, then bellowed, "Livy!"

The girl darted out of the crowd, beaming and wearing the apron Haley had made her.

She approached, and Maddox whispered something to her. She squealed and ran off to the kitchen.

While she was gone, Maddox started clearing off the picnic table. Haley helped, but when she asked what he was up to, he half-grinned and said nothing.

A few minutes later, Livy climbed on top of the picnic table, and Haley realized what Maddox and Livy had planned. They were auctioning off five quarts of the gourmet ice cream. Immediately, a crowd gathered around.

Olivia's eyes were shining, but Maddox looked slightly pained.

Maddox started, "Okay, we've got—" Olivia murmured something to him—"Chocolate covered strawberries, folks. Who'll give me fifteen bucks for this quart?"

It had been one of the most popular flavors of the day, and Haley wasn't surprised to see several hands go up.

Maddox got the bid up to thirty before his voice boomed, "Sold, to the gal in the yellow shirt." Within a few minutes, the rest of the quarts were auctioned and, with some cheesing up to the audience and Olivia chipping in about the ingredients she'd put into each different ice cream, sold for top dollar.

Handing out the prized ice cream, Olivia was bouncing

with joy.

Haley watched from the edge of the yard, swelling with pride for Livy. All the work they'd put into this event had been worth it. And when Maddox's eyes met hers, that pride was replaced with something entirely different.

The party was winding down when Haley brought Maddox a bottle of water. He'd been sitting at the same table, though finally, he'd been left alone for a little while. He grabbed the water, twisted off the cap, and downed it. "Thanks."

"You looked thirsty."

He was wiping his mouth with his sleeve when Rob Shepherd, one of the loan officers from the bank, moseyed by.

"Got a neat little operation here," the man said. "I hope it pays off for you."

"It's all Livy," Haley said, sliding onto the bench beside him. Thank God she hadn't caught the man's undertones.

"Place is looking good, Michaels," he said. "I heard the medical bills might keep you from putting in that irrigation system you were talking about last winter."

Maddox could only imagine who he'd heard that from. Small-town gossip.

"Not this year," Maddox said, gritting a smile out.

The other man lifted one foot onto the bench opposite theirs and shot the breeze for another few minutes before moseying off.

"What was that about?" Haley asked.

He shrugged. "Folks around here have a long memory."

She nodded. He guessed she probably understood that, the way everyone still remembered her as Katie's friend.

She narrowed her eyes. "So...?"

"So some of them have been waiting for me to fail, just like my old man."

"Really?" She sounded surprised. "Back then, it seemed like they were all pulling for you."

"Not all of them."

She tilted her head to the side. "Are you sure you're not

projecting?"

"What's that mean?" He shook his head. "Forget it." It was about time to find a trash bag. When he stood, she followed him.

"It means, are you sure *you* aren't the one worried about failing?"

She always did have a way of cutting to the heart of the matter.

He gritted his back teeth. He didn't want to talk about his pop with her. Didn't really want to think about the man—it was a waste of time.

She stopped him in the shade of the house with a soft hand on his sleeve. "No matter what anyone else says or thinks, you've got Livy—you've done a good thing."

The way she was looking at him, like she believed in him.... Suddenly, possibilities rose like a shimmering mirage.

He just didn't know if he had the strength to hope in possibilities any more.

CHAPTER FOUR

Several days after Olivia's birthday, Haley awoke feeling somehow...off, but she couldn't pinpoint why.

It wasn't until she was driving home after picking up some prescriptions for Aunt Matilda that she realized what day it was. The anniversary of the car accident that had killed Katie.

She was coasting past the small town cemetery when she saw a lone, small figure, huddled into herself. Livy.

Grief and hot disappointment surged through her.

Haley parked around the side, not wanting to interrupt the girl.

How could she have almost forgotten such an important day? And where were Livy's uncles?

She had her phone in her hand and dialed before she could talk herself out of it. It really wasn't her business. But she cared about Livy, too.

Maddox picked up on the first ring. "Haley?"

She should've held her tongue, but the words burst out before she could even think.

"How could you leave her alone today? Even if you couldn't bring her—"

"Olivia—?"

"Did she ride her bike to town again? I would've picked her up—"

"Haley—"

"She's at the cemetery, Maddox. By herself. Where are you?"

Her voice broke as she remembered standing alone at her

mother's grave in a St. Louis cemetery, saying goodbye the day before Haley's father moved them across the country.

There was a long pause, as if he were waiting to see if she was really done railing at him.

Then, a quiet. "I'm here."

She scanned the area and saw his truck parked on the opposite side of the fence.

He lifted his hand from the steering wheel in a brief wave.

"She said she wanted to go alone."

The enormity of what she'd done crashed down on Haley. Not only had she ranted at him when he was most likely grieving too, but she'd accused him of neglecting Olivia again, this time when he didn't deserve it.

She squeezed her eyes closed, the hand that wasn't holding her phone squeezing on the steering wheel.

"I'm sorry," she whispered.

When Haley pulled around and parked beside his truck, Maddox wasn't surprised.

She was something of a pit bull beneath that friendly, smiling exterior.

He was starting to like it.

It made his voice gruff when she popped his door open.

She just looked at him for a long moment, silent and assessing.

"You okay?" Her soft-spoken question hit harder than he wanted to let on.

He looked out over the wrist he'd rested on the dash, squinting a little.

Then she shocked him by taking his other hand. Picked it right up off of his thigh, mashing it between both of her smaller, cool hands. Touching him again. Comforting him.

"I'm fine," he said.

But he wasn't. Not really. He'd spent all morning tiptoeing around Justin, who'd been more of a grump than usual.

His brother hadn't talked about the giant elephant in the room, their shared loss. So Maddox hadn't either.

Maddox's chest expanded, and he breathed out harshly.

But he didn't have time for more than that, because she was pulling him out of the truck. "What—?"

"Even if Livy told you she wanted to be alone, that's not what she needs."

He dug in his heels, unease bucking like an unbroken bronco.

She shook her head. "We've got to get you educated on woman-speak before Livy turns into a teenager."

She tugged him forward, and this time he went, mostly to save his wrist from being pulled out of socket.

He didn't know how to handle Olivia's grief. He didn't even know what to do with the hot ball lodged in own his gut.

He wasn't equipped to deal with this. Maybe he never would be.

But somehow... Having Haley at his side made the trek past all those other graves less daunting.

Olivia looked up at their approach, and the pain in her eyes nearly sent him to his knees. But she was dry-eyed, thank God.

Haley let go of his hand, and he felt the loss intensely, but she wrapped both arms around Olivia's shoulders.

The sight of them together, like mother and daughter, made his heart thump once, hard.

"I'm so sorry, baby," she said to Olivia. He could hear the pain in her words.

Olivia must've, too, because she burrowed her head into Haley's shoulder.

Then Haley looked up at him, eyes baring her heart. She motioned him closer, but he hesitated. Could he weather Olivia's emotional storm?

Haley didn't give him a choice. She reached out and grabbed his shirtsleeve and gave him such a hard tug that he stumbled toward both girls. Being close, his only alternative was to put his arms around them.

Olivia turned her face toward him and pressed her cheek into his chest. He tightened his arm around her shoulders. Haley shifted, like she might be trying to back out of the embrace, but he tightened his arm around her, too.

She'd gotten him into this. She was staying.

It felt right, having her in this circle with him.

She looked up at him from entirely too close, and her cheeks were wet. "I miss her, too," Haley whispered.

And darn if he didn't find himself saying, voice rough, "Me, too."

And Olivia burst into tears. She clutched the back of his shirt in one hand.

He looked frantically at Haley, who gave a wet chuckle. She rested her hand on the crown of Olivia's head.

They stayed like that for several minutes, in a tight huddle. Until Olivia's sobs quieted to hiccups and he was sweating through his T-shirt from being so close to two other bodies in the hundred-plus degree Oklahoma sun.

Finally, Olivia pushed away, and he let them both go.

Olivia wiped her face with her fingers, and then Haley pressed a Kleenex she'd pulled from somewhere into his niece's hand.

"Thanks," Olivia said quietly. She didn't look up.

Haley looked at the top of Olivia's head. "I haven't been back here since the funeral."

Olivia's head came up. "You knew my mom?"

Haley glanced at Maddox, then back to the girl. "Yeah. I did. I moved to Redbud Trails halfway through my senior year of high school. We were friends until she died."

Olivia's face lit up. Haley gestured to the dry, sun-baked grass. "You wanna sit for a little bit?"

Maddox made a noise, mostly to discourage her because of her dressy suit pants, but she dragged Olivia down with her and didn't seem worried about her slacks getting grass stains.

He sat with them, folding his too-long legs beneath him to complete their triangle.

"You're a lot like her," Haley said.

"Really?" Olivia's voice cracked, a sound between hope and uncertainty.

His heart ached with some of that uncertainty. Katie had

been an inferno, bright and sometimes painful, burning out too quickly. *How much* was Olivia like her mother?

"Your eyes, your hair, your nose," Haley said. "The first day I saw you, I thought you looked just like her."

He nodded, listening. But not as raptly as Olivia was, with her face turned toward Haley, her eyes glued to her.

"Everyone liked Katie," Haley went on. "Wherever she went, people greeted her by name."

That was true, too.

"On my first day of school, I didn't know a soul. Before my first class was over, Katie had grabbed me and toted me with her down the hall and to our next class. She was so nice... and she didn't take *no* for an answer."

Maddox smiled. "She never did."

Olivia's head swiveled to him, her eyes serious, hopeful...

And he couldn't deny her.

Especially when Haley kicked the toe of his boot.

"She was a prankster. She would put bugs and lizards—one time even a snake—in our boots in the mudroom. Justin and I learned to check them every time."

Olivia giggled. He and his brother had never learned to laugh at her jokes. They'd always complained loudly to their mom.

He leaned back, letting his wrist take his weight. Some of the painful pressure in his chest was deflating, like a slow helium leak from a balloon.

"She was great at math and science, like you, Olivia," Haley remembered. She leaned back on her arm as well, her fingers overlapping Maddox's on the ground. Had she done that on purpose?

"And she was a planner, too," Haley continued. "She worked for weeks on what we were going to wear to prom, where we would eat supper, who we were going with..." She trailed off, a beautiful pink flush spreading across her face.

She must've realized exactly who she was talking to.

Maddox found himself grinning. She was finally getting a taste of her own medicine—the discomfort he'd felt ever since she'd burst into his life in vibrant color.

"She was a good friend." Haley sniffed, and he realized she was blinking back tears.

Olivia sniffled as well.

"And she loved, you, kiddo," he said, through a sandpaper throat. "In the hospital with you, those first few days... she barely let anyone else hold you. She didn't want to let you go, even for a minute."

Olivia was crying again, silent tears streaming down her face, looking at him like...like she almost didn't believe him. "Why did she have to die?" she whispered.

He gathered her up, more natural about it this time. He shook his head, held her tightly. "I don't know, kiddo, I don't know."

Haley was wiping her eyes as unobtrusively as she could, but she was staying, sticking by his side, even though she probably needed to get back to her aunt.

But she was still here. When it hurt.

She placed a hand on Olivia's back, offering comfort.

Because Olivia needed her.

And then she reached out and touched his upper arm. Offering the same.

Because...he needed her.

Their eyes met and held. His insides churned like he'd ridden a whirly carnival ride. She did that to him. Discombobulated him until he wasn't sure which way was up.

But she also comforted him in a way no one else could.

She touched him, when no one else did.

He couldn't be...falling for her. Again. Could he?

He bent his head down over Olivia, the brim of his hat breaking the fragile connection of their gaze.

His heart was thundering now, he was sweating more than the baking sun really called for.

He wasn't falling for her. He couldn't be. She was just Katie's old friend. Now Olivia's friend. She'd helped him comfort Olivia, and he was grateful. That was all.

Right?

CHAPTER FIVE

"Are you going out to the Michaels' place today?"

Several days after the emotional scene at the cemetery, Haley settled in the floral-covered chair next to her aunt's bedside. The lunch she'd brought on a tray earlier lay on the bedside table, mostly untouched. She would take it back to the kitchen in a minute, but as long as Aunt Matilda was awake, she would sit and talk for a bit.

"I don't know."

Haley couldn't get Maddox off her mind. He and Livy were making strides from where they'd been at the beginning of the summer, when she'd come back into their lives.

He'd been calling the little girl every night from the road on the harvest crew.

And the last two nights, he'd called Haley. They'd talked for close to an hour each time, about her job as a marketing assistant for a big firm in Oklahoma City. About Justin and the accident and his recovery. About Livy.

But Maddox held back about himself.

"Am I getting too involved?" she asked her aunt. It was somewhat of a rhetorical question. "I started the summer wanting to help Livy with her ice cream business and maybe show her uncle what he was missing out on..."

"And now you've met the real man."

And she was afraid she was falling in love with him.

"I'm glad," Aunt Matilda smiled and a patted Haley's hand. "I was afraid you were going to be hung up on that awful Patrick forever."

"Paul," Haley corrected gently. "And I've been over Paul for a while."

After spending time with Maddox this summer, she wondered if what she'd felt for the other man had been real love. In the beginning, she'd been infatuated with him. But as their relationship wore on, sometimes the things he said made her feel uncomfortable. He didn't think she was outgoing enough. Always wanted to go to more parties, when Haley would be perfectly content to stay home for a quiet dinner. They'd been together for two years and she'd been expecting a proposal. Instead, he'd left her behind for an out-of-state job. She'd *thought* she'd been heartbroken.

But if she'd loved him, why didn't she go with him? He hadn't asked, but what had stopped her from suggesting it?

She didn't know the answer to that question.

And she didn't know what to do about Maddox.

"Open your heart," Aunt Matilda said. "Don't be afraid to fall in love again. Life's too short to miss your second chances."

Coming from her aunt, the words were a bittersweet reminder.

The doorbell rang.

"Expecting someone?" her aunt asked.

"No."

When she pulled open the front door, there were Maddox and an effervescent Livy on the front stoop.

"What are you doing here?"

Livy's answer was a hug that Haley gratefully accepted. A step behind, Maddox held up a hand-packed quart of ice cream in each hand.

"New flavor, and we thought we'd better check on you and Mrs. Matilda."

It was thoughtful...and unexpected.

"Can I take it in to Aunt Matilda?" Livy asked, bouncing on her toes. Bubbling with energy, as usual.

Haley agreed. "Grab a spoon from the kitchen," she called after the girl.

Maddox relinquished the carton to her and trailed her into the kitchen. They passed Livy on her way to Matilda's room.

Haley fished a pair of spoons out of the silverware drawer and offered one to Maddox.

"I shouldn't," he said, but he took the spoon anyway. "I had a taste at home already." He patted his stomach, and she rolled her eyes.

"It would take more than a taste to fatten you up. You work too hard."

A shadow flickered in his eyes, but he only smiled.

"So what flavor do we have here?" Haley dipped her spoon in what looked like a swirl of vanilla and caramel, but was... "Pumpkin bread?" she asked in surprise after the first bite.

"Yes, and it's addictive."

She sighed as she swallowed a few good bites. "This was just what I needed today." Both the ice cream and the visit.

"Glad we could oblige." His voice was a rumble of laughter, and Livy's giggle from the bedroom was an echo of the same.

He set the spoon down in the stainless steel sink. "Do you want to come to a rodeo this weekend? Like a... date?"

The tips of his ears had turned that endearing red.

"I thought you were on the road again."

"The kid I'm splitting shifts with needed to switch our days. I'll get back out there next week. Plus, I wanted to spend a little more time with Livy. School will start soon."

Their eyes met, and she read his sincerity. He was really trying with Livy.

He'd even changed his schedule.

Maybe he was figuring out that you never got back that lost time.

And she realized she didn't want to lose any time, either. No matter the risk.

She agreed in a whisper. "All right."

CHAPTER SIX

Two days later, the realization that Matilda didn't have much time left finally became real for Haley.

She curled in a ball on the living room sofa and cuddled beneath one of Aunt Matilda's afghans, idly flipping through a photo album. She had rarely seen her aunt during her childhood, with her father moving the two of them around often. Until her senior year of high school, when Aunt Matilda had asked her to stay. They'd become close, almost as close as the mother she'd missed for years. Even when Haley had gone to college and made her life in Oklahoma City, they'd kept in touch with frequent phone calls and Matilda's visits to the city.

Unlike Haley's father, who had grown more and more distant. She might talk to him once every three months. At Christmas. Aunt Matilda had become the parent Haley needed.

What was Haley going to do without her? She still thought of Aunt Matilda's house as *home*, even after a decade away.

It was after nine when the soft knock came. At first she thought she'd imagined it.

But when it came a second time, she knew that whoever was out there wasn't going away. She peeked out the peephole to see Maddox's strong features and opened the door without thinking. It was when he blinked, visibly surprised, that she remembered she was wearing her painting sweatpants and rattiest T-shirt, she hadn't had a shower, her hair was tucked in a messy ponytail, and she probably had bags under her eyes.

It had been that kind of day.

His eyes softened when he saw her.

She tried to smile, but the weight of the day filled her eyes with tears.

She raised a hand to cover her face or ward him off—she hadn't completely made up her mind which—but he took her elbow in one of his big hands and tugged her forward.

He wrapped her in his muscled arms, and she sank into his embrace. She let him take her weight, buried her face in his chest, and breathed in leather and horse and cowboy.

"Bad day, huh?"

His words were a rumble under her cheek and hot in her hair and she hung on tightly.

She nodded, the top of her head bumping his chin.

"She's hanging in there?"

She nodded again. "Getting weaker," she said against the collar of his T-shirt.

"Still doesn't want to go to the hospital?"

This time she shook her head. Tears burned her eyes. The end was nearing for her aunt, but Haley wasn't ready to let her go.

He held her, giving her his strength. She knew she couldn't have him, not really. He was firmly anchored here in Redbud Trails, and she was eventually going back to her life in Oklahoma City. But she could have tonight.

When she'd settled a little, his hands moved to her waist, clasping her loosely.

She let go of him and raised both hands to wipe her cheeks.

Then he tipped her chin up, used the pad of his thumb to catch the tears she'd missed.

As she looked at those infinite brown eyes, shadowed in the darkness, he slid his palm against her jaw and leaned in.

And kissed her.

Minutes later—Maddox couldn't tell you how many—they sat together on the porch swing. He'd given Haley the quart of ice cream Olivia had sent, and she'd brought out two spoons, but he'd barely tasted the half-melted sweet. He wanted to remember the taste of Haley, not ice cream.

"How'd you know I needed this tonight?" she asked. Her head lolled on his shoulder, and his arm rested around her.

They fit perfectly together.

Just like at her senior prom.

Except for the fact that she was leaving, and he was stuck here in Redbud Trails, trying to save the family farm, trying to keep his brother afloat, trying to be a father to Olivia.

"Olivia saw me heading out the door and wanted you to try it. Sorry if it's melted."

"I'm not." The smile in her voice made him smile, too, and he squeezed her shoulders.

"What's she calling it?"

He wanted to ask her about her aunt again, but he knew how sometimes when you were so deep in something, you just needed to think and talk about the silly little things in life.

So that's what he gave her.

"She said 'peach cobbler'."

"Mmm. I like it. I predict it will be popular."

He shook his head. "You'd predict that about any of her creations."

"I would not. Not the bad ones."

Haley's early predictions about the business had been right. Things were taking off. Orders kept coming in, and Olivia spent hours running her machine. She was talking about maybe needing a second deep freezer. And she was thrilled about it.

Finally finished, Haley set the quart on the floor near their feet, and when she straightened, she turned so they were almost face-to-face and laid her palms on his cheeks.

He jumped from the cold.

She giggled. "Sorry."

But she wasn't really. He took her cold hands in his and rubbed them, providing friction, and he hoped, warmth. He was certainly warm enough for the both of them.

"Can I ask you something?"

"Yeah."

"How come you've never talked about Katie? With Livy, I mean."

He breathed in deep. "After she died, Livy was so little. Mom couldn't bear to talk about her. Those first months were hard on all of us. Then mom had her stroke and just gave up, and Justin and I didn't talk about anything. We were focused on surviving.

"I guess I never realized Livy needed it. Not until you came along. Now she wants to hear about Katie all the time."

She smiled against his shoulder.

"Has Justin picked out any classes for the fall?"

"Yeah. But he still has to go to the school and register."

Maddox wasn't ready to believe that his brother would do it. But Justin was at least talking about getting back to having a life instead of moping around in that recliner all day.

It was an improvement, if a small one. Haley had made her mark there, too.

The tip of his boot dragged on the porch floor. Their swing barely moved. She didn't seem to mind.

"Don't forget about our date Saturday. Do you still think you'll be able to come?"

"Unless Aunt Matilda gets much worse. She's looking forward to hearing all about it."

"Good."

He tucked her close again and rested his chin on top of her head. He liked being with her like this. He could imagine spending all their summer nights together, talking about their days and just *being together*.

He wanted it. Wanted it so bad he could taste it.

And that was just plain dangerous.

But it didn't stop him.

Haley was wide-awake when Maddox left a half hour later. She needed sleep, but instead of climbing into bed, she stared out the window where his taillights had disappeared.

She was in love with him.

Forget about a teenager's crush on her friend's handsome older brother.

She'd seen the real man. Someone who worked his butt off

to take care of his family. Someone who held her, not asking for anything. Giving comfort.

Someone real.

Not the dream she'd imagined for so long.

How was she going to go back to her old life after this was all over?

CHAPTER SEVEN

Saturday came, right on the heels of a new pile of medical bills. Maddox had thought they'd gotten through all of them, but a phone call to their insurance company revealed the truth—here was another stack waiting to be paid.

He'd gotten complacent these last few days, talking with Haley on the phone. Kissing her.

Thinking that they might have some kind of future together.

What had he been thinking?

He had a kid, a brother, and a farm to take care of, and bills out the wazoo.

Later that night, when Haley joined him and Justin and Livy at the rodeo arena one town over, those thoughts kept him company. He couldn't get past them even though to make polite conversation.

She noticed. Of course.

Sitting next to him on the crowded bleachers, she bumped his knee with hers, smiling sideways at him. Livy was on her other side, and Justin took up another seat past her. Maddox had been shocked when his brother had asked to ride along. He hadn't wanted to get off the farm at all, and now he wanted to attend a rodeo?

But Maddox had helped him load his crutches into the truck without a word.

"Did you ever want to do rodeo as a child?" Haley asked.

"For a few weeks," he admitted. He squinted down at the action in the fenced-off, dirt-packed arena. A bell rang and a horse took off from the starting gate at one side, its rider clinging to the reins and urging it on as it raced around three barrels in a triangle, then back out the gate where it had started.

"What happened?" Haley asked after the barrel rider had finished her loop.

"Took a ride on a sheep. Fell off, and decided football was safer."

"That's my brilliant brother," Justin put in from Livy's other side.

Maddox let Justin take the conversational reins, talking about their childhood and Katie riding barrels.

Until Haley bumped him again. "Wanna take a walk? I'll buy you a pretzel."

He considered her. She was wearing a cute pair of jeans, boots, and a black Stetson he'd never seen before. It made her look right at home in this crowd. "This is my date. I'm buying."

She met his gaze squarely. "I'm glad you remembered," she teased softly.

She was right. He'd let his worry about the medical bills take over his thoughts.

But it was also his life. He had to support his family. He refused to do what his dad had done and give up.

She followed him down the bleachers, and when he started off to the food trucks, she slid easily under his arm. Her boots put the top of her head level with his chin, and she felt *right* there. Again.

One of Justin's friends called out to Maddox, and he waved, a flop of his hand on her shoulder.

"Wanna tell me what's wrong?" They stood in line behind a few people with the same idea about the pretzels, and she looked up at him with slightly raised brows, waiting for an answer.

"Nothing for you to worry about," he said. "You've got enough going on with your aunt." And being broke wasn't exactly something he wanted to own up to. He had a little pride.

"That's true." Her chin lifted toward him. "But I can still

listen."

He shook his head slightly. Not tonight. His problems were still too raw.

She looked off into the distance. "Once I get back to Oklahoma City, maybe you could drive down for a visit..."

Haley continued to speak, but he heard very little. He'd known she would be leaving, knew this was only temporary, but how could she speak of it so casually? Her words, the very thought of her leaving, felt like a punch in the gut.

It had taken Haley so long to build up the courage to ask him to visit her in the city, and then...nothing. No answer. No response whatsoever.

She'd thought...

She'd hoped his kisses meant something. That his arm around her shoulder, the way he'd comforted her the other night, meant his feelings were growing. Growing to match what hers already were.

And here they were, on a date. A date he'd requested. Not a *let's go as friends* thing, but a real, honest-to-goodness date. And yet...

Had she been kidding herself?

Was he just enjoying a summer romance? Was he being a courteous cowboy, or simply returning her kindness to Livy?

They inched forward in the pretzel line. She took a deep breath, steeling her courage, and looked up at him. He met her gaze, his eyes dark beneath the brim of his hat. He didn't smile, but the corners of his eyes crinkled.

And she knew.

He cared about her.

But something held him back.

The gal behind the counter cleared her throat, and Maddox placed their order. He bought her a paper-wrapped pretzel and a bottle of water and led her away from the crowded line.

"So that's a *no*?" she asked tentatively.

He shook his head slightly. What did that mean? Was it *no*, that his non-response hadn't meant *no*, or just *no* to her question in general?

He led them clear of the crowd, stopped, and faced her. "I'm going to have to pick up some extra work," he said. "I doubt I'll have time to come down, even if it's for a weekend."

Oh. After what he'd said the other night, she'd thought he might be cutting back on extra work.

"Livy needs you," she said in a small voice.

"She also needs new school clothes and a roof over her head," he muttered.

They meandered toward the stands, not in any hurry, finally stopping behind them, in the small patch of shadow. On the other side of the bleachers, the arena lights lit everything, but here it was dark.

"Justin said you might have a lead on a job with Livy's school. Coaching football and teaching a little."

"So y'all have been talking about me?"

"He mentioned it."

Maddox blew out a breath. She couldn't tell if he was frustrated that she'd been in his business or frustrated about the job. "I can't take that job," he said, the anger evident, though she didn't understand it.

"Why not?" She was angry, too, though not for herself. She was trying not to feel anything for herself—the last few minutes had shattered her hopes for anything with him. But Livy needed him. "You'd have more time for Livy, all summer off—"

"I'd still have a farm to manage, but that's not the point. I can't take that job."

"If it's about being on the sidelines—"

"It's not," he said, and his voice rang with hurt.

"About expectations?"

He laughed, a harsh sound.

"You want the truth?" he asked roughly.

The words hit her like a strong gust of wind. She felt like she was on her toes, almost lifting off her feet.

She reached out and touched his arm. "Maddox..."

He didn't turn toward her. He just stared into the shadows

beneath the bleachers.

Twilight had gone and darkness had fallen. She could barely see him in the dim light that seeped from the arena.

"The truth is, everyone around here thinks I finished my degree, but I'm a year short. The only reason the principal offered me that job is he thinks I've got a piece of paper with my name on it. But I don't."

She knew about a man's pride. Her own father had chased jobs across the nation, wanting to *provide* for his girl. She could only imagine how having to admit something like this was hitting Maddox.

"Without a college education, jobs like working on the harvest crew are all I've got. With Justin out of commission and medical bills piling up...if the price of cattle falls any more, we'll be butchering our own. Working is all I know how to do. It's all I'm good for."

She grabbed his arm and yanked until he rounded on her.

She looked up at him with all the love swelling in her heart and into her throat, making it impossible to speak. She swallowed and forced the words out.

"No, it's not," she whispered. "No, it's *not*."

She slid her hands behind his neck and tugged him down toward her.

He seemed to understand. His lips slanted over hers, his hands slipped around her waist, and if he held her just a little too tightly, well, that was okay with her.

A loudspeaker squealed, breaking the moment. She backed away a step, touched her lips with a trembling hand. A disembodied voice announced the start of the bull riding.

Looking down, she saw both of their hats had fallen into the dust.

She bent to pick them up and offered his to him. He took it, but she didn't let go. Their eyes met and connected over the top.

"I don't know what's gonna happen," he said in a low voice.

Neither did she. She didn't know how long Aunt Matilda would hold on, or how Livy's ice cream business would do.

FIRST KISSES

Or if she'd walk away at the end of all of this with her heart intact.

But she couldn't walk away from Maddox right now.

She entwined her fingers with his and tugged him back up into the stands.

CHAPTER EIGHT

It was over.

Aunt Matilda was gone.

Haley sat through the funeral on the first pew in the little country church. Numb.

She and her aunt had made most of the arrangements in advance, so there had only been a few things to take care of, although she'd spent the last two days in a sea of paperwork, insurance claims, and lawyers.

How could it be that Haley would never see Aunt Matilda again? That her closest family member was lost to her?

Tears spilled over again, and Haley bowed her head, covered her face with her hands, and let them come.

She missed her. If only she'd made more time to come home since she'd left for college.

She'd always thought *there's time*.

And now, there was no time left.

A warm, wide hand rested on the center of her back. Maddox.

They were seated so close, she could feel the heat of his thigh next to hers. He'd been a steady presence the last couple of days. Bringing her food when she'd forgotten to eat. Answering the door to the church ladies when Haley couldn't face their kindness for her grief. He'd answered his phone in the wee hours when she couldn't sleep.

Olivia and Justin had been in and out, tiptoeing around and whispering like she was fine china. But this wasn't going to break her.

If she'd learned anything this summer, it was that cowgirls got back up after they got bucked off. And they didn't let go of what was important.

She was in love with Maddox.

She hadn't figured out how she was going to make it work between them. She had a job, back in Oklahoma City. Her boss had granted her another few days of leave to wrap things up, but he expected her back soon.

And Maddox was very firmly entrenched in Redbud Trails. He wasn't letting go of the farm without a fight. And he shouldn't. It was their family legacy, the place where Katie had grown up and Olivia could connect with her mother.

Everything was a muddle.

But today, all Haley could do was grieve. With Maddox beside her, holding her up, she could let Aunt Matilda go.

She would wait for a chance to talk to Maddox later.

A week later, Haley was still waiting.

Maddox had had to leave for the harvest crew the day after the funeral. The four-day separation had distanced them. He'd come home quieter, more reserved. She didn't know how to get their closeness back.

This morning, he'd come to help her load her car. It hadn't taken long, and now as he stowed the last of her boxes in the trunk, she stood in the empty dining room.

Out the window, a *For Sale* sign out front was the tangible sign that nothing would ever be the same.

She hesitated inside the front door, looking at Maddox's broad shoulders as he waited by her car.

What if... what if she'd been wrong about his feelings? For several days, she'd been mired in grief. All the insurance paperwork had kept her busy, slightly on edge, and frustrated.

And now Maddox was back, and that insidious voice in her head—a voice that sounded remarkably like Paul's—kept reminding her that she *wasn't enough*. She had never been enough to keep her father from chasing the next best job. Paul had found her wanting—criticizing her because she wasn't outgoing enough, telling her she needed to be a perfect hostess when they eventually got married.

What if...what if Maddox found her wanting as well?

Steeling herself with a deep breath, she stepped outside her aunt's door, trying not to think about how it was the last time she would, and locked it behind her.

His hands rested casually in his front pockets. His Stetson threw a shadow over his eyes, and she couldn't read them. His body language was casual, friendly.

But not welcoming.

She stopped several feet away, keys jangling in her nerveless fingers.

"Well, that's it," she said on an exhale.

If he would just give her an indication that he felt the same way he had when he'd kissed her before, at the rodeo...

But he only nodded, unsmiling.

"I'm not ready," she said softly. "To say goodbye." To the house, to her aunt's memory.

But especially to him.

Maddox fisted his hands in his jeans pockets, the muscles in his arms aching from wanting to reach for her.

He kept his jaw clenched to hold back the tide. Words like, *please don't leave me.* Words like, *I love you.*

She deserved better than a cowboy who was fighting for every paycheck.

His dad had given up, failed the family, nearly lost the farm.

But Maddox refused to do the same. Even if he was one overdue mortgage payment away from losing the place, he couldn't give up.

And that meant a lot of hard work.

How could he commit to—how could he ask Haley to commit to—a long-distance relationship when he knew he couldn't commit to it himself? He couldn't. His focus had to be on keeping his family afloat.

He'd watched his mother get beaten down by life and a husband who'd ultimately failed the family. He couldn't ask

Haley to do the same.

Or worse, start a relationship with her and a year down the road, have her decide to ditch the loser who was still working his butt off for a chunk of land.

He'd die if she walked away from him. He felt about like he was dying now. Like a big ol' bull had stepped on his chest cavity.

The best he could hope for was in a few months to have made some good money, put another nest egg aside, and when he'd proved he could support his family, call her. With any luck, she wouldn't fall in love with someone else.

All those words settled in his heart, tucked away. "Drive safe." He didn't add, *call me when you get there* or *I'll miss you.*

He couldn't bear the uncertainty in her eyes, so he turned away, yanking open her car door. She slipped under his arm, silent. Watchful. Waiting.

But he couldn't give her what she needed, so he said nothing.

And she started the car and drove away.

CHAPTER NINE

"Hello?"

"Is this Maddox Michaels?"

"Speaking. Who's this?"

"Dan Crane."

Hearing the junior high principal's voice on the phone pulled Maddox up short. He was on a three-day weekend back from the harvest crew, driving to town to make Olivia's weekly ice cream delivery to the restaurant that acted as a consignment agent for her, but now he stopped his truck on the side of the state highway.

"Dan. I've been meaning to return your calls."

He took a deep breath and decided to come clean.

"Actually, I haven't," he said. "Been meaning to call."

"Look, Maddox, we need you. There's no one else around qualified to coach—"

"I'm not qualified to teach," he said. And that shut the other man up. "I never finished my degree. I was a year short. I let everybody around here think I was done because I was too chicken to admit I was so much like my father."

His free hand clenched the bottom of the steering wheel.

There was a beat of silence before Dan spoke. "I wish I'd known this sooner."

Yeah. No kidding.

More silence and Maddox wanted to get out of the uncomfortable conversation. "I'll let you go—"

"Hang on a minute, Michaels. I'm thinking. You know, if we can get you enrolled..."

"What?"

While Maddox listened in shock, the other man outlined a plan for Maddox to finish his degree and get certified to teach—by Christmastime.

He wasn't even sure what he'd agreed to by the time the call ended twenty minutes later, but he did know that in one phone conversation, hope had come back to him.

But having a job didn't make up for losing Haley.

Every time he breathed in deeply, it felt like knives slicing through his lungs. He missed her so much.

It had been almost three weeks, and he'd heard nothing. Not that he'd expected to—he'd made his wishes clear that last day. But now, he was dying inside, a little each day.

He was still mulling the new job offer over when he got home with the boxed meal the restaurant manager had pushed on him.

Only to find Justin on his feet, wrestling with the old brown recliner.

"What're you doing?" Maddox dumped the food on the kitchen table and rushed to take the weight of the chair. Last thing Justin needed was for that chair to topple over and land on his only remaining good leg.

"I got to thinking," Justin said, huffing. "That it's time to get rid of this old thing."

Their eyes met over the top of the stinky chair.

He knew what Justin was saying. More than the recliner, it was time to let the past go.

His dad had sat in the chair and drunk himself to death. Maddox barely had any good memories of the man.

Ma had sat in this chair, swallowed by her grief. After she'd lost Katie, she'd lost herself.

Justin had almost done the same. His injury had made him give up on life.

But if he was man enough to get out of the chair, he was on the road to total recovery. His hip might not be fully functional, and he might always have a limp, but he could move on.

Maddox felt a hot burn behind his eyes. He cleared his throat. "I'm proud of you."

"Yeah, yeah." Justin leaned down to pick up the crutch he'd laid across the fireplace hearth. "After you take that out to the dump, you need to get in your truck and head to Oklahoma City."

Maddox grunted. He angled the chair toward the door, eyeing the frame. The chair wasn't going to fit upright.

"I'm not kidding," Justin said. "You can't just let a girl like Haley get away."

Maddox pushed the chair across the floor. It hung up on a patch of old carpet and he almost fell over the top of it, getting a good wallop in the stomach when it rebounded.

"Mad. I'm serious."

"She's the one who left," he huffed. She'd left him behind. Again.

"And you've been moping around here for three weeks. You've got two feet and a truck. So go get her and bring her back."

His heart panged once, hard. "It's not that easy. I've got a lead on a job, but I've got to prove myself—"

"Prove what?" Justin demanded. "Prove that you're just as much of an idiot as our father? She's in love with you—if you haven't messed that up. She'll stand by you."

He wanted to believe...wanted to believe it so badly.

Maddox's heart thudded in his chest. "I've been pretty stupid."

"No kidding. What else is new? But she fell in love with you knowing that football players have a couple screws loose, so this little act of stupidity probably hasn't surprised her much."

Could he really take Justin's advice?

What if she couldn't forgive him for breaking her heart?

Worse than that, what if he never tried to put it back together?

Haley had settled into her normal routine.

Sort of.

She went to work. And stared at her computer screen all day. She wasn't getting a lot done.

She came home. And tried not to stare at her phone, willing Maddox to call.

She'd called his house and spoken to Livy several times, checking on the business, checking on the girl.

She'd shied away from asking about Maddox. When Livy had offered tidbits like *he liked the root beer float flavor*, Haley had *mm-hmmed* and moved on.

What was wrong with her?

She had a car. Gas. Keys. She could drive back to Redbud Trails any time. She wanted to take the man by the shoulders and shake him. Or maybe kiss him.

She didn't know what she'd been thinking that last day. Maybe she'd let her grief blind her, or her fear.

She *knew* there was something between her and Maddox. It had been too strong to deny, and too strong to fade away.

She'd talked herself into a weekend trip and had her keys dangling from her fingers when she exited her front door. And stopped short.

There was a big, dusty truck in her driveway.

She barely registered the truck before a tall, dusty cowboy stood in her way, too.

She threw herself at him. And he caught her.

"What took you so long?" she mumbled into his shoulder.

He rumbled a laugh. "Sorry." She felt the press of his chin in her hair. "It took this big, dumb *Ox* a little bit to get things figured out."

She tilted her chin back and squinted up at him. "Don't call yourself dumb."

He used the opportunity to rub his thumb along the line of her jaw.

"So what did you figure out?" she whispered.

"Well, the financial situation is still a little sticky," he said. "But mostly, I realized that I was focusing on the wrong things, like your dad did."

He brushed a kiss across her temple.

"And letting the best thing in my life get away, kind of like my dad did."

Now he brushed a kiss across her cheek.

"And I don't want to be like either of them."

"You're not—" she started to say.

And he sure kissed her like he agreed.

When they broke away minutes later, both panting and out-of-breath, he noticed the keys dangling from her hand. "Going somewhere?"

"I was on my way to Redbud Trails." She couldn't help the shy smile. "You're not the only one who was being less-smart than they should be." She looked down briefly but then back up at him, his overwhelming presence—and his kisses—giving her courage. "I shouldn't have left without telling you I was in love with you."

He lit up from the inside out.

"And not because of your bank account," she went on. "Or your farm."

He lifted his eyebrows.

"It's definitely because of your niece's ice cream." She stood on her tiptoes and brushed a kiss against his lips. "I want a piece of the business."

He leaned down and kissed her beneath her jaw. "You already own a piece of it."

"Hmm." She giggled and tucked her chin down when his hot breath tickled her neck. "I guess it must be something else, then."

She pushed on his shoulders until he was far enough away that she could see his face. "It's because of who you are. The man who wouldn't give up on his brother. Who redid the kitchen to make a little girl's dream come true."

The quiet joy on his face made the heartfelt confession easy.

"Wanna know why I'm in love with you?" he asked.

Her heart soared up into her throat, and she nodded.

He cupped her jaw in one hand. "Same reason. Because of who you are. Your quiet spirit and gentle heart that saw my niece's needs and found a way to meet them. You reached out to Justin when the rest of the outside world forgot him and gave him the courage to go on." He swallowed hard. "And you found a way inside my heart when I thought it was too full of worrying about everything else." His expression darkened. "I don't know how everything's going to work out."

"That's okay. We can figure it out together."

"Together." He breathed in deeply. "That sounds so right." And he kissed her again.

ABOUT LACY WILLIAMS

Lacy Williams grew up on a farm, which is where her love of cowboys was born. In reality, she's married to a right-brained banker (happily with three kiddos). She gets to express her love of western men by writing western romances. Her books have finaled in the RT Book Reviews Reviewers' Choice Awards (2012, 2013 & 2014), the Golden Quill and the Booksellers Best Award.

Lacy loves to hear from readers. You can drop her a note at lacyjwilliams@gmail.com or visit her website at www.lacywilliams.net.